Fusion

Fusion

Rochan Morgan

www.urbanbooks.net

Urban Books, LLC
78 East Industry Court
Deer Park, NY 11729

ISBN 13: 978-1-60162-329-4
ISBN 10: 1-60162-329-1

First Mass Market Printing December 2011
First Trade Paperback Printing November 2007
Printed in the United States of America

10 9 8 7 6 5 4 3 2 1

Distributed by Kensington Publishing Corp.
Submit Wholesale Orders to:
Kensington Publishing Corp.
C/O Penguin Group (USA) Inc.
Attention: Order Processing
405 Murray Hill Parkway
East Rutherford, NJ 07073-2316
Phone: 1-800-526-0275
Fax: 1-800-227-9604

CHAPTER 1

Jonathan Reed was awakened from a fitful slumber by the sweet sounding melody of a company of mockingbirds in concert. They were serenading him from the large sycamore tree just beyond his slightly ajar bedroom window, giving perhaps their last performance of the season—a farewell of sorts—before heading south over the Gulf of Mexico.

Eyes still closed, Shakey, as he had been known for nearly fifteen years now, listened as the howling of the early morning wind brought to an abrupt end the rhythmic gaiety of the palm-sized birds. The rustling of fallen leaves and fluttering of anxious wings was their final good-bye. The sadness of it all was not lost on their only listener.

Shakey rolled onto his back, eyes finally opening. Peering deeply into the scene revealed to him by the large mirror in the ceiling, he found only himself lying in the king-sized bed. The space was much too large for one.

Shakey kicked the covers from atop of him. He rose to a sitting position before swinging his legs over the side of the bed. His feet landed directly on the nose of the infamous Empress Wu, the notorious seventh century Chinese ruler that was the focal point of the brilliantly patterned Oriental rug covering the center of the bedroom's hardwood floors.

Dressed only in a pair of black satin boxers, complete with a green embroidered money symbol in the bottom left corner, Shakey embarked on the short jaunt to the bathroom. His bare feet gripped the coolness of the marble floor as he crossed the threshold of the large room.

Shakey stepped for the round, oversized bathtub at the center of the octagon shaped bathroom. He twisted the knobs of both spickets, carefully blending the waters until the desired warmth flowed from the faucet, then headed for the sink area. Next, the still waking man reached for the toothbrush and Colgate that lie in the holder affixed to the granite countertop. After squeezing a generous portion of toothpaste onto the bristles of the toothbrush, he moved the brush in small, circular motions against the twelve thousand dollars worth of gold, diamonds, and rubies for which his mouth was the display case. After rinsing, he used a felt cloth to further polish his smile.

He began his next mission by thoroughly blanketing the peach fuzz that covered his head with two handfuls of Gillette shaving cream. He then made long and careful strokes with the twin-action razor. Minutes later, the glistening bald head was groomed to the owner's liking.

The tub half-full now, Shakey reached for the bottle of bubble bath and poured it freely into the tub. The onetime aspiring prize-fighter then returned to his position before the sink, now conscious only of the boxer-clad body staring back at him.

A quite imposing figure at six foot two tall and two hundred twenty pounds, the forever vain hustler who had once dubbed himself "The Handsome Intimidator" was quite satisfied with his mirror image. The years of "good living" he had done were invisible to the eye as he carefully scrutinized each of his body parts.

The muscles of Shakey's shoulders and arms were two endless rows of highly defined contours and curves suggesting of unfathomable power. The Handsome Intimidator flexed while observing the tattoos that covered the largeness of both pectoral muscles.

Shakey's left pec bore the image of a tombstone inscripted with the message: DIED: MAY 27, 1992. This was the start date of his most recent prison sentence. The right pec was canvas to a brilliant sunrise. Under the sunrise was a single word: RESURRECTED. Under that: NOVEMBER 14, 1998. This was the date of his release.

Shakey's abdomen was an ordered mass of impenetrable steel ridges. Written in large, red,

Old English letters, arcing in a semi-circle above his navel, were the words PALM TERRACE. The housing project where Shakey had lived in as a child.

There were more tattoos. Many others throughout his body, as tattoos it seemed had once been the only avenue of self-expression accessible to him.

Shakey's left shoulder bore the striking image of his great-grandmother. The forearm of the same side contained a highly detailed dagger, the handle of which was the graven image of a horse's head. A snake wound around the length of the blade.

The opposite side of the same arm was decorated with an image of a bulldog, complete with red scarf around his neck and a most unfortunate feline caught in the grips of his powerful jaws. The inscription under the picture read: ALL DOGS EAT PUSSY!

The right side of his body was just as decorated. There was odes to dead homies, sworn allegiances to the hood, and a strikingly detailed picture of a pistol-grip, pump-action shotgun.

On his back was a large cross. Under the cross were the words: ONLY GOD CAN JUDGE ME, a tribute to the late, great Tupac Shakur.

Shakey discarded the boxers. Still eyeing himself intently in the mirror, he raised both arms until they lie straight across at shoulder level, before curling them at the bend in the elbow and striking the "muscle man" pose.

With a well-stroked ego, Shakey finally turned away from the mirror and entered the tub. Leaning back against the wall of the tub, he turned the water off before grabbing the marijuana packed Swisher Sweet cigar from the table beside the tub. Next, he pressed the power button on the remote that was mounted on the same table. The face of Sportcenter's Stuart Scott showed immediately on the forty-six-inch flat screen television. Shakey needed only to raise the volume.

The Handsome Intimidator laid all the way back now. The warm bath and sweet smoke of the burning Swisher proved to be an extremely relaxing start to the day. With no pressing matters to tend to, Shakey could see himself moving no time soon.

The cars passed before Joe's Burgers with much less frequency now as the steady stream of early morning commuters thinned with the start of the new work day. The rising sun provided just enough warmth to combat the frigidness of the wind's whisper, whose nearly audible voice echoed from over the Gulf. The salt-filled fog that still hovered over the outside dining area dissipated into barely visible droplets of precipitation that felt sticky on the skin of the four patrons of the yet to open burger shack.

"Girl, you need to put some clothes on before you catch pneumonia!" Kitty couldn't help but smile at Shay, who wore only her trademark two-piece bikini while dancing provocatively on the street corner, unsuccessfully attempting to divert the attention of the driver of the white Protégé that whistled along Seawall Boulevard.

"Shut up, tramp." Shay returned to the table she shared with the other three. Despite the griping, Shay reached inside the small, orange gym bag she carried and quickly donned the gray shorts and white t-shirt she had packed.

"I'm getting tired," Sharon added, still holding on to the hope that enough money would soon come her way to avoid a return to Dale's.

Jessica graced them all with trademark silence.

Joe's Burgers was a small, privately owned burger stand situated on the corner of Thirty-fourth Street and Avenue S, just a block from Seawall Boulevard and the beach that was the main attraction for the majority of the restaurant's patronage. The small, square-built, brown-brick building was equipped with a single sliding window, manned usually by a family member of Joe, the burger stand's balding, middle-aged owner, who performed all cooking duties. It was at the sliding glass window where all transactions took place.

All orders at Joe's were handed through the window in brown paper bags. Fountains drinks were poured into large Styrofoam cups. Eight wooden tables and a bench for two on each side were located outside the establishment for customer use. There was no inside seating at Joe's.

The "women of Joe's", as the group of prostitutes who congregated year round at the burger
stand were known, were a varied group of street-
walkers, each of them survivors of their own personal horror stories. The roads that brought them
together at Joe's were as diverse as the tragedies
that would one day spell their doom. There were
the young and pretty part-time hoes, still naïve
enough to believe that a savior was yet to come,
and the middle-aged, past–their-prime women of
the night, who had long ago given up on thoughts
of Prince Charming or any other type of fairytale
endings. Nearly two dozen prostitutes used Joe's
as home base. At the moment, four were present.

Shay was a twenty-year-old Louisiana thorough-
bred. Big boned with beautiful red-tinted skin and
shoulder-length black hair, Shay was a favorite
amongst island drug dealers. Her many lovers read
like a who's who list of Galveston street hustlers.

Kitty was a thin but sexy dark-skinned beauty
with short-cut curly hair, large brown eyes, and
a brilliantly white smile. Having once, with the
help of a boyfriend, risen to the topmost heights
of neighborhood drug peddling only to fall swiftly
to the bottom rung of the street hierarchy, Kitty
was well versed in the ups and downs of life on the
streets. Moreover, Kitty was a survivor.

Sharon was a heavy-chested, caramel ex-dancer.
Cute though not pretty, the sheer volume of Sharon's amiable personality had always endeared

her to the biggest spenders of the island's adult entertainment network. Though greatly preferring women over men, Sharon had always ascribed the full routine of smiling, fawning, and cooing she would do in the presence of tricks to the natural talent she obviously possessed for acting.

Jessica was an unsolvable riddle to the other Women of Joe's. A striking redhead, Jessica had a face full of freckles. And from the fullness of her slightly pursed lips, to her smallish, perfectly centered nose, to the long dark lashes sensuously accentuating the large green emeralds with she viewed the world, Jessica had been blessed with flawless beauty. And with a more than ample body to go along with her facial beauty, Jessica could have her pick of tricks, though she wanted none. In fact, the sullen and often helpless acting white girl seemed to have a quite serious aversion to the idea of turning tricks for a living. Fortunately for her, the sometimes unsteady patience of her best friend Sharon had yet to fail her during the most tumultuous period of her life.

The tie that bound the four was their use of crack cocaine; and save for Jessica, the unconscionable bartering of their own bodies to attain the devilish concoction.

"Damn, it's slow out here." Sharon was speaking mainly to herself, angry at having spent every dime she had made in the pre-dawn hours, saving nothing for the day's provisions.

"Slow? It's barely eight o' clock," Kitty informed her. "The day just beginning."

"Maybe for you," Sharon returned. "I been up all night."

"You up every night," Kitty quipped. "Fo', five nights in a row sometimes."

"Fuck you, Kitty."

"You payin'?" Kitty joked and all the women laughed.

"Heeey!" Shay was quickly up and dancing for the benefit of the middle-aged white man driving the burgundy Ford Taurus. The car slowed briefly before Joe's then passed the eatery. The brake lights illuminated once more before the car ran the stop sign at the corner and turned left on Seawall Boulevard.

"Fuck!" Shay's disappointment was obvious as she returned to table six. "He would've stopped if I didn't have on this old funky T-shirt and shorts."

The fast rising sun was fully aglow now just below the eastern horizon. The only fog remaining was that which stubbornly clung to the women's skin. A new day was upon them, and not a trick was in sight.

"Somebody give me some change," Shay demanded. "I'ma call my sugar daddy."

"Yeah, hurry up and get yo' worrisome ass away from here." Sharon reached in her pocket.

"Hold on, ho!" Shay kicked herself free from the gym shorts and hurried to the curbside stage. The dirty dancing beginning even as she ran. "Here comes my man."

The '80's model Delta Eighty-Eight had seen better days, as evidenced by the layer of rust covering the sky blue paint of the hood and roof of the vehicle. The fast spinning chrome disk rims were worth more than the value of the rest of the car. Two heads bobbed rhythmically to the sound of rap music as the Eighty-Eight wheeled curbside to gain a better view of Shay.

The pace of Shay's dancing slowed to coincide with the music played by the Eighty-Eight's driver. The curvaceous sexpot seductively enticed her young male audience. So much so that a long, spindly arm protruded from the passenger side window, reaching desperately to touch the front of her bikini.

Shay shoved the large hand away, took a step backward, and continued dancing. She had drawn the wrong man's interest.

The music was lowered and the arm that protruded from the passenger side window was replaced with a head. "Come closer, girl, so I can bite ya," the smooth and slender black face requested.

"What's up, Jamaal?" The dancing stopped and the negotiations began. Shay stepped closer to the car. Bending slightly at the waist, her attention riveted to the shirtless young man driving the Eighty-Eight.

"What's up, Shay?" Jamaal answered, looking right past the half-naked beauty before him. "Who is that?" he asked.

"Oh, her?" Shay stammered while eyeing Jessica, quite unfamiliar with the twinge of jealousy she felt at Jamaal's interest in Jessica. "That's Sharon's ho."

"You can't afford her, nigga." Sharon was too far away to hear the conversation, but knew well from Shay's body language and the look in Jamaal's eye what was happening.

"Shit. Name it," Jamaal offered, speaking loudly enough to be sure that Sharon could hear him now.

Shay made no attempt at hiding her frustration while stepping back from the window.

"Fifty dollars." Sharon knew that Jamaal had never spent as much on a prostitute. But she would accept no less.

"Get out, fool." Jamaal whispered to his passenger before turning to Sharon. "Cool."

"What you mean get out?" Jamaal's friend was not happy with the instruction.

"Get out, chump."

"And go where?"

"Sit with them?" Jamaal told him. "I'll be right back."

"That's fucked up." The furious young man clutched the forty ounce of Colt 45 that had been resting between his legs. The rest of his statement was an angry, incoherent string of murmurings as he stepped from the car.

"Go ahead, Jessica," Sharon spoke from the side of her mouth, just loud enough so that only Jessica, seated next to her, could hear.

Jessica stood quickly, but needed a moment to muster the resolve to take the first step toward the Delta Eighty-Eight. She was sickened by the thought of what would be expected of her after climbing inside the car with the smiling young man. Her fear of Sharon's wrath was the stronger of conflicting emotions, however, and Jessica trudged slowly for the Eighty-Eight.

Dazed and numb by the time she climbed into the vehicle, Jessica was oblivious to the Eighty-Eight's movement as Jamaal made a U-turn and pressed hard on the gas.

"Fifteen minutes, nigga," Sharon yelled behind the car. She was already regretting her decision to allow Jessica to leave alone with Jamaal.

The shrill ring of the Motorola cell phone nearly succeeded in stirring Shakey from the bath, but the warmth and comfort of the smoke-filled bathroom held him firmly in its grip. And after a dozen or so rings, the early-morning caller realized the Handsome Intimidator was not yet open for business.

Shakey lie back even farther, now totally submerged, save for the front of his face and the right hand which dangled over the side of the tub. He toked hard on the Swisher, squeezing his eyes tightly to impede the progress of the water that rose just past the corners of his eyes. The burning end of the Swisher was now so close to his face that the heat of the fire could be felt against his lips.

Shakey lay with the stillness of a well-trained corpse. His beating heart eclipsed the sound of Stuart Scott's explanation of the stellar play of the New England Patriots. Not a ripple could be seen from the waters concealing the large frame, as not a muscle moved from the concealed.

The Motorola beckoned again, the caller obviously refusing to be ignored.

Shakey puffed hard on the butt of the Swisher. The use of his right hand was necessary to keep the cigar from being lost in his mouth. Reluctantly standing to leave the tub, Shakey took one last smoke then placed the doobie in the ashtray.

Shakey stepped from the tub. The large brown towel that hung from the rack was now in his hand. He toweled himself as his bare feet once again traveled the marble. Naked and half-dry, Shakey entered the bedroom.

Shakey flipped open the face of the cellular phone. "Yea," was the simple, gravel-voiced greeting.

"Where you been, nigga?" the familiar voice of a longtime friend and business partner questioned. The relief at finally finding a line of communications was obvious.

"What's up, Glenn?"

"I been tryin' to catch you since last night," Glenn chatted nervously.

"Whatcha got?' Shakey didn't want to talk much on the phone.

Glenn took the hint. "Two bigs."

"I'll hit you back when I'm ready," Shakey answered.

Glenn struggled to hide his frustration. After spending an entire night trying to contact Shakey, he would now be relegated to the pauper's end of the waiting game. "OK," he responded as cheerfully as possible, knowing he had no choice.

Shakey pressed the button marked 'end' and closed the phone's face. He stepped to the solid oak dresser drawer, standing momentarily in place before opening the top left drawer. He grabbed the first pair of boxers he touched. The silk robe lay atop the dresser.

Shakey exited the bedroom and traveled the length of the hallway. He reached for the banister once at the head of the stairway then slowly descended the alternating strips of black and white marble.

Shakey's first stop was the kitchen where he grabbed a red tumbler from the counter and filled it with ice.

His next stop was the living room—more importantly, the aquarium that served as the crown piece of the room.

Before tending to his own needs, Shakey observed the male betta who was the solitary inhabitant of the eight foot tank, the base of which grew out of the glass topped bar. The Chinese fighting fish slowly swam the depth and perimeter of his uncontested territory, stopping with each evolution to flash its most threatening pose, complete with a full display of its multi-colored fins whenever passing the mirror positioned in the bottom corner of the tank. Capable of extreme violence whenever confronted with anything that remotely resembled itself, the betta would relax only once satisfied that he was still the most dominant fish in the tank. Shakey had always marveled at how the betta's behavior so closely resembled the behavior of the black men he had spent the majority of his life around, himself included.

Shakey sprinkled a generous amount of food into the tank then watched as the betta attacked.

Next, it was time for his own setup.

Shakey reached for the tumbler before stepping behind the bar. He poured freely from the bottle of Bacardi 151 that he kept on the counter. Next, he twisted the cap of the two liter Coke, pouring just enough in the tumbler to change the color of the drink.

Now Shakey walked to the front door of his home.

The coolness of the November air caused Shakey to close the front of his robe. He kneeled to lift the two newspapers from the ground. The first was The Dickinson Herald, the daily publication of the small Texas town that he now called home. The second was The Galveston Daily News, the Texas island that would always be home.

Shakey reentered the home and shut the door behind him. With drink in hand and newspapers tucked securely under arm, he headed for his favorite place in the fifteen-room estate.

Shakey's study was his pride and joy. The nerve center of his empire. The only place in the world he could ever be completely of himself.

The floors were hard oak. The ceiling was a massive collection of Old World maps. A telescope protruded from the large bay window in the north wall.

The library was as extensive as it was varied, consisting of philosophy from Aristotle to Machiavelli. There were historical accounts of every major military conflict of the modern world. There were religious teachings from Abraham to Jesus to Mohammad to the Dhalai Lama. There were science titles from Darwin, Einstein, and Tesla, as well as autobiographies of Malcolm X, Colin Powell, and Bill Gates. There were six-hundred books in all, and Shakey had read each of them—many of them more than once.

The desk on the opposite side of the room was also oak. A large gemstone globe, the back of which was a pen stand, was positioned in the left corner of the desktop.

The room was decorated with life-sized bronze sculptures. Standing in the northwest corner of the room was a medieval knight, complete with chain mail armor, shield, helmet, and sword. A striking replica of The Trojan Horse, complete with an opened belly revealing a peeking Trojan warrior, was located in the center of the room. Shakey's favorite statue was found along the east wall of the study.

Harriet Tubman sat with both arms on the armrests of the rocking chair. A Winchester lie across her lap, and a knowing half-smile graced her well-chiseled features. The tiny woman was the epitome of all for which Shakey stood.

Shakey sat at the old woman's feet. He opened first to the sports page and read aloud. He read to Harriet every day.

Suddenly excited with the anticipation of knowing the results of Ball High's first round play-off game against Houston Yates, Shakey unconsciously held his breath before yelling, "Tors thirty-one, Lions fourteen."

Shakey pumped his fist before reading the article. And as expected, he found that Allen Richards had once again been the star of the game. Shakey's favorite Tor had returned the opening kickoff for a touchdown, then went all the way with an interception in the second quarter.

"To complete the hat trick," Shakey turned to Harriet, reveling at the approval that could always be found in the old woman's face. "Richards would later line up at flanker and go sixty-five yards and a score on an end around play."

The rum tasting much better now, Shakey took a hearty drink before turning the page.

Unfortunately, the rest of the day's paper proved anticlimactic as Shakey flipped disinterestedly through the pages of the county's oldest periodical. Anti climactic that was, until Shakey reached the obituaries. There, Shakey encountered a face from the past. A face in which he could associate the full gamut of human emotion. There, he found the face of Vikki Washington.

Shakey and Vikki had once been Ball High's most talked of couple. And though a decade had passed since their love affair ended, Shakey would readily admit that he had never seen a more beautiful woman.

Deeply smitten with passion known only to teenage lovers, Shakey and Vikki became expectant parents. The first pregnancy, aborted at the not-so-subtle suggesting of Vikki's father, happened the summer before the lovebirds' sophomore year. A year later, Vikki was expecting once again. This time, her teenage body, still not quite ready for the burden of childbearing, terminated the pregnancy itself.

Despite the many strains on their young love, Shakey, just three months after high school graduation and two months shy of leaving for Navy Basic Training, pledged his life-long commitment to Vikki with a five-hundred dollar engagement ring. She happily accepted.

A happy ending was not to be theirs, however, as a Dear John letter just four months into Shakey's naval career set the stage for his first and most bitter heartbreak.

Throughout the years, despite the many twists and turns of his tumultuous life, Shakey had never forgotten his first love. He had always wondered if Vikki felt the same. He had spied her countless nights on the streets, a mere shell of the beautiful young woman who, after winning Galveston's annual Juneteenth bathing suit contest three years in a row, was asked to no longer enter the pageant. She was out there hustling ten dollar tricks to purchase the crack rock her mind and body so desperately craved. Shakey's only thoughts were of taking her in his arms and confessing the still flickering flame that was still at home in his heart. And maybe, he thought, just maybe his love alone could free her from the raging demons that were fast winning the war for her tortured soul. He could always dream.

But now she was gone. The obituary read that Ms. Washington had succumbed to a lengthy illness. Shakey knew that illness was AIDS. But AIDS didn't kill Vikki. It had only succeeded in decimating an already hollow corpse. Crack cocaine had killed the Vikki Washington to which Shakey had pledged his undying love. And that Vikki Washington had been dead for quite some time.

Numb with the news of tragedy, Shakey folded the newspaper and placed it on the floor in front of him. He opted instead to fill his hand with the comfort of the tumbler. Sipping softly, the battle weary man filled the hollow in his chest with the warmth of the rum.

"See ya later, baby." Shakey kissed Harriet before leaving.

His palace now a prison, Shakey hurried toward the bedroom. His intent was to get dressed and leave as quickly as possible. With nowhere in particular to go, 'outside' was his only destination.

"Bitch! Get yo' ass out my car!" The Eighty-Eight rounded the corner and came to a screeching halt. The passenger side door was opened and the passenger was catapulted from the car.

Jessica's hands and knees landed against the pavement. Her teary eyes focused on the trio of women standing in front of Joe's.

"You ain't gotta do her like that, Jamaal!" Kitty was first to speak.

"Fuck that bitch!" Jamaal threw the transmission into park, leapt from the car and slammed the door shut behind him. "Ho gon' smoke up my shit then wanna play crazy when it's time for me to get mine." Jamaal drew closer to the prone young woman. "I oughtta kick yo' ass."

Sharon jumped quickly between Jamaal and Jessica. "Well, kick mine too!" The heavy-chested prostitute pushed the teenage boy with both hands.

The young drug dealer took one step toward Sharon then thought better of it. Sharon was a large woman. "You need to stay out my business, Sharon." Jamaal retreated in the direction of the Eighty-Eight, stopping only to allow his partner to climb into the passenger seat. The Eighty-Eight then sped away.

"You OK?" Kitty helped Jessica to the curb and immediately began wiping at her knee."

"She all right." A frustrated Sharon nearly bumped Kitty from her feet before snatching Jessica by the arm. "Bring your ass on here."

"I'm sorry, Sharon," Jessica whined pitifully. Her unfamiliarity with walking in the borrowed six-inch heels made her struggle to keep pace with Sharon's Amazon-like strides an impossible one.

"What did I tell you, Jessica?" Sharon fussed, totally oblivious to Jessica's lack of maneuverability. "What did I tell you? Huh?"

"I can't help it." Jessica did a series of awkward stumbles before finally tumbling onto the pavement. Embarrassed, she sat upright in the street, the laughing of Shay and Kitty making her pain all the worse.

"I'm sorry! I can't help it! Can't you say anything else?" Sharon turned to Jessica. "Take the damn shoes off, Jessica." Sharon took a deep breath in a gallant attempt to regain her composure.

"Get that ho right, Sharon," a man's voice cackled from the alley.

Jessica unstrapped the shoes and slid them from her feet. Holding the heels in one hand she asked, "What do you want me to do with them?"

"I don't give a fuck what you do with them!" Sharon stormed toward Broadway Boulevard.

Jessica was running to match pace.

"I told you! I told you! I told you!" Sharon was still fuming. "I'm tired of carrying your ass!"

Jessica was crying. "I'm sorry, Sharon."

"Would you please stop saying that?" Sharon yelled at the top of her lungs. "That was a fifty dollar trick you just messed up! We have no money! No money! Do you understand that?"

"We'll be all right," Jessica said with the wide-eyed innocence of a small child who had just been told that her family had lost its only source of income.

"Look." Sharon, exhausted with being angry with her friend, took another deep breath. "Let's find a trick so we can get a room and something to eat, OK?"

"OK." Jessica was determined to prove her worth to the only friend she possessed in the world.

"Here comes Snake." Sharon adjusted Jessica's shirt and blouse. "You just look pretty, I'll do the talking."

"What's up, Sharon?" A voice came from inside the black Range Rover. "Who's the snowbunny?"

"Hey, Snake." Sharon approached the vehicle, an exaggerated smile covering her face. "This is my friend Jessica."

"'Y'all wanna roll?" Snake took a burning Swisher from the ashtray and placed it between his lips.

"Open the door." Sharon smiled at Snake before turning to Jessica. "Don't embarrass me, bitch!" she hissed under her breath.

The two women climbed inside the Range Rover and were quickly whisked away.

The raging blackish-gray clouds covering the island skyline parted just enough to allow the heavens a peek at the chrome disc rims of Shakey's Cadillac Fleetwood. The eight-thousand dollar car accessories stopped revolving once in front of Sanovia's main entrance. Shakey, his complete array of street survival skills fully activated now, scanned every crack and crevice of the area visible to him before turning his attention to the Cadillac's rearview mirror, and more specifically, the non-descript dark blue sedan that came to an immediate stop behind him.

From the driver's seat of the sedan, Jazz peered back at him. Shakey smiled confidently to quell the intense nervousness present in the beautiful mocha-colored face.

An instant later, a gold-colored Mercedes pulled in front of the Fleetwood. The time for business was at hand.

The edges of the tattered brown paper bag carried by the long-limbed sexpot were folded at the top and rolled down. Following Shakey's instruction to the letter, Jazz, a favorite at Sanovia's, stepped for the passenger side of the Mercedes and climbed inside. Moments later, she climbed from the car, now carrying a blue and gray duffel bag. She moved swiftly for the entrance of Sanovia's.

The two high-pitched yelps Glenn's Mercedes made while zooming away were Shakey's cue to enter the club.

Madame Sanovia's was a small strip club, or "buttnaked" as it was more apt to be called in these parts, located just beyond Palm Terrace on Forty-fourth and Avenue H. Shakey, along with co-owner and manager of day-to-day operations Sanovia Jackson, had used the establishment to carve out a small fortune catering to the perversions of island ballers.

Just inside the entrance of the club, a step and a half to the right, was a small bar framed by an L-shaped counter top and complete with twelve unevenly placed stools. Further right, on the opposite side of the bar was a small deejay booth.

The floor of the club consisted of sixteen tables and an assortment of portable chairs—some wooden, others aluminum, all seldom used. As any regular customer of Sanovia's would tell you, evenings at Sanovia's were standing room only.

Past the floor of the establishment, on a raised platform, was the stage, complete with two poles, countless larger-than-life mirrors, and a wooden rocking horse.

Seated at the bar, a calculator and an open note-book before her, was Sanovia.

"'Bout time you brought yo' black ass in here," Sanovia sounded off as soon as Shakey entered the building.

Sanovia Jackson was a piece of work. At five foot ten and now nearly three hundred pounds, the fifty-one-year-old, rapidly graying grandmother was a far cry physically from the caramel-flavored delight who had in her day been a Market Street favorite. But despite no longer possessing the looks that had mesmerized two decades worth of Galves-ton seamen, the knowledge and insight Sanovia acquired into the often fragile psyche of men had more than adequately prepared her for her present career.

"Hi Mama." Shakey kissed Sanovia's cheek.

"I don' told you about that shit nigga!" Sanovia would never admit to appreciating the moniker. "Where yo' black ass been?"

"Chillin'." Shakey reached for the bag that Jazz held between her arm and side of her body. He laid the bag atop of the bar, and then hopped to the other side. He decided to fix himself a drink before doing anything else.

"Look at yo' hair, bitch!' Sanovia started on Jazz.

"What?" was Jazz' weak sounding protest.

"What nothin' cow! You workin' tonight."

Shakey poured freely from the just opened bot-tle of Hennessy. He took a sip then decided to issue

Jazz a temporary reprieve from Sanovia's wrath. "Count that for me, Jazz." Shakey pointed to the bag on the counter.

"Shakey, you need to talk to that bag of bones A-one before he get us closed down!" Sanovia possessed lashing enough in her tongue so that no one who knew her would feel neglected.

"What'd he do?" Shakey smiled, having already heard well of A-one's transgressions.

"That stupid-ass boy got these ignorant-ass bitches doin' live sex acts," Sanovia explained, as only Sanovia could do. "You know we can't have that shit."

A-one was the club's master of ceremonies. The ploys and tactics employed by A-one to arouse the crowd at Sanovia's were fast becoming legends of their own. But Sanovia was right; A-one was going too far.

"I'll talk to him."

Shakey watched as Jazz diligently counted the money. He found himself becoming aroused at the roundness of her rump, accentuated by the tight-fitting dress she wore.

"And the next time you bring this tramp in here with her hair lookin' like this, its gon' be me and you." Sanovia was not about to let rest the issue of Jazz' hair.

Jazz' lips smacked loudly. Sanovia's scolding obviously causing her to miscount one of the stacks of money.

"Smack 'em again, bitch!" Much faster than should've been possible for a woman her size, Sanovia was out of her seat. Her hulking presence hovered over the still seated Jazz, backhand at the ready position.

"Why you trippin'?" Jazz whined girlishly, smiling though mortally afraid of Sanovia.

"I'll show you trippin'." Sanovia returned to her seat. "Make me kick yo' ass in here." A few more mumbled expletives and Sanovia's outburst was complete.

Shakey and Sanovia settled to watch as Jazz continued to count the stacks of money. She systematically took the rubber band from each stack, counted it, and then repositioned the rubber band before placing the stack back inside the sports bag. She was barely able to conceal her amazement throughout the process.

Shakey drank aggressively, quickly finishing his first glass of Hennessy, and pouring himself a second.

"Twenty-eight thousand dollars!" Jazz' mouth was almost as wide as her eyes.

"You know the spot." Shakey put the stacks of money back into the bag and slid it toward Sanovia.

Sanovia grabbed the bag from the countertop, never taking her eyes from Jazz. Finding it impossible to resist giving the dancer one more scolding, she said "Dry yo' twat, bitch!"

Shakey laughed loudly and Jazz smacked her lips again.

Shakey strolled through the narrow opening leading from the bar to the DJ booth. Moments later, Tweet's "Oops, Oh My" played loudly.

Next, he reached in his pocket, collecting both lighter and Swisher.

Shakey sat still, save for the rhythmic nodding of his head. The Swisher and Hennessy combined with the music to form a most intoxicating elixir. His attention now belonged to Jazz.

Jazz had already taken to the stage. The twenty-year old gyrated seductively to the track, dancing with total abandonment of self-consciousness.

Shakey felt himself sinking into the leather interior of the deejay booth, but quickly peeled himself away. Though Jazz looked delicious, he felt a sudden disinterest in the whole scene.

Jazz continued to dance, oblivious to all but the music and her own body. The sensuous smile she wore while turning to face the DJ booth instantly became a disbelieving frown.

The Handsome Intimidator was gone.

CHAPTER 2

Christoper kicked at the empty beer can as he and his three cohorts crossed the intersection of Thirty-eighth and Broadway. The four boys were returning from the "hood store," the small Korean owned convenience store located on Thirty-eighth and Broadway. Inside the store was a small grill and fryer used to prepare take-out orders. And on this Saturday morning, an hour before noon, the hood store was where Christopher and his friends purchased their breakfast. Between them they shared two cheeseburgers and two orders of onion rings.

"Bingo!" Cedric pointed, barely able to get the words out, the mobility of his weighty jaws inhibited by the bite and a half of cheeseburger he chomped on. The object of his affection was a gold-colored Lexus.

"Man." Christopher kicked the can a little harder. "That ain't no gangsta ride."

"Whatchu talkin' about?" At twelve years of age, a full three years older than Christopher, Cedric felt it a must, at the very least, to contest the words of his friend, despite the fact the interest and effort necessary for him to sustain an effective argument had already been monopolized by the cheeseburger and onion rings he shared with Boo. "You don't know nothin'."

"Shut up, jelly belly," Christopher continued. "I'm down with them G-rides, nigga. I'm talkin' about them 'llacs."

"Jelly belly?" The overweight young boy had been struck in a highly sensitive area, and was quite sure that an equally insensitive counterattack was his only redress. "What you know about a G-ride, whiteboy?'

Christopher's pain-filled wince was accompanied by a clearly audible sigh.

Christopher's parents were black. At least as much could be said of the man and woman who Christopher had been taught were his parents. But there were rumors. Rumors that young Christopher was the product of his mother's stepping out with a white man. With his fair complexion and curly black hair, Christopher was hood exhibit number one—evidence enough to convict his mother of an unpardonable ghetto crime.

"Leave that li'l nigga alone." Boo, the oldest of the bunch, and closest to Cedric's size, spoke in Chistopher's defense. All who knew Christopher pitied him due to the circumstances of his birth. Unfortunately, their pity made his quest for self-validation all the more difficult. "You know that's some fucked up shit."

"Here." Wesley, Christopher's best friend, as well as Boo's younger brother, handed Christopher the tray of onion rings. Christopher handed him the remainder of the cheeseburger and both boys stuffed their faces.

The four boys continued their trek down Thirty-eighth Street, crossing Avenue H and heading for the mouth of the alley that lay to the right of the street.

Boo was first to reach the football the four boys had left under the pecan tree that stood next to the alley's entrance. He threw the ball a few feet in the air and caught it himself. He repeated the process again, each time tossing the ball a little higher, five times in all before suggesting to his friends. "Me and Cedric against y'all two."

"I don't play games." Christopher accepted the small remaining portion of cheeseburger from Wesley's hand, took a bite, and handed it back; leaving the last bite to his preschool playmate. The two of them sat on the curb.

"Oh, I forgot." Boo resumed the tossing of the ball. "You's a gangsta."

"That's right, fool." Christopher broke the last onion ring in half before sliding the tray in Wesley's direction. "And I'm about my scratch."

"What scratch, fool?" Boo laughed. "You broke."

"That's why my big homie gave me some work," Christopher answered.

"What work, fool?" Boo, obviously unimpressed, threw the ball on the ground.

Fully anticipating his friend's next question, Christopher was already taking his left shoe from his foot. He lifted the insole, revealing a small crumpled piece of aluminum foil. Once unraveling the foil, Christopher proclaimed, "This work, fool."

"Ooooh," was the collective response from the trio of boys as they huddled to get a better view of the two smallish tan-colored rocks and pile of crumbs that lie on the aluminum foil.

"Is that crack, Christopher?" Wesley's voice was a melody of confusion.

"Shut up, fool," Boo admonished. "What do you think it is?"

"Boy, you goin' to jail," Cedric told Christopher.

"We 'bout to come up." Christopher, though the youngest of the four, had obviously received a much better indoctrination into the world of the streets.

"How much can we make off that stuff?" Boo asked.

"My big homie said if I bring back forty dollars," Christopher refolded the foil and returned the package to its designated place inside the battered Nike Cross-trainer, "he'll give me an eightball."

The boys nodded, though not understanding any of what Christopher explained to them.

"How we gonna sell it, Chris?" Wesley asked.

"Let's go around Bull's." Christopher stood and tied his shoe. "It's always jumpin' around there."

Christopher crossed Thirty-eighth Street and then entered the Thirty-ninth Street alleyway. His three co-conspirators followed closely. The four of them were a clique now. A clique with a business plan. And Christopher decided he would be the un-disputed leader when it came to business.

"But Sharon." Jessica made a futile attempt at persuading Sharon to spare her the agony that awaited her inside the darkened closet. "Get in there before I strangle your ass!" Sharon shoved her inside then closed the door.

Jessica was terrified. The crack she had just smoked with Sharon caused her to imagine that a multitude of creepy crawlers inhabited the cramped closet with her.

"Heeeey baaaby." Jessica frowned at the exag-gerated warmth with which Sharon greeted the john.

"Hey yourself." Jessica easily discerned that the voice in the room with Sharon belonged to an older white man.

"Take your coat off, baby," Sharon instructed the john. Jessica shook with anger. She had totally forgotten about the creepy crawlers that had fright-ened her so just moments before. "There . . . that's better. . . . now sit down."

An extended silence from the other side of the door taunted Jessica as her mind became inces-santly fertile with images of possible happenings between Sharon and the john.

Sharon finally broke the silence. "You like?"

"I like." The john repeated, obviously quite appreciative of whatever Sharon had done to him.

Jessica noted the protests of the bedsprings as a substantial weight was suddenly added to their burden. Her anger at its peak now, she was stricken with the urge to spring suddenly from the closet and bring the sordid activities in the adjacent room to a screeching halt. Having committed an act quite similar in the not too distant past, memories of the ensuing fight proved deterrent enough to hold her in place inside the closet. Instead, Jessica sat in silent anger, fingers in both ears, wishing only that the situation would pass quickly.

Moments later, despite the deep as possible positioning of the fingers in Jessica's ears, the first of Sharon's screams and moans of pretended ecstasy could be heard. Quite familiar with the routine, Jessica could, if she wanted, perfectly imitate Sharon's entire performance. But while sitting in a hotel room closet, listening as her only friend engaged in sex for money, the mood for good-natured mimicry was lost on her.

The act was soon mercifully complete, and moments later the john was evicted with a simple "good-bye". The exaggerated warmth Sharon had shown earlier was now replaced by a barely civil impatience.

The door to the closet was opened and Jessica was allowed to enter the bedroom. She chose to sit in the chair closest to the door, deciding that she would for the rest of the day avoid the hotel room's single bed.

The two women sat in silence, the only sound in the room coming from the engine of an occasional passing car.

Finally Sharon reached for the phone, thick fingers proceeding to press violently on the push-buttons. "Kevin," she said when the occupant in room 117 answered. "Bring me a twenty." She slammed the phone into the cradle then stepped in Jessica's direction. Hurt deeply by the condemnation in the eyes of her ungrateful friend, she resigned herself to show no evidence of the pain she felt. "Pay Kevin when he gets here." Sharon dropped a twenty dollar bill on the table before rushing to allow herself the slight redemption that a hot shower would provide.

"Bitch!" was all Jessica could say as Sharon ducked into the bathroom.

"Here you go right here, J.C." The dope was already in Christopher's hand as he dashed to meet the passing bicyclist.

"If you don't get yo' bad ass somewhere." The would-be customer was not interested in the young boy's wares. J.C.'s ten-year-old Schwinn Cruiser did, however, stop in front of the crowd of young men standing in front of Bull's bar.

"Punk-ass mothafucka!" Christopher fussed before returning to the rickety wooden stairs leading to the corpse of the old Floyd's Café.

"Chill out, man." Cedric was the voice of apprehension.

Christopher said nothing, choosing instead to silently simmer.

The first day of business for the foursome had been an uneventful one. No one, it seemed, was willing to purchase crack from a group of school-aged children. At least not while a horde of older, more established drug peddlers waited across the street.

"Kitty and the white man." Christopher was off and running before even the words had left his mouth.

The three others watched in amazement at Christopher's maniacal sprint for the cream-colored Mazda Protégé rolling past the stop sign a full block away. They were further amazed when Christopher continued his full-speed approach toward the front of the car, despite the steadily increasing speed of the vehicle.

The tires screeched and Christopher veered toward the driver side of the car. He shoved his hand through the open window, stopping mere inches beneath the nose of the bug-eyed man. He once again displayed his product. "I got it, man."

The startled man said nothing.

"Get your mannish ass away from this car right now, Christopher!" Kitty snapped.

"I got it though, Kitty," Christopher pleaded while positioning the crack so she could get a good view. "Tell him I got it, Kitty."

"Christopher . . . !" Kitty fruitlessly searched for words to describe her anger. "Wait 'til I see your mama!"

"C'mon, Kitty!" Christopher clutched the window frame tightly as the car began to move forward.

"Let go of the car, Christopher." Kitty reached past the driver of the car, attempting to peel away the death grip with which Christopher held the door.

The driver of the car pressed heavily on the gas, his drug-frayed nerves rendering him incapable of dealing with the present challenge.

Christopher felt the rapidly progressing speed of the car just in time, releasing his grip before being carried too far. Unable to keep balanced, he fell forward, sliding across the pavement.

Christopher sprang quickly to his feet, looking first to the scraped knuckles of his left fist. The same fist which still clung tightly to the dope.

"You all right, Christopher?" Wesley was first to his side. The other boys followed closely.

"Bitch!" Christopher yelled to Kitty and the man. He was limping now as he made his way to the stairs.

"That's what yo' bad ass get!" someone yelled from across the street.

"Fuck you!" Christopher was defiant to the end.

No sooner than Christopher was becoming aware of the many scrapes and bruises he had been subjected to was he up and running again. This time in the direction of a woman exiting the alley a few feet to his left. "I got it, Wanda Lynn," was Christopher's oft-repeated sales pitch.

"I need a twenty," the wide-hipped woman explained while reaching inside her pocket.

"I got two of 'em." Christopher opened his hand. "Which one you want?" The nine-year-old could not conceal his excitement at having found his first customer.

"Let me see." Wanda Lynn used her index finger to examine the pebbles Christopher held. "They're so small."

"It's that good stuff," Christopher promised.

"Gimme all of it." Wanda Lynn's hand went deeper into her pocket.

"All of it. That's forty dollars," Christopher told her.

"Give it here."

Christopher placed the dope in her palm.

Wanda Lynn's hand closed instantly around the dope and she took a full step backward.

"Gimme my money, Wanda Lynn." Christopher stepped toward her, both fists balled.

The hand that had been stuffed in Wanda Lynn's pocket appeared suddenly. It was empty. "I'ma give it to you."

Christopher's partners stepped closer to the scene. They had no idea what to do.

"Gimme my dope if you ain't got my money," Christopher demanded.

"Look, boy." Wanda Lynn pushed him hard in the chest.

"I told you I'ma give it to you. G'on now." Wanda Lynn stepped around the boy and called to a man standing across the street. "Flap, you got your pipe?"

"You got me fucked up, bitch!" Christopher grabbed at Wanda Lynn and swung with all his might, landing a blow to the back of her neck.

The much bigger woman turned to face her attacker, shocked by the child's sudden burst of anger.

Christopher swung again. This time he struck the woman in the mouth.

The much larger woman reached out with both arms, wrapping them around the maddened boy. The ensuing wrestling match drew riotous laughter from nearby onlookers as the woman and boy tussled back and forth. Finally, a rapidly tiring Wanda Lynn fell onto her back at the last of Christopher's bull rushes.

"Gimme my money, bitch!" Christopher rained blows on the woman. Though many of them were blocked, he continued punching. He swung wildly until he felt himself being pulled from atop the woman.

"Getcho' bitch ass on," a husky male voice raged at Christopher while tossing him onto the gravel.

Christopher snapped to his feet, ready for battle. He stopped in his tracks upon sight of his opponent. Flap was a large man.

Christopher retreated to the opposite side of the alley, putting enough distance between himself and Flap to allow time for a plan.

"You all right, girl?" Flap bent at the waist to help Wanda Lynn to her feet.

"I'ma kill that li'l bastard!" Wanda Lynn threatened.

"Fuck him," Flap said. "You got the dope?"

"Yeah." Wanda Lynn finally opened her hand, looking inside as if feeling the need to verify the claim to herself.

Christopher quickly gathered a supply of stones, and while his unsuspecting targets inspected their treasure, he moved a little closer—just close enough to be sure of his mark. Without warning, the first of the stones were cast, smacking Flap solidly on the side of the head.

"You li'l bastard! I'm gonna—" Flap's threat was cut short by the second stone's impact. A small cut was opened just above his left eyebrow.

Christopher struck Flap again before pelting Wanda Lynn with the last two stones. Once out of ammunition, the young boy ran for his life.

"Run now, ya li'l fucka!" Flap chose not to chase the boy despite the wounds that had been inflicted upon him. The crack Wanda Lynn possessed was of much more significance to him now. "I'll get yo' ass."

Christopher ran until he was back on Thirty-eighth Street, not stopping until leaning safely against the pecan tree. Moments later, he could see the other boys running in his direction.

Wesley, shaking with amazement at his best friend's bravado, was first to speak. "You crazy, Christopher."

"For real, fool," Boo concurred. "Somethin' wrong with you."

"That dude gon' kick your butt," Cedric warned.

"Fuck that nigga!" Christopher answered. "If I woulda had my gat, I woulda bust a cap in that fool."

Normally Christopher's farfetched threats would have been immediately dismissed by the three boys. But after observing his recent actions, none of then knew just what to expect from him.

"We The Underdogs," Christopher said as if just being given a startling revelation.

"What?" Cedric spoke to Christopher in a much different tone now.

"That's right," Christopher went on, "from now on, we gon' call our clique The Underdogs. And if we catch anybody else using that name we gon' beat they ass."

The other boys were silent.

"And we gonna kill Flap!" Christopher added.

"Say Christopher, I'm down." Cedric stumbled over his words. "But I gotta go, my mama say she gon' check my homework when she get home." Cedric was already making tracks toward the Thirty-eighth Street entrance of the Sandpiper Cove apartments. "C'mon, Boo."

Christopher watched helplessly as one-half of The Underdogs instantly defected. Once the turncoats had entered the security fence and were out of sight, he turned to Wesley. "You got homework too?"

Wesley looked down at the street, contemplated for a moment his next words, and then looked his friend straight in the eye. "We The Underdogs." He whistled through the gap left by two missing front teeth.

"Underdogs," Christopher repeated before sitting on the curb.

Wesley joined him, and the boys spent the rest of the evening until nightfall, trading their favorite gangsta fairytales.

Shakey's Cadillac Fleetwood eased across the intersection at Thirty-fifth and Broadway. Sky blue with white interior, the 2002 Cadillac was Shakey's favorite of his small collection. He placed the R. Kelly CD in the player and raised the volume. He took a sip from the twenty-two ounce bull sitting between his legs and rolled the window down. Shakey waved at the smiling faces of Mr. and Mrs. Rittell, the grandparents of a childhood friend, as the Fleetwood continued down Thirty-fifth Street. The Cadillac slowed to a crawl as it approached Avenue H, its progress impeded by a woman stepping from the curb and positioning herself in front of the car, open palm speaking to the driver of the vehicle as if belonging to a traffic cop.

"You better get yo' ass out the way!" Shakey warned as the Cadillac, just a few feet from the woman now, continued to idle forward.

"You better stop this damn car, Shakey!" Sharon demanded after taking a couple of steps backward.

"What do you want?" The Fleetwood was finally still.

"I need to talk to you, Shakey." Sharon ran for the passenger side of the car.

"About what?" Shakey hit the switch that opened the door then motioned with his head for Sharon to join him inside the car.

"Let me tell you." Sharon's smile was wide as she stepped into the car.

"This better be good." Shakey made a U-turn.

"I need a job, Daddy." Speaking in her sweetest voice, Sharon squeezed gently on Shakey's thigh.

"We don' been there before," Shakey answered.

Sharon had once been a star attraction at Sanovia's. Unfortunately, like so many other girls in the business, she had fallen too deeply in love with drugs and Shakey had been forced to let her go.

"I know, Daddy." Sharon leaned a little closer. "But I learned my lesson." Her lips were at Shakey's ear now, while her hand traveled further up his thigh.

"Watch it before you waste my beer!" Shakey pushed her back into the passenger seat.

"You a trip, Shakey!" Sharon leaned against the passenger side door now. She pouted while staring straight ahead.

Shakey observed Sharon through the corner of his eye while redirecting the Cadillac once more. The cut-off shorts and T-shirt Sharon wore were dirty and her hair undone. But Shakey knew that dressing her and getting her hair fixed was only a formality. A quick look at the smooth chocolate skin covering Sharon's long thick legs, and the print of the nipples resting on her large, D-cup breasts, and Shakey knew that Sharon was still a winner. He also knew that crack cocaine was a pimp that no player could compete with.

"When was the last time you got high?" Shakey asked suddenly.

Sharon was honest. "This morning. I've got something else for you too, Daddy." Sharon turned back to Shakey.

"What?" Shakey's disinterest was obvious.

"It's a package deal, though," Sharon barked. "I don't want no shit out of yo' black ass!"

"What is it, girl?" Shakey chuckled.

"Pull up in front of the liquor store, and I'll show you."

Shakey turned left when he made it back to Thirty-fifth Street. Though knowing Sharon's claims were probably no more than the empty promises of a desperate woman, he would see this to the end.

"Wait here." Sharon hurried from the car.

"Hurry up." Shakey's impatience grew while watching Sharon approach the group of girls standing on the corner of Thirty-fifth and H.

Shakey looked to his right. A group of men, some standing, others bent at the waist, and still others kneeling, were huddled together in the storefront corner. One of the kneeling men rolled a pair of dice against the wall.

Shakey turned the engine off and stepped from the car. As he approached the crowd of men, a familiar face hurried in his direction.

"What's up, big-timer?" The man offered Shakey his hand.

"Nothin' much, Smitty." Shakey smiled.

"I ain't seen you in months." The much shorter man used a comb to sift through his beard. "I guess you don't fool with us li'l peoples no more."

"You know it ain't like that." Shakey was laughing now, not so much at Smitty's comment as he was at the noticeable stiffness in Smitty's neck. Smitty suffered a gunshot wound to the neck a few years ago. His misfortune was the result of a summer fling with a married woman. Extremely cautious of Smitty's sensitivity regarding the matter, Shakey veiled his amusement as much as possible. "Shit's been hectic, playa."

"I feel ya." Smitty turned his entire body so that he could face the crap game. "Check it out, Tee. My boy Shakey don' popped up on the scene."

A tall, burly man glanced quickly in their direction. After a quick swipe at the beads of perspiration which formed on his forehead, the man offered a disinterested wave.

"Nigga don' lost sixteen hundred." Smitty spoke from the side of his mouth while spinning to face Shakey. "So what's up?"

"Just cruisin'." Shakey pointed at the Fleetwood. "What you think?"

"Nigga, quit cappin'!" Smitty felt Shakey was just showing off.

"Who cappin'?"

"Comin' around here in a tricked out Caddy talkin' about 'what you think?'"

"Come on, man." Shakey laughed genuinely for the first time in days.

"Seriously though." Smitty's demeanor was instantly humorless. "Everything all right?"

"I'm just ridin'," Shakey repeated. "I'm waitin' for that crazy-ass Sharon."

"Oh." Smitty thought he had it all figured out. "You tryin' to get your freak on."

"Naw, man." Shakey laughed again. "She was suppose to be showin' me somethin', then the crazy bitch disappeared."

"There she is." Smitty pointed at the corner. "She got that li'l fine-ass white ho with her too."

Shakey turned quickly toward the direction in which Smitty pointed and was caught totally off-guard by the stunning beauty walking beside Sharon. Smitty had been correct when declaring the girl white. But calling this girl fine was like professing to the world that Michael Jordan could slam dunk.

"Shakey." Sharon carefully noted the beach-ball sized gleam in Shakey's eyes. "This is my friend Jessica. Jessica, this is Shakey."

"Nice to meet you, Shakey." Jessica gingerly offered a hand, and along with it a highly suspicious smile.

"The pleasure's mine." Shakey was held captive by the brilliant smile of the she-devil. He unconsciously wrapped both hands around hers all the way to the wrist, causing her to blush while pulling away.

"Do me a favor and get me a wine cooler, boo." Sharon pulled two one-dollar bills from her pocket and handed them to Jessica.

"OK." Jessica hurried for the store's entrance, accepting instruction like a well-disciplined child.

"That girl got some black in her," Smitty whispered in Shakey's ear as the two men watched the bouncing pockets on the back of Jessica's blue jeans disappear inside the liquor store.

"Now what's up?" Sharon crossed her arms, sensing that control was now hers.

"She all right." Shakey was conservative as the negotiations began.

"All right?" Sharon pursed her lips. "Nigga, don't front!"

"She all right." Shakey was unable to hold his smile. "Where y'all chilling'?"

"At Dale's," Sharon answered.

"Dale's?" Shakey frowned. "That old freak still lettin' all y'all hoes smoke and trick out his house?"

"Dale's our friend."

"And ain't none of y'all givin' him no pussy." This comment from Shakey drew riotous laughter from Smitty, which in turn drew a murderous glare from Sharon.

"Everybody ain't like you, Shakey," Sharon told him.

"You sho' right." Shakey was back on his game.

"Anyway." Sharon dismissed the comment with a wave of the hand. "We'll be at Dale's."

"I might swing by."

"It's a package deal." Sharon pointed her index finger at Shakey's face. "Don't try to fuck me over."

Jessica exited the store and handed Sharon the drink before being told, "Wait for me at the corner."

The three of them watched Jessica all the way to the corner.

"She ain't been out there either, nigga," Sharon said once Jessica was out of earshot.

"Right." Shakey knew that the "out there" Sharon spoke of was turning tricks. He also knew that Sharon's claim was quite unlikely. "I'll check y'all out," Shakey said to her before turning to Smitty. "What you drinking?"

"Shit, whatever." Smitty followed as Shakey started for the liquor store entrance.

Neither man spoke another word to Sharon.

CHAPTER 3

It was well past dark when Shakey finally pulled the Fleetwood in front of the small wood-frame house that Dale called home. The last few hours had been spent drinking, smoking, and talking it up with the crowd that transited the street corner. Not wanting to arrive too soon, lest Sharon discern his anxiousness, Shakey contented himself with the daily pleasures and excitement of life on the streets of Galveston Island. In the process, he had become quite intoxicated.

Shakey reached for the brown paper bag that lay in the passenger seat before leaving the car. He cast his gaze immediately upon the figure on the porch. It was Dale.

Dale was an elderly white man who had for years allowed the prostitutes of Galveston's East End district full access to his modest living space. And while there had been more than a few grumblings from women who had been awakened by the feel of Dale's hands exploring various parts of their bodies, Dale's hospitality was without charge. The girls would usually help Dale out with a beer or two, an occasional cooked meal, or an even rarer house-cleaning. However, Shakey had surmised long ago that the old drunk was just desperate for a little company. It was a fate Shakey feared would one day be his own.

"What's up, Dale?" Shakey called out to the old man while traveling across the short litter-strewn walkway.

"Heey, Shakey," Dale slurred, flashing the hand-ful of yellow-stained teeth he had remaining. "Long time no see."

"Too long." Oddly enough, Shakey had grown to like Dale over the years. "How's it hangin'?"

"Hangin's about all it's good for now days." Dale's smile widened.

"You lookin' good." Shakey told a lie. Dale's face was wrinkled and weather beaten. His hair was un-kempt, and Shakey was unsure of the original color of the multi-stained T-shirt the old man wore over dirty, too short pants.

"Uhhh," Dale moaned his dissatisfaction. "You ain't never been shit for a liar, Shakey." The old man turned up a tall plastic cup.

Shakey laughed before asking," What's going on around here tonight?"

"All the girls are gone." Dale took another sip of lukewarm beer. "Except Jessica."

"Jessica's here?" Shakey's eyes lit up.

"She's inside watching TV." Dale finished the beer. "Jessicaaaa!"

"What!" the young woman yelled from inside.

"Come here!" Dale yelled back with equal intensity.

Shakey smiled at the scene.

"What do you want now?" Heavy footsteps approached quickly. "You sure are one worrisome old man! I bet—" Jessica's scolding ceased in midsentence upon noticing Shakey.

"We got company," Dale laughed.

Shakey stared at the remarkably tanned legs that were visible beneath the cut-off shorts Jessica wore. "Hi, Jessica," Shakey finally spoke. He pulled the unopened bottle of Bacardi from the paper bag.

"Hi." Jessica smiled.

"Can we trouble you for a cup of ice?"

Jessica hesitated for a moment, her face framed by an expression Shakey found totally unreadable. "Just a second," she told him before disappearing through the screen door.

"Sweet as she can be." Dale looked deep into the night. "Don't mistreat her, Shakey."

"What do you mean?"

"I know what you're up to." Dale turned to Shakey. "And I know the things you don't know."

"I bet you do, old-timer."

"She's a sweet girl," Dale repeated himself.

Jessica bolted through the screen door with two old jelly jars filled with ice. She placed them both on the banister in front of her and reached for the bottle of rum. After filling both jars, she replaced the top. "I'll put this up for you." Jessica handed each man his drink before turning for the door.

"You comin' back out?" Shakey asked her.

Jessica observed Shakey, her face masked with the same impenetrable mask as before. She left without answering.

"Still as smooth as ever, huh Shakey?" Dale's hoarse laughter turned into a nasty sounding cough.

Shakey sat on the stairs. "That girl's crazy."

The two men drank in silence, both taken by the most beautiful star-filled night in ages. Since youth, Shakey had preferred the night. The daytime had always made him feel exposed. As if the world could see right through him. Free to read the deepest secrets of his heart. His every thought, feeling, and fear totally transparent.

With nightfall came the cloak of anonymity. And with that came the ability to be whoever he wanted. The nighttime crowd was never interested in the true substance of an individual. The nighttime crowd cared only for what one could bring to the party.

Dale finally broke the silence. "Beautiful night, huh Shakey?"

"Yeah." Shakey took a sip and felt the rum burning deep into his chest. "Beautiful."

Shakey thought of the times on the prison rec yard. He would stare into the night and consider the future he would carve for himself once released. So many dreams had since been deferred. And although Shakey, for his part, had left the Texas Department of Corrections with the truest intentions of changing his life for the better, fate would have it differently. And with the revelation of that fate came the slow and painful disintegration of everything dear to his heart.

Shakey drank in bigger gulps now, staring into the bottom of his cup while doing so. Standing suddenly, he said, "I'm going to talk to Jessica."

"I know," Dale said. "Just remember what I said."

Shakey walked around Dale and pulled on the screen door. Once inside the house, he saw Jessica laying across the couch in the living room. She sat up immediately upon sight of Shakey.

"Where's Sharon?" Shakey asked.

"She went out for a while."

"And left you here?" Shakey sat down next to Jessica and placed his drink on the coffee table.

"I didn't feel like going anywhere." She moved closer to the corner of the couch—a safe distance away from him. "I don't bite." Shakey took a drink. Jessica didn't reply. "I took a bath today." He slid just a fraction of an inch closer before placing his drink back on the table. Jessica, notably tense now, managed an uneasy smile. Shakey, pretending not to notice her emotional distress, feigned interest in the television. All the while, he carefully plotted his next advance. "I'm sorry," Shakey said after figuring upon a workable approach.

"Sorry for what?" Jessica held her pose.

"For whatever I've done to cause you to hate me so."

"I don't even know you," Jessica said.

"Well, why are you trying to make me feel so shitty?" Shakey played his part well.

Jessica took offense. "I haven't done anything to you."

"Like hell you haven't." Shakey took a sip from his jar.

"You know how much I like you."

"What?"

"I come all the way over here to see you and you act like I'm just disgusting or something."

"Disgusting?" Jessica frowned. "Look, I don't know what—"

"Don't you care about anyone's feelings but your own?" Shakey turned back to the television.

The two of them sat in silence. Each stealing glances of the other as safety permitted. Finally, after being driven to the brink of insanity by the juvenile game of cat and mouse, Jessica said, "Look, I'm sorry if I was rude."

"Rude?" Shakey frowned and shook his head. "What do you want from me?"

"Another cup of ice." Shakey slid the jar in front of her.

"You've got some nerve."

"You should talk."

Jessica snatched the jar from the table and stormed for the kitchen. Shakey laughed while listening to the jar fill with ice. His amusement was cut short by Jessica's approach. He watched her closely as she placed both the jar and the bottle on the table in front of him then reclaimed her spot on the couch.

"Thank you," Shakey said sarcastically.

"Don't mention it," Jessica said with equal attitude.

Shakey filled the jar to the rim. He could sense the peaking curiosity of the redhead. Finally, he sat back on the couch, drink in hand, and leaned in her direction. He leaned a little closer when she showed no visible signs of distress.

"You tired or something?" Jessica didn't ask until Shakey's head touched her shoulder.

"A little." Shakey sat up suddenly, grabbed a pillow from the back of the couch, placed it on her lap, and lay his head on it.

"I don't believe you," Jessica told him.

"Shhh." Shakey laughed where she couldn't see. "This is my favorite part of the movie."

There was an old Western on the television. A group of Indians had surrounded a stagecoach while a teary-eyed damsel pleaded with the movie's hero not to go through with a plan that involved using himself as bait while the others escaped. There was no sound in the room to accompany the weeping damsel until a light snore came from Shakey's direction.

Jessica gently wiped at the beads of perspiration flowing freely from Shakey's brow. She was amazed that he could be sweating as she froze to death.

She carefully observed the large black man whom had decided that her lap is as good a place as any for a nap. Though still extremely wary of Sharon's warnings regarding this man named Shakey, Jessica was grateful that the demons that tormented her whenever in close proximity to men had yet to voice their displeasure.

Shakey sat up suddenly, took another drink from the jelly jar, and then took to his feet. "Come on. Let's go," he mumbled while heading for the door.

"Go where?"

"I'm hungry," Shakey told her.

"I'm supposed to wait here until Sharon returns." Jessica knew she sounded ridiculous.

"Wait for Sharon?"

Shakey's words made her feel all the more childish. "We'll be right back."

Jessica stood momentarily in place before grabbing her purse from the table. "I guess it's all right."

Shakey continued onto the porch. He smiled at the sight that greeted him. Dale's head was back and his mouth was wide open. His legs were straight out in front of him with both arms flung to his side. The snoring was like a lion's roar. Shakey withdrew a ten-dollar bill from his pocket and placed it into the pocket of the flannel shirt the old man must have grabbed from the pile of rags lying in the corner of the porch. Shakey then took Jessica by the hand and led her down the stairs, toward the waiting chariot.

Shakey wheeled the Fleetwood into the Stop-N-Go parking lot at the corner of Twenty-sixth and Broadway. "Want something?" he asked after turning the music down.

"A soda."

Jessica was left alone as Shakey strolled for the store's entrance. She watched him closely, still surprised at her lack of anxiety, yet fully expecting the hammer to fall at any moment.

Moments later, Shakey returned carrying a plastic bag. "I got you this." He reached in the bag once seated.

Shakey handed her the four pack of White Zinfandel wine coolers.

"I asked for soda." Jessica stared distrustfully at the side of Shakey's baldhead.

"That's all they had." Shakey backed clear of the car next to him then drove the length of the parking lot before turning right at Twenty-fifth Street.

"Where we going?" Jessica untwisted the cap on the first wine cooler and took a drink.

"To eat." Shakey let the windows down. "You can grab my coat from the backseat if you're cold."

"I know that, but where?" Jessica reached for the coat.

"I don't know." Shakey grabbed a bottle of beer from the bag. "If we keep driving, something'll smell good."

"You're impossible." Jessica shook her head.

Shakey drove to the Seawall and made a left. In a while he would drive them to get something to eat. But first, there were other things on his mind. "Reach in the glove compartment and grab that plastic bag for me."

Jessica opened the glove compartment and froze immediately.

"What's wrong?" Shakey asked impatiently.

"There's a gun in there." Jessica told him.

"No shit." Shakey almost laughed. "Just grab the bag."

Jessica reached around the large chrome fire-arm, finally grabbing the plastic bag. Not noticing the contents of the bag until she had closed the glove compartment. "Is this marijuana?" The over-sized zip-lock bag was half-filled with a green substance that smelled very much like marijuana. Five overstuffed cigars lie atop the pile of grass.

"Here." Shakey handed her a lighter.

Jessica was flabbergasted. Lighter in hand, bag in the other, the young woman was frozen in place.

"Hurry up." Shakey snapped.

Jessica flicked the lighter, but the flame didn't take. She tried again, and again before finally looking to Shakey for help.

"Put it in your mouth." Shakey told her. "It's just like lighting a cigarette."

"I don't smoke cigarettes." Jessica responded defiantly.

"Well, inhale when you light it."

Shakey watched in silent admiration as the full-ness of Jessica's rose-colored lips wrapped around the Swisher Sweet cigar. He forced his eyes back onto the road once her lips turned inward and the first time weed smoker had inhaled.

Jessica exhaled loudly, turned her face to the open window, and held the Swisher in Shakey's direction.

Shakey took the Swisher then asked. "You have that much trouble lightin' your crack pipe?"

"What?" Jessica was angry.

"Lightin' a Swisher must be easier than lightin' a crack pipe," Shakey spoke while inhaling. Though the next line of questioning would be harsh, it was necessary. Shakey must measure the size of the monkey on the girl's back.

"Well actually," Jessica's anger caused her to take much larger sips from the wine cooler. "I like for someone to hold the lighter for me."

"Who? Your tricks?" Shakey held the Swisher out to her.

"I don't smoke marijuana." Jessica waved off the offered Swisher. "And I don't trick."

The Fleetwood turned right, then right again, then left and was on a single dirt road.

"What the fuck do you mean you don't trick?" Shakey was still holding the Swisher out to her. He believed her much more than he let on.

Jessica's voice was low but full of emotion. "I never did it."

"So why do you hang out with prostitutes?" Shakey asked.

"Sharon's my friend."

"And pimp?"

"My friend!" Jessica's voice was low no longer.

"Here." Shakey tapped her arm with the hand holding the Swisher.

"I don't smoke marijuana," Jessica repeated.

"Fine." Shakey smiled while inhaling. "I'll smoke by myself then."

The Cadillac turned onto a smaller gravel road and the beach appeared directly ahead of them. Shakey drove the car onto the sand, stopping just at the edge of the water before twisting rearward on the ignition.

Shakey was not quite finished. "How much crack you smoke?"

"I don't know." Jessica placed the empty bottle in the carton and grabbed a new one.

"Fifty dollars a day? A hundred? Two? How much?"

"What the fuck is your problem?"

"Just curious," Shakey answered. "I don't usually fool around with crackheads. And don't ever cuss me again."

Something about the way Shakey spoke the last part of his statement telegraphed an explosion of warning signals to Jessica's nervous system. And though what she felt came nowhere close to matching the intensity of "IT", the message was easily decipherable: This man was not one to play with. She did manage however, a weak sounding, "I am not a crackhead."

"When's the last time you smoked crack?"

"I don't know," Jessica lied. "About a week or so ago."

"A week?" Shakey knew she was lying. A major offense. One he would overlook just this once.

The two of them sat quietly back in their seats, both immersed in private thoughts as the soothing melody played by the oncoming waves intermingled with Smokey Robinson's silky smooth rendition of "The Quiet Storm."

Shakey thought of his problems with Trevino. Less than twenty-four hours before, in that exact same spot, he had come within a hair's width of squeezing the trigger on the .38-caliber revolver concealed within a large bag of Lay's barbecue potato chips, liberating himself for eternity from the cancer that was Jorgé Trevino.

Fortunately for Jorgé, the laughter of lovebirds, oblivious to all save for their own existence while dancing in the shallow water just an ear's shot from the potential death scene, had granted him a temporary reprieve from the never expected bullet.

Jessica thought of the insanity that was her young life. She was in disbelief over the fact that just three years out of high school could find her so far away from the Arkansas community in which she grew up. She was filled with wonderment at how the road she traveled had led to this place— sitting in a Cadillac parked on a Texas beachfront with a black man reputed as both a pimp and drug dealer. She was amazed that this man, who she hardly knew, could be the first man since Stu who could come so near to her without awakening "IT."

Shakey stepped from the Cadillac, traveling all the way around to the passenger side of the car before speaking. "Come on." He offered his hand.

Shakey led her to the front of the car. He lifted her gently from her feet and placed her atop the Cadillac's hood before sitting next to her.

"What did Sharon tell you about me?" Shakey asked.

"Why?" Jessica took a drink from the wine cooler. Tipsy already, she smiled at Shakey. "You have something to hide?"

"Just curious."

"She told me what you are."

"And that's what?"

"A hustler," Jessica said after searching the corners of her mind for the right word.

"Right." Shakey was prepared to lay down the law. "You know what that means?"

"Yeah." Jessica nodded then giggled. "I know what it means."

"What?" Shakey was grim-faced.

"I don't know. What?" Jessica giggled loudly.

"Somethin' funny?" Shakey paused then continued once significantly satisfied by Jessica's lack of response. "That means I'm about my paper." Shakey emptied the bottle of beer then tossed it in the sand. "You ain't tired of doin' yourself like this?"

"What?"

"Look at you. Ain't you tired of doin' bad?"

"Yeah." Jessica's attention was taken by the sudden squawk of a fast moving seagull. The bird swooped down with blinding speed, and after snatching its unsuspecting prey from the water, vanished just as quickly into the star-filled night.

"Roll with a winner then, baby," Shakey told her. "Leave all that bullshit behind."

Jessica nodded her head.

"How long you known Sharon?"

"Cool it with the questions." Jessica slid closer to Shakey, kissing him on the cheek before grabbing his arm and placing it around her shoulder. "I know the deal."

Jessica wrapped her arms around Shakey's waist and interlocked her fingers. She pressed her body firmly against his. Partly to see if "IT" would happen, partly because it felt so good.

The feel of the redhead's lips on his face rocked Shakey at his core. The warmth from her body compelled him to draw her nearer. The Handsome Intimidator lifted the she-devil's chin enough to brush her lips with his; pausing to read whatever message may lie in the woman's green-eyed gaze. Accepting the invitation, Shakey engaged her in a series of passionate kisses. Inertia placed them horizontally on the hood of the Cadillac. Him atop of her. Shakey kissed her again, and again, then stopped. Things were not going as planned. The king was in anything but control.

"What's wrong?" was Jessica's shallow-breathed query as she sat upright beside Shakey. "Did I do something?"

"Everything's straight." Shakey went to the driver side of the Fleetwood and climbed inside. "Get in."

Shakey played the music loud enough to discourage conversation. He was extremely upset with himself over the way he was acting. There was no doubt that the redhead was a real moneymaker. But first it was essential to establish just who would be Macking who.

"Christopher!" Barbara Ann Simmons leapt from the couch upon hearing the disengagement of the deadbolt lock. She ran to the door while working to shed the blanket she had used to cover herself. "Where have you been?" The thirty-year-old mother was deathly ill with worry. She wrapped both arms around her only child.

"Playin'." Christopher pushed her away then stepped around her.

"Do you know what time it is?" Barbara let her anger be known to him.

Christopher hurried away from her, bumping his leg on the coffee table as he made his way to the kitchen.

Barbara followed closely. "Do you hear me talking to you, Christopher?"

"I hear you." Christopher frowned while pulling at the handle of the refrigerator door. He was instantly incensed with himself for setting up such disappointment. He peered into the refrigerator a moment longer—there was only a half-filled pitcher of water there.

"Well act like it then." Barbara had no idea what she meant, but it didn't matter. What mattered most to her was that her nine-year-old son had finally come home.

Christopher turned to Barbara, prepared to shift the argument toward the lack of food present in the Simmons household, but was stopped in his tracks upon sight of the purplish-green atrocity that was his mother's left eye. A torrent of super-charged rage surged through every inch of his body.

"I know, baby." Barbara spoke in hurriedly hushed tones. She hoped to calm her son before he made the mistake of announcing his return to Winston.

"But nothin', Mama!" the boy yelled.

"Shhhh!" Barbara continued. "He's in the bedroom."

"Man," Christopher scanned the kitchen for a workable weapon, "y'all gon' make me do something."

Just then the door opened. The squeaking hinges sent a million shards of terror knifing through Barbara's heart.

"Where the hell you been?" Winston's wiry-frame hovered just over Barbara's shoulder. He was still outfitted in the oil-stained blue jeans and T-shirt he'd worn when Christopher had last seen him. Sweat poured from the edges of his uncombed Afro, and his gap-toothed scowl was aimed squarely at Christopher.

Christopher said nothing. He was unafraid, but wanted to say or do nothing to instigate more violence upon his mother. He would continue to bide his time while praying daily for the size and strength to dispose of Winston once and for all.

"You ignorin' me, boy?" Winston took a step toward Christopher.

Barbara moved quickly, effectively forming a blockade between the two with her body. She stood firmly in protection of the only thing she had in the world worth fighting for. "Christopher, answer him please!"

Christopher maintained his defiance, wishing with all that he was for the gun his big homie had promised him.

"I'll deal with your ass later." Winston waved him off, suddenly behaving as would a man with matters of much more significance to tend to. Turning his attention to his wife, he asked, "Where that money at, Barbara?"

"Money?" The remainder of Barbara's heart crumbled to pieces before falling to the floor. "That money's for my baby's shoes."

"I don't wanna hear that shit!" Winston yelled, then hurried for the living room, remembering that he had seen Barbara's purse atop the television.

"Winston, please!" Barbara pleaded while running into the living room. She arrived just in time to see Winston dumping the contents of her purse onto the coffee table.

"Where the fuck is it?"

"I'll give it to you!" Barbara cried. She snatched the purse from him and quickly produced the hundred dollar bill, lest Winston find the money she had placed aside to feed herself and Christopher until the food stamps came. "Here." Barbara placed the money, and along with it, her only chance to purchase for Christopher a Christmas present that would put a smile on his face.

"You'll get it back." Winston spoke a little softer now, perhaps reacting to a chord of resentment that struck somewhere deep within him. A chord hopelessly buried beneath the all-powerful need to satisfy his own cravings.

Money in hand now, Winston moved quickly for the door, not even bothering to close it behind him.

The beaten woman followed him to the door. She pushed it softly shut, then rested her forehead against the peephole. She sighed deeply before locking the door behind her deeply troubled husband. She had no clue as to the words that would comfort her child.

Sparing her the burden, Christopher stormed for his bedroom. He slammed the door behind him with enough force to shake his pre-school graduation picture from the wall.

Alone with the pitch darkness of his bedroom, the tears could now fall freely from the young boy's face. The slow and steady rising of the rage he felt laced yet another calloused layer of bitterness around his once innocent heart. His anger was temporarily pacified by the violent, vengeance-filled images in his mind.

A gentle breeze called Christopher's attention to the fluttering sheet used to cover his drapeless window. The boy took to his feet, moved the sheet aside, then climbed through the window. He broke into an all-out sprint as soon as his feet touched the ground. He knew not where his midnight run would take him, but was certain that any destination was better than home.

The Fleetwood pulled into the Denny's parking lot. Once nestled securely between a beige Ford Escort and red Jeep Cherokee, the Cadillac's occupants both stepped from the car.

The temperature was in steady decline now, and the kiss of the northern wind caused Jessica to burrow deep inside Shakey's coat. The two of them walked briskly for the restaurant's entrance.

A small congregation of customers was in the lobby awaiting seating. Shakey and Jessica took their place at the end of the line.

"I have to use the restroom," Jessica whispered into Shakey's ear before heading for the lighted sign at the far end of the lobby.

"Damn." Shakey was drunk and merry. "The more I drink, the more you piss." The small crowd laughed along with Shakey.

The line moved swiftly, and Shakey was already standing before the greeter's podium when Jessica returned from the restroom.

"Table for one, sir?" a polite, rosy-cheeked young man sang through two full rows of braces.

"Two." Shakey held up two fingers on his right hand while placing his left arm around Jessica.

"Smoking or non-smoking?" There was a barely perceptible change in the young man's demeanor. It was a change noticed only by Jessica.

"Smoking." Jessica answered.

"Right this way." The man led them to a table along the back wall of the building. "A waitress will be with you in a second."

Jessica offered a smile as the greeter turned to leave. It was not returned.

The two of them were seated. Moments later they were approached by a beautifully olive-complexioned Hispanic woman bearing the genuine smile of a friend. The waitress placed a glass of water and a menu in before each of them. "And how are you two tonight?" The waitress' heavily accented voice was both deep and sexy.

"Fine, and you?" Shakey checked the fit of the woman's uniform. "Never seen you before. How long you been working here?"

"A while." The waitress blushed.

"Naw, can't be." Shakey leaned back in his seat. He shook his head before saying, "I would definitely remember you."

"I work days." The waitress took careful note of the chilling glare coming from the eyes of the angry redhead seated across from the black man. "You guys let me know when you're ready to order."

"Let me get a Sprite right now," Shakey requested.

"No problem." The waitress dashed from the table.

"You know, that was some kind of rude." Jessica said immediately upon the waitress leaving the table.

"Rude?" Shakey looked as if genuinely surprised. "What was rude?"

"Noticing another woman while with me," Jessica snapped. "That was downright rude."

Shakey smiled at how country the redhead sounded once angered. "With you?" he asked before proposing, "My apologies."

Jessica started to say more, but refrained upon noting the approach of the waitress.

"I would say thank you," Shakey said as the waitress placed the soda in front of him. "But I'm not supposed to say anything else to you."

The waitress laughed in spite of herself. "Just let me know when you're ready to order," she said before leaving.

"Why did you do that?" Jessica reached for her menu.

"What?" Shakey feigned surprise.

"Why'd you say that?"

"Say what?"

"You know what I'm talking about." Jessica would have smiled if she wasn't so angry.

"I just told the truth," Shakey laughed.

"You're a jerk. You know that?"

"That's an upgrade." Shakey produced a bottle of Tanqueray Gin from somewhere under the table. He had purchased the pint from a bootlegger on the way to the restaurant. "Let me know when you're ready to order. I know what I want."

"I do too." Jessica was shocked at how Shakey could have such little regard for the number of watching eyes as he pouted freely into the glass of Sprite.

"Call J-Lo." Shakey placed the remainder of the gin in his pants.

"What did I tell you, Shakey?" Jessica scolded.

"Oh, yeah." Shakey sipped from the straw. "Let's order."

Jessica motioned for the waitress to return to the table.

"Ready?" The waitress looked directly to Jessica.

"Yes, ma'am. I'll have the grand slam breakfast," Jessica said then looked at Shakey.

"Tell her I want a steak and potato." Shakey sipped from the straw while eyeing the rear of the waitress.

"A steak and potato for the jerk." Jessica smiled at the woman.

"Girl, your hands are full," the waitress said before asking, "Anything else?"

"I think that's it." Jessica looked to Shakey for confirmation.

"All right then." The waitress collected the menus. "Be back shortly."

Shakey leaned farther back into his seat, drink in hand, staring intently at the beautiful creature in front of him. He wished that he could simply content himself with sipping from the glass, and admiring the redhead's beauty. But the time for further interrogation was at hand.

"Where you from?" Shakey asked.

"Malverne, Arkansas," Jessica whispered.

"Malverne, Arkansas?" Shakey repeated, took a sip from his straw, and then returned the glass to the table. "How does one get from Malverne, Arkansas to Galveston, Texas?"

"I came here with my husband."

"Husband?" The lines were far and deep across Shakey's forehead. "You married?"

"Separated."

"What happened?" Shakey lifted the glass again. This time he ignored the straw and turned the bottom of the glass to the ceiling.

"He started using drugs." Jessica squirmed in her seat. "One night he left with some people and I never saw him again."

Shakey could feel the sadness in the young girl's eyes. "And before he left, he turned you on," Shakey deduced aloud.

Jessica nodded slowly.

The greeter passed swiftly by Shakey and Jessica's table, followed closely by three college-aged young men. The trio of men was seated at the table next to Shakey and Jessica.

"Here you go." The waitress was encumbered with a large platter. After removing Shakey and Jessica's dishes from the platter and placing them on the table she said, "If you guys need anything else, just let me know."

Shakey and Jessica both murmured "thank you," and the waitress moved to the table next to theirs.

"How long has it been since you've seen him?" Shakey placed a large portion of steak in his mouth.

"Can we talk about something else?" Jessica's appetite waned.

"Sure." Shakey was nearly moved by the pain in her eyes. "Let's talk about you."

"What about me?" Jessica spoke in lifeless monologue.

"How old are you?"

"Twenty-one."

At this, The Handsome Intimidator was shaken. He wondered at how a girl so young could possibly have accumulated such sadness in her eyes. He thought too of her present predicament: far from home with a growing crack habit. And if that wasn't bad enough, he was now planning to exploit her for his own selfish purposes. Thinking of it all caused him to hate both himself and the world that created him.

Jessica started at the eggs, small bites at first, then much larger ones as she was reminded of the famished state of her body. She looked approvingly at the man across the table from her. Though he had already showed the tendency to be both arrogant and rude, Shakey could also be a real charmer when he wanted. More importantly to her was the fact that she felt secure in his presence. Jessica smiled to herself at the thought that she just might get laid tonight.

"Somethin' funny?" Shakey never appeared to take his eyes off the steak.

"Just thinking." Jessica smiled wider.

"Yeah." Shakey leaned back in his seat, now trying desperately to read the redhead's devilish grin. "About what?"

"Nothing you'd find interesting." Jessica laughed so hard that egg fragments flew from her mouth. "Excuse me." She was still laughing.

"Maybe I should have had wine coolers." Shakey laughed too.

"That's not it." Jessica wiped at her mouth with a napkin.

"Shit," Shakey reached under the table for the bottle of gin. He emptied the remainder of the bottle into his glass before saying, "Could've fooled me."

"You're the one with the hollow leg," Jessica told him.

"Third leg?" Shakey frowned into his cup.

"Not third leg, silly." Jessica laughed loudly. "Hollow leg."

"We'll see."

"We'll what?" Jessica raised an eyebrow. It had been a long time since she had had as much fun.

"I said." Shakey hesitated, stricken suddenly with Jessica's beauty.

"You said what?"

"I have something I would like to show you later." Shakey laughed at how corny he sounded.

"You're terrible, you know that?" Jessica's eyes darted to her left just long enough to catch a glance at the angry blue eyes of the young man staring at her from the next table. The angry man said something to the other two, and now all three of them looked at Jessica.

"You OK?" Shakey grabbed Jessica's hand, and with it, her attention.

"Yeah." Jessica was slightly startled, but found the large black hand covering her own to be reassuring. "I was just thinking about Sharon."

"Sharon?" Shakey squeezed her hand then went back to his steak.

Jessica looked to the table once more. The look in the angry blue eyes told of unspeakable hatred. The young man spoke again to his friends, and once more they looked in her direction, this time laughing loudly. Though not able to hear the man's comments, Jessica knew that she was the object of their ridicule.

Jessica watched as the three of them stood suddenly. Her heart beat rapidly when the three of them stepped in her and Shakey's direction. She once again caught the gaze of the angry young man. The hatred she saw caused her to shudder in her seat.

"Be nice, Randy," one of the laughing young men urged just as the party was passing the table.

"Hey." Randy's gaze burned into the side of Jessica's head. "Somebody has to take out the trash."

The three men roared with laughter, finally alerting Shakey to their presence. Shakey eyed the three men uneasily, but was unsure of what was happening.

"Did they say something to you?" Shakey's fork fell onto his plate as he prepared to stand.

"They're just assholes." Jessica grew more nervous. "It's nothing, Shakey. Really."

Randy looked once more to Shakey and Jessica's table. He found Shakey glaring in his direction. The aggression left Randy's eyes immediately. The laughter of his companions stopped also as one of them made haste to settle their bill. The three of them quickly exited the establishment.

"What'd they say?" Shakey sat down.

"Something stupid," Jessica told him. "I don't know. Let's not let it ruin our meal."

Shakey agreed. The short time spent with Jessica had been quite pleasurable. On most nights, dinner out would mean a table for one. And as Shakey had come to learn, one was a very lonely number. The two of them finished their meals in silence. Both content with the presence of the other. Both strengthened by the knowledge that neither of them would be alone tonight.

CHAPTER 4

Christopher slowed to a trot once crossing Thirty-seventh Street and Sealy Avenue. He stopped altogether at the mouth of the alley. He breathed rapidly while watching the cars whiz along Broadway Boulevard, only now becoming aware of the night's frigidity.

"Say, li'l one, what's up?" a gravelly voice beckoned from the darkness of the alley.

"Nothin'." Christopher strained to see the owner of the voice.

"Come here and give me a hand." Christopher could hear the rattling of the fence that enclosed a small yard behind a small, nameless auto shop.

Christopher backpedaled instinctively as the gravel crunched beneath the heavily approaching steps.

"It's a couple of dollars in it for ya, li'l one." The sweat suit clad man moved with great urgency. "Come on." A large meaty paw waved for Christopher to enter the alleyway. "Gimme a hand."

Christopher treaded cautiously into the alleyway. His curiosity was piqued by his own wonderment at the hairy-faced man's mission in the alley.

"Check it out, li'l one." The man pointed toward the small yard. The weight of the man shifted from one foot to the other as he waited for Christopher to join him. "See that battery?"

Christopher moved closer to the fence in order to gain a better view of the yard. A Diehard battery lay against the rear wall of the building. "Yeah." Christopher placed both hands on the fence. "I see it."

"I'm too big." The man pulled at the bottom of the fence to verify his claim. "But you can crawl under and get my battery."

Christopher considered the request. Though certain the battery was not the property of the unconvincing man, he would retrieve it anyway. But first things first. "Show me the money."

"I got the money, li'l one." The anxious man spoke as if offended. He pulled harder at the fence before saying, "Just get the battery."

Christopher lay flat on his back and positioned himself parallel to the fence. He slid slowly across the ground until he was inside the yarded area. He sprang quickly to his feet, then began the short trot across the yard, navigating his way around an assortment of debris enroute to the prize.

"C'mon li'l one," the man urged.

Christopher used the plastic handle to lift the battery from the ground then cradled it in both arms before turning to the man.

"Let's go li'l one." The man was still holding the bottom of the fence. "Come on."

Christopher's body stiffened upon hearing a loud clanking noise, followed immediately by the sound of something heavy being dragged across the ground, coming from the side of the building. He hastened his pace at hearing the guttural growl of the intruded upon beast, but found running with the encumbrance of the battery to be a quite difficult task.

Christopher ran as hard as he could. He was frightened to near death at feeling the heavy-breathing beast nipping at his heels.

"Run, li'l one! Run!" the man holding the fence yelled.

Christopher took a peek over his shoulder, taking his eye from his course just long enough to stumble over a radiator hose. Unable to regain his balance, the boy dropped the battery in order to free his hands and brace himself for the fall.

A violent snap signaled the limit of the animal's progression as the chain had been extended to the fullest.

The maddened dog was able to snare the cuff of Christopher's pants. The dog's neck jerked wildly to and fro, briefly lifting the boy's lower body from the ground.

Christopher somehow managed to roll onto his back. He nearly fainted upon sight of the two-hundred pound Bull Mastiff.

"Mama!" Christopher kicked wildly at the dog's face and head with his free foot, finally striking pay dirt with a solid thrust to the monster's nose.

The stunned canine released its grip for just a moment, but recovered quickly. The dog lunged forward before even the thought of escape could form in the boy's mind. This time the dog's vicious bite covered the back of Christopher's Nike Cross-trainer.

The feel of the dog's teeth pressing against the skin of his foot caused a surge of adrenaline to rush through Christopher's body. He struggled mightily to free himself from the powerful clutches of the Mastiff's jaws.

The dog was equally tenacious as the pull of the large chain attached to its collar was all that prevented a fatal advance upon its victim.

Christopher's foot came free from the tennis shoe, leaving the enraged Mastiff with a glaring reminder of the one that got away.

Christopher scrambled on his hands and feet in the direction of the fence.

"Get the battery li'l one,"the man reminded him before adding, "He can't get you."

Christopher looked behind him. The Mastiff's vehement struggle failed to garner progress against the unyielding metal.

Christopher calmly lifted the battery from the ground, cradling the treasure once more before stepping toward the fence.

A surrendering splinter of wood screamed loudly into the night as the dog's assault on his restraint intensified.

Christopher was running now. He dropped the battery onto the ground before sliding in one precise move onto his torso. His motion didn't slow until safely on the other side of the much welcomed barrier. He left his unnamed crime partner to slide the battery underneath the fence.

A resounding crack of wood caused them to both look in the direction of the dog. Another ear-splitting snap and the carnivorous beast ran freely for the fence, dragging behind him the thirty-foot chain. The opposite end of the chain pulled a utilities meter.

Both Christopher and the man ran from the alleyway. The two of them laughed once standing safely on Thirty-seventh Street.

"Here ya go, li'l one." The man gathered the three one-dollar bills from his pocket and gave them to Christopher. "Good job."

"Thank you." Christopher tightened his fist around the bills.

"Holla at old Scrip when ya need a hustle." The man walked hurriedly toward Sealy Avenue. "I'll be around."

"All right." Christopher stood undecidedly at the alley's corner, again clueless as to his destination. The barking of the still frantic dog suggested to him a path south toward Broadway. He was still quite sure that despite a shoeless left foot and the coolness of the night air, the streets were a much better place to be than home.

"Mothafucka!" Shakey shouted at the site of the Cadillac's two airless tires.

"What's wrong?" Jessica had yet to see the damages.

"Punk-ass bitches!" Shakey inspected the passenger side of the car. As expected, he found the two tires on that side flat also.

"Oh, no." Jessica was finally able to view the object of Shakey's despair. "Who would do such a thing?" Jessica's question was answered by the memory of hate-filled blue eyes.

An eruption of ground shattering music turned both Jessica and Shakey's attention to the black Escalade creeping slowly in their direction. Jessica felt her insides vibrate with the vehicle's continued approach. The Escalade stopped directly behind Shakey's Cadillac and the window came down.

"What's up, homeboy?" The music was lowered just enough for the voice's call to Shakey.

Shakey stepped to the window. A husky dark-skinned brother wearing a black leather coat was seated behind the wheel. A black beanie cap was pulled down to just above his eyebrows.

"Some haters slashed my tires," Shakey told the stranger.

"That's fucked up." The man eyed the slashed rear tires as if they were the mortal wounds of a dear friend. "You need to call somebody?" He offered his cell phone to Shakey.

Although he had his own phone, Shakey accepted the stranger's gesture with a "Thank You." He quickly dialed the set of numbers then waited anxiously for the voice on the other end. While waiting he noticed the fifteen pack of bull in the backseat of the truck. "Say, man," Shakey spoke into the phone. "I need you to come rescue me and my shark." Shakey moved the phone a few inches from his eyes in an attempt to put some distance between his eardrums and voluminous yells that echoed through the earpiece. "Yeah, I'm at Dennys. I know what it is. It's an emergency. Yea . . . yea . . . all right then . . . solid."

Shakey hung up the phone and handed it back to the man. "How much to add one of those beers to my bill?" Shakey reached into his pocket.

"You don't owe me nothin', playa!" The young man placed the phone beside him before grabbing two beers from the box. "Take these beers, my nigga."

"Thanks, fool." Shakey grabbed the beers.

"Later." The window went up and the Escalade was on the move. The ground rumbled to the funky bass line coming from the truck's monster sound system.

Shakey returned to his broken chariot. His anger rose once more when he looked at his car. "You can sit inside if you're cold," he told Jessica before opening the door for her.

Jessica stood still. She struggled desperately to find the words that would ease her new friend's burden, but found herself to be paralyzed with fear. The only thing that she feared more than men was angry men. Despite her apprehensions, Jessica closed the car door and cautiously approached Shakey.

"I'm sorry about your car," Jessica whispered into Shakey's ear once seated next to him on the hood of the car. "It's all my fault."

Shakey turned to her, gazing somewhat suspiciously in her eyes before saying. "Don't worry about it."

Jessica slid closer to him but didn't say anything.

Shakey, perhaps sensing her discomfort, placed one arm around her while using the other to feed himself the malt liquor.

Jessica was at ease within the security of Shakey's embrace.

After just a minute of stillness, Shakey stood in recognition of the purple and green wrecker truck bouncing over the incline of the parking lot's entrance. Shakey stepped into the driveway, waving frantically to signal the wrecker's driver.

The wrecker pulled just in front of the Cadillac and two men climbed from the vehicle.

The driver of the truck was David Erving. David was a five foot two, 140 pounds, a constantly chattering ball of energy. A long-time acquaintance of Shakey's, David owned a small garage and wrecker service.

The second man was Fred. He was an employed whipping boy of David's.

"What's up, Shakey?" David's deep, throaty voice was reminiscent of Wolfman Jack.

"Somebody slashed my tires."

"You know that sayin' about scorned hoes." David's laugh was loud and obnoxious.

"Yeah." Shakey smiled briefly.

"What you waitin' for?" David scowled at Fred. "Get yo' dopefiend ass to work!"

"What you want me to do?" Fred asked his boss.

"What I want you to do!" In an instant, David was in Fred's face. "Ask me another dumb-ass question and watch me break my foot off in yo' ass! Air up the damn tires so we can tow it!"

"Aw right, man." Fred searched the front of the wrecker for the needed supplies.

Shakey shook his head while laughing.

David was a champion shit-talker but could back up none of it. The many scars throughout his face and head served as a written record to his winless fight career. Never short on courage, David had been known to challenge the entire crowd at the bars he frequented. The result was always the same: a painful whipping for David.

Despite a true fondness for David, it had been quite some time since Shakey had ventured into public with his friend; a night out with David almost always guaranteed involvement in a brawl of some type.

"Hurry up, crackhead!" David watched as Fred filled the back tires with fix-a-flat.

Fred mumbled something just a little too loud in return.

"What you say?" David ran behind Fred. "Say it again, bitch!" David challenged, then stood over his employee until certain there would be no further defiance. "I ain't think so!"

"Is he crazy?" Jessica whispered into Shakey's ear.

"He all right," Shakey assured her.

"Want a drink?" David pulled a bottle from beneath the driver side seat of his truck.

"I'm cool." Shakey held his beer out in front of him.

David looked at Jessica. "What about you, princess?"

Jessica shook her head before burying her face deep into Shakey's chest.

"Fuck y'all then." David poured from a carton of grapefruit juice into a label-less bottle. He shook the bottle vigorously before drinking. "I'll drink my own shit."

"You gotta car at the garage?" Shakey asked suddenly.

"My daughter's BMW," David answered.

"Think I can borrow it until tomorrow?"

"Cool." Droplets of David's concoction slid from both corners of his mouth. "Say, princess."

"Me?" Jessica asked timidly.

"I sho' ain't callin' this big rusty mothafucka' princess."

David's laugh was long and loud. "But serious business though, princess, let me ask you a question."

Jessica studied the insane midget standing before her.

"You ever been licked by a man under five-five?" David asked with apparent sincerity.

"Have I what?"

"Chill out, David," Shakey protested while struggling to stifle a laugh.

"Once you been licked and stamped by the D-a-v-i-d," David made loud slurping noises with his mouth then laughed. "You'll never be the same."

"All ready to go, boss," Fred spoke from behind the Cadillac.

"You ride in the car," David told Fred. "You two ride up front with me," he said, and they piled into the vehicles.

Shakey pulled the BMW into a parking spot directly across from the hotel's office. "Wait here," was his only instruction to Jessica before heading for the office entrance.

Jessica sat still in the car as the first pangs of "IT", so mercifully absent so far this night, now caused a not so subtle change in the rhythm of her breathing.

Shakey tapped on the window. "Get the keys," he spoke from outside the car. Jessica did as instructed then locked the door behind her. She stepped quickly to keep pace with Shakey as he rounded the corner. She continued to follow as he strode down a long, dimly lit walkway. There was a seemingly endless row of doors to their right, and Jessica eyed the numbers on the doors as she walked. Their seemed to be a full company of acrobats performing in the pit of her stomach, and despite the temperature, there were large beads of perspiration forming on her brow.

Shakey stopped once in front of room 184. He pulled the key from his pocket and opened the door. He prodded her inside with a gentle hand to the back before entering the room himself. Once the door was closed behind them, Shakey headed immediately for the restroom.

Jessica stepped further inside the room. The furnishings were cheap and simple. There was a queen-sized bed with dark-colored linen, a nightstand attached to the wall, and a table with four chairs positioned before the sliding glass patio door. The wall opposite the bed had attached to it a small dresser. A television sat atop the dresser.

Jessica sat at the table. She struggled desperately with the demons within as the sound of the man urinating in the next room pushed her to the brink of total terror. She closed her eyes as tight as she could, then used her hand to wipe away the single tear that slid down her left cheek while listening to the flushing toilet.

Shakey entered the room. His shoes were off, his belt was unbuckled, and his pants were unfastened. He inhaled deeply from the burning Swisher that hung from his mouth. "You cold?" Shakey moved for the thermostat control, sure that he knew the reason for the woman's trembling. "It'll warm up in a second." Shakey stepped to the table, kissed her on the forehead, then headed for the television. He turned on the power then flipped through the channels until finding ESPN. He was just in time for the NBA highlights.

Jessica watched as Shakey sat at the foot of the bed. Though still stiff with apprehension, she was amazed at the calming effect of his kiss. Though clueless as to the source or reason of the apparent power he had over her, she found herself longing for more of his attention.

"Damn." Shakey sat straight upon seeing the whipping the Rockets had put on the Lakers. He had placed a sizeable wager on the Lakers but found it hard to upset about the outcome of the game. After all, the Rockets were his favorite team.

"What?" Jessica appeared under his arm.

"Steve Francis." Shakey turned and kissed the redhead's lips. "He picked a hell of a night to play Oscar Robinson."

Jessica smiled. She had no knowledge of he names Shakey mentioned, but assumed that they were both basketball players.

Shakey was growing quite fond of Jessica's habit of sliding up beside him and placing herself under his arm—an act she committed with such quick and subtle movement that she would already be adjoined to Shakey's hip before he could ever notice her approach. There was something so different about having her next to him; something right, something true.

Shakey brought the Swisher to his mouth again. He took a puff before turning the cigar around and placed the lit end in his mouth. "Let me blow you a charge."

"A what?" Jessica laughed at how silly he looked.

"Just breathe in slowly when I blow the smoke in your nose." Shakey placed the butt end of the Swisher just under her left nostril. He covered the other nostril with his thumb.

Before being given the opportunity to protest, a steady stream of smoke was floating freely through Jessica's nasal passage.

Jessica breathed inward as instructed. She inhaled until both lungs were overflowing with Swisher smoke then continued to inhale. She inhaled the Swisher smoke until it was no longer possible for her to do so.

Jessica finally backed away from the Swisher. Her head was light, and a pleasure-filled half-smile covered her face. "Damn." She said softly before lying backwards onto the bed.

"Damn," Shakey repeated then laughed. He turned the Swisher around and took for himself one last toke before reaching over Jessica and placing the cigar in the ashtray.

Shakey began to unbutton the coat that he had given her earlier to wear. He found the glossy-eyed redhead, who was still smiling absently at the ceiling, to be more than helpful once the time had come to slip the jacket from her body.

Jessica had never been so relaxed. The sweet smoke of the Swisher had induced a quite pleasurable paralysis. At the same time, the heightened sensations to every nerve in her body caused her to quiver with delight upon each touch from Shakey. Both her smile and gaze were aimed at the top of Shakey's glistening bald head as the nimble-fingered magician quickly unbuttoned her blouse.

Shakey kissed the redhead softly then backed away to observe the firmness of her deeply tanned skin. He pressed the palm of his hand against the rigidness of her torso then used his fingers to delicately trace the outline of each abdominal muscle until reaching the base of her bra. Shakey kissed her again, this time deep and hard, while working the hook on the front fastening bra.

While sliding the bra back over both shoulders, he continued to cover her face and neck with gentle kisses, taking into his hand one of her perfectly formed breasts.

Jessica felt the warmth of Shakey's breath against her breast. She thought she would succumb to spontaneous combustion at the feel of the moist tongue tracing small circles around her fast hardening nipples. She clasped both hands around

the back of his head, pulling him deeper into her
bosom. A soft moan escaped her lips as he took her
nipple into his mouth.

Shakey bit down softly on the tip of Jessica's
nipple before feeding on a mouthful of soft flesh.
His nature was already beginning to rise while tugging at the buttons alongside her skirt.

Jessica's body was on fire. Never had she known
such desire. She unfastened the last two buttons
and freed herself from the skirt.

Shakey's pulse quickened with the slow back
and forth movement his hand made against the
moistness at the center of the black lace panties
that were now Jessica's only clothing. He continued massaging while feeling the slow and rhythmic
rotation of the redhead's hips.

Jessica had never had a comparable experience
and found herself completely consumed with desire. She pulled Shakey nearer to her. She kissed
the top of his head and wrapped both arms tightly
around his neck.

Shakey ignored the vibrating phone in his pocket
while delighting himself with the feel of the small
soft hands that gently stroked the broadness of his
back.

Shakey placed an open mouth atop Jessica's
belly button then worked his way down with slow
and soft kisses until his lips touched just above the
waistband of the lace panties. The kissing stopped
and Shakey used his hand to pull the waistband of
the panties away from her skin.

The phone vibrated again and Shakey snatched it from his pocket. He decided to take a quick peek at the display window before flinging the Motorola across the room. The page was from his closest partner Red: Red's number was followed by 9-1-1—a page not to be ignored.

To Jessica's dismay, Shakey rolled suddenly from the bed and placed the phone to his ear. A split second later she could hear a man's voice on the other end.

"What?" Shakey couldn't believe his ears. "When? . . . Fuck!" He slammed his fist into the nightstand. "I'll be right there." Shakey closed the phone and placed it back in his pocket before taking a seat on the edge of the bed.

"What's wrong, baby?" Jessica reached over his shoulder and used both hands to slowly massage his chest.

"Nothing." Shakey pushed her off of him before standing to fasten his clothes. He grabbed the keys from the nightstand and hurried toward the door. Saying only, "I'll be back in a while," before closing the door behind him.

Before Jessica could protest, Shakey was gone, and the magical moment was finished. Now the redhead kneeled on both knees in the center of the bed. Never had she felt so naked, or alone.

Shakey parked across the street from the Harris County Jail. The radio played softly, and the Handsome Intimidator sipped from a warm bottle of beer. He had been parked there for nearly four hours.

Red's phone call had elicited a full range of negative emotions from Shakey. Initially there was shock, which was followed immediately by anger powerful enough to induce heart palpitations. Now there were the twin tormentors of worry and regret as Shakey feared that he had once again proved capable of ruining another's life.

D.D., or Doris as was her given name, was the first cousin of Shakey's ex-wife Evette. A friend for years, Shakey had always joked to Doris that she was the only woman he had known for any measure of time while maintaining a platonic relationship. D.D.'s reply would always hinge on the proclamation that their relationship would forever stay platonic.

D.D.'s position in Shakey's organization was simple but fraught with peril. Her responsibility: the transporting of drugs from a location designated by Trevino to a spot chosen by Shakey. D.D. was the best, and Shakey paid her handsomely. Tonight, she was busted while traveling south on Interstate-45 at about the halfway mark between Houston and Galveston.

The thirty thousand dollars forked over to Rebecca of Allied Bails Bonding to secure D.D.'s release was of little consequence to Shakey. Truth be told, his love for money—like his once unbridled passion for hustling—had grown cold and stale.

Shakey had indeed grown quite weary of the game. But unknown to even his closest friends, the Handsome Intimidator was trapped into ballin' by a most precarious set of circumstances.

Shakey leaned back into the BMW's leather seat. The streetlight directly above the car's windshield began to dim as Shakey's eyes grew heavy. His mind floated freely to a time long since past.

Shakey replayed the only period of his adult life in which he had displayed any semblance of personal responsibility. Not so surprisingly, it was also the only period in his adult life in which he had known happiness.

Nookie was a newborn then, and Shakey a fresh-faced twenty-one-year-old, just a year removed from his first prison stint. He and Evette owned nothing of tangible value. Each night, after working ten or more hours at Wendy's, Shakey would make the six mile trek to sleep next to Evette on her mother's living room couch. Their offspring would sleep in the car seat placed atop the glass topped coffee table. Never again had Shakey known such contentment.

But Shakey would soon trade the safety and contentment of Mrs. Jackson's living room for the bright lights and loud promises of the ghetto streets. Life was instantly better financially for man, woman, and child. Shakey purchased for Evette a house of her own, along with all he fathomed to be her heart's desire. Nookie possessed all in which he expressed a passing interest, save for the attention of the father he loved so dearly. And Shakey was King of the Jungle, partaking freely of all that befitted a ghetto superstar, yet totally unaware of the destruction that awaited the end of his reign. In hindsight, Shakey could see that he had been locked aboard a constantly descending rollercoaster the entire time. And thirteen years later, the ride was still gaining speed.

"Shakey." A tap on the window snatched Shakey into the here and now. "Open the door, nigga. It's cold out here."

Shakey smiled at the woman running around the front of the car. No sooner had he unlocked the door was she seated inside.

"Shit." D.D. struggled to slam the door against the howling wind. "You surprised the fuck out of me, Shakey. A bitch was just getting ready to lay down on that nasty-ass mattress!" D.D. was a lovely shade of milk chocolate. Her full, round lips and smooth, seamless skin was as inviting as the track star-like legs that threatened to burst the side-stitching of jeans she wore. Add to the mix a fun-loving attitude, and "around the way girl" personality, and it was a sure bet that D.D. was the 'thug girl' made famous by a score of popular rap tunes. When referring to herself, third person "bitch" was D.D.'s reference of choice.

Shakey couldn't believe his ears. "You thought I'd leave you there?"

"Nigga, when they told me my bail was $300,000, I didn't know what to think." D.D. unbuttoned the denim jacket she wore. "Shit, the average motha-fucka woulda left a bitch stuck out."

"I ain't never been the average mothafucka," Shakey reminded her.

"I know a bitch happy to see yo' ass!" D.D. squeezed tightly on Shakey's neck and planted a kiss on his cheek. "If you wasn't married to my cousin, a bitch'a put you in this pussy."

Shakey smiled before saying. "I think I know the answer to this question, but are you OK?"

"I've been better." D.D. was now in the mirror fretting over her fallen hairdo. "Look at my hair."

Shakey started the engine. His mind raced with the thoughts that he hoped would fix D.D.'s pre-dicament as he wheeled the BMW away from 1301 Reasner. "I mean . . ." Shakey started, paused for a moment then finished. "Are you OK?" Shakey looked at her.

D.D. returned his gaze. She was initially un-sure of what he was asking, but felt herself grow instantly angry once his question became clear to her. "I know you ain't askin' if I'm snitchin'."

"Naw," Shakey lied to her. He thought for a moment then said. "I talked to Nelson already, so don't worry.

"What you mean, don't worry?" D.D. was still upset.

"Just stick to the story I gave you." Shakey guided the BMW's ascension onto the interstate. "I got the rest."

"I hope so." D.D. turned back to the mirror. "'Cause a bitch ain't tryin' to do no time."

"You won't," Shakey assured her. "You hungry?"

"Uh uh." D.D. shook her head. "Take me home. My baby gotta go to school tomorrow. I bet she worried to death about her mama."

Shakey thought of D.D.'s thirteen-year-old daughter.

"How the hell is Nelson anyway?" D.D. asked of Shakey's cousin, who was also now her criminal defense attorney. Nelson had always had a crush on D.D. "A bitch need a workin' man."

"He's doin' all right." Shakey laughed before asking, "I thought Nelson was a square?"

"He is." D.D. put the comb and brush back in her purse. "That's what a bitch need, 'cause this gangsta boo shit is played out."

Shakey laughed but said nothing. There was no need. A bitch had said it all.

"Why the hell are there dishes in the sink?" Stan's drunken roar shattered the short-lived peacefulness that had resided in the Reardon home. "And this house is filthy!"

Twelve-year-old Jessica Reardon was frightened to tears at the sound of her stepfather's voice. As she had done on countless nights before, Jessica prayed fervently in hopes that some great calamity would suddenly befall her mother's third husband. Or maybe Jessica hoped God would see fit for Stan to peacefully bypass his stepdaughter's bedroom and enter the room he shared with her mother. Unfortunately, neither of her prayers would be answered on this night.

"You hear me talkin' to you, missy?" Stan shoved the bedroom door open and stepped inside the darkened room. "Why in God's creation are there dirty dishes in that sink?"

"I'll wash them in the morning before I go to school." Jessica pulled the blanket to her chin.

"You'll do no such thing, young lady!" Stan snatched the blanket from her grasp. "I want that kitchen scrubbed spotless, tonight!"

"OK, Stan." Jessica took a glimpse at the clock radio that was on her nightstand. 9:00 P.M. At least two hours before her mother's return from work. "OK. I'll do it now." Jessica leapt from the bed, her progress impeded by the vise-like grip that clamped her shoulder.

"You're goddamn right you'll do it right now." Stan shoved her back onto the bed. "It's about the time you all showed some appreciation for me around here."

"We appreciate you, Stan." Jessica cried out. "Please!"

With no regard for the young girl's cries, Stan lie atop of her. "Don't I pay the bills around here?"

"Yes, Stan." Jessica's stomach was sick with the stench of alcohol and stale tobacco. She attempted to free herself, but Stan was much too heavy.

"Don't I feed and clothe you and that good-for-nothing piece of shit brother of yours?" Stan forced the child's legs open.

"Please Stan, don't!" Jessica fought the useless fight.

Any restraint Stan may have possessed just moments before was now non-existent. He ripped the young girl's clothing from her body then stopped to unzip his pants once her body lay bare before him.

"Noooo!" Jessica made one last attempt to escape the inevitable. She forced her legs closed with all her might.

Stan refused to be denied. He clamped one sweaty paw over the girl's mouth while using the other hand to force her legs open again. Next, he penetrated his stepdaughter with a maniac's viciousness.

With no one to hear her muffled cries, Jessica retreated deep inside her own head. She found the one place where everything was pink and blue. Where there could be no angry stepfathers named Stan, and no piercing pains between the legs of twelve-year-old girls. A place where there were only loving mothers who baked blueberry muffins, bandaged and kissed booboos, and showered their children with unconditional love and approval.

A sudden movement in the doorway snatched Jessica back into the here and now. Jessica locked gazes with the second victim of her stepfather's barbarity. Jason, her eight-year-old brother was witnessing the entire act.

Jessica awakened with a shudder. Jason's terror-filled eyes still searched hers for answers she could never give.

The tortured young woman rolled across the sweat dampened sheets. She reached for the Swisher Shakey had left on the nightstand earlier.

Trying desperately to rid herself of the tortuous images, Jessica lit the Swisher and puffed hard. She prayed for Shakey's return, longing for the newly discovered security she found in his arms.

Jessica took another puff then placed the Swisher back in the ashtray. She lay on the bed then curled into a fetal position. "God, please bring him back," she whispered into the darkness.

CHAPTER 5

Shakey pulled the BMW alongside the Ball High School field house as instructed. A black Ford Mustang made a fast approach from behind. The Mustang flashed its high beams before gently kissing bumpers with the BMW. Shakey popped the clip into the .41-caliber pistol he carried then unfastened the safety lever in preparation for whatever the situation may bring.

Shortly after dropping D.D. off at home, Shakey received a call from Trevino. Upon returning the call, it had not been Trevino who answered. Instead, it was Josephine. It was also Josephine who was now stepping from the Mustang that had nearly drawn Shakey's fire.

Shakey placed the pistol in the waistband of his pants and covered it with his coat. He unlocked the passenger side door while observing the slender but shapely caramel ex-call girl who was now Trevino's main love interest. She was also, Shakey surmised, the thriving force behind his own dire circumstance. Josephine carried a satchel on her shoulder, and Shakey was sure of the contents.

"Jonathan." Josephine's firm behind settled into the cushioned leather. She always called him Jonathan. Partly to remind him of their past intimacy, but mostly because she knew how much it annoyed him.

"Slut." Shakey was as cordial as possible. Despite the relationship the two of them once shared, Shakey was disgusted by her presence.

"You should talk." Josephine was not the slightest bit upset. The smirk on her face suggesting a fondness for the direction of the conversation. "My man is waiting for you over there." Josephine pointed to the park at their left, her smirk a full-blown smile now.

"You mean your pimp?" Shakey shot back.

"Call it what you want, nigga. But I'm always gonna have the mothafucka calling the shots. If that ain't you, don't be mad."

Shakey smiled to mask his anger. He stepped quickly from the car before finding himself no longer able to suppress the urge to strike Josephine.

Once inside the park, Shakey zeroed in on the solitary figure sitting on a swing at the center of the park. The Handsome Intimidator quickly scanned the park for evidence of another's presence.

Shakey approached cautiously. Though not known to be violent, Trevino could be extremely unpredictable.

Trevino didn't speak until Shakey was a few feet away. "What's up, Shakey? You act like you don't want to talk to me or something."

Shakey didn't respond until seated in the swing next to Trevino. "What's up?"

"You tell me." Trevino's fast opening smile produced tiny little wrinkles in the corners of both eyes. His jet black hair was slicked straight back and held in place by a handful of styling gel. The tiny specks of premature grayness were still isolated enough to be barely visible to the naked eye. "I hear you had some trouble tonight."

"Good news travels fast," Shakey mumbled.

"Wanna tell me about it?" Trevino's voice was calm.

Shakey's temper reared its ugly head. "You know what happened, mothafucka!" The Handsome Intimidator quickly recomposed himself.

"You're right, Shakey." Trevino turned to look Shakey in the eye. "I also know that you are fucking up!"

Shakey hated this man, and the grudge between them was filled with history.

Jorgé Trevino was the bastard child of an Italian police officer. His mother was an illegal Mexican immigrant. And while Officer Joseph Russo was totally enamored with mi amor, as he addressed her, the racially intolerant Russo family would never have given the two their blessing to marry. Young love honors no barriers, however, and though never making an honest woman of the mother of his child, Joseph Russo showered both woman and child with love and attention. And there was a very happy little boy who dearly loved the tall dark-haired man he called Pa Pa.

Shakey's father was a pimp, numbers runner, drug dealer, and addict, hustling his days on earth away in the section of the island ghetto called "the jungle". Officer Russo was the most feared cop in the jungle streets, known for his hard-nosed approach to policing, and he often demonstrated prowess with the billy club.

One summer day, just over a quarter century ago, officer Russo rousted the group of men congregated outside the Sweet Dreams café. As a result, Shakey's father was transported by way of Officer Russo's squad car to an isolated area of Galveston that locals referred to as The Backtrack for an intensive session of stick and flashlight therapy. Most unfortunate for Officer Russo was his failure to frisk and handcuff his victim before placing him into the car.

Before ever reaching The Backtrack, Shakey's father produced the screwdriver he carried in his sock and stabbed officer Russo repeatedly in the neck, brutally ending the young officer's life.

The offense earned Shakey's father a life sentence in the Texas Department of Corrections, thus depriving both boys of the fathers to which they had both been blessed with.

The murder only marked the beginning of Shakey and Trevino's strange-fated relationship. Their destinies were seemingly permanently intertwined by forces forever to remain unseen.

During their junior high school years, both boys found it hard to fit in with expected peer groups. Trevino because of the Caucasian features that would forever set him apart from others of Mexican descent, yet not quite render him fully acceptable to many of the white kids. Shakey, because of the tattered clothing he was forced to wear, became a magnet for the attention of every would-be comedian at Weis Junior High School.

Both boys found solace in the Galveston Boy's Club. And in boxing coach Johnny Enriquez, they both found the mentor and father figure they so desperately needed. In each other, they both had their only friend.

But with high school came the inevitable fork in the road. Trevino was the achiever: ROTC, junior police cadet, National Honor Society—he lacked only the much desired respect of his peers. Shakey was the enigma. Perfectly capable of serious accomplishment in both academic and athletic pursuits, he chose a road that lead to suspensions, street hustling, pistol-packing, and short stints in Texas Youth Corrections. He gained nothing, save for the admiration of his peers.

Not until high school did either boy approach the subject of their fathers. It was Trevino who finally pulled the cork on the bottle filled with a lifetime's worth of anger, fear, and frustration. Once he had, he would find that he no longer had control of the words fired from his mouth. He spoke badly of both Shakey's parents before predicting that his former compadre would amount to no more than the sum of the two who had produced him.

Possessing no other coping skills to deal with the sting of his best friend's words, Shakey punched Trevino in the mouth. Always stronger and faster than Trevino, Shakey won the ensuing fight in a most convincing manner.

Trevino went on to join the Police Academy. He advanced rapidly through the ranks, finally landing as the top man on Galveston County's narcotics task force.

Shakey was a high school dropout. And after a brief stint in the military, he settled into his predestined occupation of career criminal. He proceeded to rise as rapidly on the street as Trevino did on the force.

Enter Josephine.

Ethel Josephine Gilbert was a looker, and was as rotten inside as she was beautiful on the outside. She first met Shakey at the home of a young hustler named Tyrone. Being the upwardly mobile bitch that she was, not much time had passed before Tyrone had been discarded as a mere stepping stone and Josephine had sank her claws firmly into Shakey.

Theirs was a swift and intense affair of lust and deceit. Shakey found himself totally enraptured with the fantasies Josephine created for him with the array of sexy costumes and lingerie she kept in her bedroom closet. For her part, Josephine was temporarily pacified with knowing that she had snared the largest fish in the pond.

However, her eyes would forever be opened to bigger and better things.

Enter The Big Tuna.

Despite a mercurial climb through the ranks of the Galveston police department, Jorgé Trevino had never satisfied his desire for the admiration of 'his people,' nor had he quenched his thirst for vengeance against Shakey. He found himself left only with the overwhelming despair of one constantly fighting an impossible to win battle.

Trevino was haunted with the realization that while he worked tirelessly, risking his life daily in someone's proposed war on drugs—all for $48,000 a year—that scum like Shakey got rich peddling drugs and coaxing vulnerable young women into the exploitation of their own bodies. Trevino vowed to not end up like his father—a lost life in a politician's war with nothing to show for his sacrifices but a military style funeral. That might work for the white boys on the force, but not Jorgé Trevino. And after finally deciding that nice guys do indeed finish last, Trevino decided that the time was right for him to become a player in the game. Though he had yet to determine the hand he would play.

Re-enter Josephine.

Josephine met Trevino late one night while driving a Cadillac Eldorado belonging to Shakey. After pulling the car over, Trevino said enough between flirts to start the wheels churning in Josephine's mind. And in short time, the cop who would be drug dealer was smitten with the black widow's sting.

The first part of Josephine's plan called for Shakey to be sent on a long trip upstate. Then, Trevino's connections would allow the two of them to fill the void left by Shakey's absence. All this she concocted while convincing Trevino that the devilish scheme was a product of his own genius.

The result: Shakey lost it all. The years of building were brought to ruin with one swift swing of the task force battering ram. All assets were frozen, and all possessions confiscated. Shakey was instantly reduced to just another broke and incarcerated young black male, having nothing to show for his years in the game but stories to entertain the boys on the cellblock.

David and Red chipped in to secure for Shakey the hotshot lawyer that saved a life. Instead, the Handsome Intimidator was hit with a fifteen-year sentence. Six and a half years later, Jonathan Reed was a free man. Or so he thought.

A half-year into Shakey's release, Trevino showed his face again. This time he presented Shakey with a life-ending ultimatum. Armed with the necessary dirt to put Shakey away for the rest of his life, the deal Trevino offered was simple: Shakey would move Trevino's dope or spend the next ninety-nine years as a ward of the Texas Department of Corrections. Thus Shakey became a slave to the bloodthirsty cop. And Trevino finally felt the beginnings of his thirst for vengeance being quenched.

And here they were. Two men sitting on the swing set in a children's park, their lives intertwined since youth by circumstances neither of them would ever understand. Both hated the other for different reasons, with the intensity of each man's hatred multiplying itself exponentially with each passing moment.

"And about that dope your mule lost tonight." Trevino smirked. "You know you gotta make that up, don't you?" Trevino was only looking to remind Shakey of where he stood on the totem pole.

"Fuck you." If not for Josephine sitting fifty feet away, Jorgé Trevino would have been the next recipient of a twenty-one gun salute.

"I know what you're thinking, Shakey." Trevino peered into the soul of his prey. "But remember, I do have a partner on the force. And he knows everything." Trevino placed emphasis on the word "everything," then went on to list just a few of the bag's contents. "The bitch that OD'ed in Corpus, the Rastas in Houston, and then there's that other thing."

The thought of the other thing caused Shakey's ulcer to burn.

"Yeah." Trevino's eyes were smiling a defiant symphony. "Fuck with me, and Governor Perry'll give you the needle himself."

Shakey was a beaten man, and he knew it. Trevino was not bluffing. Trapped by his past, the King of the Jungle was now a monkey doing tricks at the command of the sickest of circus masters. No more words were spoken as both men knew they were locked into their respective positions until the day one of them grew truly tired of it all.

"The satchel Josephine is carrying contains ten birds." Trevino stood and brushed the wrinkles from the Armani suit he wore. "I want twenty-two a ki."

"Twenty-two a ki?" Twenty-two thousand dollars was three grand more than Trevino usually made him pay for a kilo of cocaine. It was also seven thousand dollars more than he would pay elsewhere.

"That's right, and I want my money in seven days." Trevino told him. "None of this bullshit you've been pulling lately."

"What about D.D.?"

"What about her?" Trevino started his stroll for the Mustang. "Tell her to keep her fucking mouth shut."

"She has a child, man," Shakey yelled behind him. "She can't do no time."

"That's up to you." Trevino kept walking.

"What you mean it's up to me?"

"If I'm happy, maybe I'll let her CI on some other ass-holes and get probation." Trevino stopped, then turned to face Shakey. "A real playa like me got it like that." Trevino's love for the power he felt showed all over his face.

"CI?" Shakey was in no way willing to expose D.D. to the dangers that came with snitching. "If you're happy?" He was finding it hard to believe how sick his nemesis had become.

"Yeah, if I'm happy." There was no compromising Trevino's position. "And the only thing that makes me happy is money. So go make me some more money, bitch!" Trevino frowned before turning for the Mustang once more.

Shakey's blood boiled. His hand gripped the handle of the death tool. His eyes focused on the spot in the back of Trevino's head that would bear the gaping hole.

"When you do," Trevino said without looking back, "just pick the vein you want the Governor to tap."

Jessica had been here before. Many times before. Forced to revisit the images of childhood miseries that totaled to shape her past, the marathon matinee of fiendish horror porn always culminated with the same twisted scene.

It would always start with the voices. Jessica could hear Stan and the others before they had even stepped onto the unpaved walkway leading to the front door of the trailer home. The fourteen-year-old trembled at the noise made by the laughing men. She knew that with her mother at work and Jason attending a high school basketball game, no buffer existed between herself and the horror that had entered the Reardon household.

Jessica pulled the covers over her head, then jammed both index fingers as far as she could into her ears in an attempt to shield herself from the raucousness of the adjoining room. The young girl shuddered when the conversation turned to the pretty little redheaded thang in the other room.

With the boldness of a drunken fool, Stan confessed to his friends that he had already "tried the little slut out." The revelation caused Jessica's heart to shrivel with shame.

One thing led to another as the alcohol and sordid conversation fueled the lust of the roomful of drunken men. Minutes later, the five of them entered Jessica's bedroom. They were as merry as a group of school boys viewing their first naked pictures. Bottles were passed, jokes were told, and insults were hurled as each man took his turn with the horrified child.

The special place that had been Jessica's safe haven in the midst of past violations was now unreachable as the thunderous sounds of the men's voices, the musky stench that emanated from their sweat covered bodies, and the salty taste of her own falling tears proved sensory reception enough to keep the teenage girl hopelessly trapped in her bedroom. Her mind's eye vividly recorded every detail of the unfolding atrocity.

Five days, and a million breakdowns later, Jessica hurled herself into her mother's arms. She informed the woman whom birthed her of the gang rape that had taken place under her roof. She told also of the ongoing abuse Stan had inflicted upon her since her last year of elementary school. The two women cried and hugged. Then Jessica was pushed away suddenly with great force.

A string of obscenities were passed from mother to daughter. There were accusations of seduction to go along with the labels of harlot, slut, and Jezebel. Jessica found the sting of her mother's words to be the most painful of all she had endured.

A little over a year later, just three days after her sixteenth birthday, Jessica wed the forty-seven year-old forklift driver who would become her means to escape the Reardon house of horrors.

A full seven years later and Jessica was no closer to understanding her mother's rejection as she had been on the day she first revealed her stepfather's transgressions.

Jessica wiped her eyes and snatched her purse from the table. She ran from the hotel room as fast as her legs would take her. She ran from the memories of Stan and her mother. She crossed the hotel parking lot and was on Seawall Boulevard. East into the night she ran, in search of whatever peace that would be afforded her in this cold and lonely world.

God was dead! There was no other explanation, Shakey surmised, for the disastrous pattern of events that constituted his thirty-four year existence. Shakey drank straight from the gin bottle while meditating on the impossibility that was his life.

Shortly after his father's incarceration, Shakey's eighteen-year-old mother packed the meager belongings that she and her three-year-old son possessed and moved into the home of Ben Massey. Ben was the forty-year-old longshoreman who would soon make Delores Reed his wife. The unhappily married couple would soon bring three more children into their tempest of dysfunction.

The relationship between stepfather and stepson was cursed from the beginning. Ben detested Delores' bastard child from the day he first laid eyes on him. The hatred was returned by the toddler with equal measure.

Child abuse did not begin to explain the mistreatment the young boy was subjected to at the hands of his mother's husband. Words were sparse but cruel. Discipline was issued with open hands to the face and closed fists to the chest.

Rebellion it seemed had been deeply ingrained in the heart of Delores Reed's eldest son from the beginning. At four years of age, young Jonathan swung the claw end of a hammer in his stepfather's direction. A year later, the bedroom Ben and Delores shared was set ablaze by the angry child.

The many incidents of insurrection committed by the young boy resulted in the absorption of massive beatings and humiliations. But nothing Ben did seemed able to extinguish the flame that burned in young Jonathan's eyes and heart. Nor were the flames merely fanned. But the abuse endured by Shakey served the same purpose as pouring a tanker full of gasoline on an already out of control brush fire.

The young boy's mind became a breeding ground for violent thoughts as he indulged himself with endless fantasies about the vengeance to be extracted once he was bigger.

At seven, Jonathan ran away to his mother's grandmother's house. His Big Mama, apparently cut from the same cloth that had produced the warrior in her great grandson, refused to allow Jonathan to return to a home where he would be mistreated. Big Mama was quite adamant about her stance, as evidenced by the single shot fired from her double-barreled Winchester.

With Big Mama's gunshot, the only period of normalcy in Shakey's childhood began. The eighty-year-old woman adored her great-grandson, and the love was returned a thousand times over by the small child. Finally loved and care for, there was a marked change in the behavior of young Jonathan. His second grade teachers were awestruck at the soft-spoken and well-behaved seven-year-old impersonating the hellion whom just two months into the school year had already caused two young teachers to break down in tears. Even more astonishing to the group of educators was the true brilliance he now exhibited.

Shakey took two more sips from the bottle before replacing the top and positioning the bottle between his legs. He smiled broadly as the memories of Big Mama's small and cluttered apartment passed through his mind.

The two of them shared a bed in the apartment's only bedroom. Each night before they slept, Big Mama would tell Shakey Bible stories. Shakey was fascinated with the way Big Mama could make the characters of the Bible seem as real to him as the men standing just a few feet outside their bedroom window, laughing and drinking their lives away under the hand painted sign that read simply ENGLISH CAFÉ.

Shakey's favorite story was the one about a wise king named Solomon, and how he decided between two women who lay claim to the same infant boy. To this day, Shakey marveled at the remarkable faith Big Mama placed in her maker, despite the hardships of her life.

Shakey reminisced over Big Mama's sweet potato pie. Shakey loved the pies, and Big Mama prepared an individual sized pie to eat with his dinner every evening. He could smell Big Mama's kitchen now. And the songs Big Mama hummed while working were as sweet as any melody ever heard.

Shakey laughed at how he and Big Mama would never miss an episode of wrestling. "Get 'em, Tommy!" he could hear Big Mama yell through a mouthful of snuff. Big Mama loved Wildfire Tommy Rich, and loathed Gino Hernandez. Shakey on the other hand, had always preferred the bad guys.

Shakey remembered that day in the seventh grade. The day he came home from school and there was no smell of sweet potatoes cooking. There was also no sweet sounding melody coming from the kitchen. There was nothing but the loud echoing stillness that filled his heart with fright. "Big Mama," was the boy's call as he stepped into the kitchen and found that nothing in the room had been touched. Shakey walked rapidly across the hallway and pushed the door open. There he found Big Mama.

Big Mama was seated in the wooden rocking chair that faced the television. Her favorite bible was in her lap. Shakey's fifth grade school picture was lying on the open page. "Big Mama," Shakey called once more, though already knowing that the woman who had taught him to love was dead. The serenity in Big Mama's face was his only solace in her passing.

Shakey could still conjure the image of Big Mama's not quite smiling face. A single tear stain traveled a path that started at the corner of Big Mama's left eye, ran through the small black freckled dots on her cheek, and finally entered the corner of her mouth.

A single verse was highlighted on the page opposite Shakey's picture. The young boy read aloud, "Every word of God is pure. He is a shield to those who put their trust in him." These words the young boy placed securely in his heart. These words the world conspired to rip from his heart.

Big Mama's passing meant that Jonathan would once again be forced to live with Ben and his mother, along with the two younger sisters and baby brother he had seen only occasionally during the last five years despite the fact that only eight blocks separated the Massey's four bedroom home from Big Mama's small apartment.

The enmity between Jonathan and Ben was obvious from the day Jonathan returned to the Massey household. The older man still possessed an intense hatred for the child who was the spitting image of Delores' first love. And so did Shakey hate the old man, even more so now that Ben had taken to physically abusing Shakey's mother and younger siblings.

A large kid for his age, and still armed with the boldness of spirit that had enabled him to swing the hammer at his stepfather nearly nine years ago, Shakey quickly let it be known that the beatings his mother and siblings were forced to endure would stop immediately. To demonstrate his seriousness, the next time Ben came home drunk, and with the intent to fight his mother, the thirteen-year-old Jonathan balled his fist as tight as he could, then punched the longshoreman in the face with all his might. What followed was a knockdown drag-out fight that left no portion of the Massey household untouched. The longshoreman finally outlasted the boy.

The year was 1986 and crack cocaine had taken the Galveston streets by storm. The jungle's biggest hustlers—guys with names like Tim Tim, Meat-head, and Snake—took a liking to Jonathan. This resulted in the young boy spending considerable time on the jungle streets. If not for Johnny and the Galveston Boys' Club, the outlet he found in boxing, and his best friend Jorgé Trevino, Shakey would have succumb to the streets at a very young age.

Ben's beatings of his wife and children increased in both frequency and severity over the next year. Once again, Shakey was forced to show his disdain for his stepfather's behavior with a right hand to the mouth.

And what a difference a year's worth of growth and rage would make.

Again the two tumbled throughout the house. But this time the boy was getting the better of it. And when the wood-framed house could no longer hold the youngster's rage, the two men tumbled through the screen door, breaking the porch banister before landing on the ground. Not once did Jonathan stop pummeling the longshoreman's face, the cries and pleas of his mother and siblings so far in the distance they may as well have been coming from a neighboring planet. If not for the passing group of men than ran to his rescue, Ben Massey would surely have perished on that day. And he knew it.

A week later, the longshoreman surprised his stepson in the kitchen. He used a .38-caliber revolver to issue Jonathan a brutal pistol-whipping. The writing was now surely on the wall. One of the two would not survive this war.

The next two and a half years was a study in contrast for the two. Jonathan, who was now referred to only as Shakey, was a powerfully built sixteen-year-old who stood just over six feet tall. His developing reputation as a ladies' man was his claim to fame since discovering the latent talent for smooth-talking with which he had been blessed. The gift for gab it was called in the jungle streets.

Shakey also made strides as an amateur boxer, though his poor work ethic ensured that he would never reach his full potential. The teenager began spending the lion's share of his time on the streets, and while not yet a full-blown hustler, the felony education he received was substantial.

At school he was the enigma. Abundantly endowed with the potential to learn, Shakey could choose any career path. However, Shakey was a teenager who had decided that he had no interest in educational achievement. He would complete no homework, participate in no projects, and would sleep through any films or videos shown in class. Ironically, and even more frustrating to the educators that attempted to reach the young malcontent, Shakey would still retain more information than his classmates. He almost always led the way in test scores.

As for Ben, alcohol took a rapid toll on the longshoreman's body. In two years, he had aged twenty. And with the decline of health and appearance, came a rapid rise in the viper's evil. While not still healthy enough to physically abuse his family, there was no limit to the extent to which Ben would seek to inflict mental torture upon his wife and children. Once, Shakey's ten-year-old sister Brittany was forced to place an unloaded pistol to her own temple and pull the trigger.

But as with all things, the writing on the wall would eventually be read.

Early one Thursday morning, Shakey, late for school, eyed his stepfather stumbling home after a night's worth of drinking and gambling. The seventeen-year-old boy continued to observe as his lifelong tormentor struggled down the hallway toward the master bedroom, cursing no one in particular as he went. Once inside his bedroom, Ben Massey lay across the bed, fast asleep, not even burdening himself with the untying of his shoes.

Shakey followed his stepfather down the hallway leading to the bedroom. He leaned against the doorway while watching the old man's chest heave upward then fall with each labored breath. The room reeked with the smell of cheap wine.

The wickedest of thoughts crossed Shakey's mind, and before finding time for conscientious debate, his feet were already moving toward the bed. Now hovering over his mother's slumbering husband, Shakey grabbed a pillow from the bed. He used both hands to press the pillow against Ben's face. The short struggle of the washed up drunk was no match for the focused rage of the much stronger young man. In a matter of minutes, the reading was done, and Ben Massey lay dead. His work now complete, Shakey made the fifteen minute walk to school.

A day or two later, the cops briefly questioned Shakey, though it was quite obvious that the death of the drunken ex-longshoreman didn't rank as high priority with the Galveston police department. Natural causes were cited, and with that, Jonathan Reed had gotten away with murder. He confessed his sins to no one, save for Jorgé Trevino.

Ben Massey was not to be Shakey's only murder victim. Nor was Ben's murder the only one that Trevino eventually found out about.

Shakey had once administered a fatal drug cocktail to the veins of a girl who worked for him. Her life was ended due to her suspected cooperation with the police. Another time, he filled two would-be Jamaican robbers with enough lead to start a pencil factory. There was a cop in Austin. A Mexican inmate in prison, and a man he had fought with in a Virginia bar. There was no mistaking the fact: Jonathan Reed was a killer. And while he often dreamed of living a much different life than the one he felt had been forced on him, he knew too that the mere dreaming of a brighter future was much less complicated than actually escaping his darkened past.

So much thinking had left Shakey drained. He walked toward the hotel room door while picturing the nakedness of the redhead inside. He could feel the warmth of her body as he envisioned himself lying next to her. He surprised himself with the good feelings that came from knowing she was there for him.

Shakey closed the door behind him then placed his coat on the dresser before turning for the bed. His heart sank into the pit of his stomach. The redhead was gone.

CHAPTER 6

"Wesley," Christopher called quietly into the small crack in his best friend's bedroom window. "Wesley." He waited for a moment, and when no answer came, he tapped softly on the window.

"Wesley!" He tapped a little harder before raising the window as much as would be allowed by the small board that was jammed between the top base of the window pane and the window's frame. "Wesley!" Christopher's voice rose along with his frustration. "Prob'ly in bed with yo' mama!"

Christopher let the window close then walked along the narrow passageway running between the backside of the Sandpiper Cove apartments and the security gate that encircled the perimeter of the complex. He passed one darkened window after another before reaching the corner section of the fence that had been cut to allow access to all who wanted.

Christopher broke into a slow trot once on Winnie Avenue. He didn't stop until sure that he was safely away from the apartment complex. Once on

Thirty-seventh Street, the young runaway stopped to kick the one remaining cross trainer from his foot, picked it up, then reached his hand inside the shoe to grab the half a Swisher that was hidden there.

Christopher stepped behind the two-story fourplex on the alley corner. Finding the cover he desired, the young boy sat on the stairway leading to the back doors of the upper level apartments. He reached for the lighter in his front pocket then lit the marijuana stick.

Christopher took small puffs of the Swisher so as not to choke himself while viewing the world from the comforting darkness of the secluded stairway. He lay all the way back against the stairs, relaxing a little more with each toke from the Swisher. The entire night's fatigue rushed him all at once and he found it hard to keep his eyelids open against their own heaviness. His mind grew dim, apparently not the least bit interested in the struggle.

A light from the window closest to Christopher stirred him to an instant state of alertness. He lay as flat as possible against the stairs, using the banister as a shield while working to discern the nature of the threat.

Christopher watched in awe as a long and slender shadow maneuvered inside of what he could now see was a bedroom. The silhouette of a naked woman brushed its shoulder-length hair backwards in long deliberate strokes.

Christopher slid slowly down the stairs until his feet were on the ground. He took another puff from the Swisher before moving toward the window. The young boy pressed his face against the glass, maneuvering until he found a crack between the closely drawn drapes.

Christopher studied the naked woman from behind. She was tall. Even taller than his father. Her thin, shapely body was unmarked by scars or blemishes. Her skin tone was identical to his own.

Christopher marveled at the way her behind protruded and spread at the middle of her body. He ducked lower as the woman paused her brushing. His heart raced with the larceny of his actions.

A second woman entered the room. This woman was shorter and much wider than the first. Her skin was two full shades darker and her hair was 'crew cut' short.

The second woman wore a pair of dark-colored men's slacks, suspenders hanging at the sides. Her large, sagging breasts were uncovered.

Christopher watched as the first woman turned to acknowledge the presence of the woman with the crew cut. In the process, she unwittingly displayed the front of her nakedness to the child voyeur. The young boy's eyes were now trained upon the neatly trimmed triangular patch of hair now visible to him.

Christopher couldn't believe his eyes when the two women began to kiss. He watched with open-mouthed amazement as the women's tongues intermingled. He thought he would stop breathing when the woman with the crew cut caressed the tall woman's palm-sized breasts.

The woman with the crew cut led the tall woman to the foot of the bed. She first sat her on the edge of the bed, then pushed softly until the tall woman was lying flat on her back.

The woman with the crew cut unbuttoned the slacks she wore, then quickly shed both pants and boxers. In doing so, she granted Christopher his second look at the most private part of the female anatomy.

The second woman lie atop the first and the kissing resumed. She kissed the taller woman's breast, paying close attention to the fast growing nipples.

Shocked to the point of paralysis, Christopher continued to watch as the woman with the crew cut kissed the taller woman's stomach. He was sure he would faint when the kisses continued to travel south.

The first woman's entire body writhed against the bed with great intensity. Her head tilted backwards until she was face to face with Christopher. Her eyes opened wide.

Before the first woman could warn the other of the voyeur's presence, Christopher was gone. The Swisher was still burning in his hand as he shot from behind the house and sprinted full speed down Thirty-seventh Street. He had no destination in mind, and had not yet entertained the thought of returning home.

"Look what the cat drug in," was Sharon's not so cheery response to seeing Jessica step through Dale's front door.

"Hi Sharon." Jessica had no desire to argue with her friend.

"Where's your boyfriend?" Sharon couldn't help but ask despite not wanting to ignite a full-blown argument in front of her company.

"Asshole left me at a motel." Jessica barely noticed the two men in the room with Sharon as she headed for the back of the shotgun house. She entered the home's small kitchen and poured herself a glass of orange juice. She then rejoined the others in the living room.

"Left you alone in a hotel room?" The man seated on the couch next to Sharon sang with a good ole boy accent. "What the hell was he thinkin'?" The small toothless hole the man had for a mouth was barely visible through the wildly growing red foliage that covered his face. "You come on over here and sit next to ole Dennis." The bath-needing seaman patted a spot on the couch next to him.

Jessica hesitated for a moment, but was urged on by the wicked movement of Sharon's head. She glanced at the large, clean-cut man seated in the corner. When Jessica attempted to make eye contact, the quiet young man looked hurriedly in the other direction. Jessica nearly laughed while taking a seat on the couch, knowing full well the cause of the man's foolish behavior.

"Yeah. You come on here." Dennis grabbed the Budweiser can that was sitting next to the ashtray. The ashtray lay next to a crack pipe. "I might do a lot of thangs to ya, but leavin' you alone ain't one of 'em."

At this, Sharon stood in protest. "You what?" She placed both hands on her hips and stood directly in Dennis' face.

"I'm just funnin', sweetheart." Dennis slapped Sharon's large, fleshy rump. "You know I loves my chocolate."

"Well don't forget it." Sharon swiveled her hips so that the side of her behind brushed Dennis' face. Once satisfied that her claim was properly staked, Sharon returned to her seat in the corner of the couch.

"I guess that means red ridin' hood's with you, junior," Dennis said to the other man before reaching for the crack pipe.

Jessica tried not watching as Dennis broke a small piece from the crack rock he pulled from his top shirt pocket. She continued her attempt as Dennis placed the rock on the tip of the four inch glass cylinder. She tried to turn her head when Dennis grabbed the lighter from the table. She even tried to close her eyes when Dennis' thumb prepared to strike the lighter to life.

It was the flame. It had always been the flame. And now Jessica was hopelessly at the mercy of the flickering orange, blue, and yellow silhouette. The sizzle of the rapidly heating crack cocaine caused the hair on the back of her neck to stand on end. Her heart quickly filled with wonderment at the steady stream of white smoke that made its way from one end of the transparent tube to the portion that was attached to Dennis' mouth. All the while she noticed the rapidly bulging discs that had once been the drug-addicted seaman's eyes.

Jessica had been introduced to the pleasure and pain of crack cocaine by her ex-husband Harold, the man whom Jessica had once viewed as her personal savior.

On an otherwise uneventful Tuesday evening, after working a twelve-hour shift on the waterfront, Harold Turley purchased fifty dollars worth of crack from a coworker before returning home to his young bride.

Jessica was seated on the living room couch when Harold came through the front door. The wide-eyed, heavily breathing man was cloaked in a most unusual silence while taking a seat on the couch. Deeply concerned, Jessica was immediately at her husband's side.

Before the young bride could inquire about her husband's strange behavior, Harold produced the crack pipe. He placed the small remaining portion of the earlier purchased crack on the pipe before placing the pipe in Jessica's mouth. With a trembling hand, Harold struck the flame that had been a permanent part of Jessica's tortured conscience ever since.

In just a few weeks, the few meager possessions Harold and Jessica had managed to acquire quickly became a casualty to the couple's drug habit. With the following month came eviction notices and discontinued utility services as the entirety of the newlywed's income was used to purchase crack cocaine. A short while later, Harold left early for work one morning, never to return. Leaving his young bride to fend for herself. Far from home with no income to support herself, no friends or family to call upon, and a rapidly growing baby gorilla clutching fiercely to her back.

"Hey, Dewayne." Dennis' voice was hushed now, though still possessing the arrogance of before. "I think your girlfriend wants a hit." Dennis was conscious of the blatant display of primal hunger present in Jessica's eyes. "I'm smokin' with Hot Chocolate."

Jessica turned in response to the tap on her shoulder. Dewayne's mouth quivered but could accomplish no sound. His shaking hands offering to Jessica both crack pipe and lighter.

Jessica accepted the pipe and lighter then waited with stomach-churning anticipation as Dewayne's hand disappeared into his shirt pocket. Moments later he placed a small plastic bag containing an assortment of small crack rocks and crumbs on the table before Jessica.

Jessica was conscious now only of the crack rock she had taken from the bag and placed onto the pipe. With her left hand, she placed the pipe against her lips. Her right hand held the lighter less than an inch away from the rock encumbered end of the glass cylinder. The beads of perspiration swiftly formed on her brow as she anticipated the megablast that her mind and body so desperately craved. Her right thumb rolled forward and she was instantly mesmerized by the flame. There was no sound or smell. And no feel or consciousness for any existent being, save for the undead fire demon and the wickedly seductive jig it did at the end of the crack pipe. Even as the numbing effects of the pipe worked on her mouth and throat, Jessica knew only the flame. And the flame was good.

"Oooh, bitch!" Sharon's voice was not quite potent enough to break the hypnotic hold of the flame. "Suck blood from that mothafucka then!"

Jessica finally leaned back onto the couch. Sharon and Dennis's laughter was drowned out by the raging whistle of a nearby train. Their ghastly smiling faces drove her to near panic while her body suffered through a most ecstatic paralysis. Her head turned in Dewayne's direction. She wanted desperately to say something, to pass him the crack pipe, to thank him for the pleasure she felt, but knew that words and motion were still an impossibility.

Jessica and Dewayne made eye contact, and all that needed to be said, was, as the companions of the fire communicated through the telepathic lines available only to crack smokers.

"Damn, Red, you gon' burn all the lighter fluid." Dennis's drawl turned Jessica's attention to the still burning lighter in her right hand.

With great effort, Jessica was able to release the button on the lighter, quieting the voice of the flame. The train whistle now reduced to the sound of a frantically pleading cricket.

Moments, no years later, Jessica finally handed the pipe and lighter to Dewayne, who wasted no time in resurrecting the spirit of the flame.

The four of them smoked in silence. Each of them romanced the stone in their own particular way. Jessica sucked greedily at the pipe her and Dewayne shared whenever she was able to pry it from his hand. None of them gave any thought to the amount of crack that was smoked until Dennis finally ended the silence. "Time for you to take a ride, junior."

Dewayne's expressionless stare gave no hint to whether or not he had heard Dennis speak.

"Shit, it's time to quit fuckin' around!" Dennis' hands separated a stack of bills. "Here's four hundred bucks, son. See what Big Boy'll give us for that." Dennis threw the bills on the table.

"I'll conduct the business." Sharon scooped the money from the table, placed it in her bra, and plopped her large rump down on Dennis' lap in one soft, protest killing motion. "I'm prettier than him." She grabbed Dennis by the neck and kissed a whisker covered cheek.

"You sure are, Hot Chocolate," Dennis answered while dangling the car keys in Dewayne's direction. "She's right, junior, just drive."

Dewayne was as still and passive as a deer caught in the headlights of a fast approaching Mack truck.

"Dammit I'll drive." Sharon snatched the keys from Dennis' hand and hurried toward Dewayne. She yanked him from the chair and all but dragged him through the front door.

Jessica listened at the slamming doors of Dennis' Ford Ranger. A moment later the engine roared. Next, there was the sound of scratching gravel, followed immediately by most maddening silence the young woman had ever experienced. Her intense longing for the flame had now been replaced by the guilt that bombarded her. Having promised herself just days before that the drug use was behind her, the fire demon had proved her a liar once again.

"So what's a li'l ole thang like you doin' in a dump like this?" Dennis placed his arm around Jessica's neck. "I woulda reckoned some sly cassanova been don' bought you a house on the hill somewhere."

Jessica's body tensed and her heart skipped a beat. She was unable to breathe as the bile rose from the pit of her stomach, threatening to gag her.

"Calm down, sweetness." Slobber dripped from Dennis' beard as he flashed what was meant to be a reassuring grin. "I only bite when the lights is off."

Jessica sprang from the couch. She banged her knee on the couch while running for the safety of the kitchen. She snatched the refrigerator door open then poured herself another glass of orange juice. Her eyes closed in response to the burn of welling tears.

Jessica opened her eyes long enough to become disgusted with the black marks covering the fingertips of both hands. She placed her glass on the counter in order to reach for the dishrag that was inside the sink.

Jessica wiped hard at her hands. The tears flowed freely now as she cursed herself for returning to Dale's.

"Jessica. Ohh Jessica." Dennis stood in the door less passageway that separated Dale's living room and the shotgun house's only bedroom. He held a crack pipe and two rocks in his right hand, in his left rested the Bic lighter. "You left before I showed you what I had for you."

Jessica looked despite herself.

Dennis stepped closer, allowing his prey a better look at the meat that baited the trap.

"No thank you." Jessica shook her head before burying her face into the pillow.

"Have it your way." Dennis told her before breaking one of the rocks and placing it on the end of the pipe. "But I'm smoking."

Jessica heard the scratching sound the Bic lighter made as the fire demon sprang to life. The tears flowed again as she struggled against the call of the flame but the sizzling of the burning crack proved to be much more than her fragile resolve could withstand. As if hypnotized, Jessica rolled over and sat up in the bed.

"Change your mind, princess?" Dennis turned the puffing end of the crack pipe toward Jessica.

Jessica's first inclination was to flee for her life. To put as much distance as possible between herself ant the crack pipe. But instead she sat motionless, allowing Dennis to part her lips with the glass cylinder. Another strike of the Bic and the last chord of Jessica's self-control was severed.

Jessica sucked softly as the first of the smoke made its way to her lungs.

"Hold on, Red Ridin' Hood." Dennis abruptly snatched the pipe from her mouth. "Ain't we forgetting some-thin'?"

Jessica was speechless, save for the boisterous pleading in her eyes.

"I gotta get somethin' outta this too." Dennis flashed another slobber-filled grin. "Take off your clothes."

"But you're with Sharon." Jessica could think of no other protest.

"I'm not going to tell her." Dennis turned the pipe around again. He then placed the fire to the rock and sucked hard.

Jessica watched closely. Never needing anything as if badly as she needed the crack pipe in her mouth. The sizzling sound caused her entire body to tremble.

"Whew!" Dennis' eyes were impossibly wide. "This one's for you." Dennis took a large rock from his front shirt pocket. "Soon as you take care of me, I'll take care of you."

Jessica debated the situation with herself as much as was possible being that the only matter of consequence was the intense urge she felt to smoke crack. And as of present, there was nothing she wouldn't do for the rock in Dennis' hand.

"Hurry up, Red, 'fore they get back," was Dennis' final urging.

Jessica unfastened the buttons along the front of the cutoff shorts she wore, then backed away far enough from Dennis to slide the shorts from her body. She pulled the white T-shirt over head and placed both pieces of clothing on the nightstand beside the bed. She then lay back on the pillow.

"The bra and panties too, Red." Dennis was kneeling beside Jessica, slowly stroking his member through the open zipper of the Wrangler jeans he wore. "What ya cryin' for? I ain't gonna hurt ya."

Jessica reached for the fastener of her bra. The urge to flee had returned, along with it came the bitter taste of rising bile, but neither of these forces were as strong as her desperate longing for the devil-smoke.

"Ooh yea, baby." Dennis placed both drugs and paraphernalia on the nightstand. He stroked himself with more aggression now while reaching for one of Jessica's exposed breast.

Jessica's body convulsed under the shrimper's touch. A multitude of memories and emotions flashed through her mind at once. She let out a pain-filled shriek of despair when Dennis peeled the panties from her body. Her cries of despair fell on deaf ears as the shrimper's only concern was the satisfaction of the part of him which lay in his hand.

"What the fuck!" an angry voice pierced the perverted silence. Next, a loud crashing sound came from the direction of the porch.

"Dale?" Jessica leapt from the bed and quickly clothed herself.

"What's up, Red?" Dennis was still stroking himself.

"Who the fuck's trying to lock me out of my own house?" Dale was yelling and jerking on the screen door.

"Coming, Dale," Jessica promised. She quickly buttoned her shorts before starting in the direction of the old man's voice.

"What ya doin', Red?" Dennis clamped onto Jessica's wrist.

"Let me go!" Jessica pulled free from the shrimper's grasp then ran for the front of the house. "It's OK, Dale." Jessica unhooked the latch on the screen door.

"What are you doin' here?" The old man struggled through the door, pausing long enough to inquire. "I thought you left with Shakey."

"I came back." Jessica placed an arm around the old man's waist. "You were passed out drunk," she fussed. "You bumped your head too, you old fool." Jessica gently touched the multi-colored lump on the side of the old man's head.

"Somebody tried to lock me out of my own house," Dale explained, thoroughly enjoying the beautiful young woman's scoldings.

"Let's get you to bed." Jessica took a small step then waited patiently for Dale to match pace. In that fashion, the two of them made slow and progress in the direction of Dale's bedroom. "Tomorrow we'll see to it that you get a bath and a shave."

Jessica and Dale paused before the bedroom entrance to allow for the passage of the angry shrimper.

Dennis glanced in the direction of his escaped prey. Unwilling to meet the smirking man's gaze, Jessica lowered her eyes to the floor.

"I bet it wasn't worth my dope anyway." Dennis spat forth a mouthful of sour grapes. "Probably got nigger rings around your stinkin' cunt like the rest of the whores in this town."

"Who the fuck are you, asshole?" Dale was more than willing to return the shrimper's gaze. "And what the fuck are you doin' in my bedroom?"

"Shut the fuck up!" Dennis forced his way between them before returning to the couch and the lukewarm Budweiser he had left on the coffee table.

"What'd you say? You young punk!" Dale spun around angrily. Only Jessica's grasp prevented him from falling to the floor.

"Come on, Dale." Jessica gave a gentle rub to the old man's back. "Let's lie down."

"You'd better listen, old man." Dennis finished his beer and crushed the empty can in his hand. "'Cause I'm already in the ass-kicking mood."

"A tough guy." Dale chuckled, allowing Jessica to reroute him in the way of his bedroom. "Time'll tell how tough you are, punk!" The old man prophesized. "Always does."

No sooner than the beauty and the drunk made their way into the bedroom had Dale fell onto the bed and rolled onto his back. "Sweetheart, can I trouble you for a glass of ice water?"

Jessica made the short walk to the kitchen. She took the jar she had used earlier, quickly rinsed it, and then filled it with ice. She returned to the sink and filled it with water. She felt the first symptoms of her own fatigue as she made her way back to the bedroom. The young woman smiled at the sight that greeted her.

Dale's mouth was open and snored with a rhythmless roar that would surely cause panic to the faint of heart. He smelled terrible and his

dirt-stained body was ghastly sight to behold. But
tonight he had been her guardian angel. And she
would never forget what he had saved her from.

Jessica placed the glass of water on the nightstand before lying in bed next to Dale. She lay
awake for only a few minutes, her mind touching
upon dozens of issues in that time. She thought
of Shakey and the contentment she had felt with a
stranger. She laughed at herself for missing him.
Her last thought was of the rapidly increasing volume of the old man's snoring. Seconds later, her
own cattle call was added to the concert.

Shakey pulled the BMW into the spot directly
behind the sloppily parked Ford Ranger. He surmised the reason for the haste of the driver while
looking to Dale's humble abode. The chair that had
earlier seated the old man was turned on its side
in the yard next to the stairs. The light was on in
the living room, and Shakey counted two bodies
through the open window. He took a hearty drink
from the bottle of gin before stepping from the
BMW.

It had long been joked that Shakey had been
blessed at birth with "spider senses." He always
seemed to possess the ability to sense the presence
of latent danger in the most innocent situations.
And while Shakey had always chuckled at the notion of being endowed with qualities attributed to
a cartoon character, he knew that his talent for dis-
cerning danger was no laughing matter. It'd saved

his life on countless occasions in the past, and Shakey felt the first stirrings of his spider senses while approaching the house.

Shakey considered retrieving the .38-caliber revolver he had left in the glove compartment of the BMW, but thought better of the idea. He tapped lightly on the screen door, listening closely for even the subtlest of sounds. Hushed whispers could be heard coming from the living room, yet no footsteps approached the door.

Shakey tapped harder, then placed his face against the screen. Sharon and a scraggily looking white man were seated on the couch.

"What you want?" Sharon spoke first.

"Open the door."

"We're busy."

"Where's Jessica?"

"She sleep. Come back tomorrow." The man seated next to Sharon whispered something into her ear and the two of them shared a laugh at Shakey's expense.

Shakey took a long drink from the bottle, his anger instantly charged. "Open the door Sharon." He instructed.

"You still there?" Sharon and the man laughed again. "I thought I dismissed you already."

"Dismissed me?" Shakey jerked on the door with a swift, violent pull. In the process he broke the latch that fastened the screen door to the door frame, granting himself entrance to Dale's living room. "How the fuck you gon' dismiss me, bitch?"

"I think you better watch your mouth when talking to my lady." Dennis sprang from his seat. "Now take it back."

Sharon wrapped both arms tightly around Dennis. "Don't worry about it, baby." Knowing Shakey well, she was now wary of the fire she saw in his eyes.

Shakey drank from the bottle again. He noticed for the first time that a large, profusely sweating man, clad only in Fruit of the Loom briefs, was sitting in the corner of the room. "What's up?" Shakey's cemented gaze smacked the large man in the face.

The nervous acting man shook his head quickly then turned his attention to a spot on the carpet.

"So you gonna take it back on your own, or am going to have to make ya?" Dennis was serious.

"Don't play yourself." Shakey brought the bottle to his side. Every hair on his body stood on end as he awaited the other man's advance.

"Shakey," Jessica called from the doorway. "In here."

The sound of Jessica's voice touched Shakey in ways he would never understand. Without ever taking his eyes from the man in front of him, Shakey sidestepped in Jessica's direction.

"Come on, baby." Sharon rubbed both the shrimper's shoulders then pulled him back onto the couch. "Fuck them."

Shakey followed Jessica into the bedroom before the two of them continued the ten or so steps necessary to get to the kitchen. Once in the kitchen, they stood inches apart, each of them hesitant to voice the questions in their mind.

Shakey looked directly into the she-devil's face. Her hair was a mess, and both eyes had crust in the corners. There were deeply indented lines running across the left side of her face. But despite it all, she was simply beautiful. "Why'd you leave?" Shakey fired the first shot, careful to maintain the frown on his face.

"You expected me to wait all night?" Jessica asked, returning his frown, though not really wanting to. Though her mouth would not speak the words, Jessica really wanted to apologize for leaving the hotel room. To promise to Shakey that she would never do it again, and to beg him to lead her away from Dale's.

"I expected you to wait until I got back," Shakey said before adding, "That's what I told you to do."

"Guess I'm not used to taking orders," Jessica fired back.

Shakey twisted the cap on the gin, pouring the last of its contents into his mouth. He replaced the cap and returned the bottle to his pocket. It was the only weapon he had. "What's up with them?" Shakey motioned with his head in the direction of the living room.

"I don't know." Jessica's heart sank. She sensed that Shakey had slipped into interrogation mode. "They're Sharon's friends."

"You smoke with 'em?"

"What?" Jessica's eyes met Shakey's briefly then she quickly turned her head.

"You heard me?" Shakey was angry again. "Did you?"

Jessica nodded slowly. The tears made yet another appearance.

"Trick with 'em?" Shakey was relentless.

"What?" Jessica rubbed her eyes, shuddering to forget how close she had come to giving herself to Dennis.

"Answer the fuckin' question!" Shakey demanded.

"No!" Jessica looked at him. "Who the hell do you think you are?"

"Anything in the house that belongs to you, get it. I'll be waiting at the front door."

"What?" Jessica's puzzlement was increased.

"Hurry the fuck up!" Shakey headed for the living room.

Shakey stepped into the living room and stood opposite the couch where Sharon and the scraggily looking man was seated. Though totally engrossed in laughter and conversation before Shakey's arrival, the two of them grew silent upon sight of the Handsome Intimidator.

The hovering tension that filled the room threatened to erupt into uncensored violence. Shakey pretended not to notice the stares aimed in his direction. Though quite angry over all that happened, he still preferred to leave without incident.

Jessica entered the room with a large brown paper bag tucked under one arm. In one hand she carried a large stuffed animal. Two fingers of the other hand secured a well worn pair of Reebok tennis shoes. This was the entirety of her worldly possessions.

"Where you think you goin', bitch?" Sharon snapped at Jessica.

"She rollin' with me now," Shakey intervened. "So any questions pertaining to her should be directed right here." Shakey slammed the palm of his hand against his chest.

"Well wait just one goddamn minute." Dennis was on his feet once again. "I got a fuckin' question."

Shakey faced Dennis. The Handsome Intimidator turned the palms of both hands toward the ceiling, gesturing for the shrimper to state his case.

"Whatcha gonna do about all the money my friend spent on that whore of yours with no services rendered?"

"You talking about me?" Jessica asked, resulting in a chastising gaze from Shakey.

"You think the crack you smoked was free?" Dennis asked her.

"How much you spend?" Shakey asked the half-naked man.

"Three or four hundred." Dewayne said the first numbers that came to his mind.

Shakey looked at Jessica then reached into his pocket. He withdrew a wad of money, quickly peeled five bills from the top, and threw them onto the table. "Five hundred bucks." Shakey bent at the waist and slid the money to the end of the table closest to Dewayne. "Debt paid."

"You better drop out over here too, nigga!" Sharon was furious. "The bitch belonged to me. Respect the game."

Shakey paused to check his anger before turning to Sharon. "Come by Sanovia's Monday. I got work for you." He shoved the wad of money back into his pocket before turning to Jessica. "Let's go." He pushed the redhead softly in the back, urging her in the direction of the front door.

"You ain't goin' nowhere, bitch!" Sharon made an ill-advised lunge at Jessica, only to collide solidly with the back of Shakey's hand. The force of the blow sent the large woman crashing into the wall. The entire room was still.

"Mothafucka!" There was an easily discernible change in the pattern of Sharon's speech as the first of the blood could be seen running between her fingers. The stunned streetwalker whimpered like a small child before saying. "You bust my lip!"

"Your ass is mine, boy!" Dennis yelled while hurdling over the coffee table.

Shakey dodged the flying shrimper while snatching the bottle from his back pocket. In one swift and powerful motion the gin bottle was smashed against the base of the shrimper's skull. Dennis lost consciousness without ever knowing what hit him.

Shakey turned to face Dewayne.

Dewayne shook his head.

Shakey grabbed Jessica by the arm and led the terrified woman toward the door.

"All right, goddammit! Let's have it with the racket!" Dale yelled before rolling over and instanstly falling deeper into his drunken slumber.

"Yo' black ass don' fucked up this time, Shakey!" Sharon threatened between sobs. "I'ma get yo' ass!"

Shakey continued toward the car, not at all concerned with the trifle of Sharon's threats. There were matters of much greater relevance to wrestle with. The first of which was what to do with Jessica.

CHAPTER 7

Shakey eased the BMW into the two car garage, careful not to scrape the paint of the fire engine red '64 Impala that was already inside. Once sure the back of the BMW was clear of the garage entrance, Shakey hit the button on the keychain that lowered the garage door. He sat still in the driver's seat for a moment, observing Jessica while finishing off the last of yet another Swisher.

After leaving Dale's, Shakey drove about the island for over an hour while trying to decide what he would do with Jessica. The exhausted young woman had fallen asleep shortly after the joyless ride had begun. Probably, Shakey surmised, staying awake only long enough to be sure the man in the car with her fully quenched his thirst for violence. Once tiring of the fruitless drive, Shakey headed home. He decided to take Jessica with him.

A painful prick to Shakey's conscience accompanied thoughts of Sharon. Despite his lifestyle, Shakey had never gotten off to assaulting women. She brought it on herself, Shakey rationalized for his conscience's sake. The thought offered no comfort.

"Hey." Shakey shook Jessica gently while taking one last pull from the doobie. "Wake up."

Jessica stirred, then mumbled, then asked, "Where are we?"

"Paradise." Shakey laughed softly, then thought to himself that after what Jessica had endured in her lifetime, the inside of his home may very well seem like paradise to her.

"Where?" Jessica could discern nothing through the wall of darkness before her.

"My house." Shakey opened his door and exited the car. "Come on."

Jessica climbed from the car and stepped instinctively for the front of the vehicle. She still could not see a thing.

"Over here." Shakey opened the door leading to the rear hallway of his home. The light from inside his home provided Jessica with much needed illumination.

Jessica followed Shakey down the hallway, then through what seemed to her to be a never-ending maze of twists and turns, finally ending in their ascension upon a winding staircase. Another set of twists and turns, and Jessica followed Shakey into the master bedroom.

"You gonna just stand there and hold that shit or what?" Shakey turned on the light and television then fell back onto the bed.

"What do you want me to do with it?

"Put it wherever you want." Shakey kicked his shoes off and rolled in the bed until within arm's reach of the answering machine. He pressed the button on the answering machine that would play his messages before saying to Jessica. "Make yourself at home."

Jessica placed the larger than life panda bear on the floor next to the dresser. She then sat at the front of the bed and began sifting through the brown paper bag while eavesdropping on Shakey's messages.

"Say, fool, we need to holla!" The first message was from Red, Shakey's long-time friend and ace crime partner. "What's up with you? Call me when you get in. I don't care what time it is."

Shakey looked at the clock. It was 4:18 in the morning. He would call Red tomorrow.

"Hi, Daddy." The second message was from Rosa. "We got a small problem. Not over the phone. See you when you come by." Shakey's mind wandered as to the nature of the small problem. The fact that she had called him at his home meant that the problem was anything but small. Tomorrow was once again the verdict.

"Hey, Fuckwad!" Trevino's voice boomed from the answering machine. "I bet you—"

Shakey hit the next message button.

Jessica noted the tension that now strained Shakey's face. She crawled on all fours across the bed until she was next to him. She placed herself beneath his right wing.

Two relatively trivial messages played followed by one that caused Shakey to sit upright in his bed.

"Daddy, where are you?" Jonathan, Shakey's son and namesake spoke with trademark enthusiasm. "I did it, Daddy. I'm in the finals. It's December fourteenth at 5:30. Please be there. I'm gonna win. It's at the Ball High auditorium. Bye. Did I say December fourteenth?" Jonathan giggled wildly before message ended.

"You OK.?" Jessica squeezed softly, feeling great sympathy upon seeing the pain of Shakey's face.

"Yeah," Shakey was already rewinding the message. "I just forgot something, that's all."

Jessica knew that Shakey would prefer a few minutes to himself. She reached inside her bag for a fresh pair of panties and a large black T-shirt. She then left the room in search of the bathroom.

Shakey couldn't believe he had forgotten Jonathan's spelling bee. He would make the finals for sure. Proud to tears, he reviewed the tape and listened to the message again. And again and again.

Jessica stood under the straight stream of warm water, thoughtfully considering the conclusions that could be drawn from her new friend's phone messages. For one, he had at least one girlfriend. A Hispanic seductress named Rosa. Thinking back to his actions at Denny's, Jessica figured her new friend had a thing for Hispanic women.

Jessica had also deduced that Shakey did not place great significance on returning messages.

The voice that spoke the first message was filled with urgency and placed no time restraints on a return call. From Jessica's viewpoint, Shakey had simply ignored an obvious plea for help.

Shakey also possessed at least one enemy—a professional type with a filthy mouth. After witnessing the short work Shakey made of the shrimper, Jessica pitied the fate of the enemy.

Shakey was also a father, and an obviously not so perfect relationship with his son was a tremendous source of pain.

Jessica turned off the water and stepped from the tub. She then gently towel dried herself using a towel she found in the linen closet.

Jessica's mind traveled shortly back in time before resting on the magical moment in the hotel room she had shared with Shakey. Having never known such pleasure from the touch of a man, Jessica's heart had been broken upon being left alone in the room. But now she was here, and the anticipation of the next magical moment with Shakey caused her body to tremble. She was unsure if it was anticipation, or the cool breeze that blew from the small vent just above the light switch that was responsible for the rigidness of both her nipples.

Jessica stepped into the purple bikini underwear and donned the oversized T-shirt. She sprayed her neck, wrists, and the crease between her breasts with the perfume Sharon had given her.

Jessica turned off the light before opening the bathroom door. She stood in the doorway for a moment before finally stepping into the bedroom. Her heart raced with still heightening anticipation then slowed with disappointment as Shakey came into view. Lying on his side, with one arm hanging from the bed, Shakey was sound asleep. A twenty-two ounce bull was still firmly in his grip.

Jessica slid Shakey's loafers from his feet before prying the bottle from his hand. Now seated next to him, she drank the remaining beer in the bottle as fast as she could before lying down beside him. Cuddling as closely as possible, Jessica too, was soon fast asleep.

"What are you doing?" Jessica awakened to find Shakey fumbling around in the closet.

"Mindin' my business," Shakey spoke in a nonchalant manner. He entered the bedroom fully dressed and drinking from a small Styrofoam cup.

"Where are you going?" Jessica sat up straight in the bed.

"Same answer as above. " Shakey was always cranky before finishing his first drink of the morning.

Jessica leapt from the bed. "I'll be ready in a minute." She had no intention of being left alone in such a large, unfamiliar house.

"Who said you were going anywhere?" Shakey's admiration for Jessica's near-naked body would have been plainly noticed if the young woman was paying any attention to him at all.

Jessica peeled the T-shirt from her body then pulled flower print, cream-colored dress from the brown paper bag. She dressed hurriedly then placed her feet into the sandals. The one thing she didn't do was answer Shakey's question as she was learning that there was but one way to deal with him. And that was with equal attitude and arrogance.

Shakey didn't bother to repeat his question. He nearly smiled as he drank the last of the straight Bacardi. The sound of the tumbling ice alerted him to the urgent need of a refill.

"You have just enough time to fix you another drink while I brush my teeth." Jessica informed him before running for the restroom with toothbrush, paste, and washcloth in hand.

Shakey's brow furrowed with exaggerated confusion. He could not remember the last time he had been handled that way. Without protest, he did exactly as instructed. Once in the kitchen, he filled his cup with ice, then headed for the bar to pour himself another drink. He had taken only a couple of sips before hearing Jessica's approach.

"Ready?" Jessica leaned against the door frame.

"Who said you were going anywhere?" was Shakey's last ditch token argument. His full attention was now riveted upon Jessica's drop-dead figure. He was also becoming aware of the fact that she was fully capable of attaining from him whatever her heart desired.

Jessica smiled.

"Look, I got a lot of business to take care of," Shakey spoke with his most authoritative voice. "You can ride if you want, but keep your mouth shut."

"Yes, Daddy." Jessica smiled in response to her own sarcasm.

"Daddy?" Shakey gulped half his drink, then filled it again for good measure.

"That's what your girlfriend calls you." Jessica was unable conceal the slight tinge of jealousy she felt. "Rosa, right?"

"Not my girlfriend." Shakey stepped toward the doorway, fully expecting Jessica to move from his path. She didn't. Each staring deeply into the other's eyes, the two of them stood so close their lips touched. Shakey's attraction to her was unlike anything he had felt in years. He wanted nothing more than to lead her back to his bedroom and have the two of them spend the entire day there. But that would have to wait.

Jessica finally broke the spell. "Liar."

"What?" Shakey was unable to recall the topic of their conversation.

"Let's go." Jessica kissed him softly before turning away.

Shakey's eyes followed her closely. He paid close attention to the shifting of her butt in the tight-fitting dress. Smitty was right. Someone in this girl's ancestry was definitely from The Motherland.

The two of them climbed into the borrowed BMW. Shakey would exchange it later for his Cadillac.

Shakey eased the BMW from the garage and down the driveway. He nodded to Mr. Bouldin, the next door neighbor who had been busy trimming the Japanese Barberries that bordered his front yard before hearing Shakey's garage door open. The older man was obviously quite curious about the only company he had known Shakey to have in a very long time.

"Can you grab the paper for me, baby?" Shakey asked while pointing to the morning's edition of The Galveston Daily News. He had decided to give Mr. Bouldin heart palpitations.

Mr. Bouldin was a product of the sixties. The first in his family to attend schools that included white students, the chubby and fast-balding man had been saddled with a life-time of emotional baggage as a result of his experiences. Put bluntly, Mr. Bouldin hated white people. Or so he claimed. The mere mention of anyone with Caucasian heritage would often time elicit a string of obscene declarations from Mr. Bouldin. But Shakey found it hilarious how Mr. Bouldin now stood still and quiet while staring at Jessica's shifting hips and sister-like booty.

Shakey laughed out loud when his neighbor tugged at the front of his pants and wiped at the newly formed beads of sweat on his forehead.

"What's so funny?" Jessica returned with the paper.

"Just trippin' on my neighbor."

"Why?"

"I think he likes you." Shakey backed out of the driveway and turned left, passing directly in front of the two-story brick home Mr. Bouldin shared with his wife.

Shakey tapped the horn twice and waved at his neighbor. The newly reformed radical responded by removing his baseball cap and bowing to the passing car. Shakey thought his head would explode with laughter.

"Quit lying!" Wesley stopped wiping at the handlebars of his bicycle long enough to look at his best friend's smiling face. And though not quite believing of the tale he heard, Wesley was amused by the story.

"What I gotta lie for?" Christopher, tending to the business of cleaning his own bicycle, never looked up. "They was gettin' it, fool."

The two boys stood in the driveway of the Chevron service station located at Thirty-third Street and Broadway. As they often did, the boys came here to clean their bikes in preparation for cruising the block.

"Gettin' what?" Wesley's face was the picture of puzzlement.

"Booty, dummy." Christopher explained. "They was gettin' booty."

"Oh." Wesley nodded then thought for a moment before saying, "Two girls can't get booty."

"That's what you think." Christopher wiped hard on the frame of his bike. He would have agreed with Wesley if not for the education he was granted by peering through the window of the two unsuspecting women. "One of these days, I'ma take you by there so you can see what's up."

"You stayed out all night." Wesley changed subjects, suddenly uncomfortable with the thought of himself peeking through an open window at two women "getting booty".

"'Til the son came up," Christopher said proudly.

"And yo' mama wasn't mad?" Wesley was amazed; his own mother never allowed him to stay out past the moment the streetlights would suddenly spring to life.

"I run this." Christopher stood tall, patting his chest with the palm of his right hand to emphasize his boldly proclaimed independence. "She asked where I went, I told her I been handlin' up on a little business."

The truth of the matter is that neither Christopher's mother or father stirred in their beds when the nine-year-old boy returned shortly after seven P.M. It was doubtful, Christopher figured, that they had even noticed his absence. It was a discovery that filled Christopher's heart with more anger, despair, and loneliness than any ten boys his age should know in a lifetime.

A prolonged silence hovered about the two boys as each of them became suddenly serious with the scrubbing of their bikes. Wesley concentrated the bulk of his efforts on the grips that adorned the handlebars of his last year's Christmas present from his grandmother. Meanwhile, Christopher paid close attention to the rims of the "lo-lo" he had built from scratch using parts that were either given, found, or stolen.

A police cruiser rounded the corner and entered the driveway of the service station. The car passed slowly in front of the boys and a red-faced officer stared at them through the open window.

"What?" Christopher stood quickly, rag still in hand as he held both arms out at his side.

The officer continued past the boys, slowly pulling the police cruiser into the drive-thru carwash at the opposite end of the lot.

"I hate them mothafuckas." Christopher flung his rag onto the ground.

"Who?"

"The police! Don't you?"

"Why I'ma hate the police for?"

Christopher thought hard before saying, "'Cause we supposed to!" The young malcontent used his foot to raise the bicycle's kickstand, then jumped aboard the freshly shining chariot. "Let's go!"

The first stop on Shakey's agenda was Red's. Shakey and Red had been friends for years, and no one in his life, save for Red, had gained anything close to Shakey's total trust. Since adolescence, the six foot four, 245 pound behemoth had stood by Shakey's side through a variety of precarious situations. From a suspension saving false confession of stealing Katy Heimberger's pen in the sixth grade, to doing five years on an eight year sentence of a manslaughter conviction that rightfully belonged to Shakey, Red's loyalty had stood the test of time.

A family man now, Red separated the streets from his life during Shakey's last prison stay. But upon finding himself ensnared in Trevino's dastardly trap, Shakey's first turn was to Red. Reluctantly, for his old friend, the husband and father of three agreed to enter the game once more.

"Be right out." Shakey parked the BMW directly in front of the two-story brick home sitting on the corner of Forty-first Street and Avenue M. The house was home to Red, his wife Michelle, and their three kids.

"I hope so." Jessica decided to not waste energy with protest.

"Chill." Shakey was already out the car and headed for the gate of the cyclone fence that encased the roomy front yard. The door opened before Shakey even had a chance to knock, and Red greeted with a frown.

"Nigga, you don' lost your damn mind?" The light-skinned man was obviously very upset with Shakey.

"Good morning." Shakey smiled broadly then walked right past his old friend. His arms opened wide for the approach of Red and Michelle's twin five-year-olds, Rodney and Roderick, so named for Michelle's deceased uncles.

"Uncle Shakey!" Each boy leapt into an arm and giggled as Shakey lifted them from the floor and rocked them back and forth.

"Where you been, Shakey?" Rodney, the oldest by five minutes, asked once Shakey returned the boys to the floor.

"I went to talk to Santa about speeding up his delivery process." Shakey chose a fairy tale sure to delight the small boys.

"My mama said you was busy whorin'," Roderick said matter-of-factly, seemingly not the least bit interested in fairy tales.

"Boy, get y'all bad asses outta here 'fore I get my belt!" Red took a step in the direction of the madly scurrying little boys as their glee filled giggles and fast drumming footsteps filled the house was mischief.

Shakey laughed out loud. As a child, Red had been afflicted with a variety of serious speech impediments. The teasing by the other children was relentless. Shakey had spent countless hours with Red practicing the speaking exercises Red was given by his teachers. For the most part, Red's hard work paid off, though there were still many words Red struggled with on occasion, especially once excited. Belt was obviously one of these words.

"Hi, Kashandra!" Shakey's goddaughter stood at the head of the stairs. Clad only in a slip and nightgown, the young girl smiled while rubbing the sleep from the corners of her eyes. Shakey had always had a special fondness for the beautiful, dark-skinned little girl.

"Get in that room and put some clothes on your narrow behind." Michelle, appearing suddenly, struck the young girl on the arm with an open hand.

"Owww, Mama," was the girl's painless plea before dragging her feet in the direction of her bedroom.

"I told your ass about walkin' around here with no clothes on."

Michelle was Red's wife, and if Shakey's version was the standard, she was a real Prozac taking bitch. At just over five feet tall and a little over a hundred pounds, what the pitch dark-skinned woman lacked in size, she more than made up for with tenacity. And while Michelle could indeed become pleasant to look at whenever any attempt was made on her part at doing so, it was only on occasion that she did so. More often than not, and today coincided with the often, Michelle showed absolutely zero interest in her appearance.

Michelle stomped with the force of a two-hundred fifty pound man as she came down the stairs. With gathered portions of her hair pointed in every direction, she wore a large pink housecoat and dirty, once-white house shoes. Once at the bottom of the stairs, she pushed her way through the two men and took a peek out the front door.

"Uhhhhh," Michelle emitted the exaggerated moan that sisters in the ghetto used for a variety of reasons. She then frowned her disappointment at her husband before heading for the living room.

"What the hell is wrong with you?" Red asked Shakey. He was even angrier now that Michelle was in the vicinity.

"I was about to ask you the same thing, Red." Shakey held his hands out in a gesture of surprise. "What's with all the hostility?"

"Have you lost your sense of reality, Shakey?"

"If you got somethin' on your mind, I really wish you'd get it off your chest." Shakey was now feeling the first rumblings of his own anger.

"How come you didn't call to let me know what was up with D.D.?" Red asked. "Don't you think I wanted to know, nigga? I ain't had a wink of sleep yet."

"It's cool," Shakey assured him. "I got her out as soon as you called.

"It's not cool, man." Red was unconvinced. "That was too close for comfort."

Red was freaked. And Shakey totally understood his reasoning. Red, nor anyone else in the world, knew of Shakey's dilemma with Trevino. Nor could Red know that the one positive of his involvement with Trevino was the protection of his crew. From

Red's perspective, last night surely signaled the fall of the Shakean Empire.

"I got it, dog."

"And what's with the white bitch?" Red knew that he had to say something about the redhead in the car outside his home if for no other reason than to satisfy Michelle, who was no doubt listening to every word the two of them spoke.

"You got something against white women?"

"No, not in their place but—"

"Not in their place? Now ain't that a bitch!" Shakey laughed aloud, while Red chuckled softly in spite of himself.

"Look, man, what I mean is," Red tried to explain, "After what happened last night, it might not be a good idea for you to be ridin' 'round the island with a white girl. I know you dirty. Then, you park the bitch in front of my house. This is where I lay my head."

Red's fears were groundless paranoia. He hadn't the slightest idea about Jessica, yet had already considered her to be dangerous. Shakey understood. The rules for surviving the game dictated that all strangers were an imminent threat. With an asterisk placed next to white female strangers.

"Chill, man." Shakey knew that nothing he could possibly say would ease Red's concerns, so he made no great effort. "It's cool."

Red went back to the door. "At least tell her to come inside."

Shakey stepped onto the porch. Jessica looked at him. He smiled, then motioned for her come inside.

"What?" She rolled the window down again.

"Grab the keys from the ignition and come inside," Shakey instructed. "And bring that bottle."

Shakey returned to the spot just inside the doorway. Both he and Red watched as Jessica strutted first through the gate, then up the stairs.

"Whatchu lookin' at, bastard?" That was Michelle, and she was none too happy about her husband's reaction to the white girl.

"Nothin', baby." Red had long been spineless when faced with his wife's wrath. This was the one trait in his best friend that Shakey despised.

"Don't you know I will kick yo' ass, Red?" The irate woman continued to yell. "Get yo' ass in that living room!"

Jessica reached the front door at about the same time Red was being ushered into the living room. She had no idea what was going on, but suspected that she was the cause of some sort of tension. Her suspicions were confirmed once making eye contact with the angry black woman.

"Come on, baby." Shakey took Jessica by the hand and led her to the living room. Partly because he could sense her uneasiness, but mostly because he was certain that the gesture would further infuriate Michelle.

The four of them entered the Lattimore living room. Red and Michelle occupied opposite ends of the sixteen foot sectional couch. Shakey and Jessica, seemingly joined at the waist, sat on the brick base of the unused fireplace.

"So you gonna introduce your girlfriend?" Michelle's face was affixed with the 'something smells bad' scowl that often afflicted the haughty.

"My bad." Shakey placed his arm around Jessica in a well calculated, rage-inducing manner. "My girlfriend's name is Jessica." He kissed her cheek. "Jessica, this is my best friend Red and his pet iguana Michelle.

"I know you didn't, nigga!" The ghetto in Michelle was never far from the surface. "Tryna talk about somebody with those ashy-ass lips."

"I know you didn't, nigga." Shakey, thoroughly enjoying himself, looked at Michelle's hair. "Lookin' like you belong in the Li'l Rascals remake."

"Fuck you, you ugly, black, peel-headed bastard!"

"Same to you, you ugly, black, anorexic skank."

Shakey and Michelle both stopped abruptly. Round one was over, and both fighters returned to their respective corners.

Shakey turned to Red. "What you got to drink around here?"

Red was all set to speak but didn't as Michelle's angry glare found its mark on the side of his head. A slight shake of the head would have to do.

"Well let's just get down to business." Shakey smiled. "I got a package, and I need some magic performed on it."

"How much magic?" Red knew that Shakey talked of putting 'cut' on a package of dope.

"'Bout two for one."

Jessica was puzzled, and she knew that the two men wanted it that way. She looked to the angry woman on the opposite side of the room and could see that she was anything but confused.

"All this talk about some magic," Michelle started up again. "What magic gon' be worked for D.D.?"

"I got that," Shakey said to her.

"Yeah, nigga, we don' all heard that one before." Michelle was unconvinced. "You'll just find somebody else to run yo' dope because that's all you do is use people up, Shakey."

"Shut the fuck up!" The truth was like the sting of a scorpion.

"How the fuck you gon' tell me to shut up in my house?" Michelle stood up.

"Calm down, baby." Red stood with his wife, placing both hands on her shoulders.

"Get yo' hands off me!" Michelle was irate. "You gon' just sit there while this nigga disrespects me in our home?"

"Hold on, Red." Shakey joined them on his feet. He knew very well what Michelle was trying to do. "You know I ain't tryin' to start no shit."

"I know." Red had barely gotten the words out when Michelle slapped him aside the head. "What the hell you hit me for?"

"'Cause you always taking his side!" Michelle returned to her spot on the couch. Arms folded like a pouting child, her frown deepened.

Jessica watched it all in silent awe.

"Look, y'all, I know what happened to D.D. is causing everyone a bunch of stress." Shakey prepared to put his oratorical skills on display. And though he used the word "y'all," his present speech was only meant to ease Red's apprehension. "But we shouldn't be at each other's throats. We're family, and family stands together through the hard times." Shakey paused for effect, then stepped toward Red, arms extended to embrace. "It's all love here, my nigga, so don't ever think I don't have your best interest at heart."

The two men embraced briefly. Red had always had the utmost confidence in Shakey. And regardless of the fears he still harbored over D.D.'s bust, he did believe Shakey could make it all right again.

Shakey held his best friend tightly, silently conveying his trustworthiness in his partner while peeking over his shoulder at Michelle. Shakey stuck his tongue out at her, then smiled.

Shakey backed away from Red. "Check it out." Shakey shifted gears, now a military commander giving orders. "I got some moves to make, so wait for me to text you. When you get the text, be at the lab thirty minutes later. Solid?" Shakey held his hand out in a fist.

"Solid." Red made a friend and they exchanged pounds.

"Catch you then." Shakey turned to Jessica and offered his hand. He gently pulled her to her feet, and the two of them moved for the door.

"Be careful, Shakey." Red's voice was much more optimistic than an hour ago.

"No doubt." Shakey allowed the she-devil to exit the house first then turned toward the living room. "Bye, Michelle," was Shakey's mockingly kind farewell.

"Fuck you!" Michelle grabbed the first thing she could get her hands on, which just happened to be a large ceramic turtle-shaped ashtray and hurled it at Shakey. Fortunately for him, he closed the door behind him just in the nick of time, and the ashtray slammed against the door.

"You hungry?" were Shakey's first words in the nearly twenty minutes since they had left Red's.

"A little."

Shakey immediately wheeled the BMW into the Wendy's drive-thru and followed the line of lunch-time commuters to the speaker.

"Welcome to Wendy's. May I take your order?" Ten minutes later Shakey was parked at the speaker.

"Hold on." Shakey spoke into the speaker before turning to Jessica. "What you want?"

"Ummm, let me try the chicken combo." Jessica chose the most appealing picture on the display board.

"What kind of drink?" Shakey asked.

"Coke." She shrugged her shoulders.

"OK. I'm ready." Shakey turned back toward the speaker.

"I don't know girl, they always do that shit." The register operator was unaware, and obviously unconcerned with the patron's readiness to order. "They always get to the speaker and wanna discuss something."

"Hey." Shakey reached a long arm from the window and knocked on the speaker. "I'm ready to order."

"Well go ahead," was the cashier's response.

Shakey laughed at the cashier before speaking loud and ridiculously slow. I would like a number three combo with a Coke . . . That's a chicken sandwich combination with a Coca-Cola."

"I know what a number three combo is, boy!" the cashier yelled back at him.

Jessica laughed merrily.

"I want four Texas Double Cheeseburgers," Shakey spoke even slower. "But on two of those Texas Doubles, I don't want no bread."

"No bread?"

"That's what I said, ain't it?" Shakey feigned frustration.

"What else?" The cashier was not feigning anything.

"A Biggie Fry, a Biggie Coke, and a Biggie cup of ice."

"I'll have to charge you the price of a Biggie drink for the ice." The cashier informed him.

"You ain't said nothing." Shakey looked at Jessica who was even redder than normal with laughter.

"Anything else?"

"Did I ask for anything else?" Before the cashier could answer, Shakey sped to the window.

The woman waited with the window open. She was anxious to view the man who angered her so.

Shakey viewed the cashier as he turned the corner that led to the window. No older than twenty, the caramel complected young woman was quite attractive. Her hair was freshly done, and her well-manicured nails drummed softly on the counter top in anticipation of her continued argument with this most obnoxious customer.

"How much is it?" Shakey was ready to have more fun with the young lady. He first smiled broadly, allowing the young lady a full view of his diamond crushed gold teeth. Next, he reached in his pockets and flashed a wad of money that probably represented half year's wages for the young woman.

"Just a moment." The young woman's scowl dissipated immediately as she carefully tapped the register keys.

Shakey laughed while watching the girl motion to another woman of similar age, hairstyle, and demeanor. The second woman stood just behind the first, looking into the BMW. The second woman looked behind her and moments later there was third.

All the while, Shakey maintained his molar displaying smile.

"That was a number three combo with a Coke, two Texas doubles all the way, two more with no bun, a Biggie fry, and a Biggie Coke?"

"And a Biggie cup of ice." Shakey reminded her.

"I wasn't really going to charge you for no ice." The young girl was somehow able to simultaneously smile at Shakey, displaying two gold teeth of her own, and frown her dissatisfaction at the white girl in the passenger seat.

"Thank you." Shakey pretended to paying more attention to the two girls standing behind the cashier.

"That'll be nine dollars and eighty-seven cents." The cashier made an obvious attempt at shielding the other two young women from Shakey's view.

The window was closed for a moment while the girls bagged the order and prepared the drinks.

"Watch this." Shakey smiled to Jessica just as the young woman opened the window.

The young girl's smile was so broad as she handed Shakey the bag that he was sure her face would crack. After handing Shakey the Coke, the girl's smile somehow grew even deeper as she had one more item to hand him. "Here's your ice."

Shakey took the ice from her, making sure to rub her hand in the process. He then peeled a twenty dollar bill from somewhere in the stack of money and told her. "The change is for you, beautiful."

"Thank you," the light-headed young woman sang.

"Would you happen to have a pen and something to write on so I can give you my number?"

"Sure." The girl was blushing now.

Shakey handed Jessica the food. He smiled at the single raised eyebrow that carefully scrutinized his actions. "Just check this out," he reassured her.

The young woman returned to the window and handed Shakey a small white card and a pencil.

Shakey took the card and pencil, once again making sure to rub the young woman's hand, then scribbled onto the card.

"Big D?" The woman was slightly puzzled.

"My name's David. But they call me Big D at the shop . . . you are going to call, right?" Shakey put the finishing touches on an Academy Award-winning performance.

"Sure, when?"

"Call me tonight."

"OK." The young woman smiled at Shakey before smirking at Jessica.

"What's your name?" Shakey asked her.

"'Trice." The song voice was used again.

"Well, 'Trice, I'll be waiting."

"OK."

"Bye." Shakey eased his foot from the brake

"Bye," the young woman said dreamily then watched the BMW exit the restaurant driveway and speed down Seawall Boulevard.

"Why did you do that?" Jessica asked once the BMW was clear of the restaurant.

"Just havin' fun," Shakey told her then quickly changed the subject. "Hand me a burger."

"With or without the bun?" Jessica was afraid to ask why he had purchased two burgers with no buns.

"With bun."

Shakey peeled the wrapping from the Texas Double Cheeseburger and chomped greedily while driving the BMW and listening to the radio. He looked at Jessica and laughed to himself at how she was neatly arranging the bag in her lap before eating. "Fries," Shakey said simply while turning right on Thirty-seventh Street.

Now it was Jessica's turn to have some fun. "Here." She touched his bottom lip with the extremely hot fries.

Shakey smiled and allowed her to place the fries in his mouth, playfully nibbling on her fingers in the process.

"Stop it, crazy." Jessica giggled.

"What?" Shakey laughed with her.

"You know what." Jessica cautiously approached his mouth with two more fries.

"Come on." Shakey opened his mouth.

"I'm not playing, Shakey."

"Me either. Come on." He opened his mouth again.

Jessica placed two fries in Shakey's mouth. He ate them without incident. She placed two fries in her own mouth while waiting for him to finish chewing. She then got two more fries ready for him.

Shakey opened his mouth again as the car rolled to a stop at Thirty-seventh and Broadway. A group of young kids strolled before the BMW and laughed at Shakey and Jessica as they passed.

Jessica placed the fries in Shakey's mouth, and once he chewed them, she found her finger trapped between his teeth.

"Oww," Jessica whined as he nibbled roughly on her finger. "Stop it."

Shakey gave her one last bite, then let her go.

"That hurt," Jessica complained. "Look, you left a mark." Jessica held her hand so he could see the indentions he had made.

"Let me kiss it for you." Shakey smiled while reaching for her hand.

Jessica shook her head. "No way."

"No, for real." Shakey's was the face of innocence. "I'll make it all better, I promise."

Jessica was hesitant, but finally placed her hand next to Shakey's lips. Shakey marveled at her propensity to trust. He kissed her hand softly then pulled her close. The two of them kissed before a voice from behind interrupted.

"The light's green, man, c'mon," the frustrated motorist yelled.

Shakey shook two fingers out the driver side window at the man, a peace gesture, then sped across the intersection.

Shakey turned right on Avenue H, then left on the next corner. Jessica could tell he was looking for someone.

After making the block twice, Shakey pulled beside an abandoned building on Thirty-sixth Street and Avenue H. He put the car in park then grabbed the Texas Double with the bun and laid it in the seat. He carried the bag and the bunless burgers with him as he climbed from the car.

Jessica watched as Shakey walked in the direction of the condemned house on the alley corner.

A pack of dogs bolted suddenly from the alley, following closely on the heels of a frightened Tom cat. Bringing up to rear of the pack was a pitiful looking mutt who had obviously once been critically injured.

The dog was totally incapable of using its back legs and dragged itself with his forepaws. The poor creature struggled to keep pace with the other dogs before spotting Shakey. Jessica's appetite was ruined upon site of the pink furless flesh of the dog's behind, the result of dragging its rear end on the pavement, gravel, and grass, all day everyday.

"What's up, Baby?" Shakey kneeled before the dog.

Jessica marveled at the love in the dog's eyes. And it wasn't just because of the meat patties Shakey was now feeding it.

"Hey, girl." The man's admiration for the dog was just as evident as he patted and rubbed. "How's my Baby doing?'

Baby was the name Shakey had given the dog at the tragic onset of their relationship. One night, after a late-night crap game at Mack's place, Shakey struck Baby with his vehicle while turning the corner of Thirty-fifth and H. The severity of the dog's injuries was immediately discernable. Shakey gathered the crumpled animal in his car and took him immediately to the veterinarian. The prognosis was grim. The animal doctor suggested a lethal dose of anesthesia be administered.

Shakey refused to heed the doctor's advice as Baby's survival suddenly became the most important matter in the world to him. For the life of a dog, the thrice convicted felon, known killer and self-admitted career sinner, bowed to his maker for the first time in years. For the life of Baby, he prayed with enough ferverance to move Mount Kilimanjaro.

The veterinarian assured the distraught man that nothing could be done for the animal. Then went on to tell him that every minute in which the dog was allowed to live constituted cruelty.

Shakey gathered Baby in his arms once again. He returned her to the porch of the abandoned boarding house that served as headquarters for the stray dogs of the neighborhood. With a bundle of blankets, an ounce of weed, and enough MD 20/20 to get him through the rest of the early morning, Shakey began his vigil.

Shakey spent the better part of the next seventy-two hours with the fallen beast. He left only for food, alcohol, and drugs. And God, who he felt had forsaken him on so many occasions before, would finally answer a prayer for him. Though severely disabled, Baby's life was spared.

"What's up, Li'l Mama?" A young boy circled the BMW on his bicycle. After giving the car the once over, he stopped directly beside the passenger side window.

"Excuse me." Jessica tilted her head to view the curly haired boy. Though no older than nine or ten, the boy appeared to be drinking from a bottle of wine.

"What's up?" The boy climbed from his bike and allowed the vehicle to rest on the kickstand. "You with Shakey?"

"Are you drinking?" Jessica was appalled. She noticed that there was second boy, also traveling on a bicycle that waited a few feet behind the first one.

"You the law or something?" The boy frowned at Jessica, not believing that she had been bold enough to ask him about his bottle of Boone's Farm wine. Before she could answer, the boy turned his attention to Shakey, who was now approaching the car.

"What's up, fool? I shoulda known you'd be somewhere around that crippled-ass dog."

"What's up, Chris?" Shakey spoke to the boy.

"Just chillin'." Christopher stepped around the car and shook Shakey's hand. "Give a nigga a cigarette."

"You know better than that." Though Shakey never scolded or preached to Christopher, he had always made it clear to him that he would not contribute to the boy's negative behavior.

"You be trippin'." Christopher smacked his lips and explained. "If you front me somethin' I could buy my own."

"If I what?" Shakey lifted his shirt, then made a move as if taking off his belt.

"Boooy." Chris jumped a few steps backward before bouncing on his toes like a boxer. "Don't make me get with ya, Shakey."

Shakey smiled and refastened his belt. He liked Christopher. He understood the wayward child. Unfortunately for Christopher, their childhoods were painfully similar.

Winston, Shakey's classmate and Christopher's "father," had never forgiven Christopher's mother for the pain he felt over her obvious infidelity. And though the two of them had gotten married just weeks after Christopher's birth, Winston hated the boy. For nearly a decade now, he had made sure to inflict nearly as much pain on both mother and son, as he himself felt. Shakey shook in his shoes a year ago when Christopher vowed to kill Winston when he got a little bigger.

"What you think about my shark?" Christopher walked toward his bicycle.

"Tight." Shakey made sure his face showed that he was duly impressed.

"See my rims?" Christopher was ecstatic. "So many spokes you can't even count 'em."

"I see you, playa." Shakey smiled.

"What about you?" Christopher turned his attention back to Jessica. He turned the bottom of the bottle straight up in the air, guzzling greedily in an attempt to further perturb the unknown white woman. "You like my ride?"

"No, but I like his." Jessica pointed at the plain Huffy dirt bike that other little boy sat on.

"What?" Christopher exclaimed, unaware that Jessica was toying with him. "That piece of junk?"

"What's your name, handsome?" Jessica spoke to the other little boy.

"Wesley Allen Shepherd." The little boy grinned widely, revealing to all that he was in the missing-front teeth stage of child development before realizing his guffaw and covering the gap with his bottom lip.

"Wesley Allen Shepherd," Jessica repeated.

Wesley nodded his head slowly, careful to hold frozen his bottom lip.

"Ooh, that's a pretty name," Jessica told him.

"Thank you." Wesley said then repositioned his bottom lip.

"Aw man." Christopher shook his head then placed his face in his hands.

"Come here, Wesley." Jessica slowly curled her index finger.

Wesley stepped to Jessica's window. He struggled to suppress another smile.

Jessica fumbled through her purse until finding a cherry Blow Pop. "Here, Wesley." She handed the young boy the candy.

"Thank you."

"You know, Wesley, you are a mighty cute little boy," Jessica added.

That was it. Wesley could suppress his smile no more and the gap where there would one day soon be teeth was visible again.

"I don't believe this." Christopher yelled then took a long drink from the wine. He studied his friend closely before scolding, "Quit smilin' so much, with yo' friendly ass."

"He's just jealous, Wesley." Jessica turned to Shakey and was surprised by the full smile he wore.

"Jealous of what?" Christopher defended himself. "I got plenty women."

"Does he have plenty of women, Wesley?" Jessica asked.

Wesley nodded his affirmation, though Jessica would have preferred another answer.

"Are they as pretty as I am?" Jessica tried again.

Wesley shook his head.

"Shut yo' mark ass up." Christopher was now furious with his buddy. "Let's go." He kicked hard on the kickstand then jumped on his bike.

"Bye, Wesley." Jessica waved.

"Bye." Wesley waved in return before mounting his bike.

"Let a playa hold somethin'," Christopher said to Shakey.

"I guess I can do something for a true playa." Shakey walked toward then passed Christopher until he stood before Wesley. He reached in his pocket and gave the boy a ten dollar bill.

"Thank you, Sir." Wesley squeezed the bill in his hand.

When turning around, Shakey couldn't help but laugh at the shocked expression on the face of the baby gangsta. If he didn't know any better, he would have thought Christopher's feelings had been truly hurt.

"You know I'ma take care of you." Shakey produced another ten and gave it to Christopher. "I was just having fun."

"Show a pimp some love, then." Christopher offered Shakey his hand after placing the bill in his pocket.

Shakey ignored the hand and gave him a hug. He did love Christopher. "Y'all take it easy," Shakey said to them before stepping for the driver side of the BMW.

"Later, Shakey." Christopher was already in motion. Wesley was at his side.

"And don't buy no wine with my money," Shakey called behind him.

Christopher turned his bottle up once more in defiance. Once the bottle was empty, he threw it in the street, breaking it on the pavement.

Shakey smiled and shook his head before climbing into the car. He was greeted immediately by Jessica's disapproving gaze. She didn't understand. There was no way she could. But Shakey understood perfectly.

It has been said that it takes an entire village to raise one child. By the same token, the collective failures of the village are required to ruin the same child. So to those who chose to view Christopher, and the many children like him, with condemnation, a more worthy course of action would be to look within themselves, diligently seeking remedy for their own shortcomings, which when combined with the shortcomings of others, has conspired to render an entire generation of urban youth utterly destroyed.

CHAPTER 8

Shakey's watch read 3:30 P.M. It had been five hours since the two of them had left Shakey's home. Jessica found herself to be totally overwhelmed by the pace of Shakey's life. After stopping to feed the dog, Shakey met with over a dozen people at various locations on the island. And though Shakey made sure to conduct his business just beyond her range of sight and sound, Jessica was sure that she was witnessing major drug transactions. Periodically, Shakey would return to a West End townhome that he would enter with a key, each time dropping off satchels, purses, backpacks, or whatever he used to carry whatever he carried. The contents of the bags was something Shakey did not volunteer, nor did Jessica inquire.

The BMW traveled now on Broadway. Shakey drank from a bottle of beer while singing along with the radio. Jessica marveled at the amount of alcohol Shakey had consumed in the last two hours. Not that Shakey was the first man she had met that was prone to alcohol abuse, but for the most part it seemed that no matter how much he drank, there would be no visible effects of the alcohol.

Jessica watched as he again checked the vibrating pager on his waist. Shakey smiled then pulled into the parking lot of the old garage on the corner of 37th and Broadway. He pulled the car directly in front of a row of payphones and without saying a word climbed from the car.

"Shakey." Jessica was tired of being ignored.

"What?"

"I need to use the restroom."

"Go ahead." Shakey pointed to the pair of portolets a few feet in the distance. He then turned for the phones.

Jessica stepped from the car, crossed her arms, and stared at Shakey. She grew more furious in respond to his indifference, but had no choice but to head for the portolets.

Jessica heard a voice coming from inside the first portolet as soon as she pulled on the door handle, yet inertia ruled all and the door was opened upon a most startling scene.

Two men were inside the portolet. One man was seated on the floor of the portolet, back against the toilet. The other man straddled the first, slapping him repeatedly. The men were similarly dressed in dirty jeans and multilayered tops.

"Oh, Butch!" The man who was standing was obviously distraught. "Talk to me Butch, please!" The man repeatedly slapped the face of the other, who Jessica could now see was unconscious.

Jessica's eyes were wide with horror. She had no idea of what she was witnessing.

"Call an ambulance!" the man screamed at Jessica once noticing her presence.

Jessica stared at the scary looking human being. The tall, brown-skinned man's hair was big and bushy, appearing not to be combed in weeks. There was enough yellow gook on his teeth to paint a racecar, and Jessica could smell his breath despite the distance between them. Paralyzed by indecision, she stood in place, watching the rest of the scene play out.

"Aw Butch! Don't die Butch!" The man resumed his slapping. "Talk to me Butch man."

"Urrrrgh."

Jessica backpedaled when the other man let out an unintelligible growl.

"Butch!" The standing man slapped harder.

"Urrrrrrgh." The ashen faced man peeked at his friend through the one eye that was now opened.

"C'mon, Butch." The standing man reached inside the toilet and splashed water on Butch's face. "You can make it, man."

Jessica's stomach did a triple gainer.

"Urrrrrrgh!" He shook his head like a wet and irritable dog.

"Butch." The standing man hugged him. "I thought I lost you, man."

Butch attempted speech before movement. "What happened, Will?"

"You put too much on the pipe, man." Will's voice was a high-pitched shrill by the time he reached the end of his sentence.

"My pipe." Butch fumbled on the wet floor in search of his crack pipe. "Where's my pipe?"

"It's under your leg."

"Put somethin' on that bad boy." Butch handed Will a small folded piece of cellophane.

"Shit, no problem." Will began unfolding the cellophane before remembering Jessica's presence. "What the fuck you want?"

"I needed to use the restroom," Jessica told him.

"Well, take yo' ass next do'." Will slammed the door on Jessica and the the laughter could immediately be heard from inside.

"Fucking assholes." Jessica stepped for the next portolet, but before she could reach for the handle, the door opened and a large woman stepped out. The woman wore a black dress that had to be three sizes too small. She also wore a blonde wig and blue contacts. She scowled at Jessica before beginning a slow stroll for the corner.

Jessica stepped inside the portolet. There was a small bag in the corner of the structure and an empty bottle of wine on the floor. Jessica lifted the lid on the toilet and her meal was nearly lost.

There had to be enough blood inside the toilet to facilitate a small trauma center. Their was blood around the lid of the toilet, on the seat, and under the lid. Jessica held her nose and mouth while running from the portolet. She returned to the car at about the same time Shakey did.

"What's wrong with you?" Shakey asked.

"Why would you send me over there?" Jessica gestured in the direction of the portolet with a violent jerk of her head.

Shakey laughed. "You said you need to use the restroom."

"You knew, Shakey."

"Knew what?" Shakey did know. And it was all he could do to not break into full-scale laughter while wheeling the BMW onto Broadway Boulevard. "Don't worry. I'm about to make it up to you."

"How?" Though still angry, Jessica was intrigued by the promise.

"Patience." Shakey gave the BMW some gas while raising the volume of the radio enough so that Jessica could pose no further questions.

The sun was just beginning to fall as the BMW pulled into the Back Bay apartment complex. "I'm gonna let you kick it with Rosa for a little while." Shakey said while holding the red end of the car's lighter to the Swisher that hang from his mouth.

"Who is Rosa?"

"A friend," Shakey told her.

"Yeah." Jessica suddenly remembered the message she had heard.

"You're a trip." Shakey had always secretly enjoyed jealousy in women. "She's going to take you shopping while I take care of some things."

"I don't have any money."

"Sometimes you say the dumbest shit." Shakey inhaled long and hard on the Swisher. Jessica eyed him suspiciously "The catch is." Shakey started as if reading her mind.

He held the Swisher to her mouth allowing her to puff softly before pulling it back and kissing her on the lips. "Tonight when we get home, you give me some of that good lovin' you been holdin' back on."

"Holding back?" Jessica repeated though her mind was still stuck on the word "home". It had been a long time since she had been anywhere that she considered "home". The mere sound of the word rolling from Shakey's lips gave her a sense of safety and security she had not felt since early childhood. "You're the one."

"Tell you what." Shakey placed the Swisher to her lips again. And as before, he covered her mouth with a kiss once she had taken a puff. "Get some lingerie too." He kissed her again. "Something sexy." Another kiss. "Make sure I don't fall asleep."

"OK," was all Jessica could say.

"Let me get Rosa." Shakey stepped from the car.

Jessica's breath came in spurts as she watched him through the rear view window. She had never wanted anyone as much as she wanted Shakey. She watched him until he took the first of the stairs leading to Rosa's apartment and could be seen no more.

Shakey knocked twice on the door then pulled the key from his pocket. He turned the lock and stepped inside, the television was on, but as of yet Shakey could discern no other signs of life.

Shakey entered the kitchen, inviting himself to the refrigerator. He grabbed one of Rosa's Budweiser beers then exited the kitchen and traveled deeper into the apartment. He could hear the sound of running water coming from the direction of the bedroom. Shakey opened the door of the bedroom then headed for the bathroom door. He tapped softly on the door. "Rosa," he called softly.

"I'll be out in a minute, Daddy." Rosa could barely be heard over the sound of the running water.

Shakey sat on the foot of Rosa's bed and turned on the television. There was a news bulletin on, something about an American spy plane captured in China. Shakey laughed to himself while opening the beer. Debo had been in office less than four months and already the nation was facing a potential war.

Debo was Shakey's nickname for President George W. Bush, so given in reference to the seedy circumstances of the president's victory over democratic challenger Al Gore. In Shakey's mind, George Bush had committed the biggest robbery in the world's history, and he would never think any differently. "But I'm the criminal," Shakey said aloud then turned the channel as Debo was preparing to address the nation. He finally settled on the only show he ever really paid attention to—Sportscenter.

Rosa entered the bedroom. "Yes, you are." She was wearing nothing except the towel that was wrapped around her hair. "And I love yo' black, no good, racketeering ass." Rosa paused to kiss him on the lips. "Hi, Daddy."

"Hey, baby." Shakey returned her kiss. "Now, what's the problem?"

"It's that bitch Vanessa," Rosa explained. "I went over there to get your money and that bitch got some mothafucka over their named Tubbs talking about he running the spot now." Rosa stopped long enough to take a breath then continued. "He say any business you had with Vanessa you gotta discuss with him now.

"Yeah." Shakey took a sip from the Budweiser. His stomach knotted with discomfort as he pictured the woman that the other girls referred to as Satan. Vanessa had long been a source of excess stress for Shakey. He considered dismissing her long ago, but didn't for fear of the street's interpretation of his actions. In his business, Shakey had to be very careful of messages his actions conveyed to the streets. And the streets were always watching. So after answering numerous complaints by his most valued customers pertaining to Vanessa's lack of social etiquette and tendency to pilfer, Shakey had finally reassigned her to the operation of a dope house. She had actually done quite well the last three months. Now this. "I'll check 'em out."

"Be careful, Daddy. That guy is mean." Rosa moved to the mirror that was atop the dresser. She untied the towel then began to dry her hair.

Shakey didn't respond.

"What took you so long to come by?" The towel was on the dresser now and Rosa brushed the large black curls atop her head. "You know I don't like having all that money here. Makes me nervous."

Shakey still didn't respond. Next to the anger he felt over Vanessa's latest transgression, Rosa's conversation was insignificant.

"There's over twenty thousand dollars in here." Rosa hadn't noticed Shakey's disinterest.

"There's something I need you to do," Shakey said suddenly.

"What's that, Daddy?" Rosa was always eager to please.

"I got this girl," Shakey told her. "I need you to take her shopping for some clothes."

"Where is she?"

"In the car." Shakey reached in his wallet for the credit card then gave it to her.

"What do you want her to have?"

"The best work clothes a ho can buy." Shakey smiled.

"That's a lotta help," Rosa laughed.

"I don't know what I am going to do with her yet." Shakey explained. "I was thinking about hiring her as a waitress at Sanovia's while I check her out more closely." Shakey took another sip from the beer. "Just get her some shit to wear to work."

"Your wish is my command, Daddy." Rosa stepped enough that a small pear-shaped breast dangled inches from Shakey's mouth.

Shakey could always depend on Rosa. The two of them went way back. Actually it had been Rosa who had taught him the art of running hoes. Of course, like all manner of evil he had been exposed to, Shakey had been the perfect student. First learning, then mastering, and finally developing his own approach to the game.

Shakey observed Rosa's naked body. Well past her prime, Rosa had been to hell and back, and her body bore the marks to prove it. There was nicks and cuts on Rosa's forehead and face. Her shoulders and arms were home to even more scars. There was a three inch scar above her left breast. But the most shocking wound of Rosa's was the long scar that ran from the top of her chest all the way down to her navel. A not so subtle reminder of the open heart surgery that saved her life after a near fatal stab wound at the hands of a john she had clipped for his entire income tax refund.

"You all right, baby?" Shakey placed his left arm around Rosa, resting his hand on her buttocks. Shakey was quite fond of this woman who had first taking a liking to him over fifteen years ago after discovering that he had the same birthday as the pimp who first turned her out.

"I'd be a lot better if you came by and fucked me every once in awhile." Rosa had always been shockingly blunt.

Shakey wrapped his arms around the diminutive woman, lifted her from her feet then turned to place her back onto the bed. He looked at the clock on the night-stand. Four-thirty. With a little time to spare, the king of the jungle obliged the lioness' request.

CHAPTER 9

"What's the damn deal?" David stepped through the door, close on Shakey's heels as the two of them entered room 112 of The Inverness by The Sea condominiums.

"What's up, David?" Red stood to greet the clown. He wondered why Shakey would bring him to the lab, but he had to admit that he was happy to see David.

"It's all good in the hood, homeboy." David was as animated as usual. His deep, throaty voice instantly transformed the atmosphere of the lab to that of a party. The small man held a half-gallon of gin in his left hand while shaking Red's hand with his right. "You know what I'm talkin' about."

"I feel ya." Red laughed.

"Damn you gettin' big, Red." David sized-up the much larger man. "You thinkin' about trying out for somebody's sumo wrestling team or somethin'?"

At this Red laughed heartily.

"All right, Doc." David stepped further inside the room, greeting another long time acquaintance be-

fore finally noticing the table full of powdered cocaine. "Damn, homeboy!" David turned to Shakey.

"Chill out." Shakey said simply while pointing to
the kitchen. "There are cups and ice in the kitchen."

"Chill out." David was no less animated as he
headed to the kitchen. "Just seein' all that dope
makes me wanna take shit!"

"What's up, Doc'?" Shakey shook hands with the
bespectacled middle-aged man. Doc was another
of Shakey's long-time business associates. A free-
lancer. If there was ever a need for the cooking or
transporting of dope of any kind, Doc was the man
to call.

"Nothin' to it. Red tells me you lookin' for a li'l
magic."

"Yeah." Shakey thought of the outrageous price
Trevino wanted for the ten kilograms of cocaine he
had dropped on him two nights before.

"How much?"

"Two for one."

"Got the whip?" Doc was already reaching for
his sack.

Shakey turned to Red, who immediately disappeared into an adjoining room. Moments later, he
returned with a sack of his own.

"Here you go." Red placed the bag on the counter
next to Doc. "We got Bolivia, B-12, and some other
stuff. Shit, there's about three thousand dollars
worth of drug paraphernalia in this mothafucka."

The three men laughed.

"Well, let's see what we see." Doc surveyed the bag's contents.

David reentered the room, his arms now encumbered with a pitcher of ice, a large can of grapefruit juice, and four glasses in addition to the gin bottle he already carried. "You niggas help yourselves." David placed everything on the small end table next to the couch. He then fixed himself a drink.

"You got everything we need." Doc looked to Red after inspecting the bag.

"You know I'ma take care of ya," Shakey told Doc.

"That's the last of my worries with you." Doc gathered the entirety of his work tools and in two trips placed everything on the table in the living room. After being seated, he pulled the table closer to him.

"Time out, homeboy." David turned to Doc. He could contain himself no longer. "Let me get a line or two of that before you fuck it up."

"You sure, Dave?" Shakey was playing with him. "That's some powerful shit!"

"Am I sure?" David frowned at him. "Nigga, set it out."

Shakey took the ace of spades from the bottom of the card deck that lay on the table. He filled the entire card with cocaine then placed it on the small table next to the gin bottle. "That's you, homie," Shakey said before reaching for the remote and turning on the radio.

David said nothing. He only stared at the playing card filled with dope. All in the room were sure they had never before seen David incapable of speech.

David leaned over the mound of cocaine and when the tip of his nose touched the powder he inhaled deeply. His head shot back immediately, his large eyes were filled with water and he wiggled his nose in every direction. "Goddamn homeboy!"

The other three men laughed at David.

"Heeeey!" David stood and clapped to the sound of Q-Tip's "Vivrant Thing." He grabbed his drink and downed it in one motion. He poured himself another drink then danced around the room.

The laughter in the room was louder than the radio now.

"Where you find this fool?" Doc shook his head.

The song changed and "Chickenheads" from Project Pat played now.

"I need me one of them chickenheads right now." David screamed at the top of his lungs before attacking his drink like a dehydrated lumberjack.

"Let's kick it on the balcony." Shakey decided to have mercy on the others in the room. "I got speakers out there, we can watch them hoes in the pool."

"Sounds like a winner to me." David poured himself another drink then carefully lifted the playing card from the table before following Shakey to the balcony.

"I'm tellin' you, I'm through with that dopefiend bitch, homeboy." David parked his daughter's BMW next to Rosa's Ford Taurus. The dopefiend bitch he referred to was his common law wife Mary. "That bitch don't want nothin', homeboy."

"You know you love that woman, David." Shakey pulled from the Swisher then handed it to David.

"That mothafucka's crazy, homeboy." David's voice grew somehow deeper whenever he was angry. "How the fuck you gon' call the law on the breadwinner?'

Shakey laughed hysterically. David and Mary were always squabbling over one thing or another. Apparently the last fight resulted in David's arrest.

"You don't call the law on the breadwinner, homeboy!" David said with slow heartfelt intensity then puffed long and hard on the marijuana stick. "I'm through with that stupid mothafucka! That's it! I'm out!

"Man, let me go get this girl," Shakey said smiling. He looked at his watch. It was 9:15 and Rosa had a very important appointment to keep.

"Yea" David sat back in the seat. His head now slightly below the height of the dashboard, he smoked hard on the Swisher. "Bring mamasita out here. I might spend somethin'."

Shakey laughed all the way up the stairs. David was a character. He didn't bother to knock this time. He stuck the key in the door and called Rosa while stepping inside the apartment.

"In here Daddy." Rosa was in the kitchen. Shakey could here the clang of dishes. "I was just making sure Cynthia has something to eat when she gets home."

Cynthia was Rosa's fifteen-year-old daughter.

Rosa wrapped tin foil around the plate she had prepared and placed it in the microwave. She then placed three pots in the refrigerator.

"So what do you think?" Shakey asked her.

"About what?"

"The girl."

Rosa looked at Shakey before saying. "She's beautiful."

"And?" Shakey had never seen the expression Rosa had just given him.

"I think she's in love." Rosa said.

"Ain't all y'all?" Shakey's attempt at humor fell deaf on even his own ears. "What else?"

"She's a really nice girl, Shakey." Rosa finally spoke the words the pricked her conscience. "Too nice Daddy. She's all wrong for us."

Shakey's anger nearly erupted again. Not so much at Rosa, but at the conviction of his heart by way of her words. "She'll be all right." Shakey motioned for Rosa to follow him. "Let's go, Mr. Popovich is waiting."

"That old freak'll wait forever." Rosa laughed while reaching for her coat. "I hope he has the earrings he promised me."

Shakey allowed Rosa to leave the apartment first. He closed and locked the door before following her down the stairway. The two of them stepped side by side down the narrow walkway until Rosa stopped suddenly in her tracks.

"Hell no, Shakey!" Rosa shook her head. "No! No! No! I am not going anywhere with that man!" David was Rosa's least favorite person in the world.

"Come on, baby." Shakey took her hand. "He'll be quiet."

"Daddy, you know I can't stand that son of a bitch!" Rosa didn't budge. "Why you do this to me?"

"I'm sorry, baby." Shakey told her then quickly conjured a well-articulated falsehood. "My car's not ready and I was in a hurry."

"Man," Rosa finally took a step in the direction of the BMW. "Tell him not to speak one word to me, Shakey! I mean it. I'll cut his ass!"

"OK." Shakey concealed his smile as he and Rosa approached the passenger side of the BMW. Shakey held open the door for her then jumped in the front seat.

"Heeey, Senorita Bonita," David started before she was even seated. "Look at those legs." David turned all the way around and was now kneeling in his seat. "Girl, you drive a mothafucka to drink!" David reached behind him for his glass.

"Shakey," Rosa called for help.

"Chill out, David." Shakey was finding it hard not to laugh. He could tell by David's hyper-animation that the smallish man had snorted more cocaine while Shakey was inside.

"What?" David flashed his most disarming 'what did I do' grin. "I got some money." David jammed his hand into his pocket and began counting a handful of crumpled up bills. "Ten . . . fifteen . . . sixteen . . . seventeen." David stopped counting and turned to Rosa. "Cuantos dineros por la pinocha?" David asked in heavily encumbered Spanish then laughed as if insane. "You hear me homeboy?" He slapped Shakey on the shoulder. "How much for that pussy? Straight up like that!"

"Fuck this shit, Shakey!" Rosa opened the door. "I told you, Shakey!"

"All right, baby, he'll stop." Shakey promised. "Won't you, David?"

"Yeah." The mischief in David's smiling blood-shot eyes was barely conspicuous over the rim of the glass. "I'll chill."

Rosa took a long hard look first at David, then at Shakey. "We'll talk about this later, Shakey," she promised before closing the door.

"So why was you and Mary fightin' in the first place?" Shakey searched for a subject that would pry David's mind away from Rosa's pinocha.

"That dopefiend-ass bitch wouldn't let me in my own house, homeboy." David finally started the engine. "Her ass locked up in the house with that dopefiend brother of hers and that fat bitch from her job." David paused to sip from his cup. "I'm standin' in the rain and these dopefiend mothafuckas won't open the door."

Rosa suppressed the burning desire she felt to comment on David's story.

"So what'd you do, fool?" Shakey found it funny that David viewed everyone that used drugs as a dopefiend besides himself.

"When I go tired of knockin' on that damn do', standin' in the rain like a fool, I kicked that badboy off the hinges." David turned to Shakey as he spoke causing the car to swerve dangerously to the right.

"Watch out, Dave." It was Shakey's own hand on the wheel that rerouted the wayward vessel.

"I got this, homeboy." David took another drink. "You shoulda seen them mothafuckas when I busted up in there. Eyes like baseballs! I caught 'em in that world." David turned to Shakey, causing the car to veer off course again.

Rosa recited something, perhaps a prayer, in rapid fire Spanish.

Shakey reached for the wheel again.

"I got this, homeboy," David said before continuing his story. "I jumped on the coffee table, right? And ran all the way across until I was all up in that mothafucka's face."

Shakey laughed aloud while picturing his friend running across a table only to find himself standing face to face with the much larger Mary. "What happened then?"

"Everybody bailed when I grabbed the lamp, homeboy," David told him. "Mary, Janet, and that dopefiendass nigga. Which way, homeboy?" David asked once the BMW rolled to a stop at the intersection of Sixty-first Street and Heard's Lane.

"Go straight." Shakey knew that Broadway Boulevard would be much quicker, but with David's current driving ability, a populated street could quickly become an expressway to disaster.

"I chased them dopefiends outside," David resumed his storytelling. "Then all of a sudden Mary stopped on the porch and bucked up to me, homeboy." David took another drink. "She put her hand in my face talkin' 'bout she tired of my punk-ass shit. See how that shit fuck with they mind, homeboy?" David turned to Shakey again. "I tried to slap her hand off at the wrist."

"Then what?" Shakey began to lose interest in David's story. His thoughts were now of Jessica, who was alone in his home. He knew from experience that he could not leave her alone for long. He had given her his cell number and gotten a solemn promise that she would call if anything at all was wrong. He was also realizing that he missed her.

"That bitch stole me, homeboy!"

"What?" David's story was suddenly reenergized.

"Haaaard too!" David rubbed his chin while turning to Shakey again. "The porch was wet, that's what made me slip and fall." David turned back to the road.

"On the porch?" Shakey asked.

"Naw, you know it ain't no banister. I fell on the ground."

Shakey was laughing again, and Rosa too chuckled softly from the backseat.

"She hit hard?" Shakey was messing with David now.

"Hell yeah, that big bitch hit hard." David rubbed chin again while turning once more toward Shakey. "What you think?"

The panicked blare of an oncoming motorist's horn interrupted David's tale. The drunken storyteller swerved quickly, barely avoiding the oncoming police cruiser. Both cruiser and BMW stopped suddenly. No other cars were on the street.

"Stupid mothafucka!" David opened his door and yelled to the police cruiser. "Why don't you watch where the fuck you goin'?"

"Chill out, David man." Shakey was nervous.

"Madre Maria," was all that could be made of the gibberish coming from the backseat.

The police cruiser was still for a moment then simply continued on its way.

Shakey turned to Rosa. "Tell Maria I said thank you." The resulting glare from the angry woman caused him to quickly turn forward in his seat.

"Stupid no-drivin' mothafucka!" David finally slammed the door shut before slipping the transmission into drive.

"David." Shakey smiled. "Can you please get us there in one piece?"

"I got this, homeboy!" David finished off his drink. He chomped on the ice once the liquor was gone. He returned to the telling of his story as if he had no cares in the world. "By the time I got up she was runnin' again, homeboy! She backed against the pecan tree talking 'bout she sorry David." David looked behind him and Shakey feared that he would once again start in on Rosa. But then he said, "You see that bottle?"

"Here." Rosa handed the bottle to Shakey.

Shakey twisted the cap then filled Rosa's cup.

"I ran up on that mothafucka, homeboy." David took a hearty swig. "And I started wearing those legs out."

"What?" Shakey was unsure if he had heard David correctly.

"Hooks and uppercuts homeboy. I beat them legs up. David took another drink. "I ain't gon' hit her in the face, she gotta work." David laughed to himself then turned to Shakey. "I'ma pimp too, homeboy!"

While Shakey couldn't quite decide if he thought David's story was funny or not, he had long ago decided that David was amongst the maddest of men.

"She called the laws on me, homeboy." David reiterated in disbelief. He then turned to Rosa. And for all practical purposes, left the BMW to drive itself. "You a woman. Don't you know better than to call the laws on the breadwinner?

"Yeah." Rosa had no interest in any conversation involving David. "Turn around and watch the road."

"Don't be no backseat driver, baby girl." David turned around, bringing the BMW to stop at the corner of Forty-first and R before turning back to Rosa. "But you wouldn't have to worry about none of that, sexy."

"Shut up!" Rosa attempted to deter David before it was too late.

"I'd treat you like good barbecue."

Shakey had the notion to stop David, but was much too interested in finding out exactly what it meant to treat a woman like good barbecue.

"First, I'd season you all over." David wiggled his fingers while moving his hands up and down as if massaging and caressing some unseen object.

"Stop it," Rosa demanded.

Shakey smiled.

"Then," David paused, truly believing that his words were sexually enticing. "I'd get everything good and hot before I lay you down."

"I said stop it, you fuckin' idiot!"

"Once I start cookin', I'll make sure to turn you over and over and over so I can get every piece well done." David was now exciting himself. He yelled loudly, "Ooh girl, you just don't know."

"Tell him to shut up, Shakey."

"The light's green, David," Shakey laughed.

"And once I know that meat is tender, it's time to bite, lick, nibble, and chew." David made a slurping sound while moving his tongue outside his mouth. The accompanying hand gestures only added to the comedy.

"Stop it." Rosa's smallish hands were used to cover her ears.

"And I'll even let you suck on the bone."

"Ahhhhhh!" Rosa screamed as loud as she could.

Shakey finally broke down with laughter, and the circus car continued on its track.

"My main man Shakey! What's up?" Mr. Popovich offered Shakey his hand. The balding and overweight businessman was always excited to visit with his favorite drug-dealing pimp.

"What's up, Pops?" Shakey had always been amused by the Polish man's use of outdated slang. Shakey was smiling also because Mr. Popovich had also been one of his biggest spending customers.

"Nothing worth rapping about." Mr. Popovich used his hands to brush the wrinkles from his suit. He took a step backward to make room for Shakey and the woman he referred to as his Aztec princess to step through the door. "Been spending a little time with the wife and kids."

"Nothing wrong with that." Shakey stepped aside in order for Rosa to appear center stage. "Now its playtime."

"Hiya, my little Aztec princess." Mr. Popovich held his arms wide for Rosa.

"Ooh Daddy, you feel so good." Rosa's voice and demeanor were the epitome of female seduction. She ran her fingers through the curly locks that were alongside the head of the supermarket chain owner. Mr. Popovich had once been quite proud of the head full of curly black tufts he possessed. But with middle-age came male pattern baldness and his source of pride and joy had now been reduced to two small patches of gray located on both sides of his block-shaped head. Totally aware of this highly sensitive area, Rosa was always sure to resurrect the pride he once felt in his hair. "How come you been gone from me for so long?" Rosa was now a saddened high school princess.

"I had some urgent matters to deal with." Mr. Popovich felt sheepish at the defending of his actions to a prostitute, but knew he was powerless against Rosa's spell.

"Too urgent to come and see me?" Rosa took Mr. Popovich's hand and stroked her own face with it. She then placed his thumb inside her mouth and sucked softly. "I've been so lonely with no one to be naughty with."

"Well I'm here now, mi princessa." Mr. Popovich eased his thumb from her mouth and reached into the pocket of his sportscoat. "And look what I have for you."

Magical. Shakey had always been a big fan of Rosa's performances.

The hopelessly ensnared man produced a jewelry case which, once opened, displayed a brilliantly shining pair of diamond earrings.

"Oh Daddy, they're beautiful." Rosa's words were filled with such emotion that it was doubtful to Shakey that he was still watching a performance. "Put them on for me."

Shakey thought of Jessica while watching Mr. Popovich's trembling hands struggle with the small holes in Rosa's earlobes. She had yet to ring his cell phone. He was beginning to worry. He also missed her more.

"They're beautiful," Rosa said again, now standing before the mirror behind the bar. "And they make me feel so sexy, Daddy." Rosa did everything but purr like a kitten.

Rosa mixed two martinis, one for Mr. Popovich, the other for herself. She then placed the drinks on the table before seating herself on the sofa. She leaned back on the couch, raising her skirt until the skin of her thickly rounded thighs could be seen above the black stockings she wore. From one stocking she pulled a plastic bag containing a full ounce of crack cocaine which she sat on the table beside the martinis. From the other stocking, she gathered the pipe and a straight razor.

"I'd better be going before things get x-rated." Shakey placed a temporary block on Rosa's spell.

"Tell you what, my man." Mr. Popovich stepped for the table and opened the checkbook that lay there. He reached for the pen in his top shirt pocket and endorsed the check he pulled from the book. "I'm not sure how much time I'll be spending with mi princessa or how much stuff we'll need." Mr. Popovich handed Shakey the blank check. "So just fill in the blanks once you tally it all up."

"Gotcha, Pops." Shakey placed the check in his own pocket. "You know how to get in touch when you need me." Shakey made his way to the door.

"And we will be needing you." Mr. Popovich shook his pusher's hand once more.

"Don't hesitate to call, regardless of the time," was Shakey's last instructions before leaving.

Shakey moved quickly once outside the three bedroom Victorian style home. Just one of countless homes, apartments, and condominiums throughout the Island that Shakey owned by proxy. The structures were used to accommodate customers like Mr. Popovich, whom desired the services of women of the night, along with getting high in a safe, discreet location. Shakey's offering was one of convenience with all that was needed being found under one roof, at a location untraceable to his customers. Amongst them were some of the most affluent and influential businessmen and politicians in the area. And for Shakey's services, there was no limit to what they would spend.

Shakey stepped quickly in the direction of the Circle K store where David would be waiting. He turned the corner of Seventeenth and Broadway,

making a fast approach for the front of the store.
A large crowd was gathered around the store's entrance; the whole of them seemed to be paying ob-
servance to some great spectacle. It didn't take long
for Shakey to discover that David was somehow at
the center of that spectacle.

"Just give me a reason, Kung Fu! Give me a
reason!" David struck a fighting pose. His face was
the picture of intensity. If Shakey didn't know any
better, he too would have found himself convinced
of the miniature man's fighting prowess.

"You go." The Korean store owner, who stood
no taller than the lunatic in front of him, wielded a
broom in self-defense. "Leave now."

"Come on, you seaweed eatin' mothafucka!" David was unfazed by the broom. "I'll tear yo' funky
ass up!"

Shakey forced is way through the crowd in hopes
of talking some sense into his friend. "What's up,
David?"

"This Hong Kong Phooey mothafucka gon' tell
me I gotta leave the parking lot." David waved his
arms wildly. "He don't know me."

"Music too loud." the store owner explained to
Shakey. "Scare other customers."

"What customers?" David scowled in response
to the store owner's explanation. "They all here to
see you get yo' ass kicked!"

David made a move toward the store owner. The
frightened man instinctively raised the broom-
stick, striking Shakey between the legs. Despite the

ensuing pain, Shakey was able to use his wingspan to keep the two men apart.

"It's cool." Shakey said to the store owner once David stopped struggling. "We're leaving." Shakey pushed David toward the car before limping in the same direction.

"I'm leavin', Kung Fu!" David announce while opening the car door. "But I'll be back!" he promised. "I'll be back!" He backed the BMW away from the storefront, dotted through the parking lot, and sped along Broadway.

Shakey drove into his garage and leapt from the car. He was anxious to get inside his home. Jessica had never bothered to call. It was now 1:00 P.M., six full hours since Shakey had left her alone. He burst through the door that led from the garage to his home, disbelieving the frantic anticipation that caused his heart to race so rapidly. He was nearly running as he traveled the length of the hallway leading to his bedroom, embarrassed by his own silent prayer offerings requesting Jessica's presence.

Shakey could hear the television as he approached the bedroom door. He gathered himself then slowly turned the doorknob. He entered the room. His heart sank with relief upon sight of the slumbering woman.

Shakey stepped closer. Jessica lay on her side. She wore an oversized baseball jersey of Shakey's and used it as a nightgown. While in dreamland, the bottom of the shirt had traveled enough to not only allow Shakey a look at her bare legs, but also a full view of the white bikini underwear she wore. And more arousingly, the shapely behind with which she had been so graciously endowed. Oddly, Shakey found himself further aroused by the way she clung tightly to the pillow she hugged with both arms.

Shakey had nearly forgotten the small brown paper bag he clutched underneath his left arm. And once remembered, the spirits inside the bag were of no consequence to him. He placed the bag on the dresser, careful not to wake Jessica.

Shakey stood beside the bed, slowly unbuttoning his shirt. He then kicked the shoes from his feet and unfastened his belt. He crawled onto the bed, approaching her from behind. He lay still next to her and placed his arm around her waist.

Jessica's body jerked violently. He had startled her.

"It's me, baby." Shakey whispered into her ear.

Jessica turned to face Shakey. She said nothing.

Shakey kissed her gently. The sweetness of her lips aroused in him a need for more. He wrapped her into his arms and pulled her near. The warmth of her body was hot against his skin. Shakey kissed her again then pushed softly at her shoulder until she lay on her back.

Jessica squeezed Shakey's neck with both arms. She raised her body from the bed so that he could pull the shirt over her head. The braless flesh that had been concealed by the jersey was now fully exposed.

Shakey kneeled in the center of the bed. He swiftly peeled the shirt from his body then tugged gently at Jessica's panties. Once again, her body contoured to whatever shape was necessary to aid Shakey in unclothing her.

Shakey slid the pants from his body. Clad now only in his boxers, he positioned himself on top of her.

Jessica felt a nervous anticipation as the long, large body of the black man hovered above her own. She reached upward with both arms wide, wrapping her arms as far around Shakey's body as possible, her hands not quite touching the center of his back.

Shakey kissed her again, now using his right hand to make his hardness accessible through the front of his boxers.

Jessica gasped loudly, a pleasure mixture of pleasure and pain as Shakey entered her.

Shakey's entire body was set aflame upon entering her as he found the the spot between her legs to be even warmer to the touch than the rest of her body.

Jessica squeezed Shakey's neck as firmly as her tightness clung to his member. Shakey moved slowly, then lay totally still atop of her, allowing enough time for her vaginal muscles to relax before attempting to go deeper inside her.

Jessica writhed wildly beneath him, making every move necessary to accommodate Shakey's decension into the deepest depths of the fire within her.

The two of them touched every inch of the King-sized bed. Jessica had never known such pleasure, as she had never before given herself to a man purely upon the premise of her own desires.

For his part, sex for Shakey had long been just a physical act. A tool used for a variety of reasons. It seemed lifetimes ago since sex had been coupled with anything resembling the emotions he felt now.

Just on the other side of daybreak, after bringing each other to countless climaxes, the two of them slept. Each clung tightly to the other, both souls thankful for the night that passed. And with that night came the settling revelation that in even the coldest of worlds, their still existed brief, pleasure-filled moments of respite from their maker.

CHAPTER 10

There was a much different rhythm to Shakey's walk as he floated across the bedroom floor. The sound of the softly drumming water was nearly successful at enticing him to join Jessica in the shower. Pressed for time, he instead decided to make his way to the guestroom located at the far end of the hallway.

After a fast, hot shower, Shakey used his towel to clear a spot in the mirror he used to view himself. He smiled at his reflection while counting to himself the years since he had been acquainted with even a distant cousin of the lovebug. He then remembered the only other time in his life that a single night of sex had had such a positive effect on his psyche.

Shakey's mind instantly conjured images of Kiska and the night they had spent together over a dozen years before. Shakey was fourteen, Kiska a year younger. Just a few days before they met, Shakey, intoxicated on MD 20/20 wine, fell face first to the pavement, jarring a top front tooth from his mouth. The following days he spent sitting around the house, too embarrassed to even speak, impatiently awaiting the call from the dentist that would announce the readiness of the partial plate his mom sacrificed to buy for him.

On a night when his mom, stepfather, and other friends and family members attended a gathering, it was decided that the kids would crash at the Massey residence. Among them was Kiska, the daughter of Candace Mitchell, a woman who worked at the cleaner's with Shakey's mother.

As fate would have it, Jonathan and Kiska found themselves awake alone, long after the other kids had tired of late night television.

As was predictable, opportunity plus physical attraction plus youthful curiosity equaled sex. As well as a night that Shakey would never forget.

By no means was this Shakey's first sexual encounter. In his naivety he believed himself to be quite experienced. But the difference in the night spent with Kiska was that it was Shakey's first encounter with the female orgasm. And talk about therapy. For days, Shakey walked with a pride unknown to even the bravest of lions.

Shakey, fully dressed now, made his way back down the hallway. Jessica met him at the head of the stairs, also dressed, a radiant beauty.

The first wear of Jessica's new wardrobe was simple purple pantsuit that clung provocatively to every curve of her body. The sandals she wore were perfect compliments to both her outfit and her freshly painted toenails.

"Nice." Shakey was determined to reassume some position of authority in this relationship.

"Think so?" Jessica gave herself the once over, apparently not quite sure about her new style of dress.

"What's wrong?" Shakey stepped closer, a mistake. Before he knew it, his arms were around her again.

"Nothing." Jessica pressed her head against his chest, slowly inhaling the cologne he wore. She found herself becoming quite fond of being in Shakey's arms. "I've just never worn clothes like this before."

"Well, I like it." Shakey kissed the top of her head.

"Wait until you see your credit card bill." Jessica smiled.

"You can make it up to me."

"And how is that?" Jessica leaned back so that she could see his face.

"A few more nights like last night, and I'll owe you." Shakey wanted to introduce her to the idea of sex for money.

"Oh, yeah?" Jessica's balled fists were now on her hips. "And how much was last night worth to you?"

"Well." Shakey appeared to be in deep concentration. "If I had to quote a price—"

"You'd better not." Jessica pushed playfully at his chest.

"What?" Shakey grabbed her, leading to yet another sweet embrace.

"You can really be an asshole when you want," Jessica declared.

"You asked." Shakey laughed before saying, "Let's go."

"Where?"

"I figured we'd have a family breakfast this morning," Shakey informed her.

"More like lunch." Jessica grabbed the purse from the bed that Rosa had selected to specifically go with the pantsuit. "And what family?"

"Maybe I do need to look at my credit card receipts," Shakey joked while feigning a frown at the purse.

"Shut up," Jessica whined, still feeling uncomfortable though she knew he was only kidding.

"I figured you, me, and Baby'd eat something."

"Baby?" Jessica search her mind for remembrance. "Oh, that dog."

"Yeah." Shakey smiled. "That dog."

"Well, I'm starvin'," Jessica said.

"You oughtta be." Shakey grabbed the car keys from the dresser and turned to leave the bedroom. "Let's go."

"And just what is that supposed to mean?" Jessica followed Shakey down the stairs and in the direction of the garage.

"Nothing." Shakey laughed.

"Tell me." Jessica squeezed a healthy portion of Shakey's rear end between her thumb and index finger.

"Hey, girl!" Shakey covered his behind with both hands, disbelieving the fact that she had pinched him.

"Tell me what you meant then." The not so subtle threat was clearly audible in Jessica's voice.

"Nothin'." Shakey was blushing like a young boy basking in the afterglow of his first kiss. He quickly pondered his circumstance then motioned with his head for Jessica to walk in front of him. "You go."

"You must think I am stupid," Jessica replied. "You go."

Shakey and Jessica faced each other in the narrow hallway. Both their backs were pressed against the wall as neither of them were willing to expose the target area.

"Quit trippin', girl." Shakey felt ridiculous.

"Go ahead then."

"We'll go together," Shakey told her.

As if on cue, the two of them took well-measured side steps in the direction of the door until Shakey was stricken with the need for revenge.

In a blur Shakey lunged forward, reaching around her and aiming his hand at the abundant softness of her hind parts. As if knowing the exact moment his attack would come, Jessica easily spun away from him.

"Cheater!" Jessica shrieked as Shakey first wrapped his arms around her then palmed her behind with both hands. Her struggle caused the two of them to stumble and they soon found themselves on the carpet, her on top of him. Two hours would pass before they made it to the garage.

After stopping to feed Baby the two chopped beef poboys he purchased for her, Shakey drove east on Seawall Boulevard. Though not quite sure of his destination, he was more than happy with the company he kept.

Jessica sang along with Ashanti's "Baby," seemingly just as contented with Shakey. The clothes that Rosa selected for her did wonders for her appearance. Shakey's instructions to Rosa was to dress her for work, yet Jessica looked to be anything but a potential woman of the night. In fact, Shakey mused, it would constitute a crime to confine such beauty to the obscurity of darkness.

Shakey saw the sign that read GO CITY RACETRACK and quickly exited onto the side road that led to entrance of the building.

Jessica had yet to notice the change in routes, as she was growing quickly accustomed to the many stops Shakey made on a given day.

Jessica did notice, however, when the Cadillac rolled to a stop in the racetrack parking lot. "What are you doing?" she asked with heightening curiosity.

"Let's have some fun." Shakey's own voice sounded odd to him. Surely he had never spoken such nerdish words.

"I don't know how to drive a go-cart." Jessica doubted his sanity.

"It's just like driving a car," Shakey told her. "Gas, brake, steering wheel." He utilized the driving mechanisms of the Cadillac as props for his lecture.

"I never drove a car," she informed him.

"You'll pick it up." Shakey opened his door. "Let's go."

"No, I won't." Jessica reached past him and pulled his door shut. "Because we're not going in there."

"What?" Shakey smiled, he was not able to decipher the cause of the rising emotion Jessica now spoke with.

"I'm not getting in one of those things." Jessica watched as the small race cars zoomed around the track. Red-faced drivers screamed with glee while living out their formula one fantasies.

"Why not?" Shakey asked, though the look on her face was now speaking volumes to the "why not".

"Because it's dangerous."

"You're scared," Shakey declared.

"I am not."

"Are too."

"No, I'm not."

"Well let's go." Shakey grabbed the door handle and, with a raised eyebrow, made his final challenge.

"You really think I'm afraid, don't you?" Jessica smiled at Shakey.

The steadiness of Shakey's gaze was his answer.

"OK, smart ass." Jessica stepped from the Cadillac. "Let's go. But when I zoom around this track so fast that I leave your ass in the dust, don't say I didn't warn you."

"Let's be serious."

Shakey and Jessica entered the establishment and were immediately bombarded with a multitude of sounds coming from the video arcade. Children of all ages laughed and played while partaking in a variety of video fantasies.

Shakey walked over to the large window along the east wall of the building. There he was granted a full view of the racetrack. He looked back at Jessica, surveying her swiftly, then returned his attention to the track. The speed of the cars, along with the aggressiveness of some of the drivers, was causing Shakey to rethink his decision to place Jessica behind the wheel of one of the vehicles.

"You sure you wanna do this?" He turned to Jessica again.

"Are you?" Jessica perceived his question as further provocation.

Shakey quickly scanned the small arcade. A few feet to his right he saw exactly what was needed.

Black in color and shaped like a Ford Mustang, the patron was to sit inside the game. The appearance and dimensions inside the Mustang was identical to that of an actual 5.0. The windshield of the car was a screen that provided the sight, and the dashboard was equipped with an assortment of speakers that provided the sounds of the game play. The game allowed the driver to test his or her driving skills against the pre-programmed conditions. Shakey decided that a few dollars spent for Jessica on the driving experience would be money well spent.

"Why don't you practice over here?" Shakey suggested while pointing at the car.

"Who needs practice?" Jessica was indignant. "Let's go!"

Jessica led Shakey from the arcade and onto the racetrack entrance. She marched, without the slightest hitch in step, straight to the small counter where patrons paid to drive the cars.

"Together?" a puffy-faced, cigar smoking man asked.

Shakey was drilled with the question, as it provided him with the perfect safe-haven for Jessica. "One". Shakey answered the man.

"Two." Jessica held two fingers in the air. "I'm driving my own." She looked at Shakey.

"OK." Shakey flashed the mouthful of gold, diamonds, and rubies. "But I'm ridin' with you."

"Now who's scared?"

"I'm not scared," Shakey said hesitantly, quickly rummaging the corners of his mind for an excuse to fit the occasion.

"What is it then, chicken?" Jessica folded her arms like wings and flapped them wildly. "Buck, buck, buck."

The cigar smoking attendant laughed loudly.

"I'd just rather ride with you, baby." Shakey could think of nothing better to say.

Jessica smirked in the attendant's direction.

"Hey." The attendant happily obliged her. "Sounds like he's scared to me."

"I'll show y'all how scared I am." It was Shakey's turn to wear the hat of indignation. Shakey pulled from his pocket the ten dollars it would take for him and Jessica to rent two cars.

"Well all right!" The attendant was now gleefully part of the joking. "The big man's got a pair!" He handed each of them a helmet. Next he handed Shakey two sets of keys. "Cars six and seven."

Shakey took the keys from the attendant, handed one key ring to Jessica, and then stormed off in the direction of car number seven.

Jessica winked at the attendant before following Shakey to the pit area. She was still grinning when Shakey stopped beside his car. Hers was directly in front of his.

Shakey turned to Jessica. "Know how to put your helmet on?"

Jessica laughed at the question. "Of course I know how to put my helmet on." She placed the helmet on her head only to find that she was unable to fasten the chinstrap.

"What was that?" Shakey laughed while helping her by pulling the strap through the buckle. He adjusted the strap until the helmet fit firmly in place.

Shakey walked her to the driver side of her car, opened the door for her, and then waited for her to be seated. "Fasten your seatbelt," he instructed.

Jessica did as she was told. She loved the air of authority that Shakey sometimes used when communicating. She would never let him know that, however.

"The small pedal to the right is your gas." Shakey began the crash course in driver's ed. "The other one is the brake."

"OK." Jessica inserted the key into the ignition.

"See the stick shift?" Shakey asked.

"Yeah." Jessica thought the question to be absurd. How could she not see the foot long metal rod protruding from the bottom of the car, directly to her right?

"It won't move unless you press the button on the top."

"Gotcha." She pressed the button just to get the feel of it.

"Right now you're in park. That's what the P means."

"No shit, Sherlock!" Jessica laughed.

"Well do you know the rest of them?"

"The N is neutral, R is reverse, and D is for drive." Jessica was a schoolgirl reciting her multiplication tables.

"Very good, dear." Shakey was just as sarcastic. He turned to jump inside his own car before stopping to inform her, "I'll follow you around the first lap to make sure you're all right."

Jessica said nothing. Perhaps, Shakey surmised, her bravado was waning now that the safety gate was opening and the dozen or so racecars were manned by eager drivers ready to show their stuff.

Shakey jumped inside his own car, quickly donning his own helmet and fastening his seatbelt while watching the traffic light at the tracks starting point change from red to yellow.

"Drivers, start your engine," was the instruction from the cigar smoking attendant. Mic now in hand, the attendant's voice boomed throughout the park.

Shakey cranked his car then watched as Jessica nervously did the same. Moments later, the light turned green, and one by one, the straight line of cars left the pit area and took to the track. That is, until the line got to car number six.

"Push the button on the stick like I told you!" Shakey shouted to her.

Car number six launched backward, kissing car number seven. Shakey looked to the attendant. The chain smoker laughed hysterically.

"D is for drive," Shakey shouted louder.

Jessica shifted the transmission into drive and the small car jerked violently forward. In a panic, she pressed hard on the brake, bringing the vehicle to an abrupt stop.

Jessica pressed on the gas again before bringing the car to an immediate halt. Car number six continued in this herky jerky manner all the way out of the pit area and onto the racetrack.

Shakey pulled out of the pit and directly alongside car number six. "Relax," he called to her. "Don't push the gas, just take your foot off the brake."

Jessica followed his instructions and the car idled forward.

"Don't worry about the pedals right now," Shakey told her. "Just get the feel of the steering wheel." He idled alongside her as she shakily navigated the track's first turn.

After navigating the next two turns, Jessica was ready for an increase in speed. She pressed softly on the gas.

"Hold it steady," Shakey encouraged her.

Jessica watched as the speedometer rose to sixteen miles per hour. She smiled with fast growing confidence while carefully navigating the next turn.

"You're doin' good," Shakey told her. "Just stay calm."

The fastest set of drivers were already completing the first lap. The impatient shrill of their horns informed Shakey of their desire to pass him and Jessica. Shakey slowed enough to position his car behind car number six, a move designed to accommodate the Mario Andretti's of the track.

Jessica watched as the other cars passed her and Shakey. She gave car number six a little more gas, and the speedometer now read twenty-one miles per hour. Jessica navigated another turn then looked to the cars ahead of her.

"You doin' good." Shakey repositioned his car next to Jessica's.

Jessica's smile was a wicked one. "Ready to run?" she challenged him.

"What?" Shakey wasn't quite able to make out what she was saying, but was sure that any words accompanying the crazed look in her eyes must be dangerous words indeed.

Jessica pressed hard on the gas. Thirty-five miles per hour. A woman possessed, she was intent on catching the cars that had passed her.

Shakey struggled to keep pace with car number six as Jessica began taking the racetrack's suicide turns at full speed. Shakey would never have imagined Jessica to be capable of such reckless abandon. Within seconds she had closed the gap between herself and the lead pack of cars, forcing herself into the mix of fast moving vehicles with startling aggressiveness.

Shakey lost ground as he had not the nerve to hurl his own vehicle into traffic as Jessica had done. He grimaced while watching her attempt a pass while making a curve-hugging turn. Fortunately, the other cars were captained by drivers who were reasonable enough to make sure she had sufficient room to pass.

Jessica drove in a similar manner the rest of her time on the track. The grace of God coupled with the sanity of the other drivers prevented injury. Jessica's recklessness garnered her a third place finish, the race being not quite long enough to allow the she-devil to make up for the one lap headstart she had surrendered at the onset of the contest. In the end, Shakey found himself an entire half-lap behind her.

Once back in the pit area, Shakey threw his car in park, leapt from the car, and ran for Jessica, who yelled frantically at all who passed. Shakey was now convinced that she had lost her mind.

"That was incredible!" Jessica said to one laughing couple en route to surrendering their helmet and keys. "What in the hell is wrong with you?" Shakey pulled at Jessica's arm, turning her to face him.

"Whew!" Jessica wrapped both arms around Shakey's neck and kissed him firmly on the mouth. "I'm so hot I could take you right here!"

"What?" Shakey was frozen in place as she unfastened his helmet and took the keys from his hand.

"Come on." Jessica pulled him in the direction of the attendant. After placing the helmets and keys on the counter, she took his hand again. "Let's go somewhere and fuck!"

"This bitch is crazy." Shakey was led away in open-mouth amazement.

It was just after five when Shakey and Jessica entered the Gulf Greyhound Racetrack. While walking on the beach just an hour before, Jessica mentioned that she had never been to the dog track. Himself a gambling fanatic, Shakey needed no other motivation to make the dog races the next stop for the two of them.

"OK, explain it to me again." Jessica attempted to follow the giant display boards, but found herself to be totally overwhelmed by the information.

"Look." Shakey grabbed a program from the information booth and opened to the evening matinee. "These are today's races."

"Heat one," Jessica mumbled to herself.

"Galloping Ghost." Shakey's attention was drawn to the name of his favorite dog. The trusted canine was even more money to parlay his lane four assignment to a firsthand victory.

"Uh uh." Jessica shook her head. "Charlie's Angel."

"Charlie's Angel?" Shakey laughed. "I figured they would have shot that dog by now."

"I'm telling you Shakey, Charlie's Angel is going to win."

"That dog is a twelve to one underdog, Jessica." Shakey was losing patience with his stubborn student. "Do you know why?"

"I don't even know what a twelve to one underdog is," Jessica laughed merrily. She was joined by the silver-haired white man that stood next to them.

"That means for every dollar you put up, you will win twelve if that mutt wins." Shakey quickly scanned the rest of the crowd. He gauged the size of the crowd and anticipated their spending habits as he thought about whether to attempt to explain to Jessica the more complex bets that resulted in shared pots for the winners. He decided not to.

"Ooh, that's good." Jessica smiled at the dark-suited man who had shown earlier amusement in her and Shakey's conversation.

"It sounds good." Shakey was busy making his selections. "But he's not such a big payer because he's a regular winner.

"He doesn't have to be a regular winner," Jessica insisted. "He just needs to win this race."

"Well, sweetie, you talked me into it." The elderly man who had been nosily listening to their every word couldn't resist becoming involved in their conversation. "I think she knows something, son."

"It's your money, old school." Shakey put the finishing touches on his race card.

Jessica was excited. "Loan me twenty bucks."

"You're really going to bet on that dog."

"He's going to win, baby."

"You'd have a better chance pickin' an exacta," Shakey told her.

"What's an exacta?" Jessica asked.

"Don't worry about it." Shakey shook his head while handing her the twenty bucks. He handed her a race card then offered a few last second instructions. "You know you can bet that he places or shows. That way if he comes in second or third, you still have a chance to win something."

"He's going to win," Jessica repeatedly slowly.

"Fill out the top of the card and write your race selection here." Shakey waited for her to fill out the self-explanatory identification card, then write the name Charlie's Angel in the box designated "winner" for race number one. "Right this way." Shakey smiled knowingly as the two of them approached the desk.

After placing their bets, Shakey and Jessica made their way to the concession stand. Both ordered large Cokes, though they both had different reasons for doing so. Jessica wanted only to quench her thirst, while Shakey, not so surprisingly, was armed with a pint of Bacardi 151. The bottle was concealed in his left coat pocket.

The relative sparseness of the crowd allowed them to select a seat on the bleachers that prevented them from being blocked in on either side.

Once seated, Shakey reached immediately for his bottle and prepared his drink.

Jessica waved to the elderly man who listened to Jessica long enough to be duped into choosing Charlie's Angel. He smiled back from two bleachers beneath them.

Moments later, the dogs were in their chutes and the announcer's voice boomed through the PA system. "Welcome to Gulf Greyhound Park!" he greeted the crowd.

"You're crazy, you know that?" Shakey took a look at Jessica.

"Pour me a little." Jessica held her cup in Shakey's direction just as he was readying to reposition the cap on the bottle.

Shakey studied Jessica's face. He was discovering that she was full of surprises. "Say when." Shakey poured slowly.

"When." Jessica said after watching Shakey pour less than enough rum to change the taste of the thirty-two-ounce cup of Coca Cola. "And we'll see who's crazy."

"Right about now." Shakey said as the announcer finished introducing the eight competitors.

The dogs broke from the gate with typical canine enthusiasm, eight determined greyhounds, each with the one-tracked notion of being the one to catch the mechanical lure. It wasn't until after the first turn that the first separation could be seen, and to Shakey's amusement, Galloping Ghost was ahead, with the gap widening quickly.

Jessica clapped and yelled, "Come on, baby! Run!"

"Shakey looked for dog number five. Charlie's Angel was in a respectable fourth place, a full two lengths from being third. Shakey thought of Jessica's foolishness in not placing a 'show' bet.

"Come on, baby, you can do it!" Jessica yelled even louder.

Shakey frowned at her. She was beginning to get annoying.

"Yeah, baby!" Charlie's Angel took possession of third place and quickly closed on second as the pack of dogs approached the final turn.

Dudley Double took too wide an angle around the last curve, and Charlie's Angel seized the moment. The hapless canine accelerated to the inside with amazing quickness and was firmly in second as he neared the backstretch.

Galloping Ghost was still the frontrunner, but the rate of his gallop had slowed substantially. Or was it that Charlie's Angel was simply running much faster.

"Yeah, baby!" Jessica was having the time of her life. And Shakey thought for a moment that the equally crazy dog was listening to her.

Shakey stood, mumbling under his breath, "Come on, Ghost."

The man who had bet with Jessica was also standing as Charlie's Angel quickly closed the gap between himself and the Galloping Ghost. As if on cue, the entire section of spectators stood, cheering loudly as the two dogs ran neck to neck toward the finish line. Shakey couldn't believe his eyes when Charlie's Angel edged Galloping Ghost by the shortest of possible margins.

"Aaaiiii!" Jessica squeezed Shakey's neck. "He did it! He did it!"

Shakey could only laugh as the smiling old man, who was now leaning just over Jessica's shoulder gave him a thumbs-up.

"I have to get my money." Jessica pulled away suddenly. "When's the next race?"

"About ten minutes." The old man took a position next to Shakey. "Just enough time for us to see who you like and place another bet."

"See who she likes?" Shakey had seen the man at the track on more than a few occasions. Surely an experienced racegoer like himself would know that the happenings of the first race were a fluke.

"I'm betting with the lady."

"My name's Jessica." Jessica extended a hand. "What's yours?"

"Monroe Jameson," the old man said. "Pleasure's mine." "Well, Mr. Jameson, I guess this makes us partners."

Jessica placed her arm before her, gesturing for Mr. Jameson to become her formal escort to the betting area. "Shall we?"

The old man played the gentleman. "Why certainly."

"It's your money, old school." Shakey shook his head as Jessica and the old man bounced away with great enthusiasm.

The sun had fallen, and the darkness of the night had engulfed the city by the time Shakey and Jessica exited Gulf Greyhound Park. Shakey, numb with the shock of losing all eight races on which he wagered, could only smile at his plight. On the other hand, Jessica and the old man made one trip after another to collect their winnings; profiting again and again with wagers on ridiculously over-matched underdogs. If not for one loss in heat six, Shakey would have been convinced that he had been witness to a well-choreographed set-up. All told, Jessica stung Gulf Greyhound Park for nearly four thousand dollars.

Both Shakey and Jessica climbed into the Cadillac. Shakey quickly started the car, having had his fill of the track for one day.

The toot of a horn alerted Shakey to the presence of an approaching visitor from Shakey's side of the car. Not so surprisingly, it was the old man.

"Just wanted to give the lady my thanks," the old man said through the half-opened window of the late model Chevrolet Impala. "I had a great time."

"You're welcome, Mr. Jameson." Jessica waved. "Bye."

"You kids don't have too much fun with all that money," Mr. Jameson said and was gone.

"Here." Jessica placed the whole of her winnings in Shakey's lap.

"What's this?" Shakey looked closely at her as she prepared to answer.

"I want you to have it."

"You don't want to keep some of it?" Shakey probed her mind.

"Uh uh." Jessica placed her head on Shakey's shoulder, then wrapped her arms around his waist. "I know you'll take care of me."

Shakey was stricken by the sincere innocence of Jessica's response. Something unexplainable was happening to the Handsome Intimidator. He attempted no response. He preferred instead to enjoy the feel of Jessica's body as it pressed against his own, and to allow whatever spell it was that had worked its way into his system to freely run its course.

Shakey could hear the music as soon as he turned the corner leading to the parking lot of Club Entice. The remix of Missy Elliot's "Get Your Freak On" instigated a collective sway amongst the well-dressed young men and beautiful young women that lined the pavement directly in front of the building, awaiting entrance to the club. All heads turned when Shakey's Cadillac wheeled onto the parking lot gravel.

Shakey pulled up to the sign that said RESERVED FOR MANAGEMENT. He then reached for the half a Swisher that lie in the ashtray, lit it, took two quick puffs, and handed it to Jessica.

Jessica took the marijuana stuffed cigar from Shakey's hand. Already slightly intoxicated, she found it easy to draw a long, steady stream of smoke into her lungs. While doing so, she contemplated the full day of activities she and Shakey had shared. From racing cars, to the dog track, to dinner out, all sandwiched between repeated bouts of passionate lovemaking. Never had she known so much of a man's attention, never had she given so much of her own. Though having nothing in her past to compare it to, Jessica was sure that the stirring in her stomach was the first stirrings of the fast blossoming love she was developing for the owner of the glistening bald head beside her.

"Ready?" Shakey took the Swisher from her hand and put it out in the ashtray.

"Always." Jessica leaned farther in his direction, kissed the side of his face, and ran a hand across the width of his chest.

"Chill out." Shakey turned to gently kiss her lips before taking the key from the ignition and opening the door. "You're starting to remind me of how old I am."

Shakey closed the door behind him then knocked the wrinkles from the pants he had earlier changed into. The tight-fitting black silk shirt he wore more than accentuated the contours of his shoulders, chest, and arms. His favorite pair of loafers were on his feet.

He stopped to wait for Jessica, whose late-night apparel consisted of a white dress that clung to her body even tighter than Shakey's shirt clung to his. Shakey took a moment to admire her figure, finding that he was becoming more enchanted with her with each passing moment.

"Come on." Shakey took her hand in his, leading the way to the club's entrance. As the two of them approached the waiting crowd all eyes were on Shakey and his latest acquisition.

"What's up, Shakey?" a male voice called from the crowd.

"Slow boogie baby," was Shakey's standard response while leading Jessica past the waiting crowd and into the club.

"Another winner, fool," a second onlooker voiced his opinion of Jessica.

A tight-lipped smile was Shakey's response.

"That nigga there ballin'!" The excited young man went on to inform his not-so-up-on-things companion.

No words were spoken by the women in the crowd. Not verbally anyway. But the piercing stares of envy that bore into the side of Jessica's head were clearly audible. That is, if Jessica had been paying the jealous-hearted any mind at all.

"What's up, Shakey?" the man at the door greeted.

"Nothin' to it, Big Sam." Shakey walked by the man, still leading Jessica by the hand. "What's going on with you?"

"Shit, I can't call it." The larger man's eyes were riveted to Jessica's dress. "As usual, you doin' all the good."

Shakey led Jessica down a short hallway that led to the party ahead of them. The song changed just as the two of them entered the club. D-12's "Purple Pills" boomed loudly as Shakey and Jessica stepped in the direction of the dance floor.

"Hold on to my belt loop," Shakey instructed as the two of them navigated the ridiculously overcrowded dance floor. Crossing the floor was a necessity to get to the bar and tables located on the other side of the room.

Initially apprehensive about approaching the mass of gyrating bodies, Jessica found quickly that her concerns were completely unfounded as she was obviously the last thing on the minds of anyone on the dance floor.

"Shakey!" The short, Hispanic man standing behind the bar spoke as if genuinely happy to see Shakey. "What's up?"

"Slow boogie, Jesse." Shakey accepted bartender's handshake.

"I was just beginning to worry about you." The clean-cut bartender had tiny specks of gray sprinkled throughout his curly black hair and spoke with the smallest hint of an accent. "Where you been?"

"Just chillin', Jesse." Shakey watched as his old cell-mate at the Gib Lewis High Security facility fixed the rum and Coke before Shakey had even ordered it. "You know I lay low sometimes."

"I know, but—" Jesse placed the drink on the counter in front of Shakey. A slightly perceptible frown could be seen despite his cheery demeanor. "Next time give us a call. It's been two weeks."

"Will do, amigo." Shakey appreciated the concern. Jesse was another in a long line of Shakey's undeniably loyal business partners, and the bond between them had been forged by years of shared grief. And while most onlookers of the present scene between Jessica Reardon and Jonathan Reed saw only a bartender servicing a patron, a select few in the crowd knew that the men were, in fact, the co-owners of the establishment.

While the two of them languished in the most unyielding hell Texas prisons had to offer, Jesse taught Shakey loads about the business of restaurants, night clubs, and hotels. Shakey was duly impressed with the wealth of knowledge Jesse had incurred while climbing from dishwasher to regional manager of a national restaurant chain. Shakey could also relate to the hardships experienced by this bone-hard little chicano as a small child, who along with his mother and siblings, experienced both poverty and homelessness on the streets of Chicago.

The proposal Shakey presented to Jesse was a simple one indeed: your brains, my money. Jesse agreed with a handshake though, figuring his cellmate's promises to be nothing more than the idle conversation of a bored convict. Especially since the only thing the Handsome Intimidator owned at the time was the four gold teeth in his mouth.

To Jesse's utter astonishment, upon his release, not quite four years after his and Shakey's handshake deal, Shakey had not only secured a building, obtained a liquor license and all needed business permits, but also handed his ex-cellmate two keys—the first to a west end Galveston condo, the other to a '98 Mustang 5.0. The gesture had won Jesse's lifelong, undying loyalty.

"And you, beautiful?" Jesse smiled at Jessica. "What would you like to drink?"

"Uhhhh . . ." Jessica was unsure. She felt the desire for something stronger than a wine cooler, but had no experience ordering drinks.

"How about a sex on the beach?" Jesse suggested.

"Been there, done that." Jessica smirked while moving closer to Shakey. She found that his mere presence filled her with a boldness she had never before known.

"Oh." Jesse's mouth was a perfect circle as he quickly looked to Shakey for assistance.

"Long Island Iced Tea." Shakey took a sip from his own perfectly mixed drink.

"Comin' right up." Jesse was swift about fixing Jessica's drink and placing it before her. "Here you go."

"Thank you." Jessica enjoyed knowing that she had knocked the man off balance.

"Come on, crazy," Shakey said to Jessica while stepping away from the bar. "Catch ya later, Jesse."

"Be careful, Shakey." Jesse had now regained his composure. "That one has fangs."

Shakey was beginning to regret his decision to introduce Jessica to Long Island Iced Tea. She had drunk three of them in the last hour. It was not so much her drinking that was the problem, but it now seemed that she was totally incapable of sitting still.

Shakey had readily agreed when a friend of a business associate asked to dance with Jessica. He needed the space to speak with the dozen or so familiar faces wanting to ask him where he had been for so long. And more importantly, when could they score.

But now that all of Red's next day's deliveries were set, Shakey was beginning to feel silly sitting alone, watching as Jessica drank and laughed it up, dancing with seemingly every man in the building.

Twice Shakey had considered intervening when Jessica's dance partner played it a little too close for Shakey's likings. Both times he thought better of it. He laughed to himself while admitting the presence of an emotion he would never have thought possible. The Handsome Intimidator was a little jealous.

"Heeey!" Shakey recognized the deep baritone without having to turn around. "What's up, homeboy?" David placed his drink on the table and gave Shakey a handshake that quickly became a hug. He acted for all the world as if he had not seen Shakey in ages.

"What's up, David?" Shakey smiled, always happy to see David, moreso now as the presence of his friend eased the awkwardness he felt at sitting alone while Jessica continued to entertain the crowd.

Shakey hadn't noticed Mary standing behind David.

"What's up, Mary?" Shakey spoke warmly. It was nice to see David and Mary enjoying a night out together. After all, this was the woman who had borne David five children. On a lighter note, Shakey found it amusing that just two days before when he vowed that their relationship was forever terminated. Such was the nature of their love.

"Hey, Baldy." Mary responded with the nickname she had christened him with upon first seeing his shaved head. A mood necessitated by the asserted dominance of the Reed family genes.

"Y'all sit down." Shakey motioned first to the empty seats across from him then at the waitress. "What y'all drinking?" He directed his question at David.

"Gin makes me sin, homeboy!" David was typically loud and obnoxious. "It might even make me wake up with this ugly mothafucka in the mornin'." He turned to his common law wife of over a decade.

"Fuck you, David." Mary was more than capable of rebuttal. "Who you callin' ugly with yo' Beetlejuice lookin' ass!"

Shakey and the just arriving waitress shared a laugh at the constantly quarreling mates. "A gin and . . ." Shakey looked to Mary.

"Hurricane," Mary said.

"Oh, Lord." David put his face in his hands. "I know I'ma have to fight yo' ignorant ass tonight!"

"One gin on the rocks, one hurricane, and you?" The exotic looking waitress smiled at Shakey.

"Rum and Coke."

"Anything else?" The waitress had that unmistakeable gleam in her eye.

"Any suggestions?" Shakey flirted.

"Anything you see that you like." The young woman stepped away from the table.

"What the fuck?" David watched as the waitress stepped for the bar. "I don' heard stories of fish jumpin' in boats, but goddamn, homeboy."

"You better watch your mouth, David," Mary fussed.

Just then the song changed. Young girls from every corner of the room scurried for the dance floor as Mystical's "Shake Dat Ass" played through the sound system.

"You here by yourself, homeboy?" David danced in his seat, snapping his fingers, swaying from left to right. He was even more comical when he exerted no effort.

"Naw." Shakey grimaced once his attention turned back to Jessica. She had taken up with a group of young girls who instructed and demonstrated to her the nuances of Shaking Dat Ass. Though severely lacking in the rhythm department, Jessica energetically shook, lifted, twisted, and rolled her ample romp in every direction. "Jessica's over there."

"Ooh wee, man!" David exclaimed. "Ass jigglin' everywhere."

"Mothafucka!" Mary delivered a backhand slap to the smiling midget. "You ain't gon' just sit here and disrespect me, nigga!"

"See why I don't take this crazy mothafucka nowhere, homeboy?" Both David's voice and facial expression seemed chiseled in granite, but it was obvious that he was thoroughly enjoying himself.

The waitress returned carrying a tray with the three drinks. After first serving David and Mary, the young waitress turned to Shakey. She spoke no words, but her eyes said it all. Before Shakey, she placed the requested rum and Coke along with two napkins. One napkin was for personal use, the other contained the young woman's phone number and a short message: I live alone. The beautiful young woman turned to leave, satisfied that her case had been sufficiently stated.

The song changed again and after promising to her many new friends a swift return, Jessica hurried for the table.

Shakey closely observed her approach. Her face was covered with a light coat of perspiration that made its way down her neck, chest and back, converting the white dress she wore into a see-through negligee.

"Whew, I'm hot." Jessica used her hand to fan herself while taking a seat next to Shakey.

"You should be." Shakey was almost able to hide his anger.

Jessica tilted her head in Shakey's direction, pursing her lips while studying Shakey's coal black face, seeking to confirm her preliminary perceptions regarding his statement. She was tempted to toy with him regarding the clearly discernible jealousy in his face, but decided to spare him further aggravation while in the presence of his friends.

"Hi, my name is Jessica." Jessica offered Mary her hand, reminding Shakey of his rudeness.

"Mary." David's woman completed the introduction.

"We already met." David made a play for Jessica's attention.

"I know." The she-devil rolled her eyes and contorted her face into a twisted mass of pain and disgust.

The women laughed loudly.

Juvenile's "Set It Off" was the DJ's next selection, and it was obvious that Jessica couldn't wait to make a return to the dance floor. "You two clowns gonna dance with us, or do we have to go looking?" She elbowed Shakey in the ribs.

Mary laughed again, this time even louder, amused at witnessing Shakey being handled in such a fashion.

"What you laughing at?" David turned to Mary. "Don't nobody in here wanna dance with you."

"Wanna bet?" Jessica had made another friend and was more than willing to come to her defense. She took a sip from Shakey's drink. "Too strong." She told him before turning to Mary. "What about those two, girl?" Jessica pointed at two handsome young men standing just at the dance floor's edge. "Let's ask them to dance."

"OK." Mary smiled while sliding her chair away from the table.

"Bullshit!" David stood up even quicker than the two women. "This the only mack you dancin' with." David finished his drink in one turn of the cup then took his woman by the hand. He led her to the dance floor.

"What's up with my mack?" Jessica looked at Shakey.

No dancer to speak of, Shakey had no desire to grace the crowded dance floor. However, his disdain for seeing Jessica dance with others trumped any self-consciousness he felt.

Jessica pulled Shakey to a spot on the floor next to David and Mary. Salty Water's "Make it Hot" played loudly.

"Ahhh!" David held both hands out and shifted from side to side. "You ain't know your man could get down like this, huh?"

Mary, the only decent dancer of the four, smiled then turned her back to her insane gangsta midget.

Bending at the waist, she did herself no shame with her own version of booty dancing.

Shakey grooved in a subdued manner while enjoying Jessica's hyper-animated movements. She couldn't dance at all but was having the time of her life. Shakey laughed openly while Jessica danced something resembling a combined effort of marching in place, and the old 'wop' dance craze of years past, all while clapping her hands loudly.

Jessica's enthusiasm was clearly contagious, as all on the dance floor clapped and cheered her on. Shakey smiled through his discomfort, reigned to his fate as all attention turned to him and Jessica. Moments later, the music mercifully stopped, and Jessica bowed to a thunderous ovation.

CHAPTER 11

The fall of night was complete by the time Shakey's Cadillac turned off Broadway Boulevard at Thirty-fifth Street and thrust both he and Jessica upon his favorite corner store. Despite the briskness of the mid-November air, the PennySavers corner store was alive and bristling with activity. Shakey pulled the Cadillac close to the curb as a fanatically waving Smitty motioned for him to stop.

"Man, you need to find Li'l Chris!" Smitty shouted into Shakey's ear; the concern on his face registering clearly.

"What's up?" Shakey asked.

"The boy runnin' 'round here wit' a pistol!"

"What?"

"He lookin' for Winston!" Smitty gave a full report. "Li'l Chris gon' shoot him when he find him. Winston dun broke Barbara Ann jaw!"

"Damn." Shakey's mind was already outlining the course he would take to search for his nine-year-old friend. "How long since you seen him?"

"He just passed through here," Smitty explained. "Hollering and screaming, waving the gun around; look like a .25."

"Which way'd he go?" Shakey shifted the Cadillac transmission into drive while lifting his foot from the brake.

"He went toward Parkland," Smitty shouted behind the Cadillac before adding. "He's on a bicycle."

Shakey snatched a Newport from the pack of cigarettes on the dashboard and stuck it in his mouth. Jessica dutifully flicked the lighter and held it to the cigarette. Shakey's Cadillac zoomed down Winnie, rolling through stop signs while heading toward Parkland.

"Look out, Black," Shakey called out to a familiar face amongst the small group of men seated outside Kimbro's Lounge. "You seen Li'l Chris?"

"Yeah," Black answered. "That li'l crazy bastard gon' toward the park. Came through here—."

Shakey drove off before catching the rest of Black's statement. He had to find Chris before Chris found Winston, or the young boy's life would be forever altered for the worse.

Shakey circled Wright Cuney Park twice before patrolling the Palm Terrace housing projects. No sign of Chris anywhere. Shakey next traveled the backside of the projects, carefully monitoring every nook and cranny of the landscape as he passed.

"There's his bike!" Jessica pointed toward Bull's Café.

The Cadillac launched forward before Shakey double-parked in the middle of the street and leapt from the car. "Hey, C!" The relief Shakey felt at locating his friend was short-lived as he realized that the pistol was still in the young boy's hand.

"You better come get this li'l mothafucka, Shakey, before something bad happens to him!" a man yelled in frightened anger.

"You ain't gon' fuck with me!" A large green vein sprang from the side of Christopher's neck. He lifted the gun; causing the small crowd to disperse instantly.

"C! Chill out, homie." Shakey stepped between the boy and the man Christopher was arguing with. "What you wanna draw your piece on Jack for?"

"He messin' with me!"

"Ain't nobody messin' with you, li'l nigga!" Jack was furious, yet not nearly foolish enough to approach Chris. "You the one comin' around here with a gun, accusin' people of helpin' Winston hide from you, like you some bad mothafucka or something!"

"Come on, Chris," Shakey urged his young friend. "Let's walk."

Chris lowered the gun to his side, giving Jack the dirtiest of looks before following his idol to the Cadillac.

"Watch my li'l homie's bike for me," Shakey instructed Jessica. "We're gonna take a walk around the block".

Neither Shakey nor Christopher spoke for a full block as Shakey waited for the boy to break the silence, to explain his thoughts and feelings, and to release the cap on the lifetime of anger, disappointment, and rage that was capable of producing a nine-year-old killer.

"I'ma kill that ho-ass nigga, Shakey!" Li'l Chris' voice broke with the pain of living in such a dysfunctional home.

"Then what?" Shakey asked calmly.

"What?" Chris frowned, tilting his face at an upward angle to face his friend.

"What are you gonna do after you shoot him?"

"What am I supposed to do?"

"About twenty years." Shakey was grim-faced.

The two of them stopped in front of an old wood-framed building that should have been demolished years ago. Shakey was first to take a seat on the stairs, and Christopher sat next to him. Gun still in hand, the young boy sobbed softly.

"It's OK, man." Shakey had never seen his young friend cry before. But due to the circumstances of his life, Shakey was sure that crying was something Christopher did quite often when alone. "It's OK."

"I'm tired of that nigga shit, Shakey!" The young boy's cry for help was filled with emotion.

"I know." Shakey shivered with the empathy he felt for Christopher's plight. "But you can't just kill everyone you get tired of, C."

Both were quiet again, each examining Shakey's words from entirely different perspectives. Shakey hoped that Christopher would find much more use for his advice as the years passed than he had himself.

"C, I want you to give me the gun," Shakey announced. Though sure that he could easily take the gun from his young friend, he knew the importance of having the youngster hand the gun over voluntarily.

Christopher was silent, but his body tensed noticeably at the thought of surrendering his weapon.

"You're not gonna solve the problem that way," Shakey continued. "You're only gonna create a bigger problem."

There was silence again before the young boy turned to Shakey, suggesting "Kick that nigga ass for me then, Shakey!"

Shakey stared into the wounded child's eyes. He was speechless at the boy's request. Getting into Winston's personal business with his woman violated every code of street ethics Shakey was ever taught, but there was no way he could deny Christopher's plea for relief—nor the growing rage he himself was starting to feel for Winston.

Chris handed Shakey the gun. Shakey took the weapon and tucked it into his pocket, thus sealing their agreement. The questioning of the origin of Chris' gun crossed Shakey's mind, but the answer was a moot point. Chris was a ward of the street, and there was nothing in or of those streets that was unattainable for him.

Shakey stood suddenly. "Now, let me tell you what I want you to do for me."

"Aw man, here we go." Chris was a nine-year-old boy again.

"We're gonna walk back around this corner, and you're going to apologize to Fat Jack and everyone else you just scared half to death."

"C'mon, Shakey, that's embarrassing," Chris whined as the two of them started the short trek back toward the café.

"Not nearly as embarrassing as all those people seein' me take a strap to your behind." Shakey unbuttoned his belt for emphasis.

"OK, Shakey." Christopher giggled while wiping the last of the tears from his eyes.

"You got some money?" Shakey wanted to make sure Christopher at least had a little change to purchase something to eat when he got hungry, though he knew that the young boy's problems ran much deeper than his next meal.

"Two dollars," Chris answered.

Shakey thought about the grave dangers that could come Christopher's way once Winston was informed of the pistol and the death threats. "Tell ya what, C." Shakey thought quickly, he would never forgive himself if he allowed anything to happen to Chris. "After you apologize to Fat Jack, we'll go get a pizza and rent some movies. You can spend a few nights at my house."

"For real, Shakey?" Christopher leapt with excitement.

"For real." Shakey rubbed his hands once across the large brown curls that nested atop the young boy's head, touched at the core that anyone could find such happiness at the mere prospect of being in his presence. The two of them turned the corner toward the reassemblin' crowd. "Since you're in such a good mood, how 'bout a cigarette?"

"Not on your life, kiddo." Shakey couldn't help but smile while pushing the young boy toward Fat Jack for a much-needed lesson in humility.

Rosa's whole heart belonged to the man who had rescued her from a life of crack smoking and corner hustling. The same man was also the thriving force in the life of the well-adjusted teenage daughter who had become Rosa's only source of pride. What Rosa felt for Shakey was a love and devotion that would always guarantee her one hundred percent loyalty; regardless of the perils involved.

Rosa shook a Virginia Slim cigarette from the pack and placed it in her mouth before knocking on the front door of Vanessa's home.

"What's crackin'?" a man's voice shouted from behind the door.

"Where's Vanessa, bitch!" Rosa spoke back.

The voices behind the door conferred, Vanessa amongst them, before the lock turned and the door was opened.

A squat, muscular dark-skinned youngster, all of twenty-one years of age, mind completely filled with self-deluding ideas of personal supremacy, leaned in the doorway grinning at Rosa. The bald-headed youngster wore shorts, a tank top, and a large gold chain that contrasted magically with his coal black skin. "I'm Tubbs," he spoke deeply.

"I don't give a fuck!" Rosa voiced her disinterest before forcing herself through the doorway. "Vanessa!" Once inside the house, she continued to the living room.

Vanessa and another young man sat on the couch. The young man's sock covered feet rested on the coffee table. He wore designer jeans and was shirtless. Both arms were spread across the couch, with Vanessa tucked under his right arm. She placed a burning Swisher in his mouth, held it still until he was satisfied with the amount of marijuana smoke that filled his mouth, throat, and lungs, then pulled it back, obviously intent on holding the Swisher until he was ready for another puff.

"Bitch, where my Daddy money?" Rosa got straight to the point.

"Yo' Daddy?" the shirtless young man on the couch questioned after Vanessa had taken the Swisher from his mouth once again. The young man pulled his arms in front of him, and sat forward on the couch. "Look like you old enough to be his mama." The honey-brown skinned young man grabbed a hair brush from the table and brushed vigorously at the well-groomed waves in his shiny black hair.

"Shakey wants his money," Rosa told her coworker, undaunted by the boy who wanted be King of the Jungle.

Vanessa stood and stepped around the couch, heading for the kitchen, talking as she did so. "I ain't got nothin' that belongs to that nigga."

"You what?" Rosa's voice rose as she took a step forward in response to Tubbs' approach from behind. "What you mean, ole stupid-ass girl?"

"She mean," the boy who would be king spoke up again, still brushing his hair, closely checking the results in a small, hand-held mirror. "She mean what she said. She ain't got nothin' for that nigga." He placed both the brush and the mirror on the table, lay back on the couch, both hands clasped behind his head. "And if he got a problem with that, he can come holla at D-Ray."

Rosa winced; actually feeling sorry for the kid. The youngster had no idea what that evil bitch Vanessa was getting him into.

"You need to come in the back and let a nigga beat that pussy up," Tubbs said from behind Rosa. "I know that Busta ain't fuckin' you right!"

"You a perverted mothafucka, Tubbs!" D-Ray laughed loudly.

"Shit, I wanna fuck something." Tubbs stepped closer to Rosa, massaging his crotch.

"Back off!" Rosa barked before taking another couple of steps away from Tubbs.

D-Ray was still laughing when he said, "You better get on back to yo' Daddy."

"That's exactly where I'm going." Rosa made eye contact with Vanessa, who was just returning from the kitchen with two cups of ice, a bottle of Bacardi, and a twenty-ounce Coke. She watched as Vanessa sat both cups on the table. She first poured Bacardi in the glass she had placed in front of D-Ray, stopping only when instructed to do so by his subtle hand gesture. She then filled the glass the rest of the way with Coke. She stirred the drink with her finger, then held it to his mouth. "If you got any sense left, bitch, I'll have his money when I get there."

"She told you she ain't got nothing for that nigga now." Tubbs stepped closer to Rosa again, this time wrapping his arms around her, pressing his hardness against the small of her back. "Come on, let a nigga fuck!"

Rosa pulled away from him, spinning around suddenly, anger running unchecked. She slapped Tubbs on the cheek.

Tubbs smiled wickedly at Rosa then returned the assault with a closed fist. Rosa's body skimmed the surface of the rug, not stopping until her head crashed against the base of the floor model television.

"Goddamn, Tubbs!" D-Ray showed only a slight annoyance at his friend's behavior. "What you slide that ho for?"

"That bitch hit me," Tubbs explained before leaning over Rosa and reaching for a breast. "I still want some of that pussy, though."

With a swiftness the envy of Copperfield, Rosa produced a barber's razor from out of thin air and sliced the side of Tubb's face. The young man backed away instinctively, eyes as large as two dinner platters.

Rosa was on her feet and going at Tubbs. Two more swings of the razor sliced into the young man's large, powerful arms as he desperately shielded his face and neck.

Rosa heard the sound of broken glass a split second before feeling the sharp pain in the back of her head. Turning to face her new attacker, she was met with a crushing blow to the face. On the floor once again, she looked up in time to see D-Ray lift his right leg and send the bottom of his foot crashing against the side of her head. She covered her face and head best she could against the barrage of kicks that ensued first by D-Ray, then by both men. "Stop it, y'all gon' kill her!" Vanessa's voice was the last thing that penetrated Rosa's consciousness before she faded completely into the closing wall of darkness.

"Turn, Shakey!" Chris yelled. "Watch out for the water trap!"

"Damn." Shakey watched as the motorcycle and driver he controlled via the PlayStation 3 control pad tumbled over and over.

"Watch this" Chris was the picture of supreme confidence as he readied himself for his own motorcycle race. "I'ma show you how to do this one more time."

"You two guys are something else." Jessica stepped from the darkened hallway into the living room. She was wearing a bathrobe and house shoes Shakey had bought for her.

"Come play with us Jessica." Li'l Chris never turned his head from the television.

"It's 4:00 A.M." Jessica sat next to Shakey. "Are you guys ever going to get any sleep?"

"We chillin'," Li'l Chris told her while easily navigating the hazards and pitfalls of the game course.

"Shakey." Jessica gave Shakey a look that eliminated the need for further explanation.

"We chillin', baby," Shakey told her, slightly perturbed that she would disturb him as he tried to record each of Li'l Chris' course strategies.

"Christopher, it's time for Shakey to come to bed." Jessica stood with hands on her hips.

"Aw, Shakey. It's like that." Christopher giggled.

"Naw, it ain't like that," Shakey defended.

"It ain't?" Jessica raised an eyebrow, amused that Shakey felt the need to defend himself to a nine-year-old.

"I don't believe this." Christopher laughed loudly. "This is just like at Wesley's house."

"I'll be there in a minute, baby." Shakey smiled, sensing the position Chris and Jessica were hedging in on him.

A half-ring of the telephone provided Shakey with a much needed diversion. He hadn't even thought of the oddity of such a late-night phone call at his residence as he stepped in the direction of the telephone.

"Hello." Shakey had barely spoken when the young girl's cries filled his ears, head, and heart with her own terror and grief. "Cindy? Baby, what's wrong?"

Shakey listened as Cindy sobbed loudly. Not understanding much of what the young girl said, but hearing that her mother, who had been attacked and badly injured, was at John Sealy emergency room.

"Look, sweetheart." Shakey knew there was nothing he could say to calm the frantic girl, but tried anyway. "I'm on my way. Relax. Everything's going to be OK."

Cindy went on about broken bones and said something about swelling before Shakey cut her off. "I'm on my way!" He slammed the receiver on its hook.

Neither Jessica nor Christopher said a word to the grim-faced Shakey as he grabbed his keys from the table and headed for the garage.

Shakey burst through the doors of John Sealy emergency room and ran straight to the desk, showing absolutely no regard for those in line ahead of him. "Rosa Benavidez!"

"Sir," the visibly fatigued nurse protested. "There's a line."

"I don't give a fuck!" Shakey's nerves were strained and frayed, and he was rapidly losing a grip on his self-control.

"Carla," the nurse called to another woman who was taking the vitals of a drunk who had been found lying unconscious in a convenience store parking lot. "Call security."

"Bitch, you gon' need more than security!" Shakey slammed both hands on the desk. Though the middle-aged woman was not an enemy, the night had simply brought with it much too much stress to allow for civility.

"Shakey!" Cindy's voice pierced the howling madness of the emergency room.

Shakey turned to his right and Cindy came running toward him. Before he had spoken, the young girl was in his arms, crying uncontrollably to the only person in the world she had trusted to call in her time of crisis. Shakey's heart ached with knowing that whatever happened to her mother was surely his fault.

"What happened, Cindy?"

"They found her on the side of the Stop-N-Go on Twenty-sixth and Broadway," Cindy cried.

"What?" Shakey's mind raced for an explanation.

"Somebody beat her up bad, Shakey." Cindy was disintegrating right before his eyes.

"Where is she?" Shakey asked, knowing that there was not much understandable conversation left in the young girl.

"They're takin' her to surgery." The young girl was near hysteria. "The doctor told me—" She sobbed harder, then struggled to gather the composure to finish the sentence. "Her brain is swelling."

Shakey wrapped his arms around the frightened child again, holding her tight, wishing that it was he who had been first to be notified of Rosa's condition. "Where is she, princess?" Shakey kissed her forehead.

Cindy led Shakey through the sliding door, then down the hallway toward the hospital room where her mother laid unconscious. He held her hand.

Cindy and Shakey stopped in front of room 722. Cindy said nothing. The grief-propelled energy traveling from her body to Shakey's told him that Rosa was inside.

"Wait here." Shakey kissed the child's forehead again before stepping to the door.

"They won't let you inside," Cindy cried out behind him.

Shakey pushed the door open, stepping just inside the doorway. Hospital workers were everywhere. Their frantic chatter accompanied by the audibles produced by the assortment of technology used in the attempt to save Rosa's life.

"Sir, you need to step outside, please," a professional sounding white coat instructed.

"Rosa!" the gasp escaped Shakey's lips as the mangled mass that was Rosa's head and face permanently imprinted on his mind. A lump formed in his throat as he thanked God for not allowing Cindy to see her mother's disfiguration.

"Sir." The petite almond-colored woman's voice was much more compassionate now. "You have to leave. I'm sorry."

Shakey backpedaled slowly, the first rumblings of his next violent eruption already taking place in his heart; only a victim was needed.

"We're doing everything we can." They closed the door softly on Shakey.

Shakey stared at the plate on the door, swallowing back the tears as the dormant monster within him awakened.

Cindy touched him softly in the middle of his back. Shakey turned to face her. He held her tightly hoping for her forgiveness. He would make it right. Retaliation would be swift!

CHAPTER 12

"You look like shit." Never one to pull punches, Red opened the door to allow Shakey entrance to the Williams' residence. When Shakey didn't respond, Red asked, "Who is that?"

"Nelson." Shakey took a drink from the tightly clinched gin bottle. "Remember?"

Red nodded. Nelson was Shakey's first cousin; a lawyer, square as a knot, smart as a whip. His presence could only mean that Shakey was ensnared in some sort of serious legal quandary. "What's up?"

"Not here." Shakey's bloodshot eyes communicated to his most trusted ally.

"Let me get dressed." Red quickly climbed the stairs leading to the family's sleeping quarters. "Hi, sweetheart." Red kissed his eldest child on the cheek before passing her at the head of the stairs.

Kashandra remained at the top of the stairs. She stared at Shakey.

Shakey returned the young girl's gaze. Her dark, deep set eyes sending chills up and down his spine. *"She knows,"* the voice inside his head whispered softly.

"Beep! Beep!" The first twin waved while running past Shakey.

"Beep! Beep!" The second little boy followed closely as the giggling toddlers continued their chase throughout the house.

Shakey took another look toward the top of the stairs. Kashandra was gone, but the image of the young girl's smooth black face and eerily stern gaze remained in Shakey's mind. *"She knows,"* the voice repeated before being drowned by a hearty drink from the gin bottle.

Shakey stepped into the living room. Michelle sat alone watching an early morning talk show.

"You look like the trash you are." Michelle glanced briefly from the television set. "Where's Barbie?"

There was no response from Shakey. An oddity. Michelle looked to Shakey again, this time taking a serious inventory of her long-time nemesis, finally deciding that this was not the time to mess with him.

Shakey's thoughts were of the twelve-year-old girl upstairs. He needed to ask Michelle the question that painfully seared his soul but lacked the nerve. A long drink from the gin bottle, and his mind refocused on the battered condition in which he had seen Rosa. A second drink and he was contemplating the dire circumstances Nelson had advised him of regarding D.D.'s drug charges. Another drink and he was pummeling Winston to a pulp. The next and he wanted to speak with Jonathan.

"You all right?" Michelle asked in a voice belying no hostility.

Shakey said nothing, honestly not knowing the answer.

"Let's roll, man." Red was at the bottom of the stairs.

Shakey maintained his silence while following Red out the door. When the two of them reached the Cadillac, Nelson climbed from the passenger seat and stepped toward the back of the car, volunteering to occupy the back seat.

"You all right to drive?" Red asked. He was becoming more concerned for Shakey's mental and physical state with each passing moment.

Shakey handed him the keys, took another drink, then walked over to the passenger side of the car and climbed inside.

Red settled behind the wheel of the Cadillac, cranking the engine and readying himself for whatever horror was to soon fill his ears.

The Cadillac eased away from the curb and Shakey began to speak immediately. "Rosa got hurt," he spoke evenly.

"How"?

"Beaten." Shakey's fire-red eyes watched Larry as the Cadillac passed the mad, basket-pushing boy. As usual, Larry was involved in a heated conversation with people whom only he could see.

Among them, no doubt, was his fallen friend Tony. Now, more than ever, Shakey understood Larry, and perhaps even envied the teenager just a bit.

"Bad?"

"She's in a coma." Shakey's eyes blurred as two renegade tears broke free from his eyes and landed in his gin bottle.

"Who?" Red's anger rose rapidly. He too had known Rosa forever.

"Two youngsters hustlin' out of Vanessa's." Shakey had only needed a couple of hours to learn the identity of Rosa's attackers. The young fools didn't even have the sense to get rid of her black Toyota Camry, which was parked directly behind Vanessa's three bedroom home.

"Hustlin' at Vanessa's?" Red was confused. Vanessa's was Shakey's. In Shakey's face he found all answers. No further conversation was needed as Red was quite aware he was to play the role of accomplice in the soon to be murder. "Where we goin'?"

"David's." Shakey had a job for his old friend.

Red looked to Shakey sure to make eye contact before motioning to Nelson.

"Yeah." Shakey was gulping gin at an inhuman pace now. "We gotta shut down the business for a while".

"What's up?" Red asked, not the least bit upset with the idea of shutting down the business for a while. Long since exhausted with the perils of drug trafficking, Red had accumulated the assets to live a simple, comfortable existence with his family for the rest of his days on earth. For Red, the game was played for the love of Shakey.

"D.D.'s in a fix," Shakey said.

"The half a big?" Red was familiar with the circumstances of D.D.'s arrest.

"The Feds picked it up," Shakey said, then turned to Nelson for the details.

"Doris is in a rather precarious position." The eloquently speaking Nelson Mathis III, complete with his suit, shoes, and briefcase was out of place amongst the two murderous drug dealers in the car with him. But Shakey trusted Nelson, and for that reason alone, was the young lawyer caught in such a dangerous web of street espionage.

"Aha." Red smiled, responding with a feigned English accent. "And just what might that position be, mate?"

The three men shared a guarded chuckle, all feeling the gravity of the matter at hand, all desperately needing the release of a tension relieving laugh. Especially Shakey.

"Her position." Nelson was serious again. "The Feds have issued to her the following ultimatum. Full cooperation against Jonathan Reed and his cohorts, or face prosecution to the full extent of the law."

Red went numb. His mind racing with the possible consequences of what he had just been told.

Life as he knew it could instantly be over. "How much she facin'?"

"Under the present sentencing guidelines, about fifteen years," Nelson said grimly. Red winced as the number fifteen bore into his heart; a lot of time for a single mother. "What's the plan?" "We'll lay low for a piece," Shakey told him. "Minimize the damage".

"Minimize the damage?" Red sensed that he had not yet been fully informed as to the damage Shakey had referred to.

"Cut the cord now, and there'll be nothin' to corroborate Doris' testimony."

"Her testimony?" Red turned to look into the lawyer's eyes as the Cadillac rolled to a stop at the corner of Forty-first and Broadway.

"What would you have her do?" Nelson asked coldly.

Red turned his disbelieving gaze on Shakey.

"He's fuckin' her." Shakey shrugged his shoulders while informing Red of the exact nature of Nelson and Doris' relationship, speaking as if no other explanation was needed.

Red's eyes turned forward again. He had heard enough. Nelson's only concern would be D.D. once the shit hit the fan.

Red pulled alongside David's garage once the Cadillac reached Forty-fourth and Broadway. The three of them stepped quickly from the car, using the raised garage door to enter the establishment.

David and an employee were seated at a table in the middle of the floor playing dominoes.

"My nigga!" David jumped from the table and ran to greet Shakey, enthusiastically giving his buddy five.

"What's up, David?" Shakey smiled. David was always able to cheer him up.

"Just regulatin' on the bones." David's deep and level drone filled the entire garage.

"Let me pull you a way for a minute." Shakey passed David the bottle, not even bothering to ask whether a drink was desired. "Urgent business."

"You got rescued, nigga!" David pointed at his opponent; Slim was his name.

"Aw, fool, I was gonna come back with this monster I just pulled." Slim turned the two handfuls of dominoes he held onto their backs.

"You lucky, Slim!" David turned up the bottle. Liquor ran down both sides of his mouth.

"Sit yo' ass down then!" Slim challenged, already washing the dominos.

"I'll bring him back, Slim," Shakey promised. "Red'll keep the seat warm for you."

"I don't feel like it." Red walked in the direction of the pit bull David kept chained in the back of the garage.

"You play?" Slim scowled at the well-dressed man standing on the opposite side of the table.

"A little." Nelson was being modest. He was the "Singles Domino Champion" at Tulane University three years straight. Only graduation ended his reign.

"Sit down," Slim demanded.

Shakey and David entered the small air-conditioned office a few feet away, leaving the door open behind them.

"What's up, homeboy?" David took another drink then gave Shakey the bottle, his demeanor changing once finally getting a good look at his friend. This was for real.

"I need a car," Shakey said.

"What kind?"

"Non-descript."

David sat down. He didn't even want to know the answer to the first question that threatened to burst from his lips. "OK."

Outside the office, the domino game was quickly heating up.

"Fifteen points," Nelson was heard to say.

"Fifteen points?" Slim scowled while cocking a domino high above his head. "Hey, Shakey, where the fuck you get this counterfeit-ass nigga from?" Slim slammed the 'big five' against the table with such force that Nelson nearly leapt from his seat. "Three hoes and a pimp, nigga!" Slim yelled then grabbed the pencil to record the score.

"Whatever that means," Nelson shook his head while playing a blank 'in the gut.' "Twenty points."

"Bolt the mothafunckin' doors, there's a playa loose!" Slim slammed the double blank against the table even harder than he had the last domino.

"That nigga's crazy," David said with humor.

"For real." Shakey almost smiled.

"I gotta '92 Chevy Caprice I keep at the house," David said. "Dark blue, tinted windows. Never been on the Island."

"What you want for it?"

"I ain't never charged you to borrow nothin'."

"This ain't a loner, baby." Shakey stared directly into David's eyes.

"You wanna buy it?"

Shakey nodded. "Then I want it to disappear; like into a thousand pieces." Shakey took a drink. "Add the price of labor, along with any inconvenience to the price of the car."

David looked down at the floor. Shakey was getting him into some heavy shit. But how could he refuse? Shakey had always been there whenever David found himself in need. Even the garage he now owned was funded with an interest-free loan from Shakey. A loan which he had still not fully repaid. "No inconvenience." David finally looked up from the floor. "The car's a Christmas present." He reached for the bottle. "And the labor's on the house."

"Thanks, David." Shakey took the bottle back.

"When you need it?" David asked as they moved toward the office door.

"I'll be back this afternoon," Shakey told him.

The two of them returned to the garage area of the building. The domino game in which Slim and Nelson competed had become quite heated.

"Come on outta there, nigga!" Slim shouted when Nelson took just a little too long to play for the mechanic's liking.

"I pass," Nelson mumbled.

"You pass?" Slim pretended not to understand.

"I can't play," Nelson spoke slowly, battling to retain his restraint.

"I knew you couldn't play when you sat yo' bitch ass down here!" Slim slammed another domino. "Feel on him he might be that way?"

Nelson looked to Shakey and David for some kind of assistance in dealing with this fool named Slim.

"That's y'all game, homeboy." David showed Nelson two open palms.

"Yo' play!" Slim yelled. "That French for 'Go, mothafucka!"

Shakey and David laughed now, only serving to further infuriate Nelson.

"If I couldn't play on aces and deuces my last turn," Nelson spoke to Slim as one would a small child, "it would stand to reason that I can't now."

Slim observed Nelson with a guarded half-frown feeling that he had somehow been disrespected, though not quite sure how. "Well knock when you can't play, sissy!" Slim slammed another domino.

"What did you call me, asshole?" Nelson took to his feet.

Slim jumped from his seat just as quickly, stepping two full steps back from the table and well out of Nelson's reach before speaking. "I called you a punk, pussy, dick-in-the booty-ass mothafucka!"

"You think I'm a punk, pussy, dick-in-the-booty mothafucka?" Nelson was rounding the table at Slim. Everyone in the garage laughed loudly, including, it seemed, the wildly barking pit bull. Shakey was first to step between the warring domino players.

"I'll bust your ass, dude!" Nelson threatened.

Shakey laughed while wrapping Aunt Mamie's youngest son in a bear hug. The funniest part of it all was that Slim didn't stand a chance against the two-hundred pound lawyer, who just happened to also be a devout student of the martial arts.

"Janet Jackson'll be giving five dollar blow jobs on Market Street the day Mississippi Slim gets wh-upped by a punk nigga!"

"Dude," Nelson once again spoke in typical Carltonesque manner. "Consider yourself fortunate.

"Consider?" Slim frowned. "If you don't get yo' bitch ass—"

"That's enough, Slim." David was smiling yet serious as his mind focused on the important matter he was to tend to.

Slim headed for the small refrigerator in the back of the garage. The intensity of his mumblings decreased as he stepped closer to the ice cold forty-ounce. bull that awaited him. Shakey kept an arm around Nelson's shoulder as the two of them headed for the door. Red followed them outside. The father of three observed them both before heading for the driver side of the car, battling to stifle the frightening premonition that he would, in the not too distant future, be retaining the services of his own criminal lawyer.

CHAPTER 13

Shakey's head bobbed furiously to UGK and Ludacris' "Stick 'Em Up" as the Chevy Caprice came to a stop on Thirty-first Street, halfway between Avenues L and M—just over a block away from Vanessa's house. Red killed the lights. Shakey was even more animated when Li'l Jon and the Eastside Boyz' "Bia Bia" boomed through the Caprice's six by nine speakers.

Shakey was in 'da zone'—the one he would work himself into using drugs, alcohol, and meditation on the worst aspects of his life. The one where the unthinkable propensity for violence that always teetered just beyond the curtain that veiled his conscious mind became the sole controller of his every thought and action.

Shakey held the .41-caliber pistol that would shortly be used to end the lives of Rosa's attackers in his right hand, waving it rhythmically back and forth, reveling in the power he felt.

Red passed Shakey the burning Swisher. In exchange, Shakey passed Red the day's second gin bottle. Neither man bothered with conversation.

They had done this enough times that no words were needed.

Shakey sucked hard on the Swisher, and Ben Massey's face appeared in the cloud of smoke that formed less than six inches before his own face. Shakey's anger was on overload while watching Ben deliver a trademark beating to his mother and younger siblings.

While Shakey in no way believed that rap music—nor any other form of musical expression—could be blamed for a listener's violent behavior, he had learned long ago that some of his favorite songs could also be used to aid in the psych job he would perform on himself before puttin' in work. And now, as Juvenile's "Set it Off" played loudly, Shakey was finally in the manic state he desired.

Shakey returned the small remaining portion of the Swisher to Red. He took a long drink from the gin bottle then also gave that to Red. He placed the pistol in his lap then reached between his legs for the Afro wig that would be used to obscure his identity. Next, the sixteen shot clip, fully loaded with hollow point bullets, was placed into the pistol. He placed the dark-tinted Locs on his face and stepped from the car, barely closing the door before Red took off for the agreed upon post-job rendezvous point behind the car wash on Thirty-third and Broadway.

Shakey concealed the pistol in the waistband of his pants, then buttoned the front of the full-length black raincoat he wore. He kneeled briefly to tighten the laces of the dirty, once-white Nike tennis shoes he wore. Slowly he walked for Vanessa's, certain that any undetected onlooker would see only a neighborhood smoker in search of a blast.

Shakey stuck a Newport in his mouth once at the corner across from Vanessa's house. He pulled the Bic lighter from the raincoat's pocket, lit the cigarette, and then returned the lighter there. He watched as the passenger side door on the Oldsmobile Cutlass Royal that was parked alongside Vanessa's house opened. A thin, bare-footed white woman leapt from the car and ran across the lawn toward the front door of the house. Shakey watched as the woman disappeared inside the house. Puffing patiently on the Newport until he saw the door open again, Shakey dropped the butt on the pavement and smashed it with his feet before moving hurriedly for the house.

"Baby girl!" Shakey walked hurriedly toward the woman, not allowing her to venture from the area just outside the front door.

The woman, who was carefully studying the contents of her hand, looked to Shakey.

"What you been up to?" Shakey pretended to know the woman while increasing the speed of his approach. "Vanessa inside?"

The woman shook her head, not quite sure what to make of this funny looking character.

Shakey reached quickly into the raincoat, producing the firearm. He pointed it directly at the woman before instructing, "Let's go." He clamped his left hand onto the back of the woman's arm.

"Please. I don't have anything."

"Knock on the door," Shakey instructed once they were on the porch. He stood to the woman's left, avoiding the line of sight of whoever opened the door. "Tell 'em it was too small." He raised the gun high enough for her to see the hole in the barrel. "When the door opens, go on about your business."

"Oh, God." The woman cried softly while knocking on the door.

"Who is it?" a man's voice challenged.

"Amanda."

"What you want?"

The woman looked to Shakey, the gun barrel was now jammed into her side. "You shorted me, man," the woman was finally able to say.

"What?" The voice was angry.

"You know this ain't no twenty, man." The inspired young woman gave the performance of a lifetime. "And don't give me that bullshit about it's late-night."

"Bitch, you must be crazy!" The lock clicked and the door came open. "I'll kick yo' crackhead ass!" Tubbs shouted through the screen door.

Shakey grabbed the handle of the screen door and snatched it violently, easily destroying the locking mechanism that held it in place.

"What the fuck?" The words had barely escaped Tubbs' lips when the first .41-caliber round exploded his chest cavity.

The woman screamed at the top of her lungs. Oblivious to all except the job he came to do, Shakey squeezed four more rounds into the fallen young man's face and chest before running farther into the house.

Shakey's pulse raced at an immeasurable pace as he moved, gun first, into the living room. A second man, startled by the gunshots, was running from Vanessa's bedroom, arriving at the living room at about the same time as Shakey.

The young man stopped suddenly in his tracks when he saw Shakey. The .380-caliber pistol he held was of no consequence as the conscienceless killer squeezed two shots into his abdomen.

Shakey stepped closer to the dying man. His eyes were open, and his breathing was labored. D-Ray's eyes were aimed directly at Shakey's, pleading for mercy. He would find none.

Shakey trained the gun on D-Ray's face and pulled the trigger, not stopping until there was no face existing.

A flash of motion in the hallway alerted Shakey to another's presence. In a split second, the gun was aimed in that direction.

"Darrell!" was the naked young woman's frantic scream.

It took Shakey but a moment to discern that the young woman posed no threat, and it was her good fortune that he was sure she could never identify him. If not for the outlandish disguise, he would have been forced to send her with the others.

Shakey ran toward the kitchen and exited the home through the sliding glass door that led to the back yard. He placed the gun in his pants before opening the wooden gate and leaving the yard. Once on the side of Vanessa's house, Shakey walked easily across the street, waiting until he entered the alleyway before breaking into an all-out sprint for two entire blocks. Once exiting the alleyway on Thirty-third Street, he turned right, walking easily again for the Chevy Caprice. He could already hear the sirens.

Shakey slammed the door shut, and the Caprice was moving. He quickly placed the gun, gloves, Afro wig, and sunglasses into a waiting Reebok sports bag. Next, he shedded the raincoat, along with the Puma sweatshirt and sneakers. These items also went into the bag.

Shakey and Red made eye contact briefly as Shakey reached for the clothes and shoes lying across the backseat. Red had confirmation.

The Caprice turned right on Avenue S, and Shakey was a different man. He wore slacks and shirt, dress shoes, and his trademark glistening bald head. He turned the radio up and reached for the gin bottle.

Shakey was now bobbing his head again. This time to Trick Daddy's "I'm A Thug." The Caprice turned right on Forty-sixth Street, then left on Avenue R. Red carefully guided the car up the ramp that led to the cargo area of the U-Haul truck that would be used to transport the Caprice and other evidence over the causeway bridge. Once in La Marque, the vehicle would be taken to a chop shop for a complete dismantling. The sports bag would find its way to the bottommost depths of Galveston Bay.

Shakey and Red climbed from the Caprice then jumped from the back of the U-Haul onto the pavement. After raising the ramp and pulling down the door to the cargo area, the two of them headed for the rented Lexus parked across the street.

Both vehicles departed at the same time, traveling in completely different directions, a constantly widening gulf forming between the killers of the two young men and the evidence that tied them to the crimes. As the distance between the two vehicles increased, so did the likelihood that Jonathan Reed had once again gotten away with murder.

The hardest part was turning it off. The slumbering lion that stayed nestled at Shakey's core was always a threat to become animated at the slightest provocation. However, returning the monstrosity to its dormant state was an utter impossibility until the beast had eaten its fill.

Shakey puffed on a Swisher while standing on the PennySavers' corner waiting for Winston, or another unfortunate soul to cross the path of the carnivore that had once again sprang to life within him.

It was nearly daybreak, and the streets were buzzing with the news of a double homicide. The music from Shakey's Cadillac played just loud enough that he and his companions grooved to Whitney Houston's "Didn't We Almost Have It All," all taking their turn with the Swisher and the pint of gin Shakey had purchased from a nearby boot-legger.

"Whoever the nigga was, he was 'bout his business." Dre, a tall, drug-addicted playground basketball legend, was next with the Swisher. "Lit them boys' asses up in that mothafucka!"

"No shit," Ced answered. Ced was the type of guy the other brothers on the street called "fly." He also had a thing for conspiracy theories. "That had to be a professional hit." The wavy-haired man took a drink before continuing. "The way I see it, either the police, or some mob shit!"

Smitty said nothing. His drink was hardly touched, and he was carefully monitoring the streets in both directions. Only Smitty knew of the association between Vanessa and Shakey, and only Smitty knew that Shakey was undoubtedly involved—in one capacity or another— in the brutal murder that rocked the streets of Galveston. It was Smitty also who first saw the money green BMW approaching the corner of Thirty-fifth and H for the third time in the last half-hour.

The BMW was the property of a well-known and extremely feared Galveston gangbanger named Moe. Word on the street had it that the victims of the night's murders were soldiers affiliated with the Deuce-Nine Crips, the set which Moe headed.

Unlike the past two times when the BMW passed without so much as a turned head from the four inside, this time the vehicle rolled to a stop in front of Shakey and his comrades.

"Dre," a voice called from inside the BMW. "Let me holler at you for a second."

Dre was unsure what to do. He looked to the others for the answer. Shakey's subtle head motion instructed him to head for the car. Dre stepped to the edge of the curb. Once there, he leaned his long frame in the direction of the car, bending at the waist in order to peer directly inside the vehicle.

Shakey had the Swisher between his lips again, watching as Dre's long arms stretched at his sides while his shoulders shrugged once in a denial of knowledge.

"I don't know." Dre spoke loud enough for all to hear, obviously quite uncomfortable with the line of questioning that was being administered to him. "You gon' have to ask the man yourself." Dre backed away from the car.

The driver side door sprang open and the man Shakey immediately recognized as Moe leapt from the car. Shakey watched as the over-aged gang-banger stepped in his direction, attired in an all-blue pantsuit. Shakey loathed Moe, not for being a gang-banger, as that would be a quite hypocritical stance for a man with Shakey's past. Shakey's beef with Moe centered around the fact that the adolescent population of Cedar Terrace housing projects worshipped the ground the man walked on, and while that influence could be used to steer many children away from the madness of the streets, Moe, and those like him, preferred instead to use the ghetto children of America to perform whatever deeds necessary to fatten their own pockets.

"What's up?" Moe stepped to the four men, his steady gaze in Shakey's direction, the only hint he gave at whom he addressed.

None of them responded, least of all Shakey. The Handsome Intimidator leaned back against the wall, inhaling deeply on the Swisher, the contempt written plainly on his face, one sudden move from reaching for the pistol hiding under the oversized FUBU pullover.

"That's some fucked up shit went down at Vanessa's."

Moe turned to Smitty, unable to hold his own gaze upon the one that cemented Shakey's face. "Those were my Locs."

Shakey nearly responded, but found the restraint to hold his tongue; not a difficult task when knowing that any words he spoke could ultimately lead to a murder conviction.

"Can I smoke with you?" Moe's eyes turned back to Shakey.

"Fuck you." Shakey spoke as if Moe was the most insignificant matter with which he had ever dealt.

The indifference shown to Moe hurt him much more than the profanity used.

"It's like that, homie?" The lock on the passenger side door of the BMW could be heard, followed shortly by the same clicking sound from the rear of the car.

"Fuck you," Shakey repeated, totally unconcerned with Moe's feelings.

"It's cool." Moe waved off the three teenagers climbing from the BMW. He faced the four men against the wall, once again speaking indiscriminately. "All I know is whoever hit my homies is in trouble if I find out who they are."

Shakey grabbed his crotch and tugged his answer to Moe's threat. Moe, eager not to lose any more face than he already had, returned quickly to his car, slamming the door and turning the music up so loud that the ground trembled. A yella, freckled-faced young man hung his arm from the window, forming the letter 'C' with the thumb and index finger of his right hand as the BMW peeled away from the curb.

"Bitch mothafucka!" Shakey mouthed to himself as the BMW zoomed away.

The BMW was barely out of sight when Winston appeared from around the corner. "I heard you

been lookin' for me, Shakey." Winston was quite
upset with his old friend, sensing that Shakey had
had something to do with his stepson's latest dis-
appearance and tiring of Shakey's insistence upon
sticking his nose in the family business of others.

"You heard right." Shakey handed Smitty the
Swisher and placed his near empty bottle on the
ground before stepping away from the wall to meet
Winston in the middle of the sidewalk.

"What you wanna say to me?" Winston opened
his arms, inviting Shakey to whatever.

"Nothin'," Shakey answered before delivering
a lightening fast right hand to Winston's chops,
sending him staggering sideways.

"Damn." Ced stepped out of the way as Winston
slumped in his direction.

"What the fuck is wrong with you, Shakey?"
Winston stood upright again, dabbing at the blood
that flowed freely from his bottom lip.

Shakey drew the gun from his belt and handed it
to Smitty before turning to Winston and yelling the
same challenge he had presented to his stepfather
twenty years earlier. "Fight a man, mothafucka!"

Winston struck a fighting pose and plodded
straight in Shakey's direction, receiving a rapid-fire
two-punch combination for his bravado. Shakey
circled to his left, throwing three sharp jabs before
suddenly changing directions and scoring with a
punishing three punch combination. It was plain
for all to see that Winston was sadly outclassed, yet
mercy was not to be expected from Shakey.

Shakey pressed the action, finally pinning Winston against the wall then unleashing a furious barrage of punches. Winston dropped to one knee and Shakey continued punching, remembering the sadness in Chris' eyes when he had spoken of his mother's broken jaw. He revisited his own rage at the assortment of injuries his own mother endured at the hands of his stepfather, striking back at the helplessness he felt as a small child at the mercy of Ben Massey's violent whims.

"That's enough, Shakey man, damn!" Smitty didn't speak until seeing Winston's eyes roll back in his head. "You gon' kill him." Shakey stepped away from his crumpled opponent and lifted the gin bottle from the ground. He guzzled the remainder of the bottle's contents then palmed the empty bottle in his hand, cocking it at his side while once again approaching Winston.

"Naw, Shakey man!" Smitty quickly intervened. "You trippin', fool." The sight of the much smaller man wrapping both arms around Shakey's waist made for a strikingly hilarious scene. Shakey stopped. He was trippin'. His battle with Winston was finished, the obligation to Christopher fulfilled. Yet the monster within had not nearly eaten its fill.

Shakey walked along the side of the railroad track, stopping briefly to pop the cap on still another pint of gin, then continuing his balancing act amongst the myriad of trains that lined both sides of the track. In his left hand was a small, newly purchased radio, discounted to him compliments of a neighborhood crack smoker. Luther crooned softly, the only sound in the early morning darkness.

Shakey traveled The Backtrack. It had once been a booming industrial area, but now, besides for the nightly train which passed at exactly 11:15 every night, the place was a virtual train cemetery. Due to its isolated location, The Backtrack had become the final resting place for more than just a few Galveston Island hustlers.

For Shakey, it was the solitude the deserted area provided that caused him to leave his car parked on the corner of Thirty-fifth Street and walk the mile or so in search of an open train car. He knew Jessica would be worried about him, but he had no intention of lying next to her after the night's happenings. She'd be OK. Chris was with her.

Shakey jumped to enter the open car then leaned against the wall just inside the door. He looked out upon the sunrise. Despite his lifelong aversion to daylight, Shakey had always been a sucker for the rising sun. For with each rise of the sun, there was always the hope of a new beginning.

Shakey relaxed, leaning farther against the wall, the exhaustion bombarding him all at once. Prince's "Adore" played on Magic 102 FM as the lead in his eyelids grew heavier. He missed Jessica.

A sound from an adjacent car startled Shakey. In a fraction of a second, Shakey's eyes were wide open, his hand on the pistol, and his weight was on the balls of feet, crouching was he in the direction of the mysterious noise. A body appeared in the open doorway separating the two cars. It was Larry.

The teenage maniac walked slowly in Shakey's direction, never looking up from the floor of the car, an empty pickle jar held out in front of him.

Shakey twisted the cap on the gin bottle, shuddering as he poured, thinking of how close he had just come to filling Larry with holes, then becoming more intrigued by the insane young man.

Once the spirits were equally divided, Larry turned and shuffled in the direction from which he had come. There were so many questions Shakey wanted to ask, but he doubted there would be an intelligible answer given. Shakey had been shocked by the moment of intelligence he had just witnessed in Larry's eyes. Perhaps Larry wasn't nearly as crazy as he had been led to believe.

He knew how to get half my gin, Shakey thought as he settled against the wall again. Quickly drifting away, hovering just beneath the point of consciousness, he looked in the direction of the neighboring car once more before surrendering to the total darkness. A pillow sailed through the open door, landing on the floor next to Shakey. Shakey folded the pillow, placed it under his head, and plunged headfirst into the depths of a dreamless slumber.

CHAPTER 14

Michelle's Nissan Pathfinder followed the brown stationwagon into the U-shaped loading zone of Alamo Elementary School. The traffic flowed slowly as car after car dropped frantically excited kids off for their last half-day before an extended Christmas vacation.

"Don't forget we get out at twelve, Mama," Kashandra said.

"I'll be here at 11:45." Michelle used the rearview mirror to observe the dark blue tinted windows that had pulled up behind her. The car had been following them since leaving their residence.

"I need to use the restroom." Michelle turned off the ignition and climbed from the vehicle. She followed her daughter toward the school's front entrance, hoping against reason that the Regal would be gone when she returned.

A quick look behind her, and to her relief, the sedan was pulling around the Pathfinder. The highly inquisitive fifth grader noted her mother's apprehension. "Who is that, Mama?"

"I don't know."

Mother and daughter walked side by side through the double doors; Michelle would waste a few minutes for good measure. "See you this evening, baby." Michelle stopped in front of the office area, bidding Kashandra a nervous good-bye.

"See, Mama?" Kashandra fussed. "You forgot already." Kashandra's cold, dark eyes admonished her mother.

"I know, I know." Michelle was startled by her first child's resemblance to her father when angry. "I was joking."

Kashandra hugged her mother before running quickly away.

"Stop runnin', Kashandra!" Michelle called behind her daughter, knowing beforehand she would be ignored. Stubbornness was another trait the child had inherited from her father.

Michelle turned toward the front door, pausing to allow for the passing of a young Hispanic woman and two kinder-aged girls before pressing her face against the glass door. To Michelle's dismay, the sedan was now positioned directly in front of Michelle's Pathfinder, blocking any possible exit.

Michelle reached into her purse with both hands, grabbing first the fully loaded seven shot clip then jamming it into its place inside the .25-caliber semi-automatic pistol. Cocked unsteadily, she stepped from the confines of Alamo Elementary School and headed toward the inevitable conflict with the driver of the dark blue sedan.

Not so unexpectedly, the driver side door of the car opened as Michelle approached the Pathfinder. Instinctively, her sweaty hand tightened around the pistol. Every muscle in her body tensed as the unknown assailant approached, then relaxed as the familiar face was unmasked with the shedding of the Versace sunglasses then tensed again with full recognition of the face smiling at her. Jorgé Trevino.

"Michelle." Anyone without previous knowledge of Galveston's chief narcotic officer would have become totally enraptured with the warmth of the man's smile. "Been a long time."

"Not long enough." Michelle carefully peeled her fingers from the grip of the gun then closed her purse, praying all the while that some unfortunate tragedy wouldn't take place. "To what do I owe the pleasure?"

"I see you're your usual—" Trevino stopped suddenly, taking a long enough look at the purse to assure Michelle that he was conscious of the contents. "—dangerous self." Trevino took a step toward the Nissan Pathfinder then took a peek through the passenger side window. "Nice."

"What do you want?" Michelle was quickly growing angry. Next to Shakey, Jorgé Trevino was her least favorite person on the face of the earth.

"Hey, I just want to help." Trevino's voice was a capsule of pure innocence. "That is," his face hardened, "if you're interested in saving your family".

Michelle's weight shifted from one foot to another, the pursed-lip expression she wore telling just how convinced she was of Trevino's sincerity. "Look, Trevino," Michelle dropped the purse onto the driver's seat of the Pathfinder, totally disregarding it's contents. "If you got somethin' to say, I sure wish you would say it."

"OK. Trevino reached under the sports coat he wore and produced a copy of the day's Galveston morning news. He unfolded the paper and placed it directly under Michelle's nose.

DOUBLE HOMICIDE ROCKS CENTRAL GALVESTON
NEIGHBORHOOD

Michelle shook while reading the headline, though not yet sure how this all affected her family. "And?"

"And, aren't you tired of your family being ripped apart at the seams every time Shakey goes on a crime spree?" Trevino stared deep into the frightened mother's eyes, then dropped the paper on the passenger seat of the Pathfinder. "Think about it."

Michelle was speechless, knowing full well that Red had left their home with Shakey last night, not returning until the wee hours of the morning. Upon his return, her husband had been totally unwilling to answer any questions regarding the night's activities.

"Look." Trevino stared into her eyes again while gathering the complete charismatic power with which he had been so bountifully blessed. He then delivered his final sales pitch. "Your husband's not a bad man, and he's not the man I want. But somebody's going to spend the rest of their life in prison over this. And you know like I know that Shakey, if given the chance, will make sure that 'someone' is Red and not himself."

Michelle, though still speechless, was already deciding that Shakey would be the 'someone' spending the rest of his life in prison for whatever happened last night, and not Red.

"Here." Trevino handed her his card. "My home number and pager's on the back. Use them."

Michelle accepted the card. Still not speaking, the eye contact she and Trevino made assured each of the other's mutual desire to co-conspire in the orchestration of Shakey's final fall.

Trevino turned quickly away from Michelle, lest the giddiness brewing in his heart be visible to her. Smiling as he returned to the sedan, he marveled at the simplicity involved in recruiting Michelle. Then again, what choice did she have? Her family was at stake. Of course, Trevino had no intention of sparing any of them. Shakey, Red, Michelle, and anyone else Trevino could possibly implicate were going to prison.

Michelle watched from behind the wheel of the Pathfinder as the sedan exited the school loading zone and made its way down Fifty-fourth Street. As much as she hated the idea of being enjoined with Trevino in any type of partnership, Michelle had once played the role of single mother awaiting the return of a husband in prison. It was a role she would not play again.

Shakey was awakened by the stealth of early morning sunlight as it gently massaged his forehead. The peacefulness of the morning was unsettled by the momentary anxiety instigated by waking in an unfamiliar place.

Once fully conscious of his whereabouts, thus reassuming the cloak of peacefulness granted to him by such an anonymous setting, Shakey rolled over, resting shortly on all fours before finally squatting on two legs. The smell of warm donuts caused his stomach to growl.

Shakey lifted then opened the white bag lying next to him. There was also a pint of orange juice and a folded newspaper. Larry. The name had barely been imprinted upon his mind before being erased by the taste of Mr. Kovacevich's famous glazed donuts. Mr. K. was well known to an entire generation of central Galveston children whose morning walk to school almost always included a detour to The Donut King on Thirty-sixth Street and Broadway Boulevard.

Shakey bit into the second donut at right about the same time he began the slow awkward shuffle from the train car in which he had slept, to the open doorway of the car Larry had inhabited. "Thanks, Larry." Shakey stepped through the doorway then stumbled deeper into the room, taken aback by the sight before him.

Larry was nowhere to be found, but evidence of the misery with which he lived was everywhere.

To Shakey's left, against the wall, was a neatly folded dark-colored blanket. Atop the blanket was a similarly folded white sheet. A pillow lay atop the sheet.

To the left of the bed was a small brown paper bag. To the right was a large trash bag filled with aluminum cans. Straight ahead of Shakey, positioned against the far wall, was a small table, covered with a gray blanket. A large picture of a smiling young boy sat in the middle of the table with dozens of smaller pictures surrounding it. A blue jean jacket hung on the corner of the table.

Shakey stepped closer; close enough to see that all the pictures on the table were of the same young man. Attached to the bottom of the largest picture was an obituary, also bearing the boy's image. Antonio Anderson was the kid's name. Shakey vaguely remembered the name as one of the victims of the past summer's rash of drive-by shootings.

The wall behind the makeshift shrine was written on in royal blue paint. One message read DEUCE-NINE FOR LIFE. Just above the first message, written much bigger were the words, TONY. ONE LOVE.

Shakey turned away from the shrine, suddenly feeling like an unlawful intruder upon the most intimate thoughts and emotions of the troubled young man the streets knew only as Crazy Larry.

Shakey returned to his own train car, standing with his back against the wall facing the entrance leading to the train yard. He opened the orange juice and took a sip before unfolding the paper. The headline whacked him in the belly with the force of a Barry Bonds wielded hammer. Pictures of the two latest African American young men to meet untimely deaths in the perilous underworld of Galveston Island accompanied the headline.

Shakey closed his eyes tightly—almost tight enough to smother the welling tears that gathered behind both overburdened eyelids. He had done it again.

Jessica peeled the slabs of pig flesh from the cardboard one by one before placing them in the skillet. In seconds, the smell of frying bacon was rapidly filling the kitchen and living room. Jessica has awakened just before sunrise. That is, if you consider the tossing and turning she had done while alone in Shakey's king-sized bed as having slept at all. After climbing from bed, the lonely young woman vainly attempted to occupy herself with a full variety of domestic tasks in hopes of blocking the onslaught of negative emotions she felt. Unfortunately, through it all, her mind and heart were battered by the most agonizing of emotions; from worry and fear, to anger and resentment, and finally, the heart stopping sense of abandonment with which she had grown so miserably familiar.

"Breakfast ready?" A just awakened Christopher peered over the kitchen counter, still rubbing the sleep from his eyes.

"Not yet." Jessica smiled, surprised by how fond she had become of Christopher now that she had gotten to spend time with him. "But, by the time you wash your face and brush your teeth, it will be."

"Hurry up," Christopher fussed while heading for the restroom. "I'm hungry"

"Didn't I tell you about demanding things, little boy?" Jessica sat the fork on the stove and made a move as if to go after Christopher.

"I'm sorry, Jessica." Christopher laughed, half his body hidden inside the doorway of the downstairs bedroom that had been declared his designated sleeping area, though Christopher never slept anywhere except on the living room floor in front of the television, usually after playing with the PlayStation 3 Shakey had purchased for him until succumbing to exhaustion.

"I'm gonna get a chance to tan your behind yet, Christopher!" Jessica's threat was a hollow bluff, and both she and Chris knew it.

Christopher's smile dissolved instantly as his mind suddenly changed gears. His voice now a pleading half-whisper, the young boy asked, "Is Shakey eatin' with us this mornin'?"

Jessica was unsure what to answer though the truth was already painfully clear. "More for us." She managed a smile.

Christopher's disappointment covered his entire face as he turned for the restroom.

Jessica returned to the kitchen. She exhaled loudly while cracking two eggs and dropping the contents into a plastic bowl. "Damn him," she whispered aloud.

Shakey had not let them down since Christopher's arrival a week ago. The three of them had begun every morning with a family breakfast.

Family. The word seemed so strange in relation to the three vastly different individuals whose only common ground was the excruciatingly painful, utterly destructive, dysfunctional set of circumstances that had produced them. Brought together under one roof by a force that could only be called fate, first learning, then longing to live together, though none of them had yet learned to live with themselves. It was an unnatural sequence of human development that would forever thwart the growth necessary to provide any semblance of long-term personal stability. But despite it all, the three of them were a family.

Shakey's head swiveled to observe the vehicle approaching from his left. The driver, obviously having no regard for the peacefulness of the early morning, rattled the walls of nearby houses with loud rap music.

"What up, homie?" The music was lowered just a little as the candy painted black Chevy Blazer pulled next to Shakey. A familiar voice yelled over Kia's "My Neck, My Back."

"Slow boogie, baby." Shakey knew the man as Moonie, just one of many anything-goes hustlers the jungle produced with frightening regularity.

"What you doin' around here this early in the mornin'?" Moonie couldn't remember ever seeing Shakey this deep in the heart of the jungle. Unknown to him, his not seeing Shakey around the jungle had much more to do with Shakey's stealth than any intentional avoidance. "And walkin' at that."

"Rough night," was Shakey's tight-lipped response.

"Ran into a wild one, huh?"

"Somethin' like that."

"Shit, what was her name?" Moonie reached over and opened the passenger door. "I'm always lookin' for a star headhunter."

"Don't know." Shakey smiled. "My memory was in the wrong head. She left with it."

"Get in, nigga." Moonie laughed loudly while pushing the door open wide. "You still a damn fool."

Shakey was more than happy to climb inside the Blazer with Moonie. Additionally, it was with his poorest possible judgment that he had decided to wait in the projects with a pistol bulging beneath his sweater, a mere twelve hours after committing a double homicide.

"What you doin' up this early?" Shakey asked once inside the vehicle.

"Deliveries." Moonie wasn't bragging, but did want to inform Shakey that he was traveling in a vehicle containing narcotics. "Taste this." Mooney took the twenty-ounce Sprite that was lying between his legs and poured a generous portion of the contents into the Styrofoam cup that lie in the holder next to Shakey. He then handed the cup to Shakey.

Shakey sniffed, then sipped from the cup. "Candy." He had barely whispered when he took a second more aggressive gulp.

Candy, syrup, bar, or lean, as the younger generation preferred, were all street names for the drugs commonly prescribed for patients battling the common cold, was very popular amongst the youth in Southeast Texas because of its depressive potency. As little as four ounces of the relatively inexpensive drug mixed with a twelve-ounce soda, and a Bar Baby could lean for hours. Mixed with alcohol, the concoction could be lethal.

"Nigga, what?" The merriment of the Buddha-looking, brown-skinned drug dealer echoed throughout the truck as he reached under the front of his seat. Moments later, he sat a gallon jug between himself and Shakey. "Let it go right now for eight-hundred."

"Naw, I don't think I need all that." Shakey cracked a half-smile as the Blazer turned on Avenue H.

"How much you need?" Moonie grabbed a large brown paper bag from the backseat. Reaching inside the bag, he pulled out two small baby food jars filled with the colored liquid.

"Fo's," or four ounces of syrup, were commonly bottled in baby food jars, having an approximate street value of forty dollars. A fo' was the accepted standard of measure amongst dealers and users.

"Five or six of them bad mothafuckas oughta do." Shakey could think of nothing better for curing his present ills than a large dose of lean. "How much is it gonna run me?"

"Bein' you my nigga and all," Moonie twirled the hair on his chin around his right index finger, wrestling between thoughts of the later benefits of appeasing Shakey now, and the greed for cash that was always passing him, "gimme a bill seventy-five, and take you six of 'em outta there."

"Good business." Shakey could hardly wait to pour two fo's in a twenty-ounce Sprite. He reached into his pocket, quickly peeling the requested money from his wad, and handed it to Moonie. "Let me off around PennySavers'."

"Be careful, fool." Moonie placed the folded money in the top pocket of the red flannel shirt he wore. "Johnny Law is out in force this morning."

"Yeah," Shakey answered with pretended disinterest.

"Some fool wit' a Afro peeled some youngstas caps at Vanessa's house."

"An Afro?" Shakey subtly pumped Moonie for all that the pot-bellied man knew.

"Yeah, fool." Moonie laughed aloud while drinking from the Sprite bottle. "Say that fool had a blowout like Superfly. Lit them boys' ass up in there!"

"Kill 'em?"

"Dead en' a mothafucka! But, peep this. The nigga had to be a pro, 'cause he wasn't even concerned about the boppa they wuz in there fuckin'."

"Let her make it?"

"Walked by that bitch like she wasn't even there." The Blazer pulled up to the corner of Thirty-fifth and H.

"What's the word in the streets?" Shakey asked.

"You know how that shit goes," Moonie answered. "Everybody got they own theory. I saw that niggga Moe a li'l while ago; them youngstas was down wit' Deuce-nine." Moonie paused long enough to shake two Newports from the pack lying on the dashboard, then pushed in the lighter. After handing Shakey one of the smokes he continued. "Moe says he know who did that shit, and he's gonna take care of it. Other people say Vanessa owed some Colombians some money. Like I said, you know how the rumor mill turns."

"Yeah." Shakey was sure Moe indeed knew the truth, but he also knew that despite all else, Moe was a fairly intelligent man. War with Shakey was a foolish choice. That fact was plainly evident. "Probably never know the truth."

"Whoever the fool was," Moonie grabbed the lighter, offering first to light Shakey's cigarette, "I suggest they quit fuckin' wit' that nigga." Moonie laughed again while placing the red end of the lighter to his own cancer stick.

"For real." Shakey opened the door to step from the truck. "Appreciate the ride, fool, and the drink."

"You know how we do it." Moonie would expect twice the same discount on his next crack purchase. "Take it easy."

"Later." Shakey tapped the side of the Chevy Blazer before stepping toward the already fully-inhabited store corner.

Shakey first stepped toward his Cadillac; a quick once-over assured him of the car's wholeness.

"It's just like you left it," Butch assured him. Butch was the royal guard of Shakey's ghetto chariot. "I ain't even let nobody sit on it."

"I see you took care of your business." Shakey peeled a fifty-dollar bill from his stash and handed it to Butch.

"Whew." Butch's eyes widened and he flashed his broadest jack-o-lantern grin while accepting payment for his services. "Thank you, Shakey!" Butch was was off and running. "C'mon, Will."

"Smoke!" Smitty appeared at Shakey's side. "'Til you can't smoke no mo'!" Smitty laughed so hard his entire body shook.

Shakey gave his stiff-necked friend some dap, then laughed just as hard, though his amusement was not of the same origin.

"I was wonderin' when you was comin' for your ride."

"Shit, I just woke up," Shakey told him. "How long you been out here?"

"Since you left." Smitty motioned for Shakey to step away from the crowded corner and follow him toward the alley. "You know all of us ain't got it like you; some of us still hustle for a livin'."

Shakey smiled, knowing that the long hours Smitty put in were nine parts greed to every one part need. His smile was cut short by the grim expression that now framed Smitty's face. "What gives?"

Moe been back around here," Smitty informed him, not bothering to mention why he felt it necessary to do so. "Him and about four more of his toy soldiers. They packin' heavy heat."

Shakey was slow to respond, finally deciding he would think about Moe later. "It's cool," Shakey assured his buddy.

Smitty nodded slowly, obviously not agreeing with Shakey's assessment of the situation.

"You get the Big Red." Shakey reached a hand in each of his jacket pockets, withdrawing four baby food jars. "I got the drink."

"You ain't gotta tell me twice." Smitty hurried toward the entrance of PennySavers.

Shakey followed a few paces behind Smitty. The rational thinking man in him loathed the possible war he had started. The murderous monster within embraced the promise of further violence. In any event, Shakey had staked claim to these jungle streets long before the toy soldiers Moe was capable of deploying had even considered packing guns. And, as much as Shakey hated the thought of hurting more kids, he would wipe the streets clean of Deuce-Nine Crips if Moe decided to attack.

"One more, Jessica, please." It hadn't taken long for Christopher to discover that Jessica was powerless against his pleas.

"I'm tired, Christopher," Jessica protested meekly, although fully aware that she would soon give in to Christopher's every whim and fancy.

Christopher and Jessica had been playing Mortal Kombat for nearly three hours now, and the aching that had begun at the tips of her fingers had now traveled across her hands, settling at the bend in both wrists. Not to mention the fact that her ego could take no more of the evil laughs that came from Christopher each time he won a game.

"C'mon, Jessica, please." Christopher was all smiles.

"One more, and that's it!" Jessica asserted for the fifth time in the last forty-five minutes.

Both cohabitants chose their warriors, and the one-sided battle continued. It wasn't long before the warrior princess Jessica had chosen was fallen once again.

"That's it, Christopher." Christopher's jeering laughter so perturbed Jessica that she turned the

power off to the game and pulled the game car-
tridge from the system.

"Whatcha doin', Jessica?" Christopher was still
laughing.

"That's it." Jessica turned the television station
until locating The Young and the Restless. "You
and Shakey can play when he gets home."

"Sore loser," Christopher jabbed, noting the
sadness in Jessica's face when speaking Shakey's
name.

"Forget you, boy." Jessica had picked up a slew
of delinquent language skills from hanging out
with Christopher.

"Forget you, carrot top." Christopher giggled
then asked, "You miss him, huh?"

"Yeah, I miss him," Jessica answered.

Christopher's face was suddenly covered with an
expression much more serious than Jessica would
ever have thought possible—not anything like the
face of dread, but more like the face of one suddenly coming to grips with the complexities of life.
Finally, the nine-year-old asked, "Y'all in love?"

"What kind of question is that?" Even as she
spoke, the butterflies performed a frantic tango
deep within the pit of her stomach.

"Y'all sleep in the same bed every night," Christopher reasoned. "So, y'all married."

"We are not!" Jessica was embarrassed by the
child's observations. Through flushed cheeks, she
admonished, "You sure are a smart little boy"

"Y'all better get married." Christopher's voice was full of warning.

"And why is that?" Jessica couldn't wait to hear.

"'Cause fornication is a sin," Christopher instructed. "And you don't want God mad at you."

"Is that right?"

"Yep." The curly-haired young boy nodded assertively. "That's right."

"You're somethin' else, little boy, you know that?"

Christopher smiled. Jessica was, without a doubt, the only person in the world that could get away with calling him little boy. In an instant, Christopher's countenance was solidified with the complexities of his young life once again as he finally get around to broaching the issue that had been at the forefront of his mind all morning. "Jessica?"

"What, little boy?" Jessica was yet to discern Christopher's inner turmoil.

"When y'all get married, y'all gonna have a bunch of kids?"

"You just don't stop, do you, Christopher?" Jessica ran a hand through the softness of Christopher's tightly curled locks. "I would imagine." Jessica went along with the youngster's scenario not only for the child's appeasement. "That's if." Jessica emphasized the word "if" so as not to allow either of them to forget that the projected scenario was purely hypothetical. "We were to marry, we would have kids."

"Lots of kids?"

"I don't know." Jessica was just now becoming aware of the weight of emotional investment Christopher had in the questions he posed to her. "Why do you ask, sweetheart?"

"'Cause I wanna stay with y'all." Christopher was unable to hide the pitiful little boy that spoke through his mouth.

Jessica's face lit with a glow she hadn't felt since she and Jason were small kids—before her mother's rejection, before drugs, before her disbelief in Santa Claus. Jessica basked in the unmistakable feeling of being completely and unconditionally loved and needed. "Oh, sweetie." Jessica opened both arms, welcoming the frightened little boy to a warmth he had never known.

Christopher allowed himself to be held. Finally, after letting go the last visages of pretended self-reliance, he returned Jessica's embrace as tightly as he could. Despite himself, he sobbed softly into her bosom.

"It's OK, sweetheart." Jessica softly kissed the top of his head. Tears of her own stinging both eyes, surprised by the intensity of the love she had developed for the tender-hearted little boy she had found hiding under the layer upon layer of false bravado and feigned arrogance with which he had been forced to insulate himself. "We'll always be together." Jessica's voice broke. "We're family."

"Shakey too?" Christopher wanted to know.

"Shakey too," Jessica confirmed before saying, "and just wait until we get our hands on him."

Christopher managed to smile, sniffing hard to stifle the tears before pulling away from Jessica. He said, "I know where we can find him."

"Where?" Jessica too had a sudden case of the sniffles.

"PennySavers," Christopher said.

"Think so?"

"Know so." Christopher didn't waver.

"He's lucky we don't have a way there."

"We got a way there, Jessica." The light bulb that went off inside Christopher's head illuminated his entire face.

Jessica eyes asked the question.

"The Impala," Christopher suggested.

"He'd be so angry." Jessica knew that taking off in a car she had yet to see Shakey himself drive was not a good idea.

Christopher shrugged, the smirk that covered his tear-stained face seeming to say . . .

"Serves him right," Jessica finished the thought.

"Well?" Christopher lifted both arms, palms up at his side.

"Let's go." Jessica hurried toward the garage, and with Christopher following closely, she was determined to find Shakey and give him a piece of her mind.

CHAPTER 15

"Po' a fo' in a can soda, I can do that." Shakey, 'buzzin' as he hadn't in quite some time, sung along with Li'l Flip as his Cadillac was used to turn the PennySavers store corner into an instant block party.

A passin car honked its horn while passing the crowd. Upon recognition of the driver, Shakey threw both hands in the air, slurring loudly, "What's up nigga?"

Moe, halfway through the intersection, put the BMW in reverse and sped backward until double parked next to Shakey's Cadillac.

The front driver side door sprang open a split second before the other three. Moe, along with Big Lou, his first lieutenant, climbed from the front of the BMW. Three younger soldiers spilled from the back.

The festive crowd of moments past was now a hushed collection of frightened onlookers. Revelers grabbed hats, keys, bottles of beer, and whatever personal belongings they had to gather before stepping quickly away from the much anticipated confrontation, not stopping until sure they were spectating from a safe distance. Of the score of acquaintances who had attended Shakey's party, only Smitty remained by Shakey's side.

"What you say to me?" Moe wore an angry scowl as he stepped onto the curb. The four flunkies followed closely, even imitating Moe's facial expression.

"What's up, nigga?" Shakey repeated, unmoved by the face that Moe wore, nor the faces of the four flunkies who would surely commit to violence at the gang leader's command.

"What you want to be up?" Moe threatened.

Shakey laughed while sipping from the Sprite bottle. Moe was a joke. Shakey knew it. Worse yet, Moe knew that he knew it.

"Somethin' funny? You think Deuce-Nine is a joke?" Moe yelled.

Shakey laughed harder.

"One of y'all show this nigga what's up," Moe spoke at the three youngsters standing behind him.

The largest of the three kids stepped forward. The rangy, well-built youngster couldn't have been any older than seventeen. "Catch a square," the boy challenged.

Instantly, the smile in Shakey's eyes was gone and was replaced by a gaze so dark the teenager nearly wet his pants. "Don't do yourself, son." Shakey's slow, deliberate warning sent chills down the spine of all within earshot.

"Bring it on." The saddest part of it all was that the teenager was so dependent upon the acceptance of his gangbanging peers that he would rather face the certain destruction of tangling with a known killer than enduring the rejection he knew would be his if he backed down.

Shakey shook his head, taking another sip from his drink, then handing the bottle to Smitty before taking a step in the waiting fool's direction. As much as Shakey would love to allow the kid a free pass, he was mindful that the streets were watching. The streets were always watching.

"Damn." Smitty placed both bottles against the brick wall he had been leaning against, freeing his hands in case he was needed to combat an intervening Deuce-Nine Crip.

The teenager stood flat-footed, hands at the ready; much too low to combat a puncher with Shakey's hand speed. Shakey sized up the youngster, hoping that he would not be forced to hurt him badly.

The Handsome Intimidator bounced slowly on this toes, loosening up. The youngster circled timidly to his left, both eyes and body language telling of his lack of desire to fight.

"Get him, Herk," another young Crip yelled, he too voicing the dread he knew his mate was facing.

At Moe's urging, the teenager advanced on Shakey, lunging wildly with an overhead right. Shakey easily dodged the frightened boy's punch, then countered with two punishing hooks to the body. The teenager's hands dropped even lower.

The Crips cheered loudly for Herk; everyone else maintained complete silence. Herk threw a looping right hand. Shakey slipped the punch then effectively countered once more with a solid left hook to the body, this time followed by an equally powerful punch to the side of the teenager's head.

Herk stumbled backward, and Shakey closed in. His first instinct was to finish the youngster off, but intent on not hurting the kid any more than necessary, he held steady, granting Herk the option of ending the fight while still on his feet.

"Get the fool, Herk!" was the not so encouraging yell.

Herk, his morale all but non-existent, tiptoed gingerly in Shakey's direction.

Shakey peppered the teenager's face with a series of jabs. He was angry now with the boy's foolishness, but instead of unloading with a fight-ending right hand, Shakey backed away once more.

Herk, his nose now oozing a steady stream of crimson, looked to Moe. Moe tapped the shoulder of the soldier standing next to him.

"Rest him up, Loc."

Another youngster, this one two inches shorter and twenty-five pounds lighter than the Herk, took Herk's place before Shakey.

"C'mon, man." Shakey shook his head disbelievingly at the child. "You win, fool." Shakey turned away from the boy, searched for his drink, then lifted it from the ground.

"C'mon, ho!" The second boy was a bigger fool than the first. Shakey could find no anger within himself despite the blatant disrespect shown to him. "Go home, son." Shakey leaned back against PennySavers' wall.

"My Li'l Loc' callin' you out," Moe told Shakey.

"Well, I'm callin you out bitch!" Shakey was off the wall and heading for Moe. Big Lou quickly cut off Shakey's path, causing Smitty to cock the brick he had found at his side.

"Hold on, Shakey," Big Lou spoke peacefully. He was the biggest Deuce-Nine Crip of them all, and was obviously not looking to force an altercation with Shakey.

"Get yo' mothafuckin' hands off me!" Shakey slapped Big Lou's hand from this chest.

The crowd of spectators scurried to a safer distance as Big Lou stood at full height. Shakey didn't flinch; he wasn't the least bit daunted by the anger of the first lieutenant. Smitty squeezed the brick, Moe palmed the handle of the .380 in his pants, and the stage was set for tragedy.

A passing patrol car slowed upon sight of the impending melee. Not at all anxious to abandon the safe confines of his squad car, the policeman hit the squawk button on his sound system. Once sure the stage was his, the two-year veteran turned his right index finger in a circular motion above his head, gesturing for the crowd to disperse.

"You don' fucked up this time, Shakey!" Moe threatened, not sure himself what he meant, but knowing Deuce-Nine must boldly answer Shakey's transgression.

Shakey's gaze showered Moe with fire and brimstone, his countenance as black as the day after judgment day. "I killed yo' homeboys, bitch!" His intense, low-volumed whisper was a double-edge sword of hatred and doom.

Total stillness enveloped the melee participants, as all were disbelieving that Shakey would readily declare that what they all very well knew. "And you ain't gonna do a mothafuckin' thing about it!" Shakey could be as ignorant as any.

Let's go, Locs." Moe's troops gathered for departure. "Deuce-Nine'll be payin' you a visit, Cuz," was the gang leader's final threat before hurling himself behind the wheel of the BMW.

Shakey watched as the BMW traveled down Thirty-fifth Street to Broadway Boulevard. He then aimed his scowl at the eyes of the young patrolman, and, after watching the patrol car leave, the same as the BMW, Shakey returned to his spot against the wall.

Smitty stood silently next to Shakey, totally unsure of what should be said after such a startling turn of events. He was not yet aware of the brick he still held until leaning to reach for his drink and finding his hand encumbered.

Sipping at his drink now, and peeking attentatively over the rim of the plastic cup, the next sight that met Shakey was a must unbelievable one. His beloved red, candy-coated '64 Impala was speeding in his direction.

His pride and joy screeched to a nerve-grinding halt at the corner of Thirty-fifth and H. Jessica was driving, and Christopher was in the backseat. "This bitch is crazy!" Shakey was finally convinced.

The Impala pulled next to the Cadillac and parked; neither Jessica nor her accomplice stepped from the car.

Shakey stepped from the wall, his shock subsiding now, more than adequately replaced with anger. "What the hell are you doing?"

"Wanting to know what the hell you're doing?" Jessica, pumped for the moment, stood firmly.

"What you doin' in my Impala?" Shakey was an angry adolescent discovering a younger sibling's unrequested fingering of a prized baseball card collection.

"We needed transportation." Jessica turned to Chris. "After all, you did abandon us."

"Abandon?" Shakey's eyes fell on Christopher. His young friend smiled sheepishly, obviously under the influence of the she-devil's bewitching.

"And for what?" Jessica fussed, attracting the amused onlookers whom once again gathered closely, amazed at her handling of Shakey. "Look at you. You're all dirty, you're drunk, your hands are all scraped." Jessica could have went on, but felt no need.

"Get out!" Shakey reached for the handle on the door, only to find that Jessica was just a little too quick for him. She hurriedly locked the doors, then quickly rolled the windows up before allowing Shakey the opportunity to do anything about it. "Quit playin', girl." Shakey's fist banged the window.

Jessica motioned for Shakey to make his way to the passenger side of the car.

Shakey yelled, "Open this damn door, girl," as he was now beginning to feel embarrassed by the laughter of the crowd.

Jessica said something to Chris. The young boy rolled his window down then positioned his entire upper body between the window "She said get in or she's leavin'."

"Ya better open this door, you crazy mothafucka!" Shakey slapped hard against the window.

Jessica shifted the transmission into drive and lifted her foot from the brake.

"Stop!" Shakey's palms struck the window. The Impala remained still just long enough for him to run around the rear of the car and leap into the passenger seat.

A roar of laughter accompanied Shakey's mad dash for the open passenger side door.

Jessica's foot grew heavy atop the gas pedal, and the Impala launched forward.

"What's yo' damn problem, girl?"

"What's your problem, Jonathan?" Jessica had decided along the way to PennySavers that Shakey was a ridiculous name for a grown man.

"You the one trippin'!" Shakey had never seen anything resembling anger from her until now. As angry as he felt over his car, he found himself to be much more intrigued by the she-devil's fire than he was fueled by his own.

"Oh, am I?" Jessica turned left on Winnie. "You could've at least called, asshole!"

"I was comin' home soon." Shakey watched the dots of green that eyed his two red, dingy half-slits. The she-devil was beautiful; much too beautiful for any prolonged anger to be aimed in her direction.

"When, Jonathan?" Jessica too lost her steam. Now that Shakey was in the car, she was much more settled. "We waited all night and morning for you."

Shakey looked to his watch. 3:30 P.M. He had been gone for over twenty-four hours. A phone call would have been much less than reasonable. "Well you got me. Now what?" Shakey couldn't bring himself to confess the errors of his ways.

"Now I want you to come home." Jessica's plea was malice-free.

"I'm comin'," Shakey told her.

"Right now," Jessica insisted as the Impala passed alongside Sandpiper Cover apartments.

Christopher slumped sideways in his seat, placing both index fingers in his ears, quietly voicing his displeasure at the fireless war of words.

"My Cadillac's around PennySavers." Shakey watched a group of small boys as they tossed an airless football back and forth.

"We'll go and get it." Jessica rolled to a near stop at the corner of Forty-third and Winnie before making a left turn.

Shakey's eyes were riveted to his rearview mirror. As suspected, the patrol car that had been parked behind the beat-up green Ford LTD was now trailing the Impala.

Before having even the chance to worn Jessica of the cop's presence, the blue and red lights whirled atop the car.

"Fuck!" Shakey exclaimed.

"Oh, shit!" Jessica nerves made it difficult for her to pull the car to the side of the street.

"Just relax." Shakey reached to her side of the car and killed the ignition, glad that he had left the pistol he carried in the glove compartment of the Cadillac.

"I don't have a driver's license," Jessica whispered while eyeing the approaching officer.

"Don't worry about it." Shakey faced forward.

Christopher's heart sank. He and Officer Bluitt knew each other quite well.

Three taps to Jessica's window with his billy club was the first communication from the tall, blonde officer.

Officer Gary Bluitt looked a long while at Jessica before speaking, silently simmering upon site of the beautiful redhead driving the car of Galveston's most infamous scumbag. "License and registration." The officer's demeanor was a brisk New Year's Day on Mars.

"I don't uh . . ." Jessica stammered while reaching over both Christopher and Shakey to reach into the glove compartment.

"What?" The officer frowned.

"It's my car," Shakey told the officer what he already knew.

"Yeah." The blue-eyed officer smirked, took a step back from the car, feigning admiration while observing the classic Impala, finally spitting on the ground in disgust. "License and registration." He scowled at Jessica.

Shakey took the vehicle registration from the glove compartment and handed it to Jessica.

"License," Bluitt demanded after snatching the vehicle registration from Jessica.

"I don't have one." Jessica's voice broke with nervousness.

"What's your name?" Bluitt took a small notepad, along with a pen from his top shirt pocket. "Birth date?" After finishing with Jessica, the officer looked to Shakey.

"You know my name," Shakey snapped.

"Damn right I know your name! What's with the juvenile delinquent?"

"Fuck you, Bluitt!" Christopher responded, instantly forgetting the civilized person he had become.

"What'd you say crack baby?" Bluitt leaned closer to Jessica's window, obviously enjoying the bantering with the child.

"I said—" All but the very beginning of Christopher's reply was muffled by the firmness of Jessica's hand against his mouth. "Mutavukka."

"That's enough, Christopher," Jessica chastised.

"Hmph." Bluitt sounded through the smile that still framed his face. "Wait here until I run a check on you," he told Jessica.

"What's gotten into you, Christopher? You don't talk to police officers that way."

"He always trippin'." Christopher felt that his explanation gave total justification to his actions.

"Aren't you going to say something?" Jessica turned to Shakey.

"'Bout what?" Shakey was disinterested.

"About the disrespectful way Christopher spoke to that police officer."

"Bluitt?" Shakey viewed the John Wayne wannabe through his rearview mirror.

"Yes, Officer Bluitt." Jessica was obviously disturbed by Shakey's nonchalant attitude toward Christopher's recalcitrance.

"Fuck him." Shakey turned the mirror away from the patrol car, confident by the officer's body language that he was in no real danger.

Jessica shook her head in disgust.

Officer Bluitt slammed his door and strolled slowly back in the direction of the Impala.

Jessica rolled her window down again in anticipation of the officer's instructions.

"Ms. Reardon," he rapped the billy club against his palm. "I'm afraid I have to take you in."

"What?" Jessica couldn't believe her ears.

"For no driver's license?" Shakey asked.

"Nope." Blue-eyes opened Jessica's door as another patrol car arrived on the scene. In this car were two officers; one was a female. "Seems Ms.Reardon has a habit of lifting things that don't belong to her."

"What are you talking about?" Jessica eyes watered while stepping from the car.

"You have an outstanding warrant for shoplifting, Ms.Reardon—a Class A misdemeanor in this state."

Jessica turned to Shakey for help.

"I'll come and get you." The fear in her eyes caused Shakey to laugh. "Quit trippin'!"

"This isn't funny," she told him.

The reinforcement officers approached swiftly, drawing their billy clubs in unison, looking for all the world like a choreographed dance team.

"What ya got?" the burly, bush-haired male officer asked Bluitt.

"Right now just an outstanding warrant for shoplifting." Bluitt pointed a finger at Jessica then motioned with his head at the Impala. "There's bound to be more." Bluitt was sure. "Much more."

The attractive thirty-something female officer bent forward at the waist to get a better look inside the car. She lifted the visor on the front of her hat a few inches then pulled it down as the cool air sent chills through her long brown hair. "Jonathan Reed." The female officer spoke as if utterly surprised to see Shakey. "You still runnin' whores?" She sized-up the redhead standing beside the car.

"I guess you can pat her down and put her in my car," Bluitt said to his female coworker. Turning to her partner, he added "We'll search the car."

"Gimme the dope." Christopher tapped Shakey's leg.

"What?" Shakey grinned.

"I'ma take the case."

"Ain't no case to take, ya li'l fool." Shakey chuckled.

"All right ,Shakey, you and the juvenile delinquent step from the car," Bluitt instructed.

"I don' told yo' ass about playin' with me, Bluitt," Christopher fussed while climbing from the car.

"Shut up!" Bluitt had the passenger side door wide open, already leaning inside the car.

"Chill, baby." Shakey urged Christopher to be quiet; now wanting only to end the inconvenience as soon as possible.

"Come with me, girlfriend." The female officer led Jessica to Bluitt's patrol car. Once at the car, the officer conducted a quick pat search before opening the rear door and pushing Jessica inside.

Shakey watched as the two male officers tore at the inside of his Impala, the rage building steadily as the violation progressed. Simmering in the three decades of anger, distrust, and hatred his heart bestowed for police officers while directly to his right, the constantly recycled seeds germinated in the mind of nine-year-old Christopher.

A silver-haired man, clothed in civilian attire and bearing crinkled weather beaten skin, approached the holding tank. He wore black horn-rimmed glasses and beckoned for Jessica to join him at the opposite end of the corridor.

Jessica had been a resident of the City Jail's holding tank for two hours now. She was huddled in the corner of the bench along the north wall, her arms tucked inside the sweater she wore. She looked helplessly at the slew of drunken and battered bodies strewn across the floor, lying between herself and the gate.

"Let's go, missy. I don't have all damn day," the man snapped with impatience.

Jessica stood slowly, carefully stepping over the catatonic bum nearest her before hopping over another. Her second trip to Galveston City Jail was already proving to be just as unpleasant as the first; and while Jessica was unable to completely capture in words her feelings pertaining to the co-ed house of horrors that was the City Jail holding tank, the adjectives disgusting, horrid, and filthy were amongst those that immediately sprang to mind.

After having successfully navigated the obstacle course filled with slumbering bodies, Jessica reached for the gate. The sounding of the buzzer just a second before her hand touched the gate, assuring her of no further impediments to her progress.

"What's the matter?" The older man was quite proud of his obnoxiousness. "You act like you're not very fond of our fine establishment."

Jessica shook her head.

"Well quit stealin'," the old man said loudly.

A scatter of laughter came from the uniforms seated behind the desk to Jessica's left.

"Right this way, missy." The man pointed to a small room located just a few paces down the dimly lit corridor. The light was on, and the door was open.

Jessica moved toward the room as instructed. While passing the man, she noticed his eyes being carefully trained to her own backside. Her entire body shook with nervousness.

"Jessica Reardon," the man called Jessica's whole name while closing the door behind them.

The sound of the clicking lock caused Jessica's heart to ignore a full cycle of beats.

"My name is Mr. Hopson, and it is my job to photo and fingerprint you," the old man explained. "But then a working girl like yourself already knows all that."

Jessica backed into the corner farthest from Mr. Hopson.

"I guess we'll print you first." Mr. Hopson neatly arranged the print cards on the table; normally choosing to photo the accursed first, it was Mr. Hopson's desire for closeness to the redhead that led him to shuffle the normal order of procedure "Well, c'mon, missy."

Jessica didn't budge, suddenly feeling the full intensity of the terror she had nearly forgotten. The constantly shrinking room grew cold and dark as the hideous monster turned to face her. Jessica thought she would faint when the man took a step in her direction.

"Christ Almighty," Mr. Hopson yelled. "I get all the damn psych patients!"

The civil employee stomped angrily in Jessica's direction. The tortured young woman attempted further retreat, but found the wall unmoving.

"C'mon here." Mr. Hopson reached to grab Jessica's arm.

Jessica forcefully jerked her arm away.

"I'm tellin' you, missy, you don't want trouble with me," Mr. Hopson threatened with a right index finger positioned just inches from the tip of Jessica's nose. "Now let's get this done with and go on."

Jessica's back was attached to the wall.

"Some people, I tell you." Mr. Hopson placed both hands on Jessica's shoulders and pulled forward.

"Leave me alone!" With a rage borne of one long suffering of fear, pain, and mental torment, Jessica bull-rushed the much larger man. "Noooo!" She screamed, kicked, and clawed the overwhelmed man.

Mr. Hopson fought to push the lunatic woman from atop of him, but she possessed the strength of ten NFL linemen.

Jessica pounded the man's head with her fist before reaching for the metal contraption that held the fingerprinting cards. She swung at his head with all her might, barely the missing dodging man.

"Hey!" Mr Hopson was just now realizing the extent of the danger he was in. "Somebody help," he yelled loudly.

Jessica continued to swing the machine. Fortunately for Mr. Hopson, he was able to cover up, effectively absorbing the punishment she inflicted with his arms and hands.

"What the hell?" Jessica was vaguely aware of the shrieking female voice.

Moments later, a half-dozen uniforms infiltrated the room. The female officer grabbed a handful of Jessica's hair, pulling hard while one of her co-workers wrestled the weapon away from her. A second later, the hair-pulling brunette had Jessica in a choke hold and though Jessica fought gallantly, the brunette's grip was firm. Jessica's last vision before losing consciousness was that of Stan, standing over her, accompanied by his drinking buddies, laughing and teasing as they prepared to have their way with her.

"Damn homeboy." David leapt from the wrecker truck and observed the Impala. "You musta' really pissed them boys off."

"Fuck them mothafuckas!" Shakey was really in no mood to discuss his latest run-in with the Galveston police department. "You gotta phone on you?"

"Yeah." David climbed just far enough inside the wrecker truck so that he could grab the cell phone from the dashboard. Before turning to Shakey, he lashed out at Fred, who was still seated comfortably in the wrecker truck's passenger seat. "What you waitin' for, crackhead mothafucka? A summons from the judge?"

"I was just tryin' to see . . ." Fred lost his train of thought once remembering the uselessness of his defense.

"Tryin' to see what?" David slammed the door, now staring through the window at Fred, somehow able to strike a pose that suggested danger from his one-hundred thirty pound frame. "Get yo' sorry ass to work. Now!"

Shakey almost laughed when accepting the phone from David. His regard for Fred's feelings kept him straight-faced.

Shakey quickly dialed the number to Allied Bail Bonding, turning his back to his pitiful looking car. "Rebecca?"

"Yeah." Rebecca was an attractive Hispanic woman in her thirties. She had been an employee of Allied Bail Bonding since finishing high school.

"Hey, baby."

"Shakey?" Rebecca's voice registered the pleasant surprise of hearing Shakey's voice before her demeanor quickly changed to one of guarded curiosity. "What's the problem?"

"What makes you so sure there's a problem?" Shakey spoke softly.

"I'm a bails bondsman, Shakey," Rebecca laughed.

"OK, OK," Shakey conceded. "I need a favor."

"Uh hmm."

"Jessica Reardon." Shakey gave her only the essentials. "Theft." He then asked. "Can you get her for me? I'll straighten you later."

"Jessica?" Rebecca repeated.

"Right."

"I guess I can do that," Rebecca told him.

"Thanks, Rebecca."

"You better bring my money." Rebecca was well-versed in the non-sensical behavior of Jonathan Reed.

"I will." Shakey promised then said. "If you need me at all, call me at 767-5967." Shakey knew David's cell phone number by heart.

"Anything else?" Rebecca asked.

"I love you," Shakey answered.

"Whatever." Rebecca hung up.

Shakey hung up the phone and handed it back to David. A little calmer now, he could now discuss the events of the last hour. "Damn, they fucked my shit up!" Shakey stepped closer to the Impala.

"You damn skippy, homeboy!" David shook his head at the car. The interior of the Impala was a mess. The dashboard and steering wheel had been disassembled. The seats had been cut, and a dog had been allowed to track mud everywhere. As a final insult, the Labrador Retriever was given the order to urinate in the driver's seat. "Yo' shit fucked up!" Bluntness was the only approach in David's repertoire.

"When can you have it ready?" Shakey asked.

"Coupla days." David took a closer look. "Gimme through the weekend; you ain't in no mood to talk price, so we'll worry 'bout that later."

The phone rang before Shakey could respond. "Hello."

"Shakey." Rebecca's voice was much more serious than was normal for her.

"Yeah."

"Looks like Ms. Reardon is a little more serious about this crime thang than you gave her credit for."

"What you mean?"

"Aggravated assault on a police officer," Rebecca told him.

"What?" Shakey couldn't believe his ears.

"Yeah. I checked, double-checked, then checked again. The bail is $100,000."

"Fuck!" Shakey was completely baffled. "Ten gees to bounce?" Shakey was talking more to himself than he was asking a question.

"That's right," Rebecca answered anyway.

"Go get her."

"What?"

"Go get her." Shakey didn't waver. "I got you."

"Must be that whip appeal," Rebecca quipped.

Shakey smiled but declined a response, choosing simply to hang up the phone without further comment. He wondered to himself how Jessica could end up with such a serious charge and was even more puzzled by his own decision to cough up ten thousand dollars to gain her release.

CHAPTER 16

Christopher awakened with a rush, his body still running full-speed in a desperate effort to escape his machete-wielding father. He sat momentarily at the edge of the bed, the physical changes that accompanied his panic beginning to stabilize as he wiped at the sweat on his forehead, relieved upon remembering that for now he had no reason to fear the drunken violence of Winston.

The barefooted young boy shuffled across the floor toward his bedroom door. Once in the living room, he stopped close enough to the entertainment center to see the time: 7:45 A.M.

Christopher stepped toward the fish tank that was home to the Chinese Beta. He reached for the fish food that lie atop the tank, opened it, and sprinkled a generous amount of the bottle's contents into the water. He watched as the Chinese Beta devoured the meal with quick, powerful stabs that made chunks of food disappear at one time. Enjoying the Beta's feeding time almost as much as the fish, Christopher was tempted to heap another serving onto the surface of the water, however, he had been well-counseled by Shakey in regards to the dangers of overfeeding.

Christopher's thoughts were of his mother now as he returned the food container to its proper place. He feared for her safety and both loved and missed her dearly.

Christopher's next thoughts were of Shakey and Jessica. He quickly climbed the stairs and headed in the direction of Shakey's bedroom until he stood before the door placing his ear against the portal to be sure he wasn't disturbing the two lovebirds while in the act of knockin' boots before softly turning the doorknob. Once the door was opened wide enough to place his head between the crack, Christopher did so. He found both Shakey and Jessica to be present and sound asleep. All was well.

Christopher closed the door just as softly as he had opened it before heading back in the other direction. This time his destination was the kitchen.

Christopher's eye was on the Fruity Pebbles on top the refrigerator. He hated when Jessica placed the cereal so high, making him feel as small as he actually was.

With the aid of the chair he carried from the dining area, Christopher obtained the box of cereal. A few moments later, breakfast was served. Christopher sat Indian style in front of the television. Bowl in lap, remote in hand, he searched for cartoons. Once he found one, he placed the remote on the floor beside him. Having never known such contentment as he now felt, life in Shakey's home was heaven on earth when compared to life in his own. If not for the absence of his mother, life at Shakey's would be perfect.

"Guess who?" A pair of hands suddenly covered Christopher's eyes.

"That's easy." Christopher giggled. Everything from the smell of Dove bath soap, to the soft melody of her voice, to the gentleness of touch, was uniquely Jessica.

"Well who then?" Jessica kneeled and kissed him on the cheek.

"It's you." Christopher smirked.

"Who?" Jessica hands abandoned his eyes and immediately proceeded to tickle him from both sides.

"You." Christopher giggled.

"Who?" Jessica tickled harder.

"OK, OK, you' gon' make me drop my cereal." The extremely ticklish Christopher giggled uncontrollably. "It's Jessica!"

"Whatcha doin', sweetie?" Jessica sat down next to him.

"Watchin' TV."

"Yeah." Jessica watched the program for a minute or so herself before asking, "Remember the movie you wanted to see?"

"Yeah?" How could he forget.

"Shakey's taking us to see it." Jessica studied Christopher's face for the reaction she knew was sure to come.

"Really?" Christopher jumped so suddenly he came close again to spilling his breakfast. "When?"

"This afternoon. After you finish your cereal, you need to get ready."

"It's only 8:00." Though anxious himself, Christopher saw no reason to prepare now for a movie when the first showing was still four hours away.

"We're going shopping, too," Jessica informed him. "Shakey's already getting dressed, so we need to hurry."

Christopher responded by quickly drinking down the remainder of his cereal and milk. He then leapt quickly to his feet.

"Don't choke yourself, silly." Jessica hugged and kissed him again.

Christopher warmly returned the embrace then ran for his bedroom. Jessica shook her head behind him; he was certainly a handful, and with each passing day, she was beginning to think of him more and more as her own.

"Come on." Shakey motioned to the large round platter that lie open at the center of the table with four slices of pizza left. It was the third platter that had occupied the spot in the last half-hour.

"Uh uh." Christopher sat back in his seat, placed both hands around his now enormous stomach, and shook his head. "I'm full."

"What about you?" Shakey asked Jessica while snatching two of the slices from the platter and placing them on the plate in front of him. "You can't hang either?"

"No, I can't." Jessica had stopped eating quite some time ago. "And I'm not ashamed to say it."

"Thought y'all wanted to eat some pizza." Shakey was already reaching for the third of the four pieces.

"I can't believe he went out like that." Christopher had went on and on about the movie while eating, and now that talking was all there was to do with his mouth, Jessica and Shakey were sure to get an earful.

Christopher was still talking when he, Shakey, and Jessica exited the pizzeria. The three of them walked toward the Footlocker store. It was now time for some serious shopping. Although they had picked up a few things before the movie, all agreed that the heavy shopping should wait until afterward.

Christopher led the way, drawing the immediate attention of the teenage salesgirl dressed in the black and white striped referee's uniform that was standard for Footlocker employees. "What's up, little man?" The fair-complexioned, freckle-faced young lady smiled through heavy metallic looking braces while welcoming Christopher to the store. Although not very fond of the 'little man' moniker, Christopher smiled at her.

"Can I help you with something?" the friendly young lady looked to Shakey and Jessica now.

"The Answer V." Christopher yearned to once again be at the center of the young girl's attention.

Conscious of the youngster's motives, the pretty young girl took Christopher by the hand and led him to the wall containing dozens of tennis shoes. "They're right over here." She smiled to Shakey and Jessica before pointing for Christopher.

"Tight." Christopher slid his hand free from the grasp of the girl then grabbed the shoe from the display stand.

"I know," the salesgirl agreed. "I bought a pair last payday.

Christopher looked at the girl's feet. She sported the latest Jordans. "You got Jordans, too?" Christopher asked.

"I got these the payday before that," the young girl told him.

"How much are these?" Christopher asked.

"$79.95 plus tax," the salesgirl answered, conveniently loud enough for Shakey and Jessica to hear.

"You gotta be kiddin' me," was Jessica's backwoodish profession of amazement, shamelessly displaying her total ignorance in regards to the pricing of basketball shoes.

The salesgirl's hand was a little slow at covering her laughing mouth.

"That's what you want?" Shakey asked Christopher while sharing a laugh with the young girl.

The salesgirl was intrigued with Shakey's smile so much so that she considered asking about the tiny pieces of diamonds that sparkled so brightly within his mouth. She decided against the idea, as she knew any questioning would be bad taste.

"I dunno." Christopher hunched his shoulders. "I like the Jordans too." He pointed at the salesgirl's feet.

"How much are the Michael Jordans?" Jessica was becoming quite hilarious. "A hundred bucks?"

"They're a little more than that." The salesgirl smiled before stepping a few paces to her left, maneuvering around another customer, and grabbing the single Jordan tennis shoe from the display shelf. She then quickly returned, shoe in hand, to her waiting customers. "Which one?" The young girl took the first shoe from Christopher's hand and held them both before Jessica, bracing herself for what she anticipated would be a most entertaining response.

"Which one comes with the guarantee that he'll be an instant basketball star and make us millions of dollars?" Jessica did not disappoint.

"He'll have to take care of that himself," the salesgirl laughed.

"Which one, Christopher?" Jessica asked.

Christopher gave no immediate response, eyeing one shoe and then the other, obviously wrestling with an impossible decision.

"Get 'em both." Shakey figured he'd spare his young partner the mental anguish.

"Both of 'em." Jessica exclaimed. "I know we can expect some slam dunkin' now." This time Christopher, Shakey, and the salesgirl all laughed.

"What size?" the salesgirl asked.

"Five and a half," Christopher answered.

"Better try 'em on," Shakey said to Christopher then did wonders for the young boy's ego by suggesting, "You might be growin'."

"Get them a half-size bigger than you wear." Jessica's words of wisdom caused her to sound twice her age.

"C'mon." Shakey laughed while pulling Jessica in the direction of the rack filled with Nike sweat suits in the far corner.

"Your mama's funny," the salesgirl said to Christopher.

Christopher didn't say a word while feeling an odd satisfaction at having the young girl mistake Jessica for his mother. He inwardly felt that to display that satisfaction would be a blatant betrayal of his real mother.

The salesgirl, totally misreading the cause of the sudden sulkiness that had befallen her young customer, told him, "It's cool, my mama's white, too."

At this Christopher's smile was wide. Though clueless, the salesgirl had made a friend for life.

"Let me get your shoes." The salesgirl presented her braces again. "We'll try a six."

Christopher took a seat. He watched as Shakey took a multi-colored sweat suit down from the rack and held it in front of Jessica. He thought both of how life would be if Jessica and Shakey actually were his parents and of how his life would be different once the present fairy tale was over. The one thing he was quite sure of was Winston's waiting anger.

"Fuck Winston." Christopher thought of the .25-caliber pistol his big homie kept hidden in the bushes alongside the Pirate's Cove apartment complex. Never again did he expect to see the .380 caliber pistol Shakey had taken from him.

"Here we go." The smiling salesgirl returned with the shoes. "I brought sixes and six and a half's."

Christopher untied the laces of his left shoe then allowed the salesgirl to slip the elderly Reeboks from his feet. The six fit perfectly, so much so that both he and the salesgirl agreed that there was no need to try the other sizes.

"I think I might get a pair of these myself." Shakey hovered over Christopher, his and hers Nike sweat suits folded over his left forearm.

"Which ones?" Christopher asked.

"The Jordans, size twelve." Shakey's answer was directed at the salesgirl. He then turned to Jessica. "Find some shoes to go with your sweat suit."

"I wouldn't even know where to start lookin'." Jessica scanned the wall full of shoes.

"Let me bag these, then I'll get the size twelve and I'll assist you if you like," the salesgirl told Jessica all in one breath.

"OK," was all Jessica could say.

"I'ma be stylin' now." Christopher stood to check the profile of his Answer V basketball shoes in the large mirror that had been propped against the chair next to him.

"Yeah, your first day back at school'll be your own personal fashion show."

"School?" Christopher's expressionless face turned to Shakey. He hadn't been to school in over a year, and had no intentions of ever attending again.

"School," Shakey repeated firmly.

"Let me go over here and wait for her." Jessica left on cue. She and Shakey talked for hours last night about Christopher, and both agreed that Christopher needed to be in school. The fact was a simple one to conclude. The challenge would be selling Christopher on the idea.

"Man, Shakey." Thoughts of school were agonizing for Christopher, the institution having become his own personal hell. The other kids hated him and made it a point to remind him often of that fact. The teasing Christopher faced was brutal as every aspect of the child's life became part of the flaming sword used to slice at the core of his already wounded soul. Christopher was ridiculed about his drug addicted mother, who was often seen walking the streets by his classmates. Daily, he was reminded that he was one of the poorest kids in school with no designer jeans, name brand tennis shoes, fresh haircuts, or any other status symbols to endear him to his tormentors. Even his classmates' parents seemed anxious to join the conspiracy against him. A few of them were even cruel enough to pass the rumors on to their own children that Christopher was a crack baby and that his true father was a white man.

Christopher attacked his mistreatment with closed fists. Much smaller than the average kid his age, Christopher received as many whippings as he gave, yet he never stopped fighting. Once the title of troublemaker became synonymous with his name, Christopher was often the only party to suffer punishment for the frequent scuffles in which he participated.

The final episode was March of last year, just two months remaining in the boy's third grade year. A classmate, who Christopher had fought and beaten in the boys' restroom, recruited his older brother, a nice sized fifth-grader, to fight the rematch in his place. After school that very same day, the older boy roughed Christopher up quite thoroughly.

The following day, Christopher returned to school armed with a six-inch buck knife. Spotting the fifth grader in the cafeteria during breakfast, the teary-eyed Christopher, open knife at his side, approached from behind his intended victim. Fortunately for the fifth-grader, a young girl who spotted Christopher long before he was close enough to do any damage, yelled at the top of her lungs, causing kids and staff members to scurry in every direction. Christopher chased his prey all around the chow hall until finally being subdued by a P.E. teacher.

Christopher was expelled for the remainder of the school year, suiting him just fine. Long before the next term was set to begin, Christopher had made the decision to forever forego a return.

"Man, what?" Shakey noted the rising emotion in Christopher's voice. And while quite adamant about getting Christopher into school, Shakey knew that kids like Christopher were not to be made to do anything.

"I don't know about that school shit, Shakey." Christopher had been so successful at refraining from the use of profanity that his present choice of words caught Shakey off guard.

"What's so bad about school?" he finally managed.

"Man." Christopher shook his head slowly. "Them li'l marks gon' be messin' with me, and I'ma have to fuck somebody up." Christopher was quickly running for the defense mechanisms that kids of his background were forced to deploy when the pain and despair that dominated their lives became overwhelming.

"Christopher." Shakey stopped short of scolding, but felt it quite necessary to let Christopher know that his language was unacceptable.

"I know, man, but they be trippin' at school," Christopher protested.

"But you'll be goin' to another school," Shakey reasoned. "You'll have a fresh start."

"What other school?"

"Once I get the OK from your mama for you to stay with me, I'll enroll you.

Christopher was admittedly encouraged by the prospect of a new school, and enormously excited with the idea of being with Shakey and Jessica for good. Yet his mind was able to immediately locate the one major hurdle to it all. "What if my mama says no?"

"Let me handle that," Shakey assured him.

"I dunno, Shakey." Christopher looked to Jessica, who was smiling and talking to the salesgirl. He then looked back at Shakey. Christopher loved the two of them enough to give all that Shakey suggested at try. And enough to be irretrievably broken if things didn't work. "I wanna go, but they might start trippin' too."

Shakey smiled. With three weeks to go until the next semester began, he decided to savor the small progress he had just made and to give the issue a rest for now. "Just think about it, all right?"

"All right." Christopher found Shakey's last words to be a much more grantable request.

Jessica and the salesgirl were still smiling and talking as they made their return. Jessica was holding a pair of multi-colored Nike cross trainers. Green, yellow, white, and black were just a few of the shoes more prominent colors. They were the perfect complement to the green and black sweat suit she had chosen earlier.

Shakey looked around the store, spotting a wall filled with baseball hats. "Say, Chris. Let's scope out the hats," Shakey suggested.

Off the two of them went. Knowing that the salesgirl received a small commission on each sale, Shakey prodded Christopher to choose all sorts of things. Once the finals were tallied, Shakey had spent over twelve hundred dollars, and quite a few stores still remained on their shopping list. One thing was for sure. Christopher's return to school would not be marred by a lack of name brand clothing.

CHAPTER 17

Jessica's eyes opened just as the first rays of sunshine reached the foot of her and Shakey's bed. She lay still a moment more before rising, enjoying the security of the powerful arm that held her close to Shakey's body. She then began the task of peeling herself away from Shakey without waking him.

Jessica placed her own arm under Shakey's, pushing upward just enough for her to roll from underneath. Shakey stirred momentarily, but never regained consciousness.

Once free, Jessica grabbed the house robe from the chair next to the bed and walked softly toward the slightly ajar bedroom door. Once safely in the hallway, she closed the door gently behind her, and then headed for the kitchen. Cooking was beginning to be her favorite early morning pastime.

Jessica pulled a large plastic bowl from the cabinet above the sink. She then reached inside the refrigerator for the carton of eggs. One by one, she cracked six eggs and dropped them into the bowl before remembering the enormous amounts of food Shakey was capable of consuming. With that in mind, she emptied the entire carton's contents into the bowl. After carefully buttering one of two skillets left on the stove the night before, she ignited the flame beneath it.

Next, Jessica grabbed the pack of bacon and slowly separated half the pack from the box, placing the slabs in the second skillet atop a low fire.

While the bacon sizzled slowly, Jessica began to pour eggs into the first skillet.

With the smell of bacon already escaping the kitchen, Jessica began to hum a sweet sounding melody. A song the likes of which was possible only when the spirit was at peace; an odd occurrence in Jessica's life.

While meeting Shakey had provided her for the first time with a man whose attention seemed to be not to her detriment, with Christopher, she found the much needed vessel in which to bestow the heart full of love and tenderness that had been dormant within her for much too long. Together, the two of them had redirected her life from the constantly descending escalator filled with heartbreak and atrocity to a stairway to heaven, lined with womanly duty and purpose. For the first time ever in her life, Jessica knew what life was like when not greeting each new day with dread.

Jessica's heart was warm with memories of the day before. Never had she seen a happier little boy. The joy given to Christopher was in itself enough to cause Jessica to love Shakey forever.

Once the eggs and bacon were finished, Jessica snatched the loaf of bread from atop the refrigerator. She used the toaster to lightly brown ten slices. Without much time to spare, the eggs, bacon, and cheese sandwiches she prepared would have to do until later.

Jessica left the food long enough to wake her slumbering men, heading first for Christopher's room. "Christopher," she called softly while pushing the door open.

Christopher was sound asleep, a single white sheet covering the lower half of his body.

Jessica smiled at her sleeping angel again, disbelieving that this was the little boy that she had witnessed that first day smoking, cursing, and drinking wine, shuddering to think of the environment that could cause such behavior from such a sweet little boy.

Jessica stepped closer, stopping at the side of the bed and kissing Christopher's forehead. Christopher's eyes opened immediately; the smile covering his entire face upon recognition of Jessica.

"It's time to get up, sweetheart," Jessica said softly.

Christopher sprung from the bed immediately, anxious to begin the day. He, Jessica, and Shakey would be driving to Houston to watch the Tors play the Elsik Rams in the Astrodome. "I gotta get ready." Christopher leapt from his bed and ran full speed to the restroom.

Jessica watched with amusement before leaving for her and Shakey's bedroom.

The climate controlled Astrodome was a pleasant relief from the wind and rain that pounded the Houston area throughout the morning. Shakey and Jessica held hands while following an extremely excited Christopher.

"What's the seat number again?" Christopher frantically searched the letter designation of each aisle while traveling the long, paved area located under the seats.

"Aisle K, Row thirty-five." Shakey's smile was from deep within as he sincerely enjoyed the excitement seen in Christopher. "It's right over there." Shakey pointed. Already quite familiar with the Astrodome, he relieved Christopher of the torrid search.

Christopher was instantly at the mouth of Aisle K, bouncing on his toes while listening to the roaring crowd. "Y'all come on. They're startin'." Christopher could barely contain himself.

"You don't wanna get somethin' to snack on while we're down here?" Shakey asked.

"Uh uh." Christopher shook his head. "Come on." He took off running up the concrete ramp, showing running-back like agility in his own right while dodging in and out of pedestrian traffic.

The highly charged atmosphere took hold of them all as the three of them made it to the top of the ramp and hurried for Row thirty-five.

"Let's go, Tors." Shakey clapped loudly.

The crowd was on its feet as the Elsik Rams prepared to kick the ball to the Tors. The frenzied anticipation was measurable in megawatts as Shakey's favorite Tor, Allen Richards, bounced up and down on his toes at the Ball High ten-yard line. The cheers became a deafening roar as the Ram placekicker placed a high, booming kick well over Richards' head, into and through the end zone.

As the Tor offense took the field, Shakey, Jessica, and Christopher were settled in their seats.

On their first drive of the game, the Tor offense found the Ram defense to be quite impenetrable. After netting just one yard on three successive running plays, the Tors were forced to punt.

The game proved to be a defensive struggle, as neither team was able to score in the first half. After three quarters, the two dominating defenses were still knotted in a scoreless tie.

Five minutes into the final period, the Elsik Rams took the lead with a thirty-seven yard field goal. Three minutes later, the Rams were threatening again as their bruising 240-pound fullback powered his way enroute to the sixth first down of the drive with a punishing five yard gain. The result was first and goal at the Tor six yard line.

"C'mon, dee-fense!" Shakey yelled, if only to deceive himself, as it was becoming increasingly apparent that the Tor defense was wearing down fast. "Stand strong, baby!"

On the next play from scrimmage, the ball was not so surprisingly given to the fullback. Number forty-four barreled into the middle of the Tor line, dragging would-be tacklers to the two-yard line.

The Ram fans cheered loudly as the dejected Tor fans stomped their feet and cursed before being consumed by a knowing silence.

On second down, the hammer fell, and the Ram lead was ten to nothing.

"Man!" Christopher miraculously suppressed the itch of vulgarity. "They sorry!"

Shakey sipped from the heavily laced sixteen ounce Coca Cola before looking up at the clock. Only five minutes and forty-five seconds remained. The Tors would need to strike fast if they were to have any chance at a comeback.

As both teams readied themselves for the kick-off, Tor fans vainly hoped for an Allen Richards explosion. Their hopes would turn to boos as the Ram kicker purposely kicked the ball out of bounds, deciding it much better to take a penalty than to allow Allen Richards a chance at a return.

"Coward mothafucka," Shakey mumbled into his cup.

The Tor quarterback picked up ten yards of his own on the drive's first play, and then found his tight-end for twelve more. The third play of the drive was an end around that netted eighteen, and the Tors were in business at the Ram twenty-five with three minutes remaining.

"Yeah! Yeah!" was all Christopher could say while pumping his fist.

Jessica clapped so hard that her hands began to sting "Whew!" She continued despite the pain.

"Let's go, Tors!" Shakey sat his drink at his feet while anxiously awaiting the snap of the ball.

The Tor quarterback dropped back to pass. No receivers were open. He drifted to his right, then took off running with nothing but pay dirt before him. The mirage disappeared quickly as Murphy's Law conspired to ruin the Tors' post season. The Tor quarterback inadvertently bounced the ball off his thigh pad, and the pigskin was loose. His ensuing attempt to field the ground ball resulted in a kick that sent the ball through the back of the end zone. Touchback. Rams ball on the twenty yard line.

"Fuck." Shakey found the only suitable exclamation for the moment.

Christopher folded his arms and sat back in his seat. His eyes quickly filled with tears.

"It's just a game, baby." Jessica stroked the side of Christopher's head.

The bleakest of scenes for the Tors grew darker by the moment.

The Ram quarterback handed the ball to the fullback once again. Number forty-four charged with a full head of steam for the center of the line. Unexpected by everyone, especially the Tor secondary who were collectively conscious only of run support, number forty-four tossed the ball back to the quarterback, who then lofted a high arcing pass that found a wide-open Ram receiver at midfield. With no Tor defender within twenty yards, a touchdown was a foregone conclusion.

But then a purple and gold blur from the opposite side of the field quickly closed the gap between himself and the running Ram. The barely visible number twenty-one on the back of the defender's jersey identified the flashing Tor as none other than Allen Richards.

Richards caught up with the ball carrier at the five-yard line and punched the ball loose from the receiver's grasp.

The crowd took to its feet as Richards ran around the baffled receiver, recovering the ball eight yards deep in his own end zone.

A head fake and sidestep made the receiver a permanent part of Richards' rearview scenery.

Shakey's favorite Tor picked up speed while surveying the position of the Ram's offensive players, a group now presented with the daunting task of tackling the most elusive return man in the state.

Richards ran by one defender before splitting two others. He evaded a fourth defender while running for the right sideline.

"Go! Go!" Christopher had regained his enthusiasm.

Richards cut back to his left at midfield and the foot race was on. Five seconds later the Tor players were celebrating the electrifying one-hundred eight yard fumble return.

The crowd was abuzz with the most exciting high school football play many of them had ever seen.

After the kickoff and a short return, the Ram offense took over at the eighteen yard line with 1:48 remaining on the clock. Two successive run plays resulted in fifteen seconds and two Tor timeouts being burned.

A third run resulted in a one-yard loss, but the Tors were out of timeouts.

The crowd took to its feet as number twenty-one jumped up and down at his own thirty-five yard line. The ticking clock now had forty-two seconds.

The snap of the ball caused the entire stadium to take to their feet. For decades, all present would tell the tale of the tragic decision made by the sixteen-year-old Ram punter.

The low line drive of a kick moved with the speed of a pitched stone as it headed straight for the arms of number twenty-one.

Allen Richards cradled the ball at the Tor forty-five yard line, running full-speed for the crease he had already spotted in the Ram punt coverage team. No Ram player had even a chance at laying a finger on him as he sprinted the Ram half of the field. Touchdown Tors.

The Tor side of the stadium was hysterical, and that included Shakey, Christopher, and Jessica. No one could believe the minute-long Allen Richards show.

The stunned Ram offense threw three incomplete passes before a fourth was picked-off by none other than: Allen Richards.

All that was left was for the Tor quarterback to kneel twice on the ball, and the Ball High faithful counted as the waning seconds on the clocked ticked away. "four . . . three . . . two . . . one," they called in unison before erupting with a collective roar of approval. The Ball High Tors had advanced to the semi-final round of the Texas High School playoffs.

"Cold-blooded, ain't he?" a squat, brown-skinned man seated in the row in front of Shakey turned around.

"Bad boy," Shakey agreed, a smile stretching across his face. He and the fellow Tor fan shook hands.

Shakey watched closely as a handful of the teammates lifted Allen Richards high enough to grab the guard rail that separated the first row of stadium fans from the field of play. With ball in hand, number twenty-one worked to reach a pretty young girl seated in a wheel chair.

Shakey, along with the rest of the Astrodome crowd, clapped softly as Allen Richards held the ball in the direction of his younger sister. The girl had been wheelchair bound since being caught in the cross fire of a drive-by shooting.

The applause, now coming from both sides of the stadium, and including the Ram players, grew in intensity as the pretty young girl in the wheel chair stood and leaned forward in the direction of her older brother. An equally pretty girl, not much older, kept a careful watch at her side.

Shakey thought the building would collapse when the young girl took a half-step forward, followed by a second full step, then a third. Shakey swallowed back his own tears as Allen Richards embraced his younger sister, handing her the football that had been clutched under his right arm.

With a hand from the young girl on her right and the older woman on her left, Allen Richards' younger sister made it back to her seat.

The ovation lasted a full five minutes.

Christopher buttoned the jacket he wore all the time to the chin in response to the not so subtle suggestion given him by the ever-increasing frigidity of the November day. He found himself quite amazed at the excitement he felt as he and Shakey stepped through the gate and under the sign reading HERMAN ZOO.

"Look, Shakey, the baboons!" Christopher, already forgetting the bite of the howling evening wind, broke from Shakey's side and ran to peer inside the baboon cage. "Dang, they big."

Shakey, charged to the height of enthusiasm himself at the happiness in Christopher's voice, quickly took a position next to the young boy. "That one kind of looks like you." Shakey pointed at the most animated of the pack of primates.

"Forget you, Shakey." Christopher quickly moved along.

Shakey followed Christopher en route to the covered walkway leading to the lion cages.

"Don't get too close to the cage," Shakey joked. "You wouldn't be but a biteful for the king."

"The king?" Christopher was unimpressed by the sluggish looking creature lying just a few feet before him, tail wagging lazily, basking in what little warmth the fast descending sun still provided. "King of what?"

"King of the jungle." Shakey had always been a big fan of the lion. In his opinion, the lion was the only creature of God truly deserving of the title of pimp. He stepped closer to Christopher and the cage, not that the lion's lair had any resemblance to a cage. Designed to provide a habitat as close as possible to the lion's own, the lion's lair was complete with two lionesses and a litter of cubs that peered curiously from the edge of the rack structured cave. "That's a bad boy you talkin' down on."

"He ain't nothing." Christopher jumped at on the concrete border surrounding the cage. With both hands clinging to the bars, Christopher caused Shakey more than just a bit of nervousness. "I ain't scared of no big cat."

"Grrrr." The threatening roar of the lion turned into the laziest of yawns.

"Shut up, punk!" Christopher challenged the king of the jungle.

"Grrrr!" In the blink of an eye, the once compla-cent lion was on his feet and moving toward the spot along the bars where Christopher was stand-ing.

"Shakey!" Without turning around, Christopher leapt straight back into Shakey's arms. "Come get him." Shakey, with frightened little boy in his arms, stepped in the direction of the lion's cage. "Noooo!" Christopher kicked his feet frantically. "Put me down, Shakey!"

"But you so bad." Shakey finally placed Christo-pher on his feet a safe distance from the lion's cage, sharing a laugh with the handful of witnesses to the fear exhibited by Christopher.

"Wasn't nobody scared." The swagger had re-turned to Christopher's walk as he strolled in the direction of the hyenas.

"What?" Shakey stomped a foot behind Chris-topher, and the boy was off and running. The small crowd of zoo-goers busted at the seams with laughter.

Jessica finally rolled over. She was alone in the large Marriott hotel suite, yet for once not lonely.

Jessica shut her eyes tightly in an effort to squeeze the last remnants of peace-filled sleep in which she had just been blessed. Blessings it seemed were now abundant in her life.

Jessica envisioned the beautifully white wed-ding dress that had filled her dreams. She smiled along with the thousands of guests that came to

witness her and Shakey's vows of lifelong matri-
mony. Her fantasy was suddenly interrupted by the
fullness of her loudly protesting bladder.

Life with Shakey to love and Christopher to care
for had rapidly grown to be much more fulfilling
than anything Jessica could have imagined. The
years of misery, suffering, and pain were now a
part of someone else's past as Jessica was more
than happy to live in the contentment of the here
and now. She was graciously aware of the fact that
the evil the world had shown her had done nothing
to extinguish her capacity to love.

Regrettably, nature's call refused to go unanswered as Jessica was forced to abandon the warmth
and security of the king-sized bed to embark on a
short, barefooted journey to the restroom.

Jessica reached inside the open door, running
her hand along the wall until finding the button
that provided luminance for the restroom before
entering. She was admittedly apprehensive in regards to darkness.

A glimpse in the mirror slowed her from her
final destination. Jessica turned to face the looking glass head on. She smiled at seeing that which
had never before been revealed to her: beauty, and
not just of a physical sort. Jessica saw the extreme
beauty of a woman who had endured the unthinkable. The beauty of a woman who now believed
in the reflection smiling back at her. She saw the

beauty of God's promise of a much brighter tomorrow. The glowing beauty of a woman loved.

Shakey and Christopher entered the double swinging doors leading to the large aquarium with the multitude of sea life. The last two hours had been spent viewing an assortment of members from the animal kingdom, from the colorful brilliance of the flamingo, to the stunning gracefulness of the gazelle. From the menacing stoicism of the mighty-jawed crocodile, to the hilarious cunning of the chimpanzee. It was a day well-filled and enjoyed with both Shakey and Christopher agreeing that the aquarium would mark the end of their exploration.

Shakey watched with amusement as Christopher and a girl who appeared about his age smiled at each other. "Mack Daddy," Shakey teased.

"Quit playin', Shakey." Christopher's smile was wide.

"Get her phone number," Shakey urged him on.

"What I'ma do with her phone number?" Christopher adamantly denied any interest in the pretty little girl.

"So you can call her."

"I don't wanna call her." The pint-sized actor frowned as if his head was filled with grotesque images. His countenance reconnected itself instantly, however, as he and Shakey turned in the direction of the still smiling little girl.

Christopher wondered while watching the repetitive, over-the-shoulder peeks of the little girl, if she and her mother were having the same discussion.

"Chicken," Shakey teased.

"Ya got me bent, fool." Christopher laughed aloud.

"Make your move then."

"Uh uh." Christopher's shaking head spoke volumes louder than his unsteady voice.

"Don't be scared."

"I ain't scared of nothin'," Christopher argued, then said, "I just don't know what to say."

"Why didn't you just say so?" Shakey had already figured as much.

Christopher's reply was a shrug.

"Look at the swordfish." Shakey moved closer to the glass wall of the aquarium.

"Quit playin', Shakey." Christopher knew exactly what Shakey was doing.

"What?" Shakey's was the face of true innocence.

"Tell me."

"Tell you what?"

"How to talk to girls." Christopher couldn't believe his own words.

"Ohh." Shakey's mouth opened wide. "You ready to learn about mackin' to the honeys."

"Be quiet, Shakey." Christopher looked all around him before pretending to observe the fish-filled tank.

"My bad." Shakey's voice was now but a whisper. He was thoroughly enjoying the time spent with Christopher. "Check it out." He hesitated while scanning the room for eavesdroppers.

"C'mon!" Christopher was nervous with anticipation.

"Look," Shakey told him. "Boldness."

"Boldness?"

"Yeah." Shakey scanned the room again, this time searching for the prop to reinforce his point. "Watch this."

Christopher's pulse quickened while watching his hero approach an attractive, blue jean and blouse clad woman from behind. The boy walked in the man's tracks, determined not to miss a thing.

Shakey reached forward and gently pinched the woman on the elbow, responding to the menacing sneer she aimed in his direction with an ultra confident. "What's up?"

"You gotta problem?" The sneer covered the nose of the beautiful mocha-colored sister, and Christopher began counting the moments until the slap that he knew was coming.

"No problem at all." Shakey was unflappable.

"You must have a problem." The woman redirected her eyes to the aquarium, but not before adding, "putting your hands where they don't have any business."

Shakey turned to Christopher, who was quite unimpressed with his hero's technique. After returning the face full of doubt that came from his faithless disciple with a still confident smile, Shakey pinched softly on the elbow of the woman once again.

"Boy, what do you want?" The young woman's frown was venomous.

"What's up?" Shakey spoke just as calmly as before.

The first chink in the young woman's armor was obvious when the corners of her mouth curled upwards for just a moment. "Look." The frown reappeared. "You need to go look at some fish or somethin', 'cause you are getting on my nerves."

"I didn't mean to get on your nerves, baby." Shakey stepped closer to the woman, pausing briefly when he was as close to the woman as possible without touching, then finally pressing himself against her.

"I know you lost your damn mind now!" the woman snapped but didn't move.

Christopher, breath coming in gasps now, stepped far enough to his left to gain the perfect view of show.

"I just wanted to see if you were as soft as I thought you were." Shakey's mouth grazed the back of the woman's ear.

"You about to get maced." The woman fumbled with the purse dangling from her shoulder.

"Hold on, baby." Shakey wrapped his arms around her, placing both of his hands atop of hers.

"You ain't gotta mace me." He squeezed gently, moaning softly into the ear of the stricken young woman. "Just let me get a number to call, and I'm outta here."

Another long moment passed before either of them moved a muscle. Finally, the woman pulled away. She turned to face him then reached inside her purse without speaking. She scribbled her number on the small notepad inside the purse. She handed the folded piece of paper over with a smile.

Shakey looked at what the woman had written. "Ki Ki," Shakey mouthed while watching the smitten woman walk away. Once she had left the aquarium area, he turned to Christopher.

"You crazy, Shakey." Christopher was finding it hard to believe all he had just witnessed.

"Here." Shakey gave Christopher the number. "Let's find you a honey."

"Yeah." Christopher was confident now that he could use "boldness" the way Shakey had, sure that he would someday be the player his hero was.

CHAPTER 18

The moon was still high in the sky as the sun made its first peek from the bottom corner of the east horizon. Seated on the stairs leading to the deck he had himself built onto the back of his home, Shakey puffed lightly on a Swisher, watching the night's retreat from the rapidly advancing daylight finding a God-like peace in the stillness of the early Thanksgiving morning.

Shakey had awakened in the middle of the night and was unable to secure a second ride to slumber land. Not wanting to disturb Jessica, he donned a pair of shorts and T-shirt, stepped into a pair of Nikes, and after peeking in on Christopher, headed for the back porch.

The stirring started days ago, and had grown into the burning fire in the pit of his belly that one felt when enduring radical shifts in personal philosophy—shifts that for all practical purposes rendered a man a completely different creature.

Shakey thought it funny how as a young boy he had become so enraptured with the paradigm of optimism. To heart did he take every word of encouragement and promise of opportunity that he had been given. How deeply did he believe as a young boy that good would always conquer evil? How readily did his daydreams manifest his unwavering belief in the great life that would be his? How reasonable it had sounded to him when a middle-age white youth basketball coach told him he could rise from the jungle streets of Galveston, Texas, and keep rising all the way to the post of Commander-in-Chief of the most powerful nation on the planet? Only time, the boy Shakey surmised, separated him from the big house with the back yard swimming pool, a well paying job that would make him a well respected pillar of the community, and most importantly, a beautiful wife and family. Family not just in word, but in thoughts, feelings, and actions.

The world honors not the childish dreams of innocence. The reality of Jonathan Reed's childhood was a horror story that would have hardened the hearts of the most dedicated Christian martyrs. The flames of optimism that fueled the young boy's hopes and dreams for the future had been slowly extinguished by the evil of never enough. Never did there seem to exist the love and encouragement needed to sustain the life of the boy's adolescent dreams. Never did there seem to be, after his younger siblings were provided for, any resources remaining to address Shakey's material needs. Never, it seemed, would God grant any relief from the torture that was his very existence.

Anger, bitterness, and hatred are the last lines of defense for the chronically mistreated, and the teenaged Shakey quickly constructed an impenetrable fortress. The world was fucked, and nothing could change that fact.

While in prison, Shakey began again his longing for the American dream. Even, against all logical reason, convincing himself that the dream was still an attainable one for him. And upon his release, for a short time, his most desired dreams gained fruition. No longer desiring the money, cars, and jewelry that had first served to distract, then permanently stagnate his entire generation, Jonathan Reed, the man, desired only the titles of husband and father to secure his happiness. But happiness in a world full of Jorgé Trevinos would always be a short-lived phenomenon.

The Handsome Intimidator peered into the sky. The last of the stars were invisible now, and the moon stood shoulder to shoulder with the much larger sun.

Shakey loved Jessica. A fact he dared not mention lest he tempt the fates to crush the last of the pebbles which had once served as his heart.

He loved Christopher too. And though he knew better, having long since abandoned any hopes of happiness, he found himself truly believing that the three of them together could truly be happy; not only believing, but at this very moment committing himself to the idea of the three of them fused together forever as a family.

And so it was from optimist, to cynic, to fool, the metamorphosis was complete.

Shakey pressed the Swisher against the hardwood floor, putting it out before throwing the butt in the yard. He smiled to himself before returning to bed, amused at the thought of how good Baby would look in his backyard.

"He did it." Michelle flicked the ashes out of the Nissan Pathfinder while leaving the Kroger parking lot.

"Think so?" Her passenger, Jorgé Trevino, had already concluded as much. It was the physical evidence that Michelle could possibly obtain that interested him.

Michelle nodded while rolling to a stop at the intersection of Sixty-ninth and Broadway. Despite the intense hatred of Shakey she was sometimes able to summons, she did not enjoy what she was doing. She did not cooperate with policemen, especially Jorgé Trevino. Yet unlike everyone else in the life of Jonathan Reed, she would not allow all that was dear to her to be destroyed to prove her loyalty to a man who cared only for himself.

"Red drove the car?" Jorgé really didn't have to ask. Whenever Shakey was involved in something that could earn him a life sentence, Red would be there to play A.C. Cowlings to Shakey's O.J. Simpson.

No response as the Pathfinder began moving again. Michelle would not implicate her husband.

"What do you know?" Trevino asked in a way that made it quite clear what he wanted.

"What do you know?" he had asked to mean, "What can you prove?"

"The car came from David Irving," Michelle spoke easily. "The gun could have come from anywhere."

"Where's the car now?" Trevino sensed the closeness of the much-needed breakthrough.

"Chop shop," Michelle relayed somberly, knowing that a barrier had been reached.

"Damn." Trevino pounded a fist into a palm. He knew that the doom he so desperately desired for Shakey was within grasp. He would not be denied.

Trevino reached into the pocket of the coat he wore, grabbing, then placing in his lap, a small gold case, flipping it open so Michelle could see the small mound of white powder. Next he grabbed the small straw that matched the case, and after using the razor blade to separate a line, he ingested it with two short, powerful inhalations.

Michelle wheeled left on Forty-fifth Street.

"Here." Trevino offered to Michelle the case and all of its contents.

Before her brain could formulate the protest for her mouth to voice, she had already grabbed the open case and placed one end of the straw at the opening of her left nostril, bending forward at the waist, just far enough to allow her to snort her first line of cocaine in nearly a decade.

"Red drove the car." Trevino knew that Michelle would clam up whenever presented with the issue of her husband driving the getaway car in a double homicide, but he also knew that it must be made quite clear to her that unless some other compelling evidence was produced that would assure Shakey's conviction, Red's testimony would be needed.

Michelle pulled into the Chevron gas station at the corner of Forty-fifth Street and Avenue S. The first line she snorted felt so good that she fixed herself a second before closing the case.

Trevino re-opened the case, tooted another line himself, then turned to Michelle, noticing for the first time the long, gentle smoothness of the large, shapely black legs that showed below the hemline of the flower print dress she wore. A most pleasant side-effect, Trevino's cocaine use had always caused in him a greatly increased sexual appetite.

"Look, it's Shakey I want, not Red." Trevino placed the gold case on the dashboard and leaned in Michelle's direction. He placed a hand on the inside of Michelle's leg, just below the knee, then slowly traveled north. "I know we can come to some type of understanding."

Michelle's hand clamped onto the narcotic officer's wrist, peeling it from her thigh and slamming it against the dashboard. Then after jamming both hands squarely into the officer's face, the housewife and mother of three shoved him with the strength and explosiveness of an NFL lineman. A loud thud resonated throughout the vehicle as the back of Trevino's head blasted into the door.

Trevino gasped at the menacing scowl that covered the surface of Michelle's dark chocolate face, his own face registering the extreme shock of the python that mistakenly attacked the mongoose. "It's like that," Trevino finally spoke. His shock became anger as his composure began to settle.

"Just like that, mothafucka!" Anger was an emotion Michelle could match with anyone.

Trevino used the rearview mirror to fix his tie and straighten his clothes. "Take me back to my car." His tone was business like. "And for the record, how far Red is dragged into this depends on what you can get for me, so I suggest you get to work."

"He's comin' over today," Michelle answered while backing out of the parking lot. In fact, the need to secure the last minute details of their Thanksgiving meal was the excuse she used to get away from home for the time it had taken for the rendezvous with Trevino. "Red invited him and Barbie over to the house for Thanksgiving."

"Barbie?"

"Some white trash bitch he done fell in love with." Michelle's words were broken chunks of red-hot ore.

"Shakey?" Trevino considered the impossibility of such a presumption. "In love?"

"Yeah. Shakey," Michelle snapped. "Trick ass ain't no different than the rest of them niggas!" It was quite unclear whether or not she was speaking to anyone but herself. "Dog out every decent sista he don' ever come across, then try to make a princess out of a crackhead white bitch!"

At this Trevino smiled, knowing surely, though not yet how, that he had just heard the information that would enable him to impale the dagger he had been sharpening for years into the deepest chambers of Shakey's heart.

"You two guys can eat." Jessica disbelievingly watched as Shakey and Red continued to scarf down entire plates of food long after everyone else in the house had eaten to capacity.

"'Round here," Red started between shovelfuls of dressings, "gotta take advantage of a cooked meal when you can." Red had complained greatly of recent in response to what he felt was Micelle's failure to consistently satisfy one of her most important womanly duties.

"Your ass, Red." Michelle was full, and in as good a mood as anyone would ever see.

"Man." Shakey sat back into his chair, his stomach popping two of the buttons on the shirt he wore. "Every Thanksgiving, I'm reminded of what you see in this wench in the first place."

"Fuck you, mothafucka!" Michelle snapped.

Christopher and the entire bunch found Michelle's profanity to be quite hilarious.

"'Scuse me, children," Michelle laughed at herself.

Cedric, the eldest of the twins by six minutes,
ran around the table, stopping at a spot between
Christopher and Jessica. He placed his mouth to
Christopher's ear. "My sista say you got good hair,"
Cedric whispered to his guest.

Christopher looked across the table at the eldest
of the children. Though pretending to study the
remainder of the cranberry sauce on her plate, the
smile she struggled to suppress was plain for all to
see. Christopher leaned to his left in order to take
advantage of the messenger service. "Tell her I said
she do too," he whispered into the five-year-old's
ear.

"Ooh ooh ooh!" Cedric ran around the table yelling loudly. "He say—"

Kashandra popped him quickly on the hand.
"Shh!" was instruction enough.

Still smiling, Cedric relayed Christopher's message to his sister.

Kashandra leaned to give Cedric another message to carry before Malcolm whined, "Let me tell
him this time."

"OK." Kashandra turned in his direction.

After listening closely to his sister's missive, the
younger twin ran around the table and whispered
into Christopher's ear. "My sista say you cute."

"Tell her she cute too," Christopher whispered
in return.

"Ooooooooooooooooh." Malcolm returned to his sister's side. Wary of the pop his brother received, the younger twin didn't have to be reminded to lower his voice before speaking. "He say you is too."

"Kashandra! Y'all go in the backyard and play," Michelle told her.

"Yeah!" the twins yelled in unison as Malcolm grabbed and pulled hard on his sister's arm. Cedric accepted the task of yanking Christopher from his seat.

The quartet of adults found more than just a little amusement in the site of the four kids filing from the room.

"Y'all finished?" asked Michelle, now anxious to clean the table.

"I'm ready for some of that lemon pie," Red answered before turning to Shakey "What about you homie?"

"Sweet potato." Shakey looked at Michelle.

Michelle rolled her eyes then asked Jessica "You want some pie?" The question was filled with a healthy abundance of animosity.

"Lemon." Jessica was beginning to realize that the attitude coming from Michelle wasn't meant for anyone in particular. "A little one." Jessica waited a moment before cheerfully asking, "Need some help?"

"I got it," Michelle answered, turning back.

"It ain't you, Jessica." Red confirmed her already drawn conclusion. "It's just that time of the month."

"Must be that time of the month every time I see that crazy-ass girl," Shakey said then laughed along with Red.

"I think nature reversed her cycle," Red responded gleefully. "She has a period of five good days a month."

Both Shakey and Red laughed loudly. Despite herself, Jessica chuckled softly.

"Fuck y'all mothafuckas if y'all laughin' at me!" Michelle yelled from the kitchen.

The laughing intensified.

Michelle returned, somehow carrying a large saucer in each hand, and balancing two others with the inside of her forearms. After each saucer was placed in front of the correct person, Michelle sat down to indulge herself in a humongous slice of apple pie.

"Ummm." Red bit into his lemon pie. "This is delicious, baby."

"Uh hum." Michelle frowned in her husband's direction.

Both Red and Shakey laughed again, causing Michelle to wonder if the joke that had obviously gone over her head. Refusing to allow them the satisfaction of knowing that she was even the least bit worried with being the obvious object of their amusement, she refrained from comment.

"Let me get a bite of that lemon pie." Shakey's fork encumbered hand traveled in the direction of Jessica's plate. His own pie just a recent memory, his sweet tooth was still active.

"Let that girl eat her pie," Michelle said. "Didn't you have a piece?"

"It's OK," Jessica said, pushing her saucer just far enough to allow Shakey access to "a little piece."

"Greedy ass." Michelle forked a piece of her own pie.

"Ain't it time for your Haldol injection?" Shakey placed the small square in his mouth.

"Boy!" Michelle glared at Shakey. "I almost told you to suck my pussy!"

"Michelle!" Red chastised.

"Don't Michelle me, nigga!" To Jessica, Michelle seemed really angry now "You know I don't tolerate nobody playin' about my emotional problems."

Jessica relaxed when all present resumed their pie eating. She would learn throughout the rest of the day that the hostility which seemed so shocking to her was as normal to them all as smiles and hugs would have been in the Cleaver household.

"Move," Michelle fussed at Red once finally beginning the task of cleaning the table.

Red, pie in hand, slid his chair backward.

"Let me help you, Michelle." Jessica stood and cleared the area of the table used by Shakey.

Michelle stared at the young, pretty white girl, her mind racing in search of a reason to dislike Shakey's latest love interest. Finding none, she finally responded, "OK."

Christopher watched from beneath the towering pecan tree as Kashandra pushed both her younger siblings on the swing set located in the back yard of the home. He listened to the gleefully giggling small boys as Kashandra used more force with each push, sending the twins soaring higher and higher with each swing.

Having finally summoned the needed courage, Christopher stepped forward from the tree, approaching the other children from behind. Before allowing himself time to reconsider, he reached out and pinched Kashandra softly on the elbow. The young girl turned her head slightly, smiling over her left shoulder in response to Christopher's touch.

"What's up?" Christopher mouthed just as coolly as he had seen Shakey do five days earlier. Kashandra's smile grew wider before she finally turned her head back in the direction of her younger brothers.

Christopher watched a few moments more as Kashandra resumed the pushing of the giggling little boys. Confidence soaring, he reached forward once more, again pinching his young love interest on the elbow.

Kashandra's smile grew wider again.

"What's up?" Christopher stuck to the program.

"Come on, Kashandra," Malcolm protested the dramatic decline in the velocity of his swinging. "Push," Cedric added. Kashandra turned her back to Christopher again. Still smiling, she placed a heavy hand in the back of each of the boys.

Filled with the boldness Shakey had spoken of, Christopher stepped closer to Kashandra. Swallowing hard to calm his nerves, he stepped closer, then, a half-step closer, pressing himself against her as he took to his toes in an effort to give himself the necessary height to whisper into hear ear.

With startling speed, Kashandra spun around and struck Christopher with a closed fist. The young boy's nose instantly began to bleed.

"Oooh ooooh, Kasandra bust that boy nose." Cedric leapt from the still moving swing.

"I'ma tell Mama!" The junior twin was next to leap as he followed his brother up the stairs leading to the back door of household.

Christopher stumbled back against the tree, eyes watering as both hand covered his nose. He blinked away tears while fixing his gaze on the girl he had loved just a few moments before.

"Kashandra, what's wrong with you?" Red was the first adult on the scene. Jessica was close on his heels. Shakey, then Michelle brought up the rear.

"Nasty self!" Kashandra scolded Christopher before turning to her father. "Hunchin' on people and stuff!"

"Michelle, get this girl before I strangle her," Red fussed as his first born passed him on the stairs.

"You better not touch my baby!" Michelle snapped at her husband.

Jessica slid around Red's large frame, forcing herself between him and the banister before running down the stairs and across the yard in Christopher's direction. "Aw, baby," Jessica said once she reached Christopher. "Let me see."

Christopher slowly moved his hands, and the blood flowed freely.

"See, Mama? I told you he was bleedin', look!" Cedric pointed as Christopher's injuries became visible. The excited young boy ran down the stairs to get a better view.

"It was loud too, Mama," the younger twin explained. "Bam! I heard it," he added before joining his brother.

Red and Shakey followed Jessica and the twins into the yard while Michelle and her daughter returned to the house.

Jessica dabbed gently at the boy's bloodied nose with the handkerchief she carried in her pocket. She could already see that there would be swelling.

"What happened, killa?" Shakey asked finding it hard not to laugh at his young friend's misfortune.

"Boldness," Christopher fussed at Shakey.

"What'd you do?" Shakey and Red looked amusingly at each other.

"The same thing you did to the lady at the zoo."

At this Shakey laughed loudly, the control he had tried so desperately to maintain now totally shaken. He looked into Jessica's face, finding no humor there. He killed his own smile immediately.

"Can you please get me a clean rag and some ice, Red?" Jessica asked politely.

"No problem." Red was more than thankful for the opportunity to make a momentary escape.

Shakey turned toward the back of the house in a conscious effort to avoid further reprimand. In doing so, his own gaze was drawn to Kashandra's cold black eyes. There he saw the truth. *"She knows."* His mind immediately formed the words that cloaked him in shame. *"Can't be,"* his ear reasoned. *"She knows,"* his soul answered.

CHAPTER 19

The call of the street was seldom ignored, and as much as Shakey had enjoyed the week spent with Jessica and Christopher, the Friday after Thanksgiving brought with it the call.

Shakey slowed to make a left on Thirty-fifth and Broadway. Shortly before 2:00 P.M., his favorite street corner was alive and bustling with activity.

The Cadillac rocked to tune of Juvenile's "She Get it from Her Mama."

The Cadillac whizzed through the intersection of Thirty-fifth and Sealy. Shakey parked alongside the old Lundy's Mortuary standing diagonally across the intersection from the PennnySavers store, far enough away from where he could be standing so as to avoid a search of his car if the corner was rousted.

Shakey reached into the glove compartment, grabbing one of three small brown paper bags, each stuffed to capacity with individually wrapped half-ounce servings of crack cocaine.

"What's up, Shakey?" Butch was first to approach from the stairs of the abandoned mortuary.

The dirty-faced man wore simple brown trousers and an oil-stained T-shirt. He carried a large plastic bucket at his side. "Let me wash your car."

Will, the other half of the famous twosome followed on the shorter man's heels.

"Hook it up." Shakey smiled at the pitiful looking men.

Shakey continued across the intersection of Thirty-fifth Street and Avenue H as Butch and Will quietly went to work on the Cadillac.

"What's up, Shakey?" Smitty leaned far enough back from the driver side window of the burgundy Nissan Maxima to say. "Where the hell you been?" he asked before returning his attention to the white man driving the car. Moments later he pulled away from the vehicle once again. This time the vehicle quickly made its exit. Smitty jammed a handful of money into his pocket.

"I hear it's all good in the hood." Shakey offered Smitty his hand.

"Rollin' like a mothafucka!" Smitty hold him. "You sho' left a nigga stuck out. Where the hell you been?"

"Chilllin' 'round the house." Shakey settled into his spot along the brick wall. "You know how it is."

"Whipped, ain't ya?" Smitty knew exactly how it was.

"Somethin' like that." Shakey showed the gold, diamonds, and rubies.

"Well look here." Smitty was ready to talk business. "Let me get five of them thangs before yo' crazy ass get away from here." Smitty stepped in the direction of the two-story house standing next to the PennySavers store.

Smitty looked toward the door of the house's second level. "Samantha!"

"What!" an attractive light-skinned woman at least a decade older than Smitty shot through the door and leaned over the banister with rollers in her hair.

"Throw me that bag on the TV," Smitty instructed.

"Hollerin' like you done lost yo' damn mind!" Samantha turned toward the door, and every man on the block stopped to watch the shifting of her ample behind in the black satin robe she wore.

"Gimme five good ones, homeboy." Smitty turned his whole body to speak in Shakey's direction.

A few seconds later, Samantha reappeared, dropping a small leather carrying case over the banister and into Smitty's hands.

Smitty's hands were inside the case as he approached Shakey. He wrapped his hands around a large wad of money and handed it to Shakey.

Shakey took the money, and without counting, jammed it deep inside his coat pocket. Reaching inside the other pocket, he withdrew the paper bag.

Shakey grabbed ten of the packages from the paper bag, paying no regard to which he grabbed, as they were all surely identical. "Check these out." He handed Smitty two handfuls of five.

"Good business." Smitty knew from experience that dealing with Shakey was always good business.

Shakey pulled another package from the bag. This one he opened. After breaking about $50 worth of crack from the rock, he resealed the package and gave it to Smitty. "Here you go, fool." Shakey knew that the times he stayed away from the corner were quite rough on Smitty financially.

"There you go, you black mothfucka!" Shakey barely had time to recognize the angry female voice when he felt a small solid club pelt the side of his head.

"What's wrong with you, girl?" Shakey used his arms to shield himself from the raining blows.

"Where's my goddamn baby!" Barbara Ann was furious and rightfully so. She hadn't seen Christopher in over two weeks.

"He's all right," Shakey took a giant step in the opposite direction, placing himself out of striking distance of the woman.

"Where is he, Shakey?" Barbara Ann stood firmly. Though rather petite at 110 pounds, she was as of present an extremely dangerous woman. The picture of intensity, Barbara Ann kicked the slides from her feet and struck a fighting pose.

"I got him, girl." Shakey backpedaled. "I just didn't want Winston to hurt him." Shakey spoke almost as quick as his feet was moving.

"Shakey." The woman stopped her chase, partly because of the silliness she felt, but mostly because despite the stupidity of his actions, she knew Shakey meant her son no harm. "If Christopher's not home by dark, I'm going to call the police."

"Come on, quit trippin'." Sending Christopher back to that environment would destroy him and Shakey knew it. More importantly, he was sure that she knew it also.

"Naw, nigga, you trippin'." Barbara Ann's voice was much calmer now, yet her stance was still solid. "I don' gave you a warnin', Shakey, bring my baby home." She finally turned to leave.

Shakey didn't answer. He knew quite well that his conversation would be meaningless.

"Crazy-ass bitch oughta be glad the boy ain't gotta live in that fucked up house no mo'." Smitty was at Shakey's side, doing what was only expected of a homie from the hood. Taking up for a partner with words or deeds, right or wrong, thick or thin.

"It's chill." Shakey could think of nothing else to say. "I'll think of something."

"Be careful, my nigga." Smitty scratched his beard. "You don't need no bullshit case behind that shit."

"Check this out." Shakey was quite ready to both change the subject and escape the prison-like atmos-

phere of Thirty-fifth and Avenue H. "There's about
fifteen halves left in here." Shakey handed Smitty the
paper bag. "Bring me two twenty-five a packs."

"Will do."

"I'm going to make a move." Shakey offered a
hand.

"Later, fool." Smitty wished his partner would
hang out a little longer, but knew that it was better
to let him go.

Shakey crossed the street from where he came.
Butch and Will scrubbed furiously on the Cadillac,
generating amazing speed as they worked their
way around the car for the umpteenth time.

"Damn!" Shakey covered his eyes with his arms,
feigning the need to fight the glare that came from
the car's shine. "Somebody gon' have a wreck."

"It's ready, baby." Will stood then bent at the
waist to wipe at the rims, popping the rag twice for
effect.

"Let me see what's up." Smitty walked slowly
around the car as if doing an in depth inspection of
the Cadillac's exterior.

With Butch and Will following closely on his
heels, Shakey walked around the car twice, every so
often stopping to view an imagined problem spot.
Without being told, one of the men would spray
and wipe the phantom smudge away. "I guess y'all
did all right," Shakey finally said.

"We do vacuum jobs, too!" Butch was sure to let
his customer know.

"I'm in a hurry right now." Shakey reached in his jacket pocket and grabbed the bundle of money just given to him by Smitty. From within it he searched for, then peeled away, a twenty-dollar bill.

"Did I mention that we also do lawns?" Will spoke in a deep and throaty Texas-sized drawl, not at all ashamed at the light that shined in his eyes while observing Shakey's wad.

"Some other time." Shakey reached in his other pocket for the fifty-dollar chunk of crack cocaine. To have one last bit of fun with Butch and Will, Shakey held both hands outs, palms up and open. In the left hand was the bill and in the right was the crack rock. "Y'all choose which one y'all want".

Will's hands moved instantly faster than anything Shakey ever witnessed, save for Butch's.

"Thank you, Shakey." Butch didn't speak until the crack was tightly closed in his fist. Seemingly oblivious to Will's hand, which encircled the smaller man's wrist.

The Siamese twins turned to leave, forgetting totally the twenty-dollar bill Shakey still held in his hands.

"Nigga, would you let me go?" Butch finally addressed the issue of the human cuff that Will's hand formed around his own wrist.

"You got my dope." Will's eyes were that of a droopy-faced dog.

"Nigga, we smokin' together," Butch reasoned. "You got the pipe?"

"Yeah, I got my pipe." Will's voice belayed his sadness. "But you got the dope."

Will turned to Shakey for the money. "Thank you, Shakey." He accepted the twenty-dollar bill.

"What you actin' like you gonna cry for?" Butch fussed as the two of them headed south on Thirty-fifth Street. "You wanna hold the dope?" Butch stopped walking and held the rock in his direction.

"Yeah," Will answered pitifully, reaching slowly for the rock in Butch's hand.

"Nigga, it don't matter who hold the dope. I told ya we somkin' together anyway." Butch quickly closed his hand, resuming his trek up Thirty-fifth Street.

"Just don't be havin' no seizures and stuff," Will said before obediently following. Shakey laughed loudly at Butch and Will.

Shakey had grown to loathe the antiseptic smell he had associated with hospitals since childhood. Not so much was the smell to blame for his dislike, but as it had been throughout his life, every venture inside a hospital signaled the destruction of someone Shakey had cared for. This time was no different.

The fifth floor of John Sealy Hospital was never as traffic laden as other areas of the hospital. The ICU had very strict rules governing visitation, though Shakey had not much use for rules.

"May I help you?" The pleasantly pump gray-haired white woman manning the nurse's station smiled as soon as Shakey exited the elevator.

"I got it." Shakey walked right past her, looking for all the world as if he belonged.

The large baldhead of the drug dealer craned upward as he found the sign that read "D." He followed the corresponding arrow until reaching room fifteen.

Shakey turned gently on the doorknob, stepping inside the room, then guiding the door closed.

"Rosa," Shakey whispered into the darkness. "Rosa."

"Turn on the light, silly." The weakened whisper that sounded nothing like Rosa chilled Shakey's spine. Shakey was undecided as to whether he should illuminate the room and face the mass of wounds that surely awaited him.

Shakey finally obliged Rosa's request, running his palm along the surface of the wall until finding the light switch. "How ya feelin'?" Shakey asked before looking.

He immediately wished for the darkness once seeing Rosa in the light.

Rosa's head and face was a hideous mass of bruises, cuts, scars, and gauze. Most notably was the long scar just under the gauze on the left side of her head. Thousands of stitches had to have been used on the still unopened wounds.

"How does it look like I feel?" Rosa answered.

Shakey tried to smile, but found it impossible to put on his good face. This was certainly one of the darkest moments of his life.

"I'm OK." Rosa could see Shakey's mental anguish. "You can come closer; it's not contagious."

Shakey's feet moved on their own, placing him in front of the seat next to Rosa's bed. He sat down slowly.

"You in pain?" Shakey hoped that at least she had been well-medicated through it all.

"You kiddin'?" Rosa's voice was weakening even more. "They got some good shit here."

Shakey thanked God.

"I've been going to surgery so often," Rosa said, "I can't tell the difference between when I'm getting prepped for surgery, or when I'm being numbed for the aftereffect."

Shakey's eyes watered shamelessly.

"Trevino." Rosa's voice was fastly fading.

Shakey perked.

"On the case." Rosa's speech was breaking. "Knows what you did, Daddy."

Shakey stood and leaned over Rosa. "What?"

"Vanessa," was all Rosa had the strength to say.

"Man, you know you ain't supposed to be in here." The barrel-chested security guard lumbered through the doorway. "Look at that woman," the brother instructed. "She ain't in no condition to have visitors."

Shakey reached into his pocket while stepping toward the security guard. He pulled the top bill from the wad in his pocket. "Five minutes." He showed the security guard the super sized face of Benjamin Franklin.

"Five minutes." The security guard folded the bill on his way out the door.

Shakey returned to Rosa's side.

"Be careful, Shakey," Rosa told him.

"Don't worry." Shakey leaned and kissed Rosa softly on the cheek. "You just get well, I need you."

Rosa's weakened whimper was the saddest of sounds.

"It's OK," Shakey lied.

"I'm scared, Shakey." Rosa began to cry.

"I know."

"My baby." Rosa cried harder.

"It's all right."

"She ain't got nobody now, Shakey." Rosa cried hysterically. "I'm all she had, Shakey."

"She'll be OK." Shakey made the one promise he was sure he could keep. "I'll take care of her."

Shakey leaned to kiss her once again. Her tears tasted heavily of salt.

Rosa's eyes closed; tightly at first, obviously taking great effort to do so. Shakey wondered if she was in great pain until the tiny wrinkles that covered both eyelids suddenly relaxed and the muscles of her face loosen. He would leave now, knowing that Rosa would need much rest to make a full recovery.

Shakey kissed the resting warrior once more before leaving. His heart heavier than the atmosphere of Venus, the tears flowed freely and constantly from his eyes now. If ever there was any doubt that he had done the right thing at Vanessa's, that doubt was now gone. His only regret: There was no one else to kill.

CHAPTER 20

The gentle sounding whistle of the soft, howling wind provided the perfect background music for the passionate love scene that took place on the sandy shores of Stewart beach. Just inches separated the impassioned lovers from the edge of the constantly rising tide.

The kissing exploded with intensity as Shakey and Jessica both took to their knees. Shakey leaned forward while kissing, gently coaxing Jessica onto her back. The force of the tide's thrust caused the water's edge to massage the side of Jessica's body from the tip of her shoulder to the side of her foot.

Jessica's body burned with anticipation as she reached out to Shakey, every nerve quivering as the fall of his weight bore down on her.

Shakey's right hand slid effortlessly thru Jessica's dampened hair as his own excitement heightened. The feelings she was capable of stirring deep within him would forever be indescribable.

A wave of cool water washed over them, totally consuming the two bodies as they rolled in the wet sand.

From atop of him, Jessica grappled with Shakey's zipper before leaning forward to share another kiss. She leaned farther still to allow Shakey to lift the dress she wore over her waist. There were not panties with which to wrestle. Her readiness allowed for easy entry.

Jessica sat up straight, head tilted back and hips rocking to and fro. The shifting clouds allowed her a brief unobstructed view of the yellow-stained full moon that hovered over them before her own lunar controlled fusion drew to it all conscious thought.

Jorgé Trevino slammed the binoculars against the passenger side door of the black Dodge Magnum. He had seen enough. Jonathan Reed had no right being so happy.

Trevino cranked the ignition and backed out of his stakeout spot. His hands, wet and trembling with anger, guided the racing car as he launched onto Seawall Boulevard.

Though rapidly moving in the opposite direction, Trevino could still see the face of torture. The evil black face of a smiling Shakey taunting Trevino while writhing in ecstasy with the white trash redhead.

The redhead. Trevino thought back to the striking beauty who had demeaned herself by allowing Shakey to touch her. Once again, Shakey had attained that which he did not deserve.

The Magnum screeched to a halt at the red light, marking the merger between Seawall and University Boulevards. Jorgé Trevino reached into the pocket of his trousers for his wallet. Inside was the photograph he wanted.

The distraught narcotics officer peered deeply into the eyes of the man who fathered him. Despite the advancing years, Jorgé Trevino was still afflicted with the same intense yearning whenever viewing the only remaining connection to the man he knew as PaPa.

"What a crazy, mixed-up world we live in." Trevino vainly fought the waters that raged from the spring of his soul. A mixed-up world indeed when good men like his father died in virtual poverty, nobly serving his community, and murderous drug dealers like Shakey obtained the full of their heart's desires.

Fortunately for the world, Trevino mused, there were still protectors of righteousness like himself to eradicate human cancers like Shakey. Now, if only for once in his life, Jonathan Reed would get exactly what he truly deserved.

CHAPTER 21

Jessica hummed a quiet melody to herself while sliding the pan of chocolate chip cookies into the oven. With the glee of a small child stricken with Christmas spirit, she closed the oven door and began to spoon a second pan full with cookie dough. The second pan was Shakey's, who would not return until late in the night, a business trip being the given reason for an absence lasting two full days.

"Christopher," Jessica paused her song long enough to call. "Can you do me a favor, hon?"

"What?" Christopher's eyes never left the floor model television, nor his hands the control pad of the Sony Playstation 3.

"I need you to run to the store and grab a quart of milk."

Christopher pressed the pause button on the control pad, the sweet aroma of baking cookie dough providing all the motivation that was needed. "OK," he said once standing at the kitchen's entrance. "What else?"

"That's it, I guess." Jessica reached for the small purse in the pocket of her housecoat.

"I got it." Christopher turned suddenly and headed for the door.

"Where's your jacket?" Jessica called when Christopher was halfway through the door. "And you need something on your head, little boy," Jessica continued in vain, only the slamming door responding to her scolding.

Christopher kicked the large rock that had somehow made its way onto the Reed family's front porch. A few feet onto the lawn, he kicked the rock again. The young boy continued to kick the rock while making his way along the road leading to the store.

The drone of a car engine eased slowly upon Christopher's left flank. Without much interest, the boy turned to view the dark colored sedan with tinted windows. Stepping to his right just far enough to allow for clear passage. Christopher took another large sidestep once it became evident to him that the driver of the sedan had no intention of passing.

The passenger side window came down and the unfamiliar face of a middle-aged white woman peered over the top. "Christopher," she called with mechanical compassion.

Survival instincts working on full throttle now, Christopher backpedaled slowly. Christopher peeked over the white woman's shoulder and saw the deeply lined faced of Beasley Reese, the black officer heading Galveston County's warrant division. At this sight, the boy turned to run for the house, inadvertently stepping on the rock that had masqueraded as a soccer ball, and twisting his ankle.

Both doors of the sedan opened, and Christopher's pursuers ambled in his direction.

Christopher was on his feet again, the pounding in his chest sending shards of pain to his injured ankle. Ignoring his discomfort, Christopher ran for the house.

The pursuers gave chase, fully intent on the young boy's apprehension.

Christopher sprinted full speed across the lawn now screaming, "Jessica," paying no mind to the curious stares of Mr. and Mrs. Bouldin.

Christopher ran through the door, shoving the fast swinging portal into the wall, startling Jessica.

"Christopher!" Jessica started from the kitchen.

Christopher never broke stride as he turned the corner from the house's front entrance, sprinted through the living room, and made his way toward the kitchen.

Jessica stepped far enough from the kitchen to see Christopher running full speed right at her. Before she could say a word, the frightened young boy leapt forcefully into her arms. She found it all she could do to brace herself so as not to be knocked from her feet. Her own heart sprinted rapidly upon sight of the large, suited black man standing in the doorway. "What the hell do you want?" Jessica placed Christopher on the floor, instinctively placing her own body between the child and the intruder.

The large man advanced, reaching in his pocket and producing a badge. "Beasley Reese," the out of breath man said as the white woman made it through the still open door. "Warrants. I'm here for the boy."

"He hasn't done anything," Jessica protested as she and Christopher were backed farther into the nearest corner.

"He's a runaway." Officer Reese inched closer, determined to eliminate any possible escape routes. "Hand him over now and no charges will be pressed again you."

"Why don't you just leave us alone?" Jessica's yell was nearly as fierce as her readiness to fight.

"Ma'am." The overweight, forty-something white lady moved toward the potential melee. "My name is Cynthia Albritton, and I am an employee of Child Protection Services. Christopher's mother informed us that he is a runaway, enticed to do so and harbored by one," the woman with the automated teller's voice shuffled the papers in her briefcase, "Jonathan Reed." The government worker paused after a heavy sigh, the brief show of emotion perhaps given in response to the abundant love seen in the redhead's eyes. "I have to take him." The woman's whisper was filled with compassion.

"He hasn't done anything," Jessica sobbed uncontrollably, knowing that her last-ditch protest was a futile one.

"It's OK, Jessica." Christopher stepped from behind her, unable to stomach the pain in her voice, knowing that this situation was his cross to bear.

"Oh, Christopher." Jessica threw both arms around his neck.

"I'll be back," Christopher spoke so that only she could hear. "Don't worry."

Christopher kissed Jessica on the cheek before pulling away. He turned to face the woman entrusted with the task of returning him to hell. Though outwardly calm, the overwhelming anger he felt was focused on the slightly graying overweight woman that approached with a smile.

"Hi, Christopher." The coffee stained teeth were just inches away from Christopher's face now. "You ready to see your mom and dad?

Christopher nodded as his mind raced with thoughts of escape. Finally, his thoughts turned to the love of his life, Kashandra, and what she would do in this situation. "Yeah, I'm ready." Christopher finally answered, then after waiting a split second longer, aimed his best right hand at the center of the bewildered woman's face.

"Christopher?" Jessica was the first to find a voice.

"Awwww." The woman was shocked by the oozing crimson that flowed through her fingers.

"You rotten little bastard!" Office Reese lunged at Christopher, barely missing him as Christopher ducked lower to the ground than the officer was prepared to go. The officer, smarter than most, regained his advantage by shuffling to cover the front door.

Christopher ran toward the living room, shocked to find his path to freedom already blocked.

"Look boy," Officer Reese eased forward, speaking in his most authoritative voice, "your ass is in enough trouble already!"

"Fuck you, bitch!" There was no intimidating Christopher. The young boy grabbed a small statue from the coffee table and hurled it at the officer's face, just missing wide left.

"That's it, you little fuck!" Officer Reese was incensed now, charging full speed at the boy.

Christopher ran around the coffee table, astounded by the nimbleness of foot shown by the large man while giving chase. Round and round the table they went, until Christopher, sure that he could out pace the furious cop no longer, broke the monotony by leaping across the loveseat and turning toward the door.

With the skill of an experienced soccer goalie, Officer Reese pivoted quickly, moving to position himself between Christopher and the door.

Christopher, seeing that he had no chance of winning the foot race to the door, leapt back across the loveseat and ran for the hallway leading to the back of the house.

Officer Reese followed closely, knowing that the young nut case had finally cornered himself.

Christopher considered the garage, but once inside there could be no escape. He stopped momentarily in the middle of the hallway, but with Officer Reese approaching quickly, there was no time to contemplate his next move.

Christopher ran into the guest bedroom, slamming the door shut and locking it behind him. Thinking quickly, he ran to the far end of the dresser that lined the same wall as the door and with a strength borne of extreme desperateness, he pushed the dresser until it formed an effective barricade of the door.

Christopher stepped back two full paces as the first heavy thuds from the battering of Officer Reese's size twelve shoe against the door could be heard. Knowing that the dresser would allow only a brief impediment to the officer's progress, Christopher's mind raced quickly for a viable next course of action.

The wood encasing the door's locking mechanism could take no more, and with each successive kick, the dresser rocked on two legs.

"I'm gonna kick your little ass just as soon as I get my hands on you, ya little punk!" Officer Reese threatened while continuing his assault on the door.

Christopher ran to the nightstand, opened the drawer, and searched for the weapon that he had

earlier found there. Not finding the firearm as desired, he raised the mattress, hoping it would be
there . . . no such luck.

Officer Reese had knocked the dresser back far
enough from the entrance of the door that he was
now forcing his oversized frame through the gap he
had made.

Christopher grabbed the remote control and
hurled it in the officer's direction, hitting him on
the bare skin that resulted from the officer's male
pattern baldness. Next, Christopher reached for
the lamp sitting on the nightstand, using it to strike
the officer in the same spot as had the remote control.

"Motherfucker!" Officer Reese fell back into the
hallway. The enraged officer quickly rose to his
feet, charging forward with the force of a Brahma
Bull.

Christopher was as still as a deer caught in the
rush of oncoming headlights as both door and
dresser came tumbling in his direction.

"I'm through fuckin' around, you little delinquent bastard!" Officer Reese stood in the doorway, no other barriers separating him and the boy.
"Bring your ass here now!" Jessica and Cynthia
Albritton observed from the hallway.

Christopher took a half step backward.

"All right, you li'l bastard, have it your way."
Officer Reese lumbered forward.

His only thoughts of escape, Christopher looked to the promises of freedom made by the shining sunlight that shone through the bedroom's large plate glass windows.

"Son, no." The anger in Officer Reese's voice was instantly replaced with that of a father's dread upon discovering the calamitous plot of a troubled child.

Before any rational thought could be spoken or heard, Christopher broke full speed for the window. With a leap, the sole of one jumpman tennis shoe landed on the window ledge. The second leap sent the sixty-seven pound boy crashing into and through the unforgiving glass. A score of cuts and scratches were instantly incurred from head to toe.

"Jesus Christ!" Officer Reese ran to the window.

Christopher's was tangled within the web of thorn bushes that bordered Shakey's home. The young boy struggled to free himself, but his efforts only served to open more wounds, and aggravate those already present.

"Jessica!" The last of the young boy's resolve escaped with his cry for help. The broken boy sobbed softly.

"Oh my God, Christopher!" Jessica's hand went to her mouth while viewing the damage Christopher had done to himself.

"Good for him." Mrs. Albritton was still holding her nose.

"Now look what you don' made him do, you ignorant-ass house nigga!" Mr. Bouldin, eyes filled with fire, and mouth spouting brimstone, stood under the broken window, next to the entangled young boy. Mrs. Bouldin followed a few feet behind.

"Just calm down." Officer Reese tried to calm the old man while figuring the best way to help the boy.

"Calm down, my dick!" Mr. Bouldin would not be pacified. "Bring yo' sellout ass down here and I'll show you some calm down!"

"Poor baby." Mrs. Bouldin was first to act positively, using the gardening shears she carried to cut the limbs that had the firmest hold on the child's body. "Let's get you out of there."

The three adults inside, led by Officer Reese, quickly ran to the front door, then outside and around the house not stopping until reaching the rescue scene.

"What's yo' problem, nigga?" Mr. Bouldin struck a fighting pose in front of the shaken officer. "Comin' 'round here with the white man's bullshit, scarin' this boy to death."

"Cool out, Pops," Office Reese warned.

"Or what, nigga?" Mr. Bouldin stepped forward, hands still at the ready position. "I ain't gonna run from ya."

"Harold, stop actin' so silly," Mrs. Bouldin scolded.

"Yo' ass is lucky, chump." Harold Bouldin was obviously well-versed in the consequences of disobeying Mrs. Bouldin. "You was 'bout to get yo' ass kicked."

Officer Reese ignored his belligerent elder, preferring instead to communicate with Mrs. Bouldin, who had already freed the young boy from the clutches of the thorn bushes and was now busying herself with the task of pulling thorns from his body and scanning the assortment of cuts and scratches for serious injury. "Think he needs an ambulance?" Office Reese asked.

"He don't need no ambulance." Mrs. Bouldin studied the scratch on the youngster's forehead. "All he needs is some peroxide, some adhesive strips, a few Band-Aids, and one or two of Aunt Gloria's blueberry muffins." A grandmother's kiss, planted on the cheek of the frightened boy, was the only pain medication needed.

"Well, he'll have to get those things later." Ms. Albritton's bitch level rose greatly. "He's going in CPS custody now."

"You talkin' shit to my wife." Mr. Bouldin was always ready for a good fight. "Why don't you leave this child alone? He ain't botherin' nobody."

"This child, and I use the term loosely, is responsible for this." Mrs. Albritton pointed at her nose which though no longer bleeding, had quickly swelled. "Besides, he's a runaway."

"Shit, you oughta thank him," Mr. Bouldin told her. "Now you got an excuse for being so ugly."

Officer Reese laughed despite himself. The sterness of the look giving to him by Mrs. Albritton caused him to instantly recall his official capacity. "I'm sorry, Christopher, but you have to go with her." Office Reese stepped forward.

"It's going to be OK, sweetie," Mrs. Bouldin assured with a kiss to the side of the boy's face.

"Shakey's going to find a way to come and get you," Jessica's kiss promised on Christopher's opposite cheek.

Officer Reese clamped a large, meaty paw on the youngster's shoulder and pulled forward as gently as possible for a man his size.

Christopher, his anger worked to a frenzy once again, would be defiant to the end. His right hand closing to become a weapon again, the youngster landed a solid, well-placed blow directly between the legs of the unsuspecting officer. In an instant, Christopher was off and running again.

Officer Reese stumbled backward a few steps before taking a knee. The rest of them were shocked to stillness. The rest of them that was, except for Mrs. Cynthia Albritton.

"What are you doing?" Mrs. Albritton, standing over the prone police officer, watched Christopher turn the corner. "Aren't you going to chase him?"

"Bitch, you chase him!" the blurry-eye police officer shouted in the woman's direction.

Mrs. Albritton recoiled as if struck with another blow to the face.

"That's right, boy," Mr. Bouldin applauded. "Quit doin' the white man's Tom foolery."

"Run, baby," Jessica, hands clasped against her chin, whispered so softly that only she could hear. "Run."

"Next." Shakey bit his bottom lip to contain the laughter within. Unfortunately, the nude, over-weight woman saw no humor in her routine, nor did she have any intention on stopping. "Next." Shakey could no longer control himself as his body shook so hard with laughter he knocked his drink from the table.

The woman danced with her back to Shakey and his companions, bending at the waist and touching her toes, she never slowed the jiggling that took place in every direction.

"That's it!" Lightnin', a good friend of Shakey and partner to his latest business venture, mo-tioned to the D.J.'s booth for the music to stop. Mo-ments after the music stopped playing, the woman mercifully stopped dancing.

"What?" The woman stood shamelessly in her nakedness, hands on hips while intensely working a wad of gum.

"That's enough." Lightnin' rubbed a hand through his Afro.

"But the end is the best part," the girl protested, then smiled and began to dance. "Let me show ya. I'm 'bout mine."

The table full of men laughed loudly at the girl though she paid them no mind at all. None of the men attempted to stop her, accepting the fact that the woman would not be denied the opportunity to finish her routine.

"Turn the music on," David's deep voice insisted.

The D.J. obliged, obviously coming to the same conclusion as the rest of them.

The Ying Yang Twins played once more, and the woman danced with unbridled enthusiasm. So enthusiastically, that Shakey began to believe the woman to have a measurable degree of potential. A minute later, the woman's routine finished dramatically. The overweight aspiring adult dancer did a split, then paused a few seconds before lying on her back, legs remaining in the 'splits' position, allowing the group of men a full view of her inner workings.

The men all clapped; partly from being genuinely impressed, but mostly to assure that the woman would leave the stage. But while there may be doubts regarding the disposition of the others, David's feelings were quite clear. He had become quite smitten with the full-figured young woman.

"Bravo! Bravo!" David clapped loudly. "Way to go, you big fine mothafucka, you!"

Lightnin' and his crew laughed loudly, finding their first dose of David Irving to be quite enjoyable.

The young woman took to her feet smiling broadly now, satisfied with her performance.

"What's her name?" David looked at the application lying in front of Shakey and Lightnin'. The name written on the application was Candy.

David rushed the stage, intent on getting next to Candy. "Good job, baby, we really liked your routine."

The young woman frowned at the small man in front of her. "Uh uh, Lightnin', what's up?"

"What you mean what's up?" Lightnin' asked.

"Who is this?" she scowled at David.

"That's the big man." Lightnin' looked as serious as was possible under the circumstances. "He callin' all the shots."

"For real?" The girl viewed David in a much less hostile manner now.

"Huh?" David smiled then stepped toward her. "That's right." He eased into a routine of his own. "I'm the big man, all those boys work for me."

"You like my performance?" the doe-eyed woman asked David.

"I loved your performance." David stepped a little closer.

"So you gonna pick me as a regular?"

"That's what I wanna talk to you about." David put his arm around the naked woman's waist while turning in Lightnin's direction. "Where can me and my new number one dancer go to talk in private?"

"The VIP room is right over there." Lightnin's

gold teeth shined brilliantly now. David was a real character.

David and the naked woman quickly descended the stage stairs and headed for the VIP room.

"Next! Please next," Shakey laughed and shook his head.

The music started again. This time it was UGK's "Take it Off." A pretty, girlish looking, honey brown-skinned young woman took to the stage clothed only in a pink lace lingerie set.

Just as the young woman who had written her name, Cream, on the application began to shake her stuff, Shakey's cell phone buzzed in his pocket.

"Yeah," Shakey barked into the phone. He was quite curious as to the caller of the ultra exclusive phone.

"They tried to take him." The voice was unmistakably Jessica's, though the sobbing made it hard to decipher her words.

"What?"

"C.P.S.," Jessica cried. "He jumped through the window."

"Christopher?" Shakey had no idea what Jessica was talking about.

"I don't know where he is, Shakey!" Jessica was hysterical.

"Give me the phone, sweetheart." Shakey heard a familiar male voice in the background. He then listened closely as the receiver changed hands.

"Shakey," Mr Bouldiln's voice boomed into Shakey's ear. "You need to get home, son. Now."

"What happened?" Shakey was glad to have someone on the other end of the phone that spoke with some degree of coherence.

"An Uncle Tom cop and some fat white bitch from

C.P.S. came for the boy." "Where'd they take him?" Shakey knew that Christopher's mother had made good on her threat.

"They ain't take him nowhere." There was more than just a hint of glee in Mr. Bouldin's voice as he told Shakey. "That boy fights like a mad Russian."

"Aw, man." Shakey moaned. "He fought 'em?"

"Hell yea he fought 'em." Mr. Bouldin laughed loudly. "He punched the pale face in the nose, and hit that house nigga in the nuts, that's what he did."

"What about the window?" Shakey developed an instant migraine.

"Oh yeah, the window." Mr. Bouldin laughed again. "I knew that boy was crazy the first time I laid eyes on him." The old man roared with laughter.

"Mr. Bouldin," Shakey spoke calmly. "What happened to the window?"

"That li'l crazy son of a bit ran right through it, that's what happened."

"Which window?" Shakey poured from the bottle of Hennessy Lightnin' had earlier placed on the table.

The one in the guest bedroom.

Shakey gulped his drink down completely before asking, "Did he cut himself?"

"Now that's a stupid question," Mr. Bouldin scolded. "What the hell do you think?" The older man paused before finishing. "Then he got caught up in all those damn sticker bushes you got out there. My wife had to snip the li'l crazy bastard loose with the garden shears." Mr. Bouldin laughed again. "That's when he punched that big nigga in the nuts."

Shakey shook his head. "Put Jessica on the phone."

"All right." Mr. Bouldin had one last thing to say. "But you get yo' behind on home now. This child's a nervous wreck in here."

Shakey listened as the phone changed hands again.

"Hello." Jessica was finally on the other end.

"Look, I'm on my way." Shakey spoke in his most reassuring voice. "Gimme a couple of hours," he told her despite knowing that the drive from Port Arthur to Galveston would take a bit longer.

"OK." Jessica wished he could make it to her much sooner.

"Don't worry. Where ever he is, I'll find him."

"Promise?"

"I promise." Shakey knew that finding Christopher would prove to be only a small task. Keeping him would be the impossibility. There was the brief pause of eternity before Shakey broke the silence with: "Let me go so I can find him."

"OK." Jessica's eyes filled with tears again.

"I love you."

"I love you too." Jessica hung up.

Shakey pressed the button that killed the power to the flip-faced phone. All, save for Lightnin', were firmly gripped by the spell woven by Cream.

"Everything chill?" Ligntnin' offered Shakey the Swisher.

Shakey shook his head before accepting the Swisher. "I gotta go," he spoke only after taking a long slow drag from the cigar. "Go ahead and finish the auditions, whoever you pick, I'm cool with it."

"What about David?" Lightnin' asked.

"Look after him for me," Shakey instructed between two more drags from the overstuffed cigar. He knew that suggesting to David that it was time to return to Galveston would be met with strong protest. "I'll pick him up tomorrow."

"Cool." Lightnin' was more than happy to keep David for a night. "I'll look out for him."

"Closely." Shakey smiled before standing. "Y'all take it easy." He shook hands with each man in the room before leaving.

"Aw right, playa. Later, Shakey. Stay down, fool." The scattered murmurings were swift and unlingering as Cream was still dancing.

Shakey quickly made his way to the door. "What next?" he asked himself aloud, regretting the question as soon as the words had escaped his lips.

Michelle's fingers trembled while dialing Jorgé Trevino's home phone number. She had uncovered the information that would save her family, and though she had never purposely chosen to harm Shakey, she could see no other way.

"Trevino speaking." Michelle's heart beat rapidly once the narcotics officer was on the phone.

"Hi," Michelle spoke somberly.

"Michelle?" Trevino sat up in his bed.

"Yeah."

"What's up?"

"I got it," Michelle said plainly.

"You got what?" Trevino was unable to hide his anxiousness. "Everything," Michelle told him. "The car, the clothes, the disguise, the gun. Everything!"

"No shit?" Trevino leapt from the bed, holding the phone with his shoulder while stepping into his pants. "Where are you?"

"Meet me at the corner of Fifteenth and Post Office," Michelle instructed, having already given much thought to the location of her next meeting with Trevino. "How much time you need?"

"Give me about twenty minutes," Trevino requested. His head filled with questions, but he would wait until he was face to face with Michelle.

Michelle hung up the phone. "Sorry, Shakey," she spoke aloud, her heart already heaving with the burden of betrayal.

It was his own fault, Michelle reasoned. He should have seen to it that the evidence was disposed of properly.

Michelle had been able to pry from Red the location of the chop shop entrusted with the job of dismantling the getaway car. Upon arriving at the chop shop, Michelle found that not only had the car not been destroyed as instructed, but was still on the premises.

The ensuing haggling resulted in an eighteen-hundred dollar transaction. Later, once Michelle had parked along the curb of an unpopulated street, she was further astounded to find that every bit of physical evidence tying Shakey to the double homicide was stuffed into the glove compartment.

So, she reiterated the point to herself, Shakey should have been much more cautious about the disposal of such highly sensitive material.

Finding Christopher proved to be much more difficult than Shakey had imagined. In retrospect, he could now see his own folly in believing otherwise. Ghetto kids like Christopher could disappear whenever they wanted, for however long they chose to do so. Dozens of homes were at their disposal, and their friends were as tight-lipped as a family of Mafiosos.

"Where are you, little boy?" Jessica called aloud from the passenger seat. Together she and Shakey had already covered every inch of central Galveston at least a dozen times, both of them putting to full use their contacts. It had been nearly ten hours now since Christopher had run away from home, cut and bleeding. The redhead was at wit's end with worry.

"Isn't that his li'l partner?" Shakey squinted as the Cadillac rolled to a stop on the corner of 41st and Avenue I. About a block or so ahead of them, a group of boys were congregated on the sidewalk running alongside the Palm Terrace Housing projects. Among them was Christopher's friend Wesley.

The Cadillac roared forward, stopping in the street when directly across the street from the group of young boys. Through the open window, Shakey called, "Hey Wesley."

The score of boys relaxed a bit. All of them driven to the edge by the fast approaching headlights. "See what that nigga want." One of the bigger boys pushed Wesley in the back.

Wesley stepped forward proudly; feeling it to be good for his status in the hood for Shakey to come calling on him.

"What's up?" Shakey spoke once the boy was in earshot.

"Hi, Shakey." Wesley displayed the two half-filled gaps in front of his mouth; gaps that just a month ago, had been clean as a whistle. "Hi, Jessica."

"You doin' all right?" Shakey knew that finesse was the key if he was to have any chance of learning Christopher's whereabouts.

"Just chillin'." Though only seven years old, Wesley was wise enough to know that Shakey's visit was not of a social nature. "What's up?"

"I'm lookin' for Chris. Seen him?"

"Chris ain't been around here in a long time," Wesley said before adding, "I thought he was with you."

"He was until today," Shakey told the child. "If you see him tell him to call me, would you?"

"All right." Wesley nodded.

"Here." Shakey peeled a ten-dollar bill from the wad in his pocket. Just for positive reinforcement.

"Thank you, Shakey." Wesley's smile was Grand Canyon wide.

"Tell Christopher we're worried sick." Jessica struggled mightily to remain quiet but found it impossible.

"OK." Wesley's face registered his puzzlement. "Is Chris in trouble?"

"Naw, he ain't in trouble." Shakey was quick to calm the boy's suspicions. "We're just worried because we ain't seen him all day."

"Oh," the wheels in the young boy's head were spinning rapidly, "I'll tell him."

"Thank you." Shakey reached at the vibrating pager in his pocket. The number in the display window was unfamiliar, but unfortunately the same could not be said for the code that followed.

With no further words, the weight of Shakey's foot grew light on the break as the Cadillac eased forward. Once at the corner of Forty-third and Avenue I, he reached for the cell phone.

"It's me," Trevino answered on the third ring.

"Who else?" Shakey wheeled left toward Broadway, instinctively knowing it was time to take Jessica home.

"Couldn't find him, huh?"

"What?" Shakey quickly caught himself, knowing that any display of emotion other than extreme confidence would be interpreted by Trevino as fear.

"I got a tip for you," Trevino said.

"What's that?" Shakey knew that Trevino was toying with him.

"Look where you haven't already," Trevino stated as if just giving the most brilliant insight ever.

"Fuck you!" Shakey was in no mood for Trevino's games.

"Fuck you, bitch!" Trevino's laugh was loud and obnoxious.

Shakey couldn't believe he had allowed this situation with Trevino to go on for so long. But what were his choices? "Come see me," Trevino said once he finished laughing.

"When?"

"When am I telling you?" More laughter.

"Where?" Shakey knew this was coming.

"Alamo playground." Trevino was all business now.

"On my way." Shakey had often wondered why Trevino seemed to enjoy meeting at playgrounds. This time he had chosen the elementary school located at Fifty-fourth and Avenue M.

"You got twenty minutes, ho." The phone clicked as soon as Trevino had spoken the words, but for the life of him, Shakey would swear that he could still hear the jerkish laughter of his long-time tormentor for another five minutes.

Jessica entered the house, closing the door softly behind her, never feeling such emptiness in her short, pain-filled life. After hitting the light switch, she stepped slowly for the living room. Doing so turned out to be a bad decision. The sight of Christopher's Answer V tennis shoes lying next to the Sony Playstation 3 was devastating.

Jessica's hand went to her mouth, an unconscious reaction to the nausea that rose from the pit of her stomach. The single loud and piercing cry of a young woman who had suffered one too many losses broke the empty silence.

Jessica staggered backward until her back was against the wall. The entirety of the emotions she was able to suppress for the last few hours came raging forward for freedom as the saddened young woman slid down the wall, falling in a heap to the floor, the waterworks lasting a full fifteen minutes.

Once emptied of tears, Jessica zombied toward the kitchen. She opened the microwave, grabbing the plastic plate that was filled to capacity with chopped barbecue beef. It was time to feed Baby.

Jessica opened the sliding patio door, fully expecting Baby to come scouting along the ground; not the case.

Jessica stepped outside the emptiness of the house. A light rain now accompanied by an already powerful gust of wind, the temperature was dropping fast.

"Baby." Jessica stepped farther into the back yard. Further puzzled by the dog's silence. "Baby," she called again while stepping toward the large doghouse that Shakey and Christopher had built for Baby.

"Woof." There was an unusual quiet to the dog's bark, and oddly, she had yet to come running toward the smell of chopped beef.

Jessica could now see that Baby was lying outside of the doghouse. "Crazy mutt." She walked swiftly toward the dog. "It's freezing out here and you'd rather lie in the rain than go inside."

Upon the sight of the plate, Baby drug herself a few inches forward from the entrance of the doghouse. Jessica couldn't believe what was revealed by the dog's movement. A single Nike Jumpman tennis shoe protruded just past the entrance of the doghouse.

Jessica placed the plate on the ground in front of Baby. The dog instantly went to work, quickly oblivious to all the world contained save for the taste of the chopped beef. Jessica stumbled forward, concerned only with the single size basketball shoe.

Jessica's heart threatened to bruise the underside of her chest as she kneeled low enough to peek inside Baby's castle. The tears flowed freely once more and Christopher was awakened by the loud sobs of relief that Jessica sounded.

Jessica fell to her knees, reaching with both hands for any part of Christopher that she could grasp. Finally clutching an ankle with both hands, she forcefully extracted the prodigal son from his hiding place.

"What's wrong with you?" Christopher eyes were wide as he pushed at the ground with both hands to lift himself to his feet.

Before Christopher could leave the ground, Jessica wrapped both arms around the boy's neck, bringing the full of her weight down on him, pressing him flat onto the ground.

The rain fell harder now as Jessica squeezed so tight that Christopher could hardly breathe. "I was so scared, sweetie," Jessica sobbed heavily.

Christopher wanted to speak to tell her that he was sorry for the worry he had caused. To assure her that he had been just fine the entire time. To promise it would never happen again, but the child found himself unable to speak through the lump that formed in his throat. Being loved felt so good; even for the most dedicated of delinquents.

CHAPTER 22

Shakey parked alongside the Alamo School gymnasium, stopping only to grab the .38-caliber revolver from the glove compartment and jamming it into this pocket before stepping from the car.

The windy briskness of the early December night, accompanied by the steady pitter patter of the large, slow falling rain drops coincided perfectly with the Handsome Intimidator's present mood.

Shakey stepped cautiously toward the playground, knowing that Trevino was somewhere near. During the quick ride over, Shakey had not even bothered to consider the possible reasons for Trevino's call. Not surprisingly, he found that he really didn't care. What he did know was that he had grown quite weary of Jorgé Trevino's bullshit, and tonight was as good as any for the reading on the wall.

A quick and quiet whistle garnered the Handsome Intimidator's attention. A quick scan in the direction of Trevino's call revealed that Galveston's chief narcotics officer was sitting at the top of the sliding board.

As Shakey neared the slide, Trevino crawled back inside the covered area. Shakey stood still once reaching a spot where he could see inside the slide.

"What's up, friend?" Trevino was almost convincing as his smiling face appeared through the back of the slide cover.

"What's up?" Shakey's greeting was filled with a much different meaning.

"What are you doing down there?" Trevino asked, then instructed before Shakey could respond, "Come on up."

Though angered by the ridiculousness of Trevino's invitation, Shakey knew it useless to protest. He climbed the chain ladder to the top of the slide and squeezed into the much too small area under the cover with Trevino. Both men had to sit Indian style to fit inside the children's play space.

Trevino took a drink from a gold flask before holding it in Shakey's direction.

Shakey declined the cop's offer with a shake of his head.

"What's wrong?" Trevino took another sip. "Too good to drink with your blood brother?"

Shakey responded with silence, unbelieving that this man, Jorgé Trevino was the same boy with whom he had once shared a buck knife; both cutting the palm of the other's hand, and allowing their blood to intermingle, a ceremony they had watched on TV between an Indian and a runaway slave the Indian had befriended in the final scene of an old movie. That day, each boy had called the other "brother," vowing to never let anyone or anything come between them. That was millenniums ago.

"We used to drink together." Trevino's eyes bore right through his one-time friend. "Bite from the same peanut butter and jelly sandwich, sleep in the same bed, fight with the whole neighborhood, just me and my blood brother, Shakey." Trevino's voice was a swirl of twisted emotions.

"What'd you want to talk about?" Shakey had no intentions of playing "back in da good ole days" with Jorgé Trevino.

Trevino's eyes snapped instantly to alertness. The serpent within now ready to devour whatever happened into its path. "You." The calm of the narcotics officer's voice failed to hide the intensity of his fury.

"I'm listening." Shakey wasn't intimidated.

Trevino's smile was wide. He regained his composure and rediscovered the joy of toying with his prey before finally asserting his ability to pounce for the kill. He took another drink before finally speaking. "You're getting old, my friend."

"What?"

Trevino reached suddenly behind him, perhaps never to know just how close he had come to being pumped full of .38 slugs. "Here." He chucked the package he had concealed directly into Shakey's chest.

Shakey held the plastic bag out in front of him. Inside the bag was an Afro wig. Shakey's heart refused to beat.

"Go ahead and take it out the bag," Trevino laughed. "Shit, put it on. Your fingerprints are already all over it."

"I don't know what you're talkin' about." Shakey threw the bag back in Trevino's direction.

Trevino began to laugh. A soft laugh at first, one that rose steadily in volume and intensity until the hollow beneath the cover of the slide echoed with the wicked laughter of the drunken lunatic. "You don't know what I'm talkin' about?" Trevino stopped laughing long enough to scoff. "C'mon, stupid, we both know better than that."

Shakey remained silent despite the millions of questions exploding simultaneously inside his pain riddled head. He had come to know Trevino much better than he knew anyone on the face of the earth, including himself, and this was no trick. The Afro wig was the real thing; but how?

"Slopppy, sloppy, sloppy." Trevino shook his head. "And from the great Jonathan Reed." Trevino turned the bottle up again. "So much more did I expect."

Trevino's maniacal laughter threatened to push Shakey over the edge.

"OK, I'll tell you how you fucked up," Trevino promised. "But first, let me tell you what else I got."

Shakey's eyes filled with murder.

"Ah ah ah." Trevino placed a stubby index finger in front of Shakey's face. "My partner, remember. He knows our every dealing, so killing me would only get you the needle." This time Trevino didn't laugh. The smirk he wore was much louder. "Anyway, don't you want to know what else I have of yours?"

"You ain't got nothin' of mine," Shakey snapped.

"Tell it to the judge, stupid!" Trevino loved the bewilderness he saw in Shakey's eyes "Your whole life is in my hands, so bow down, bitch!"

Shakey took a deep breath.

"Well OK." Trevino was calm again. "Now that we got a little understanding, let me tell you what I got so far." Trevino took another sip then once again held the flask in Shakey's direction. "Sure you don't need a drink?"

Shakey waved him off.

"Suit yourelf." Trevino screwed the top on the flask before speaking. "Now with no further ado." The wicked laughter resumed. "In Pandora's box we found an old pair of black Ray-Ban sunglasses." Trevino's eyes never left Shakey's. "Also we found one old model jalopy. More specifically, a beat up LTD." Shakey showed no outward reaction, though he struggled mightily with each word from Trevino.

"Also in Pandora's box was a very big gun." Trevino smiled. "A .41-caliber to be exact. There's more, but I'm sure you know as well as I do what's in Pandora's box."

Shakey was speechless.

"I just wanna know one thing." Trevino's voice displayed a genuine curiosity.

The "what's that" that Shakey offered in return was inaudible. Instead, spoken from one pair of eyes to another.

"Why in the world would you trust some petty car thieves with disposing of this type of evidence? Have you gone crazy?"

Shakey maintained his silence, shocked at learning the source of his betrayal.

"You know, stupid?" An obvious change in the tone of Trevino's voice signaled a change in the direction of the conversation. "I'm tired of fucking with you."

Shakey's attention was taken by a passing Jeep Cherokee. Usher's "You got it Bad" played loudly. The quartet of teenagers inside looked to be living a life filled with the type of carefree happiness that he could only imagine. The young girl in the passenger seat leaned in the driver's direction, kissed him before stepping from the vehicle, closing the door, and running for the stairs of the small wood-framed house.

"Hey, fuckhead," Trevino jeered. "I'm talking over here."

Shakey faced the executioner.

"Like I said, I'm tired of fucking with you," Trevino started again. "And like a good ho, you don' made Daddy plenty of money, so here's the deal;

the last dealing I want with your sorry ass is for you to pay me all that you owe me and send a girl to my condo, both payments accepted Friday night. After that, I don't ever want to see your sorry ass again."

Shakey was dumbfounded, totally disbelieving of what Jorgé Trevino seemed to be speaking. "A girl?" Shakey repeated, a bit confused. Though Trevino had often requested the services of women known to Shakey, there was something about the timing of Trevino's present request that didn't quite sit right with Shakey.

"Yeah, a girl." Trevino frowned. "What's wrong? You think I don't like girls?"

Shakey closely observed the madman.

"But I'm not talking about none of those skank hoes you got dancing and turning tricks for you."

"Who you want?" Shakey finally found words to speak.

"You know." Trevino lifted the gold flask from the floor again, not speaking until he had opened and drank heartily. "I think I have a sudden fetish for redheads."

Shakey recoiled as the rusty sword Trevino wielded was planted deep into his heart, then broken at the hilt.

It was true as evidenced by the agony seen in Shakey's eyes. Though unthinkable, it was undeniable. Shakey loved the redhead, and the mere thought of scum like Shakey being capable of such a noble emotion pushed Trevino's anger quickly toward the point of insanity.

"No dice," Shakey answered. Jessica was his woman. Not a whore.

"Oh, yeah, it's gonna be some dice." Trevino's anger was focused. "And some fuckin' too!" The wicked laughter erupted once more. "What choice do you have?"

Shakey thought about the pistol in his pocket.

"It's time for you to get out the game anyway, bitch!" Trevino concluded. "You've grown soft . . . look at you. . . . stressing over some crackhead white bitch you hardly know. What part of Pimpology is that?"

Shakey said only, "She's off limits."

Trevino's laughter reached a never before heard decibel level. "Like I said, I'm tired of fuckin' with you, so let me lay it out plainly for you." Trevino took another drink of whiskey. "Bring my money, and the redhead Friday night. Saturday morning, you can retrieve the used goods and you, her, and that crack baby you've grown so fond of can live happily ever after." There was a long, violent silence on the sliding board of the Alamo Elementary School playground before Trevino continued. "Or . . . you pay your debt to society for the double homicide at Vanessa's."

Trevino punctuated his ultimatum by shoving the Afro wig once more before Shakey's face. He then whirled suddenly to his right. "Whew!" he screamed while sliding swiftly toward the mound of dirt. Landing on his feet, Trevino took two steps before stopping. "I've always loved this place." Much emotion was present in the narcotics officer's voice. It's the last place my dad took me before some lowlife scum of the earth drug addict killed him." With that, Jorgé Trevino stepped briskly into the darkness, leaving Shakey alone atop the sliding board, hopeless to ponder the dire set of circumstances.

The mental images were the worst. Pain producing pictures of Jessica in various stages of ecstasy shared with another man. Blood pressure raising snapshots of the unthinkable, with no detail ignored. From the small circle shaped kisses that covered his own neck during lovemaking with Jessica, to the softness of her tiny hands as they traveled every inch of his back and shoulders; from the way her body tensed with the rigidness of cold steel just before orgasm; to the jello-like mass she became just after the mountain's peak. Through his mind's eye, Shakey had seen Trevino partake of it all; a million times.

"Whatever it is will be better tomorrow," Jessica spoke without opening her eyes.

Shakey and Jessica had been in bed for hours now. And while taking great comfort in the feel of the sleeping fire goddess lying next to him, any closing of his eyes signaled for the restart of the twisted cinematography he was forced to watch.

"I promise." The brilliant green emeralds finally rested on Shakey's own eyes. Jessica smiled before planting a kiss so softly onto Shakey's lips that he would never be sure if it actually happened.

"I'm just enjoying watching you sleep." Shakey kissed her back then wrapped her in his arms.

"Uh huh," she had barely managed before being whisked away to dreamland once again.

Shakey lie awake a little while longer before fatigue began to play its part. His last conscious thoughts were of the sweet smell of Jessica's curly red mane. Just before drifting away, Shakey inhaled as deeply as possible, hoping upon hope, that he could somehow take a piece of the she-devil with him to the other side, as the agony of the night would not be soon ending.

With sleep came a different misery; fragmented bits of hostile communications from afar. Some voices familiar, most not. Nothing to be understood by the natural mind, save the universal theme contained in them all; the unearthly torture of an already grossly overwhelmed soul.

Shakey tossed to and fro on his side of the bed. Pulse racing, and sweat pouring from his pores, his incoherent murmurings repeatedly woke Jessica from her own uneasy attempt at rest.

The years hadn't changed Big Mama a bit. The large black mole just under her well defined right cheekbone still moist from the single tear had coincided with her spirit offering to the maker; the barely perceptible smile she had taken with her to the great vast beyond still offering her beleaguered descendant the same promise of a merciful and forgiving God that still carried him through life's most trying times.

And while Big Mama smiled upon him, Shakey rested; the old woman providing a well-spring of contentment to him. The two of them silent but communicative; for Shakey, the troubled waters were calm.

But as with all good things, the end must come and the rapidly dulling of the old woman's eyes warned of her imminent departure. For Shakey, the panic set in immediately. His own battered spirit begged Big Mama to not abandon him again. The intense pleadings of a most troubled man echoing for eternity through the ethers.

The old woman's smile was gone, and there was no answer to give him; only heartbreak, worry, and despair now showed in her yes.

Big Mama's parched lips opened as if to speak, and a terrified little boy listened closely.

"I would take you with me," the old woman's voice was the sweetest of ballads, "but it's not your time."

Big Mama's face was gone even before the last of her words were spoken, leaving her lost little boy alone once more to find his own way home.

Shakey refused to open his eyes though the magic of the night was gone. He hoped with all that he had that the old woman would return, praying desperately to the creator, asking only for Big

Mama's loving presence. Yet, he already knew. In the deepest core of his being, he knew. Where Big Mama had gone, he would never be welcome. The miracle just afforded would be his last sighting of his mother's grandmother, and quite likely, his last dealing with any that was good and true in this world, or the next.

The twelve days of Shakey's Christmas began with anything but cheerfulness as Shakey found that the small sin driven business establishment he had dubbed "Baller's Paradise" held no appeal to him. After circling the building a half dozen times, he finally decided that he was not in a very festive mood.

It had been barely daylight when Shakey left his residence early yesterday morning. In a few hours, it would be daylight again. The Handsome Intimidator had spent the last rotation of the earth seeking every anesthetic known to the street in a futile attempt to numb the crippling effects of the vise-like grip that clutched his failing heart.

Sex with Jessica started the cycle. There he found no comfort; only a reminder of what he was adamantly opposed to sharing with another man. A full eight-ounce bottle of syrup was next. There was an ounce worth of Swisher doobies in the ashtray, a near empty fifth of Barcardi 151 in the seat next to him, and a completely empty box that had just a couple of hours ago been home to fifteen twelve-ounce cans of bulls. Not even the musky smell of the back seat sex he had shared with a street walking prostitute served to numb the aching in his heart.

Of course he could murder Trevino, but assuredly that act would be a virtual murder-suicide, resulting in the complete destruction of the few things Shakey held near to him. Shakey knew that Trevino's claims of a partner were not a bluff. He would be insane to deal with Shakey in such a capacity without a foolproof insurance policy.

The Cadillac re-entered Broadway Boulevard on Thirty-third and Broadway. A right on Thirty-fifth, and Shaky headed for PennySavers' corner. Not surprisingly, the first recognizable face was that of Smitty.

The sudden feel of dread struck Shakey as the cell phone buzzed in his pocket. It was nearly 5:00 A.M. No calls of pleasantry were made at such as hour. At the very least, Jessica was calling to fuss about his failure to return home last night. A notion Shakey quickly dismissed, Jessica had learned not to fuss.

"Yeah," was his reluctant answer.

"Shakey," Red spoke in a quiet business-like manner.

"Who's in jail?" Shakey made an attempt at humor, but the total lack of enthusiasm in his voice made the delivery of his routine an impossibility.

"I wish it was that simple." The somberness of his best friend was cause for alarm.

"What's up?" Shakey braced himself for the worst.

Red launched a bomb for which his partner could never be prepared. "Rosa died."

"What?" Shakey slammed on the brakes right in the middle of the intersection. "C'mon, man!" His mind rejected the news, though in his heart, he had long known of Rosa's imminent demise.

"I just spoke with Cindy," Red continued.

"Cindy." Shakey hadn't even been conscious that he had spoken her name aloud. What would happen to Cindy? What had he done to her?

"What happened?" Shakey asked reflexively, not at all wanting an answer. He was totally unable at this time to ponder the details that had ended Rosa's life.

"Complications," Red said simply, feeling the details to be pointless.

There was a long, pain bloated silence as Shakey struggled to make sense of it all.

"Shakey." Red's voice was that of a highly concerned friend. "Shakey?" he called again once sure that his first query had gone unanswered.

"I'm here." Shakey fought to maintain his composure, already tasting the small droplets of heart pain that of late had been flowing from his eyes with frightening regularity.

"You all right?" Red knew that Shakey wasn't.

"Yeah," Shakey lied. The tears were heavier now as the tragedy of the loss became more pronounced in his mind. "I'm chill."

Another roaming silence filled the phone line as words escaped both men.

"I'll take care of all the arrangements," Red told his grieving friend, his own voice breaking as he too loved Rosa.

"Thank you." Shakey knew that he could never complete a task as morbid as preparing for the disposal of a loved one.

"I'll figure somethin' out for Cindy too." Red had always been the ace of crisis management.

"Where is she?" Shakey asked, his mind thinking now of Moe and the Deuce-Nine Crips, then of Trevino and the Josephine conspiracy, the abuse of his stepfather, his abandonment by his siblings, anything to arouse the anger in him that had always proved the perfect defense for the pain and despair of the tragedy of life.

"In Kashandra's room," Red said. "Asleep. She's pretty tore up."

"Yeah." Shakey reached under the seat for the bottle of Bacardi. He was ready to end the conversation now. "I'll get at you tomorrow, dog."

"Yeah." Red too was ready to end the conversation and retreat to the safe confines of Micelle's arms.

Shakey hung up the phone then threw it from the open window of the car, his mind searching for any one of the many faces capable of triggering the anger he so desperately needed. Yet, this would be a time when anger failed him, as the only face his mind's eye could see was that of a beaten and battered Rosa.

The Cadillac veered slowly toward the side of the street. The handful of corner occupants observed Shakey from a distance, knowing from experience that there were times that approaching this man would be quite hazardous to one's health, and this was definitely one of those times.

Shakey turned up the bottle. His eyes were an uncontrollable river flow now as he wondered why it was not him that had been taken to rest and while hell was sure to be his eternal residence. Shakey was certain that the pit of Hades could possess for him no more misery than the mean streets of Galveston Island.

"Hungry?" Jessica had tried for the last two hours to extract some semblance of conversation from Shakey. She had yet to be successful.

"No thank you." Shakey spoke with the brief, effortful civility that showed just how little he regarded the presence of another human being at this time. He sat up on the couch, flipping disinterestedly through the channels of the television hoping only that Jessica would leave him alone.

Jessica returned to the kitchen, knowing not what to make of Shakey's unresponsiveness, knowing only the helplessness of being excluded from sharing the pain of a loved one.

Shakey looked across the living room, past the dining room area, and through the large open window, granting a full view of the back yard. Christopher, despite being wet and soapy in the face of the mid-December briskness, was all smiles while bathing a surprisingly cooperative Baby. The merriment of the scene angered Shakey beyond explanation, as he knew that his love for them all was the source of his vulnerability, and vulnerability was an unacceptable liability in the arena in which he played.

"Sweetie." Jessica's sing-song should have been a pleasure to the ear. "Why don't you tell me what's wrong?" Jessica sat on the couch next to him, kissed him softly on the cheek, and made a move to place her arms around him.

Shakey's response was a stiff arm to the she-devil's chest, pushing her away with only the needed force, yet inflicting more pain than he could ever imagine.

"What do you want, Shakey?" Jessica smarted from the sting of rejection.

"Nothin'," Shakey mumbled while taking to his feet, storming down the hallway leading to the garage. "Leave me the fuck alone!" he yelled before slamming the door behind him.

"Fucking asshole!" Jessica yelled in return. Crying now, the rejection she felt became overwhelming while listening to the suddenly erupting engine, followed by the opening of the garage door. The next sound was that of burning rubber, and an accelerating engine that carried Shakey farther, farther, and farther away from her.

CHAPTER 23

"Baby, make me a promise." Jessica, every nerve-ending in her body still aglow from the hour of high-intensity love-making, whispered into Shakey's ear.

Shakey held her naked body firmly against his own, fearful of speaking, not wanting her to ask of him that which he would be unable to give.

"Hear me, baby?" Jessica beckoned.

"Yeah, I hear you." Shakey was conscious only that he had somehow fallen in love with this woman.

"Well?"

"Well what?"

"You promise?"

"Promise what?"

"Nope." Jessica kissed his chest before placing her face against it. "You have to promise first."

"Nope." Shakey mimicked the rhythm and tone or her voice, returning the kiss on the top of her head. "You're gonna have to tell me first."

"But don't you trust me?" Jessica's happiness was contagious.

"Trust you?" Shakey quipped. "You are crazy, aren't you?"

"And just what is that supposed to mean, Jonathan?"

"Jonathan? Sounds like you know me."

"I know you're avoiding the subject."

"What subject?" Shakey asked with all the seriousness he could muster.

"Stop playing," Jessica insisted.

"Naw, square business." Shakey struggled to conceal his smile. "What subject you talkin' about?"

"This one." Jessica reached between Shakey's legs, closing her had around his testicles, squeezing gently to show who was in control.

"OK." Shakey was suddenly Mr. Compliance. "I know what subject you're talkin' about."

"I figured you would." Jessica applied just a little more pressure. "Now make me a promise."

"I promise, girl, damn!"

"That ain't good enough." Jessica enjoyed the present situation to the fullest. "Don't make me show you how strong I am."

"OK, OK." Shakey had no desire to witness any more of the she-devil's strength than necessary. "I say I promise."

"Repeat after me." Jessica thought it was wise to release just a little pressure, though not much. "I promise."

"I promise." Shakey smiled gingerly.

"To never again."

"To never again."

"Shut my woman out."

"Shut my woman out," Shakey finalized the promise.

"There then." Jessica kissed him on the lips, releasing her grip on the Reed family jewels, but keeping her hand in position to reassert her dominance. "Who's your woman?"

"Who's you woman?" Shakey sarcastically continued the parrot act.

"A comedian, huh?" Jessica squeezed so suddenly that she nearly caused Shakey to scream.

"You are, baby."

"Who?"

"You," Shakey laughed loudly.

Jessica kissed him before loosening her grip once more. The two of them held each other tightly, both enjoying the silent communion.

For Shakey, the promise he had made was already causing a slight pricking of his conscience. For as much as he may have wanted, there was no way he could ever include her in any more than the most superficial aspects of his life.

"Baby?" Jessica whispered softly.

"What?"

"I love you."

The room went silent now as Jessica was totally consumed with the fear of unreturned affection. Shakey on the other hand was quite leery of the increased vulnerability he would feel after having echoed the sentiments of the she-devil.

"I love you too," Shakey finally said to her, and he did, that fact scaring him more than anything in the world right now.

"Baby?" Jessica sang once more.

"What?"

"Tell me about it."

He couldn't, and he said nothing.

"Baby?"

"Tell you about what?"

"Baby, remember your promise," Jessica urged, perhaps not knowing the depths of the water in which she tread.

"Jessica," Shakey started then stopped. His heart burdened to capacity with the evils with which he had for years been forced to bear alone. The thought of telling her was second in unpleasantness only to the thought of lying to her.

"Say it, baby."

"Leave it alone." Shakey rolled over, turning his back to her, wanting desperately to share the full of his pain and frustration with the woman he loved, but feeling it best to spare her the agony. He resigned himself to sleep until hearing the near silent whimpering coming from behind him.

"What you cryin' for?" Shakey had a hard time being frustrated with her.

"Why do you keep doing this to me?" Jessica cried harder now. "I wanna be there for you. I can help you."

"You can help me?" Shakey had no problem being frustrated with her now as the sight of this whining and crying white girl suggesting that she could help, when in fact she was a large part of the problem, was enough to make him truly angry. "Help me with what?"

"Whatever's bothering you, honey."

"What's bothering me?" Shakey spoke with Ike Turner like righteous indignation. "Where the fuck you want me to start?"

"From the beginning." Jessica tried to match his anger.

"From the beginning." Shakey was a master mimic.

"Yeah, baby." Jessica could manage no emotion remotely similar to anger as it was plain to see how much her man was hurting. "From the beginning."

"Aw right then, Ms. I wanna be there for you!" Shakey was absolutely furious. "Here it is raw and uncut, from the beginning." Shakey paused momentarily before stating. "My father was a good for nothing junkie who stayed so full of that shit I doubt he even knew I had been born." Shakey was amazed at how just saying these words, how finally allowing himself to speak them to another human being seemed to have an immediate therapeutic effect on him. "My stepfather was even worse, or was it better?" Shakey took a second to allow for the impact of his rhetorical sarcasm. "He knew I was there, and he showed it daily. But instead of hugs and kisses, it was fists and choke holds. Not that I was special or anything, everyone in the house shared in the love." It was wildly fortunate that the room was cloaked in total darkness, lest Jessica become frightened to tears by the darkness that now masked the face of the man lying next to her. "Until I took it upon myself to finish his bitch ass!"

The words bounced over and over off the walls of Shakey's bedroom, now searching for a dry place to rest after having been deprived of their hiding place.

"And Mama," Shakey started with anger, but found that the intensity of that anger dissipated immediately upon speaking the word mama. "Mama." He swallowed hard, twice attempting to dissolve the sizeable lump in his throat. "Mama was a child herself. Underaged, under educated, and totally unprepared for a child at the age of fourteen. She did her best."

The dam was broken now, and there was nothing either of them could do to stop the rush of twisted emotions that had been corralled for much too long. Shakey told it all to her. Starting with his father's killing of Trevino's. The oddity of the bond that he and Trevino had forged as children. The lies, the secret betrayals, Big Mama's death, the pillow that ended Ben Massey's life. The murders, the dope, the prison time. He told of Evette and Jonathan, and how he had been forced to abandon them. He told her of Rosa's death, of the retribution he had taken in response to her attack, and finally of Trevino's indecent proposal.

Through it all, Jessica listened intently, never once wavering in her support of the man she loved as he shared with her the horror story that had somehow superimposed itself onto his life and then Jessica shared her own.

The two of them talked until day break, finding that together they were able to shoulder the burdens that neither of them had ever been strong enough to handle alone. Neither judgmental of the other, with nothing but unconditional love and acceptance being transmitted between them.

Finally they rested, each clutching the other before watching the rising sun as it took to its appointed spot in the heavens. This morning's sunrise was accompanied by a rainbow that stretched to the horizon and beyond—seemingly never ending.

Shakey was first to wake after having slept for less than three hours. The magic of early morning now engulfed by the urgency of the day. It was Friday, December Fifteenth, the date he was to answer Trevino's proposal. Finally he had a plan, albeit a crude one.

He would send Jessica and Christopher far away; Cindy to go with them. He would give them all that was his to give—a quite considerable fortune. He would man his war with Trevino alone, a showdown that had been looming for a quarter of a century now. A showdown that would surely cost both men their lives.

"I'll do it." Shakey's thoughts were suddenly intercepted by Jessica's words. "What?" Preoccupied with his own thought, Shakey was slow to figure the topic in which she volunteered her services.

Jessica pressed herself against him, knowing the sensitivity of the topic in which she spoke. "Then we'll be free," Jessica said. "We can go far, far away from here." Jessica was not quite convincing.

"You don't know what you're saying." Shakey was torn between the twinge of anger he felt at her suggesting to him that she sleep with Trevino, and admiration for the unselfishness it took for her to make such a pledge.

"It's not something I want to do." Jessica gently stroked the side of Shakey's head. "But I want to help you."

"I'll take care of it."

"I'm not going away without you." Jessica shocked Shakey with her ability to piece together the puzzle on his face.

"What?"

"Baby look." Jessica prepared her last plea. "This man is never going to stop until he feels that he's hurt you deeply. . . . He think he's found the way." Jessica had obviously thought long and hard on the issue. "Let him think that . . . I'll handle my business, then we'll have the whole world." Jessica was quite persuasive. "Let's win, baby."

Shakey couldn't believe the conversationist the she-devil had become. Obviously paying close attention as he had many times in her presence weaved him his own web of words. He was impressed, but placing her in the bed of Jorgé Trevino was unthinkable. "Let me think on it," Shakey finally responded, not wanting to argue with her.

"OK." Jessica snuggled closer. "But one more thing."

"What's that?"

"If we skip out, we skip out together.

Shakey was quiet.

"Understand?"

"I understand." What Shakey understood was that he had gotten this girl buried up to her neck in his mess, and if anything happened to her now, he would be irretrievably broken.

CHAPTER 24

The whistle of the wind was inaudible to the ear, and the only movement in the world was that of Shakey's Cadillac easing to a stop in front of the townhome, the eerie stillness of the cold December night the only witness to the tortuous surrender of self-respect that was to follow.

Shakey knew that Jessica's suggestion was his only salvation, but even freedom from his tormenter was no salvation at all from the self-loathing that singed his soul. He loved Jessica, Christopher, Cindy, Evette, and Jonathan, and he was no good to any of them wasting away in the Texas Department of Corrections. So Jorgé Trevino would have Jessica for a night, then she would be Shakey's for a lifetime. So he told himself, despite knowing that nothing in his life had ever been so simple.

"I'll pick you up in the morning," Shakey's voice knifed through the humiliating silence. "OK." Jessica attempted to say, but was unable to speak. The frightened young woman unlocked the door, pushed it open, and paused to gather herself before stepping from the car. Without any further attempt at speech, she closed the door behind her and trudged slowly for Trevino's house of horrors.

Shakey pressed hard on the gas, zooming quickly away from the biggest defeat of his life; careful not to look in either mirror, knowing that to see Jessica approaching the townhome would cause him to swiftly wheel the Cadillac around.

Jessica stood at the base of the stairs leading to the townhome. Wanting no parts of what surely awaited her inside the upscale living quarters, yet motivated by the fierce love she felt for Shakey and a commitment to do whatever it was that he needed she would do as she had promised, her love would permit nothing else.

Finally breaking the forces holding her in place, Jessica took to the stairs one at a time, an eternity between each upward step.

By the time she reached the third step, the door to the townhome flew open, and an olive complected white man of medium height and build stood in the doorway. His dark wavy hair was wet and the man was covered only by a bathrobe.

"Jessica." The man's smile was a flawless display of perfectly shaped ivory. The crow's feet at the corners of both eyes deepening in perfect correspondence with his smile. In another time, another place, with a drastically different set of circumstances precipitating their encounter, Jessica could have thought the man in front of her to be handsome. But in the here and now, the face of Jorgé Trevino was synonymous with that of Beelzebub. "Welcome to my humble abode." Trevino made an exaggerated motion of welcome while stepping from her path.

Jessica climbed the final three stairs, her pulse quickening as she walked past Trevino, briefly brushing against him while co-inhabiting the space in the doorway.

The scent of a well-prepared meal soured on Jessica's stomach at just about the same time the shifting of the deadbolt lock sent a message of dread to her heart. Music played in the next room, a love song Jessica could not place, though sounding very familiar to her.

Jessica knew nothing of home décor, but was sure that the lavish furnishings of the townhome were much too expensive to be purchased on a cop's salary.

"You like?" Trevino reached out for Jessica's hand. When his gesture went unanswered, he grabbed her hand and led her toward the large daybed.

Jessica was speechless. Her nerves whipped to a frenzied wave of paralyzing energy. Gallantly clinging to her composure, she did manage a barely discernible nod.

"Come." Trevino led her closer to the daybed, then urged her with a firm hand on both shoulders to sit on the daybed. Then the gracious host reached for the large golden platter and placed it in front of her.

Jessica observed the platter. On it were two large plates filled with pleasant smelling steamed fish. A small bowl of red sauce set between the two plates. A sharp pointed knife lie across the top of the container.

"Hungry?" Trevino took the knife, dug into a generous portion of fish, and placed it at the tip of the opening of Jessica's well-proportioned lips.

Jessica fought the urge to back herself into the corner of the daybed or even better, flee quickly from the midst of the evil one. But she had to do this. For the love of Shakey and Christopher she had to. "You got something to drink?" Jessica mouthed slowly to assure that her words were vaguely sounding of English.

"Wine or liquor?" Trevino placed a square of fish in his mouth, chewing with the slow deliverance of a devilishly calculating man. He then stood and opened the front of the black satin bathrobe. Underneath was a matching pair of boxers with a large green money sign embroidered on the bottom corner of the left leg. "What's your desire?" He stepped closer to where she was seated, the half open fly of his boxers just inches away from her face.

"Liquor." Jessica leaned backward in an attempt to qualm the fastly growing anxiety that was promising a full frontal assault.

Trevino stepped to the small bar beside the daybed, dipping the scooper twice into the filled ice bucket, each dip enough to fill a generous sized glass. Two parts Hennessy, one part Coke was then added to each glass.

Trevino turned in Jessica's direction, now carrying a glass in each hand. He placed one glass on the platter directly in front of Jessica, and the other on the platter where he was seated.

Jessica took a small sip to prepare her stomach, then a much larger one to calm her nerves. She then poured the entire drink down her throat while watching the purposeful movements of Trevino, who headed for the mantle atop the marble fireplace. Her own glass empty now, Jessica discarded it onto the table before opting for the full glass that was to be Trevino's.

Trevino was deeply entranced by the small tray fixed with already divided, well-proportioned lines of cocaine. He used the straw he kept on ready for the nasal injection of his favorite candy. In two toots, a hundred dollars worth of cocaine was gone.

Jessica, already half-finished with Trevino's drink and mindful of the next, looked up to observe the approach of Galveston County's head narcotics officer. Her own mind was magically drawn to the small tray he placed in front of her.

Jessica was struck dumb by the cocaine filled tray. Though preferring the rock form of the world's deadliest drug, a toot or two would have to do. Her indulgence was a foregone conclusion.

Trevino didn't speak. Jonathan Reed's personal tormentor quickly finished the remainder of his drink then headed for the bar with both glasses.

Jessica had already placed one end of the straw in her nose when the loud protest of her conscience threatened to interrupt the drug binge that was set to begin. But abstinence for this weakening addict, mired in such an impossible quagmire was a highly unlikely possibility. Fully aware that the action she would take in the next few seconds could lead to a downward spiral that was possibly never ending, Jessica's face lowered in the direction of the neatly separated lines of cocaine until the tip of the straw was touching the end of the nearest line. Slowly Jessica inhaled, making it slightly past a fourth of the line before stopping. Jessica leaned back on the couch, the burning in her nose lasting only a second before her face became completely numb.

Trevino returned with two more drinks. The wickedest of smiles covered his face upon sight of the glazed look in the eyes of the red-haired slut Shakey loved. Soon she would be his, and he would tell Shakey every detail of the night of sex he would have with her. Then he would arrest the nigga he loved to hate, and the hell that was the Texas Prison system would be his home for the rest of his natural born days. And for Shakey to have believed that anything else would happen was but proof positive of just how stupid the Handsome Intimidator had become.

The well-trained flash of high-beams coming from the alley to his left alerted Shakey of the near proximity of his customers. Though they had agreed to meet in front of the crowded Trans Am Club on the front face of Thirty-seventh Street, Shakey figured the obscurity of the alley was just as well for the sale of eighteen-ounces of crack cocaine.

Shakey eased the Cadillac farther up the street near the far corner of the block, parking against the curb opposite the club. The keys were left in the ignition. With him he took only the Jack-in-the-Box bag, stuffed full of crack cocaine and covered with a handful of napkins. The seventeen-shot 9 mm that had become his newest traveling companion was tucked into the waistband of his pants, resting against the small of his back.

As Shakey cruised the alley, the headlights flickered again, guiding him toward the nine-thousand-dollar pick-up.

The customer was Black, another wannabe baller who kept at his disposal a vast collection of children half his age, both male and female to perform tasks of both business and pleasure. Shakey and Black had never been friends. The grudge went back to the time they spent together in prison. But business was business, and money was money, though Shakey was wary of the assured drama that came with dealing with snakes like Black.

"What's up, my nigga?" Black stepped from the car, his large bald head a darker shade than that of the night that hovered over them, virtually invisible. Shakey could clearly make out only the light blue North Carolina Tarheel tank top the man wore over identically colored sweat pants.

Both back doors of the old school Eighty-Eight opened, and two young men stepped from the car, both joining Black on the passenger side of the vehicle. Shakey recognized one of them immediately, knowing him only as Li'l Willie. The driver of the car was a pretty high school aged girl.

"Slow boogie, baby." Shakey made an attempt at cordiality, though wanting only to complete the agreed upon transaction and get as far away from this cast of characters as possible within the next five minutes.

"What they hittin for?" Black asked a ridiculous question, Shakey's prices had been the same for four years.

"Same thing,"

"Let me see 'em." Black was pushing his luck. "I got my scale in the car." Black motioned to the car's still open front passenger door. In fact, each of the three doors the men had used to exit the car was still open.

"You don't need no scale." Shakey was growing angry as he moved toward the porch of a nearby house. He snatched the napkins from the Jack-in-the-Box bag and reached for the four oversized Ziploc bags lying within. Each bag contained four and a half ounces of crack.

"I just wanna see where my money's goin', home-boy." Black spoke as if having the most honest of intentions while joining Shakey in the small arc of il-lumination provided by the porch light of the mostly wood-framed home.

Shakey said nothing, feeling that his business integrity needed no validation. His dislike of Black blossomed into violent anger.

Black, perhaps sensing Shakey's anger, followed with a simple "I'll take 'em."

Shakey slid the four plastic bags in Black's direc-tion, leaving it to him to repackage the product if he so desired.

Black swiftly shoved each of the plastic bags back into the paper bag. Once finished, he turned to his accomplices. "Pay the man, Willie."

Shakey saw nothing. He didn't have to. The clicking sound made by the pump action shotgun was all the warning he needed. In an instant, his own weapon was cocked and in his hand, aimed in the direction of the Eighty-Eight's back passenger side door. The opening Li'l Willie used to extract the twelve gauge. Before turning the barrel of the gun on Shakey, the would-be jacker was cut down by two 9 mm slugs, one entering at the base of the neck, in the spot where the spinal cord meets the brain stem, and the second smashing directly into the back center of his head. Both shots painlessly lethal, Li'l Willie's corpse fell forward into the car, his feet still planted in the alley's gravel. Not so much as a spasm came from his teenaged body.

The carnage had only just begun as the 9 mm was turned on the mastermind of the bungled robbery plot. His canyon-like eyes screamed wildly in disbelief. Disbelief that he, a man personally responsible for the death of a half-dozen others in the jungle streets, the playa who had always escaped harm by riding on the wings of the misdirected loyalty given to him by the street's most foolish, was finally on the wrong end of the rod of judgment. Black didn't believe Shakey had the nerve to aim a loaded gun in his direction. The thought was Black's final, save for the wonderment at the burning in his chest that followed the sound of the roaring canon erupting before him. The two successive blasts were heard by all within an eight block radius. All that was, except for Li'l Willie and Black.

Black's lifeless body fell back into the arms of the third young man. The freckle-faced youngsta with the yellow-tinted skin and short, dirty-red hair proved to be quite swift in both mind and foot as he snatched the bag from Black's hand and ran full speed in the opposite direction.

He was nearly at the corner before Black's body had even hit the ground.

Shakey pointed the gun at him but was distracted by the waking engine of the Delta Eighty-Eight.

Whirling in the car's direction, Shakey aimed the barrel of the gun at the young girl driving the car. The car backed up quickly, droppin Li'l Willie's body in the alley next to Black's. Shakey lowered his gun and ran swiftly in the direction of his own vehicle.

The girl shifted the car into drive and lunged forward, the rear wheel of the car smashing Li'l Willie's head into the gravel. The mad young woman was conscious only of the fleeing man who had shot Black.

Shakey glanced behind him just in time to see both passenger side doors slam closed after hitting a telephone pole. Shakey ran as fast as he could in the direction of the fast growing crowd of spectators that was forming outside the Trans Am Club. Most of them had moments before been inside the establishment, head bobbin' to the latest club mixes.

"He's gotta gun!" A woman's frightened warning sent a scrambling panic throughout the crowd. A frantic dispersal immediately followed.

Pistol still in hand, and two tons of metal ripping at his heels, Shakey veered left in the direction of the club.

The murderous young woman, sensing the imminent escape of her prey, wheeled hard left, bumping Shakey with the side of the car before ramming full speed into the telephone pole positioned at the alley corner.

The impact of the bump from the car caused Shakey to leave his feet. The gun slipped from his grasp as his body slid across the concrete walkway in front of the club's entrance. He gasped at the pain of his own burning body parts, as entire portions of his arms were stripped skinless by the uncompromising pavement. Quickly on all fours, he scanned the ground about him for his weapon, concluding within moments that the nine millimeter had already been snatched from the pavement by one of the dozens of running and screaming club patrons.

The driver side door of the Delta Eighty-Eight opened suddenly, and the battered and bloodied body of the young girl fell from the car, bent awkwardly at the waist, and wielding the pump action shotgun.

Shakey scrambled to his feet, leaping for the cover provided him by the line of parked cars just a few feet away. The shotgun erupted suddenly, the pellets pelting the back end of the Lexus Sports coupe Shakey leaned against, sending chunks of paint into his eyes. He cursed himself for not shooting the girl when the opportunity presented itself.

The crowd was in full fledged hysteria now as the injured young woman, impervious to the pain of the assortment of breaks and fractures she had incurred as a result of the collision with the telephone pole, limped into the street awaiting

Shakey's appearance on the other side of the cars. The shotgun was cocked and ready for war.

Shakey, acting only on instinct, leapt from between two cars, unwittingly placing himself in the unhindered sights of the murderous young girl.

Shakey's time had come, and he knew it. While standing to face both the girl and her menacing tool of death, there came God's Reprieve. In a flash so swift as to be totally unrecognizable, something or someone tackled the young woman. The shotgun blast that would have ended the life of the jungle's most infamous kingpin obliterated the windshield of a nearby Nissan pick-up. Later, a most gracious Shakey would learn that the life-saving black angel that saved his life was none other than his old friend Smitty. But in the now, Shakey's only thoughts were of escape.

Running full-speed toward the corner of 37th Street and Winnie, Shakey's heart filled with despair upon seeing that his Cadillac was gone.

Still running, Shakey turned right on Winnie, traveling through the ankle-high grass and weeds alongside the old cotton shed building. The shadows of the building provided a near perfect camouflage.

Shakey heard the scream of burning rubber as a fast approaching vehicle came his way. The zoom of the accelerating engine fading into the screech of halting tires when the vehicle was directly next to him.

Shakey looked to his left, the familiarity of the black Nissan Pathfinder already leading him to run in it's direction, before even his mind's full discernment of the vehicle's owner could take place.

The door opened to allow his entrance to the chariot. Shakey peeped inside. Michelle frowned back at him. He quickly climbed inside and closed the door behind him before being quietly whisked away from his latest atrocity.

The cocaine failed to do its job, and so did the entire bottle of Hennessy she had consumed. Jessica could still feel sufficiently enough to be all too mindful of the constantly mounting anxiety that now reached the panic state.

Trevino thrust the knife into another piece of fish. In the other hand, he held a lemon slice, squeezing the juice onto the fish before placing the square under Jessica's lips.

Jessica's eyes filled with tears. She wanted so desperately to be strong for Shakey, but knew that a full fledged episode was a certainty in the not too distant future. She ignored Trevino's offering.

Trevino ran his tongue along the length of both sides of the blade. He then placed the knife on the table before lying back against the arm of the couch. His robe untied, the narcotics officer reached in the fly of his boxers, extracting his member. Tugging roughly on himself, his unromantic request was, "Come on, baby."

Jessica swallowed hard. The pounding of her heart caused her to feel faint. Her stomach was nauseous with the smell of her own fear.

Trevino, stiffened to capacity with his sadistic desire for Shakey's woman, sat up straight on the couch. His left hand massaged the bare skin of Jessica's inner knee while he still used his right to stroke himself.

Jessica's entire body was cold, rigid steel.

"Relax, baby." Trevino kissed her neck as his hand found its way beneath the hemline of the skirt she wore. "You'll like it. I promise."

Jessica's mind was a mass of conflict and confusion. Her love for Shakey, the distorted sense of perception caused by the drinking and drugging, and the stubbornly pursuing demons of her past, all combined in the center of her mind's eye. The result was spontaneous combustion.

"Shakey didn't tell me you like it rough." Trevino laughed gleefully while pushing her back onto the couch with a hand to the chest. With his other hand, he rubbed roughly on the mound between her legs.

"No," Jessica whimpered softly, heroically struggling to locate the resolve within herself that would free Shakey forever. She attempted to pull away from him, but the arm of the couch provided no means for escape.

"I like to role-play too!" Trevino was the exited lunatic. "You want me to take it?" He shed the robe completely from his body, standing over Jessica just long enough to step from the boxers and kick them away. Completely naked he dove atop of her, kissing roughly on her face and neck.

"Nooo!" she screamed louder this time.

"You're a fuckin nutcase, ain't ya?" Trevino jerked firmly on the waistband of her panties, tearing them from her body before throwing them behind the couch. "If you like it, I love it, baby."

"No Stan, stop it!"

Trevino jumped from atop of her and ran excitedly to the spot where he had earlier discarded the houserobe. Reaching in the robe's only pocket, he grabbed the Trojan condoms. "Oh, I'm Stan now. Baby, I'll be Stan, Dan, the man, or whatever else your crazy ass wants!" Jorgé Trevino snatched one of the condoms from the package and attached it to his phallus.

"No, Jason don't look, close your eyes." Jessica looked past Trevino.

"No, don't close your eyes." Trevino found it all to be hysterically funny. "Come on in and join the party. The slut can take us both!" Trevino was still laughing when he lie atop of her again. He struggled with all his might to part her tightly closed legs. "You're strong too. Ain't you, bitch?"

"Please don't do this," was Jessica's final cry before the lifetime of abuse and exploitation she had endured rendered her totally insane. Now possessing the strength of ten burly construction workers, the manic young woman flung Trevino from atop of her, sending him crashing onto the table in front of the couch, smashing it.

"Crazy bitch!" Trevino's voice was emptied of humor now as he became quite angry with the redhead.

Trevino would soon find that the fight had just begun, as Jessica was up and on him in an instant. She pounded the side of his head with her tiny fists, and though inflicting no major damage, the volume of her blows caused Trevino to use his arms for defensive purposes only.

The unbridled rage of the oft abused young woman was an uncontrollable wave of violence now. Jessica reached for the first of the large platters on the table, holding the food carrier high above her head before bringing it crashing into the side of Stan's head. The resulting gash sprayed blood in every direction.

Trevino struggled to free himself from beneath the woman, but the forces within her proved much too strong.

Jessica brought the platter against Stan's head again and again, not stopping until the platter was bent so badly that its further usage was no longer possible.

Jessica dropped the platter beside the half-conscious man and wept uncontrollably. She climbed from atop of him. Her mind raced with the thoughts of her stepfather's vengeance once he recovered from the wounds she had inflicted. No sooner had the thought formed in her mind, did Stan's hand clamp around her wrist.

"I'm going to kill you, bitch!" Trevino's voice was a low volume, high-intensity growl filled with promise.

"No!" Jessica struggled to free herself from Stan's grasp, but the strength was now his.

A reflected gleam of light caught the terrified woman's attention, and the reflector of that light was soon in her hand.

Trevino snatched her in his direction, not knowing that she possessed the knife until it had twice punctured the skin and muscle of his upper arm and shoulder.

Jessica stabbed repeatedly with the knife, inflicting scores of punctures into Stan's upper body, neck, and head. She was murderously intent on forever ending the incestuous abuse, continuing the stabbing long after Jorgé had taken his last breath.

"Hello?" Michelle pressed the TALK button. Her greeting wasn't a greeting at all, but in fact a most stern chastisement for an unwanted intrusion.

"Shakey." Jessica's cry was filled with questions.

"What?" Michelle heard her perfectly fine the first time, but wanted to prolong the situation for just a few seconds. "Who is this?"

"Shakey!" Jessica cried loudly into the phone, caring nothing for the vaguely familiar voice, save for the barrier-like blockage of the voice she needed.

"Shakey." Michelle gently nudged her slumbering prince then shook him hard when he failed to immediately awaken. "Shakey," she repeated in a nasty tone of voice. "That skank-ass white bitch you fuckin' is on the phone!"

Shakey's eyes remained closed. He hoped that his refusal to face the night would make it all just a dream.

"I know you hear me, nigga!" Michelle was the most ghetto of bitches. "Here!" She slammed the phone onto his chest then pouted like a small child just separated from his favorite toy. The ruby-red lipstick she had reapplied to her face once Shakey had fallen asleep, caused her to look quite cartoonish.

Shakey gripped the phone. His heart filled with the guilt of Peter at the hour of the rooster's crow. He knew that no words could explain his behavior. Frightened to the core, he himself had no understanding of the covert, purely sexual relationship that he and Michelle had maintained throughout the years. His feelings regarding his best friend's wife was a classic study in contradiction. Though finding no one thing about her that appealed to him, Shakey had found that he could never stay away from her for long. He often showing up at Red's home on some proposed business issue just to spend a few moments in nearness to his secret lover. Though not finding Michelle to be especially attractive, no woman had even been able to arouse the feelings in him, be it with a smile, frown, or defiant hand on the hip, as Michelle was masterfully able to do. Even their lovemaking was void of any notable exploits. But the thought of a romp in the sack with Michelle had always been an irresistible one for Shakey.

Of course there was a time when his interaction with Michelle had been of a completely noble origin. Years ago, with Red serving a short prison sentence, Shakey would regularly visit Michelle to see how she was holding up in Red's absence. Regrettably, the predictable happened. And from that moment until this one, Shakey had been locked on board the streetcar named disaster.

For Michelle's part, her position was much less complicated to decipher. She loved Red and the stable secure environment he provided. He was the perfect husband. But Shakey set her soul aflame with an excitement wielding more intensity than any drug known to man. And though the creeping she had done with her husband's best friend would surely relegate her to the lowly role of slut and harlot amongst the Winfrey talk circle, Michelle knew the truth: it was all women's longing to be with the man calling the shots.

"Hello." Shakey gathered the courage to face the music.

"Sha-ke-ee," Jessica's voice was a broken collection of off-key sobs.

"What's wrong?" Shakey sat straight up in the bed, fearful that his worst concerns had sprang to life.

"I—ka—Ka." Jessica struggled, but couldn't find the words.

"Jessica, calm down and tell me what's wrong." Shakey was already condemning himself for placing her in harm's way. He promised himself that if Trevino had hurt her in any way, all restraint would be broken. "What did he do?"

"I—I couldn't—" Jessica managed to stutter a few intelligible words. "I just couldn't. I'm sorry." She broke down again.

"It's OK." Shakey was happy of at least that much. "You ain't got nothin' to be sorry for."

"He wouldn't stop." Jessica coughed loudly. "I told him to stop. I didn't want to do it."

"It's OK, baby." Shakey was devastated, mistakenly interpreting Jessica's words to mean she had been raped, and knowing he was totally responsible for it all.

Michelle, angered by the concern and affection she heard in Shakey's voice, stood to dress. She quickly donned the tight-fitting pantsuit she had worn to the club and rushed from the hotel room. Shakey hardly noticed her departure.

"There's blood everywhere," Jessica sobbed before crying out loudly. "He's not breathing, Shakey!"

"What?"

"I killed him, Shakey!" The whole of Jessica's remaining emotional energy accompanied the confession. "I told him, Shakey. . . . I begged him to stop."

"Look." Shakey hoped to find that Jessica's words were the product of some strange psychotic delusion, but in the event that it wasn't, his mind was already shifting into murder scene clean-up mode. "Make sure all the blinds are closed, don't open the door, and don't answer the phone till I get there. Understand?"

Jessica nodded, once again crying uncontrollably.

"Jessica, you hear me?" Shakey's voice was loud but calm. "Jessica. Do you hear me?" He half-expected to hear Trevino's wicked laughter any any moment.

"Hurry up, Shakey . . ." Jessica finally answered, not much volume to her voice to begin with, the volume trailing away until the end of her plea was but a whisper. "Please hurry up."

"Just stay put," Shakey instructed before promising, "I'm on my way." He hung up the phone.

Shakey put his clothes on. His mind was now that of a totally calculating genius carefully plotting his next diabolical scheme. Picking up the phone, he prepared to execute move number one. Regardless of what he found when he entered the townhome, he would need his most trusted crime partner. He quickly dialed the seven digits that would assure Red's arrival at Trevino's humble abode.

CHAPTER 25

Red had not yet arrived when the dark blue Chrysler mini-van pulled in front of Trevino's townhome. Shakey had hitched a ride with the four high school aged kids inside the mini-van after agreeing to show them a place to purchase after hours liquor.

"Thanks, Ritchie," Shakey told the long-haired young man driving the mini-van while reaching into his pocket for a more tangible expression of his gratitude.

"Anytime, dude!" Richie was only slightly buzzed at the present, but that would be changing real soon.

"And as a token of my appreciation." Shakey was anxious to get inside the townhome, but was careful not to arouse the suspicions of the vanload of kids he rode with. "I have a special blend of herbs and spices for you kids." Shakey, after taking the pre-rolled Swishers that were in the large plastic bag for himself, handed the bag to Richie, complete with two ounces of high quality marijuana.

"Wow," the strawberry blonde girl in the passenger seat exclaimed. "Thanks, mister." She snatched the bag from Shakey's hand.

"Dude," another young man sat up straight behind Richie.

"You kids have fun." Shakey saw the approaching headlights of the rescuing battalion and knew that it was time for business.

"You too, dude!" the four of them seemed to say in unison.

Shakey slid the door on the side of the mini-van open. He unconsciously pulled his jacket closed in response to the briskness of air that greeted him.

"Later, dude," took the place of the long goodbye as the mini-van disappeared into the stillness of the island night.

Shakey didn't approach the door of the townhome until sure the mini-van was out of sight. Shakey reached inside his pocket for the door key. Unknown to Trevino, Shakey had the duplicate made long ago.

Shakey fit the key into the lock, turned slowly, then pushed softly. He entered the the townhome with the stealth of a ninja warrior.

Nothing was out of place in the area just beyond the doorway, causing Shakey's heart to again be filled with hopes of false alarm.

Shakey traveled the hallway leading to the living room. Shakey stopped suddenly, listening intently as Jessica's sobbing filled his ears.

He stepped forward again.

Shakey squeezed next to the wall once close enough to the living room to feel vulnerable. From where he stood, in a war-ready defense crouch, he peered into the living room. His heart melted immediately.

Jessica was a lifeless bundle of misery and despair, huddled into the corner of the couch, the only positive proof of life being the pain riddled sobs and incoherent mumblings she emitted.

Shakey steeled himself against the emotion he felt, knowing that it was enough to cost him his life.

Without placing himself in harm's way, Shakey attempted to gain a better vantage point for observing the room. He found himself unable to locate Trevino from outside the living room. Shakey reached for his gun before entering the room. With the gun out in front of him, he quickly rushed the scene.

Shakey nearly went into shock upon sight of the lifeless body of his one-time friend and long-time nemesis floating in a pool of his own blood. There were countless wounds from a variety of sources throughout the body and a knife of some sort was still impaled up to the hilt in the back of the dead man's shoulder.

He loved him. And the realization of that fact wasn't clear to him until that very moment. Despite the enmity between them, Shakey had never forgotten that Trevino was his first friend and blood brother. When neither of them had anything else to feel good about, they had each other. This was the real reason Shakey had never chosen to hurt Trevino.

"Shakey." Red entered the living room, gun at his side now that he was sure there was no imminent threat. He eyed the corpse with a stern gaze.

"They're gone." Shakey was in clean-up mode again.

"Who's gone?" Red was puzzled by the statement.

"Whoever killed him" Shakey said.

Red looked to Jessica, who though still not conscious of the two men's presence, had already given a full confession as far as Red was concerned.

"Jessica." Shakey tended to her, ignoring Red's preposterous accusation. "Jessica, baby, it's OK." He sat on the couch next to the hysterical young woman. She had still yet to acknowledge his presence.

Meanwhile, Red was quite curious as to the identity of the stiff. Using the tip of the shoes he wore, he rolled the corpse over onto its back. "Jesus Christ." Red's curiosity quickly exploded into his first real show of fear in nearly a decade.

"Jessica, baby." Shakey touched her gently on the shoulder.

"Nooooo!" Jessica screamed at the top of her lungs. She turned to face Shakey and with her back firmly against the arm of the couch, she kicked him in the chest with great force.

"Jessica, it's me," Shakey managed despite the absence of wind in his body. Reaching out to her with his right hand, he wanted to say more, but needed a few moments before any further speech was possible.

Jessica was in full fight mode now, her senses penetrable only by the sight of Shakey's breath deprived face. Sanity returned slowly, as she longed for the only man in the world with whom she had ever felt safe. "I'm sorry, baby." She leaned forward, resting on her knees, waiting desperately for any sign of acceptance.

"It's OK, baby." Shakey reached with both arms now, realizing for the first time that Red had correctly figured the murderer's identity. "It's not your fault."

Jessica leaned slowly, her body collapsing into Shakey's arms before losing herself once again in uncontrollable grief.

"What the fuck!" Red had no interest in the touching love scene before him. The lifeless body of Galveston's Chief Narcotics Officer was under his foot, and he wanted some answers. "You wanna tell me what the fuck is going on, Shakey?"

Shakey, still clinging tightly to Jessica, answered with a simple, "Hold on, dog."

"Hold on my mothafuckin' ass, nigga! What the fuck done happened in here?"

"I got here when you got here, nigga!" Shakey snapped back, though knowing he had no right to speak to Red in such a manner. The emotion of the moment made tact an impossibility.

Red holstered his weapon, a swarm of angry bumble bees churning inside his head, buzzing their menacing alert that life as he had known it had ended upon walking through the threshold of the East End townhome.

"Baby, hold on," Shakey whispered into Jessica's ear while attempting to pull away from her.

Jessica held onto him as if her own life depended on it.

"I'm not going anywhere, baby," Shakey whispered. "I'll be right there."

Jessica tightened her grip.

Red observed it all as if watching a most ridiculous story of romance. He wondered all the while how exactly Shakey had allowed this obviously disturbed white bitch to get them all into such dire straits.

He finally peeled himself away from her. "Ill be right back, baby," Shakey promised once more before stepping from the couch and heading in the direction of the large angry man hovering over Trevino's body.

"This is fucked up, Shakey." Red felt like he had been victimized by a monumental act of betrayal.

"Look, Red." Shakey was unable to find the words to appease the anger of his friend. Nor could he ease his own conscience for pulling such a dastardly stunt. "I know, man, but you was all I had."

Red thought hard about something for a moment, perhaps concentrating harder than Shakey could ever remember seeing. Calmly he spoke, "What's our next move?"

Shakey was relieved. Red had never before let him down. "First we'll take her somewhere." Shakey motioned to his weeping princess before turning to the bloodied corpse. "Then we'll take him somewhere."

Red listened closely, saying nothing. "Then," Shakey continued. "I'll come back here alone and clean up. Cool?" "Cool," Red responded, knowing that he was already involved much too deeply to give any other answer.

Shakey paused to catch his breath then quickly returned to the task of covering Trevino's makeshift grave with dirt, sensing more than just a casual urgency to quickly finish the job.

As earlier planned, Shakey had immediately taken Jessica home, feeding her a handful of Xanax along the way, assuring himself that she would rest until he returned. Next, he and Red returned to the townhome, and after loading the rug-wrapped body of Jorgé Trevino into the Pathfinder, the two men drove westward until finding a secluded spot for the soon christened cemetery.

Shakey worked swiftly, wanting desperately to be finished with the task of burying his one-time friend. He and Red switched places, and now Shakey held the small flashlight that provided the necessary illumination for them to complete their task. Ten minutes later, the two of them switched places again, and Shakey was left with the task of dumping the last of the dirt on the casketless body.

Shakey was slightly out of breath once finished with the last shovelful of dirt. The shovel was stuck into the mound, and left to stand alone while Shakey paused to ponder the atrocity he had just committed. He was just beginning to feel the powerful surge of guilt when the click-clack sound made by the cocking hammer of a large gun sent shivers down his spine.

Shakey turned slowly to face the bearer of the readying weapon. His bewilderment greatly multiplied by the face behind the hand gripping the .44 magnum.

"Dig another one, mothafucka!" Red demanded.

"Red?"

"She looks just like you, you rotten son-of-a-bitch!" The tears streamed freely from Red's bloodshot eyes. His hand trembled with the anguish of freshly discovered betrayal. His voice filled with imminent murder.

"Look, Red." Shakey's voice was as unsteady has it had ever been; his mind struggling to conjure the words that would save his life, shocked, frightened, and angered by what Micelle had obviously done. "What's your problem?"

"After all I don' for you, man." Red's rage was buffered by his grief. "I devoted my whole life to yo' bitch ass!" Red's yell proved the anger was quickly outpacing his grief.

"Hey, Red, it's me, man." Shakey quickly engaged his most disarming smile, but could immediately see that much more would be needed to stymie his best friend's murderous intentions. Unable to think of any other course of action, he settled on the truth. "I'm sorry, man."

Red shook his head, causing a series of tears to fall from the bottom of his chin, onto the toes of his shoes. "Why, Shakey?" The behemoth of a man's voice was now the high pitched shrill of a wounded eagle.

Shakey looked Red plainly in the eye, knowing that he owed his friend an answer—some sort of explanation as to why a lifetime of loyal friendship had been repaid with such an unpardonable transgression. He had fathered Red and Michelle's firstborn child, and even Shakey, in all his glory as the great conversationist, could muster only a pitiful "I don't know."

Red stepped closer, placing the end of the nine inch barrel directly against his ex-friend's forehead. "I'll dig the hole myself."

"Come on, Red." Shakey started to beg but knew it was much too late.

Red's eyes opened wide with murder, the veil of intolerable pain casting a total eclipse of his heart. But in an instant, the pounds of pressure necessary to pull the trigger of the .44 magnum became much more than Red was able to produce. "Get yo' black ass outta here!" was the last words Shakey would ever hear from his friend.

The paranoia had set in immediately. With each passing car, every nearby utility worker, and all casual encounters, Shakey's fight or flight mechanism went haywire with anticipation of the promised appearance of Trevino's mystery partner.

The heightened state of vigilance Shakey had maintained in the forty-eight hours since turning the last shovelful of dirt onto Trevino had already pushed him to the brink of total mental exhaustion. And that was without even bothering to consider the other fall-out from that ill-fated night.

Jessica was being kept in a drug-induced state of suspended animation with Cindy and Christopher playing the role of caregivers. They were told only that Jessica was feeling under the weather, but both kids knew that something quite terrible was amiss.

Though Shakey had spent much of the last two days near to Jessica, the two of them couldn't have been farther apart. Her being so close to complete delirium that a full recovery was doubtful, and he in constant fear of the fall of the long, swinging pendulum.

Finally tiring of the claustrophobic feeling of the coward in the closet, Shakey decided to hit the street. And now as the rented Saturn approached the corner of Thirty-fifth Street and Avenue H, he was greeted by the much welcomed sight of the hustle and bustle of his favorite street corner.

"Man." Smitty ran to the Saturn as soon as he identified the driver. "What you doin' out here?" He looked at Shakey as if baffled by his boldness.

"Chillin'," Shakey told him.

"Chillin'?" Smitty swiftly ran around the car and plopped into the passenger seat. "Make a coupla blocks or somethin', nigga."

Shakey did as instructed, driving in the direction of the old Falstaff brewery until forced to turn at the street's end. Choosing left, he made a right two blocks later and found a well concealed position along The Backtrack. He knew that his situation was a desperate one, but had learned long ago not to let anyone in the street see the extent in which things affected him. But now alone with the man representing his last trusted ally, the charade could not last. "What's the word?" Shakey knew there was no need to be more specific.

"Where you want me to start?" Smitty pushed in the lighter then unmounted the Swisher that rested behind his ear.

"Don't matter." Shakey's feigned indifference was unconvincing.

"Well." Smitty lit the Swisher. "What's left of the Caddy is at David's shop." Smitty started with what he deemed to be the least serious bit of information. "And that ain't very much." He blew a stream of smoke, pausing to allow Shakey the opportunity for comment. He took another puff of the Swisher, and once Shakey had made it clear that he would have no response, Smitty continued the report. "Two bodies."

Both Black and Willie were dead, Shakey knew as much. And though once quite proud of his ability to stomach violence, it now made him dizzy to think of the fallen bodies that forever seemed to follow him.

"You owe me two hundred bucks for the gun." Smitty offered him the Swisher.

"You got the gun?" Shakey's eyes widened as his thumb and index finger clamped onto the Swisher.

"Naw, I ain't got the gun, nigga!" Smitty was beginning to wonder about Shakey's mental condition. "You crazy?" Smitty watched as Shakey took two long tokes from the Swisher then continued. "I found the dope fiend mothafucka who grabbed it the other night," Smitty explained. "I got rid of it."

Shakey puffed again on the Swisher then exhaled slowly. He allowed the words Smitty spoke to sink in while waiting for the THC to calm his frayed nerves. "What else you got?" Shakey passed the Swisher.

"Them boys want war." Smitty rolled his window down far enough to flick the ashes then quickly rolled it up again

"What boys?" Shakey loved war. It was the only thing in which he had proved to be consistently good at.

"Deuce-Nine and them niggas from Fifrty-third."
Smitty puffed softly then passed the Swisher. "They
talkin' 'bout formin' a coalition to take you out."

Both men were quiet. Shakey was not afraid of
any of the Island's gang members, but was quite
wary of what such a situation would do to all on
the street.

Smitty, having saved the very worst for last,
finally said, "I think they know you did it."

Shakey started to say, "Did what?" but didn't
bother. Any one of a number or crimes he had committed in recent weeks would succeed in imprison-
ing him for life. The better question seemed to be,
"Why do you say that?"

"They sent a search party." Smitty paused before
finishing. "A one-man search party."

"What?" Shakey voiced his own anxiousness,
knowing beyond any doubt that his worst fears
would soon be realized.

"Some hotshot rookie." Smitty was smoking on a
Newport now, leaving the rest of the marijuana to
Shakey. He would need it. "Seems he's ridin' with
the task force since all that shit went down."

"What shit?" was Shakey's question, though his
mind was still occupied with the task of figuring the
identity of the young officer tracking him.

"What shit?" Smitty repeated not believing his
ears. "Where the hell you been?"

"Around," Shakey told him.

"Man, that ho-ass Trevino missin'," Smitty told him. "Cops is so hot, a nigga can't make shit on the street."

"Yeah?" Shakey was careful not to say much.

"Yeah." Smitty was obviously intrigued by the possible whereabouts of Jorgé Trevino. "I knew that bitch was dirty."

"What makes you think he's dirty?" Shakey asked.

"Gotta be dirty." Smitty cocked his head awkwardly in Shakey's direction. "Somebody don' body snatched his mothafuckin' ass!" Smitty let go of the loud rhythmless laugh that was as much his trademark as the stiff-necked manner in which he turned his head.

"Any signs of foul play?" Shakey asked.

"Man." Smitty laughed wholeheartedly at his friend's ridiculous question. "You need to get the last two newspapers or somethin', 'cause you for real outta touch, homie. They'll find that bitch mothafucka sooner or later."

"I doubt it very seriously." Shakey suppressed a knowing smile. If nothing else in his life ever again went as planned, he was sure of at least that as much.

Shakey reached into his pocket and counted twice the amount he owed Smitty. He then cranked the Saturn and began their return to PennySavers' corner. There was much he needed to do, and time was not on his side.

"Get up." Shakey shook Jessica hard. "Hey, baby." Jessica's slurred speech was of great welcome in that it was evident that now she at least recognized him.

Shakey quickly packed enough things to carry with them. Christopher and Cindy did the same in the other room. Shakey would hire his friends from DJ Movers to get the rest of their things later.

"Whatcha doin', hon?" Jessica sounded as if she hadn't a care in the world.

Shakey paid her no mind. He knew it wouldn't be long before the rookie arrived. When he did, he would find only an empty house.

Shakey and his family would spend the next few days at the four bedroom home he owned in the Island's West End.

"You got the key, Shakey?" Cindy was standing in the doorway, the shocking resemblance to her mother catching Shakey off-guard.

"Oh." Shakey blinked hard to separate mother from daughter. "Here you go, baby." Shakey handed her the keys.

"Me and that stupid boy ready," Cindy declared then exited Shakey and Jessica's bedroom.

"You stupid fatso!" Christopher could be heard from somewhere on the other side of the doorway.

"Shut up, punk, before I hit you in your nose like Kashandra did at Uncle Red's house."

"Fuck you, bitch!" Christopher snapped.

"Christopher!" Shakey chastised, getting only the highly amused giggles of both children in return. Next he heard the front door open then close, leaving total silence in the house beyond the bedroom. Moments later, the two children could be heard again, their gleeful voices audible through the cracked bedroom window.

Shakey was moved by the ability of the children who graced his life to always remain upbeat in the face of adversity. It pained him, however, to know that he was a major factor in their problems.

Shakey steadied himself for the completion of his task. Emotion served no purpose to him now. His very survival depended on his ability to transform himself into the cold-blooded, calculating killer that would allow nothing to chance or feelings.

Shakey threw the large duffel bag across his shoulder then lifted Jessica from the bed. He carried her through the living room and out the front door.

"Wheeee!" she yelled as they went.

"Open the door," Shakey called ahead to the kids.

After placing Jessica in the passenger seat of the car and fastening the seatbelt around her, Shakey turned to the kids. "Y'all got everything?"

"I need my cell phone." Cindy made a frantic dash for the house.

"I need my cell phone," Christopher mimicked before following in her footsteps.

"Hurry up," Shakey instructed while heading for the backyard. He had to get Baby.

Moments later, he and the family were in the Saturn, riding away to safety. They were all just happy to be together, despite it being temporary.

CHAPTER 26

It was just after nightfall when Shakey walked through the doors of the club, still hours before opening. No one was present, save for Jesse, who was half nodding, half watching TV.

"*Amigo,*" Shakey greeted with the broken Spanish that was always capable of getting a laugh from Jesse.

"*Qué arroyo?*" Jesse's smile was bright. Shakey, it seemed, always allowed much too much time to pass between visits.

"Slow boogie, baby." Shakey switched to a more familiar tongue.

"Business or pleasure?" Jesse seemed to have already decided for his best friend by quickly preparing for him a Long Island Iced Tea.

"Li'l bit of both, migo." Shakey was suddenly gripped with the sadness of a man living a lie that he had grown quite fond of. "Li'l bit of both."

"What's the matter?" Jesse could see the perplexing of his friend's mind as he placed the eighteen ounce glass on the table. "Everything all right?"

"Yeah. It's cool." Shakey drank in large gulps. Jesse was without doubt the undisputed champion of Long Island Tea making in the world. "I just need to get lost for a while."

Jesse raised an eyebrow. Though living a clean life at the time, Jesse was also a product of the street. He knew well why men like Shakey needed to get lost. "Need anything?"

"I come to ask you the same." Shakey was being only half-truthful.

"I guess I'll manage until you get back." Jesse was also being only half-honest, as he was quite sure he was speaking to Shakey for the last time.

"My end of the profit," Shakey started to explain, "is to be deposited into this account." Shakey handed Jesse all the information he needed to carry out his wishes. The account was Evette's. She will now have added to her holdings the income from Shakey's most lucrative legitimate business interest. It was the least he could do for her and Jonathan. He had failed them in every other way.

"Will do." Jesse's countenance fell while flipping through the papers given to him. He was beginning to figure that Shakey had found for himself real trouble and no doubt that trouble centered around some of the recent articles written in the local papers. "Anything else?"

"Yeah." Shakey smiled, basking in the warmth provided by the drink. "Don't let A-one get Sanovia closed down."

The two of them laughed uneasily.

Jesse stepped from behind the counter and the two men faced each other, standing just a few feet apart. "Take care, Shakey." Jesse reached out to hug Shakey, the affection of the truest nature.

"You too, migo." Shakey hugged him back then pulled away. Suddenly feeling strangely uncomfortable, he said, "I gotta go."

Jesse nodded and returned to his spot behind the counter, the sadness registering clearly across his face. "So long, migo," Shakey spoke softly while heading for the door. "Good-bye, friend." Jesse waved in response, already feeling the loss. Shakey stepped back into the night. There was still much left to do. His next stop: David's.

The light rain that had graced the island off and on for over a week now was on again. Shakey climbed inside the Saturn and closed himself inside. He cranked the ignition and pulled the car onto the street, heading west on Seawall Boulevard before making a right on Thirtieth Street.

Shakey barely noticed the blur of the swift moving blue sedan making a sudden move to pass the Saturn. The sedan's wheels screeched loudly to slow itself once directly beside Shakey. The sedan rammed the Saturn, sending it forcefully into a parked Buick Skylark. Shakey's head and face slammed into the steering wheel.

The shots erupted immediately, and Shakey scrambled in the direction of the passenger side door. He was unable to open the door as a result of the damage incurred in the wreck with the Skylark.

The bullets riddled the Saturn as countless weapons unloaded on the car. Shakey forced his body through the open window. He felt the burning of lead first in his left side, then in the back of the thigh on the right side.

Finally hauling himself through the window, he landed on the smashed trunk area of the Skylark. Struggling to breathe, he was quickly losing consciousness.

Moments later, the sound of erupting gunfire was gone, and the distant sound of sirens could be heard. He had never seen the shooter and now could see nothing at all as the wall of darkness grew closer and closer around him. Big Mama's face appeared in the wall and was gone. Then was the darkness complete.

Ralph Stephens could not believe his good fortune. After finding it next to impossible to track Jonathan Reed with the means at his disposal, the trophy fish had now jumped into the boat. Though a badly injured fish he was, Shakey was safely in possession.

Ralphy, as he preferred since angrily rejecting his childhood nickname of Opie, was in fact a dead ringer for his previous namesake. A smallish man with reddish colored hair, cheeks, and freckles, Ralph Stephens looked more like the high school kid that worked at the neighborhood ice cream parlor than the civil servant burdened with the responsibility of tangling with the various components of the Island's underworld. Though not blessed with the presence to intimidate, what Ralph Stephens lost in appearance, he more than compensated for in unbridled greed and ambition.

"Asshole still asleep?" Sergeant Michael Lute of the homicide division made his grand appearance. "Yeah," Ralphy answered, wondering if the meddlesome Lute had anything substantial on his prized catch.

"Hopefully it's eternal." Michael Lute was a decent cop with a longtime reputation for fair play and integrity amongst cops and robbers alike. At six foot five and 250-pounds, a young Lute had been known as a cop not to fool with. And now as the head full of curly brown hair he had been born with turned to gray, the detective Michael Lute was known for being a quite tenacious investigator.

"That's not very nice, Mike." Ralphy was well versed at playing the naïve kid.

"Nice?" Sergeant Lute stared at the man lying in the hospital bed. The man who he was sure was responsible for at least four murders in the last month. "I think the good Lord'll excuse any lack of discretion on my part."

Ralphy smiled the all American, apple-pie-eating smile that made him a favorite amongst his superiors; the smile that perfectly hid his truest feelings and intentions.

"He outta trouble yet?" Sergeant Lute asked.

"Yes, sir!" The uniformed officer guarding the door was finally able to answer a question. "He's in stable condition. Lucky though, a .38 slug lodged in his kidney, and a .22 an inch from his spine."

What the uniform officer had not mentioned was that Shakey had been shot a total of five times.

"Good for him," Michael Lute spat, his disdain for Shakey quite evident. "Now he can spend what's left of his sorry life in the joint."

"I second that motion." Ralphy smiled, though starting to fear that Michael Lute's plans would have grave consequences on his own plans for Jonathan Reed.

"Let me know if he comes to." A visibly upset Michael Lute left suddenly, not bothering with the formal good-byes.

"Gotcha," Ralphy said much too low for Sergeant Lute to hear. Just as well, though, as Ralph Stephens had no intentions of Michael Lute, or any other member of the Galveston Police Department, claim-jumping on his prized possession.

The criminal mind was never at rest; not even when recuperating from five gunshot wounds to various parts of the body. Through feigned unconsciousness, Shakey had provided for himself the opportunity to listen at the plans of the constantly congregating officers that frequented the doorway of the hospital room. And with the help of a young and pretty nurse he had earlier befriended, it was time for Shakey to enact a plan of his own.

David stepped from the elevator at just past 11:00 P.M. All was quiet on the Intensive Care Unit save for the sounds coming from the Gameboy played by the young police officer guarding Shakey's door. Dressed smartly in slacks, shirt, and sports coat, David carried a long leather briefcase to the nurses' station.

"Yes, ma'am," David spoke in a most professional tone. "Can you please tell me which room Walter Lewis is in?"

"Sir," the pudgy middle-aged nurse started, sure that there was no Walter Lewis on the floor, but not even bothering with the mention of such an irrelevant point. "Visiting hours are over."

"Oh, it's OK." David appeared unfazed. "I'm his lawyer."

"Well, you'll have to come back tomorrow." The nurse was quickly losing patience.

David frowned as if angry, then quickly regained his composure. With a wide and effortful grin, he spoke, "Look, ma'am, I know it's late, but my flight was delayed in Atlanta. Mr. Lewis' paperwork needs to be filed first thing in the morning."

The officer seated in front of Shakey's door took note of the potential altercation. But after deciding the elfish-looking black man to be no threat, he quickly resumed his game playing.

"Sir, we have rules at this hospital. Visiting hours start at eight, please leave now."

"Please leave now?" David's large eyes were wide with surprise as he looked to a second young nurse for help.

Not speaking again until the younger woman shrugged her shoulders. "I need to talk to Walter Lewis right now," David spoke loudly.

"Am I going to have to buzz security?" The nurse's threat was reinforced by her hand covering the orange button on the control panel in front of her.

"Tell you what!" David yelled loudly. "Call your supervisor."

"I am the night supervisor," the nurse returned with equal volume.

"Well call the president of this mothafucka!"

The muscular blonde officer placed the Gameboy down beside him and took to his feet, angered with having his game play interrupted. "What's the problem here?" The officer swaggered toward the disturbance.

"Look, Hercules, mind your business." David slammed the briefcase onto the countertop then turned to the nurse. "I need to see Walter Lewis, that's the problem!"

The puzzled officer also turned to the nurse.

"I told him it's after visiting hours and he'll have to come back tomorrow."

The officer thought for a moment then turned to David. "Come back tomorrow," he said as if the solution to the problem was quite obvious.

"Ain't that a bitch!" David jumped then stomped both feet on the floor. "Does anyone around here have any goddamn sense?"

"Look, go ahead about your business while you still can."

"What?" David frowned menacingly at the officer. "You think because I'm a professional now, makin' two hundred thousand dollars a year, I won't put my foot in yo' big ass?"

Shakey uncovered quickly, laughing at David's performance before a searing pain ended his amusement.

Cloaked in the surgical scrubs Penny had dressed him in after his bath, he quickly made it to the door leading to the adjoining room. With the key already in hand, he opened the door and stepped into the next room. He maneuvered through the darkness, as the room was identical to his own.

"Nurse?" a hoarse and weakened voice called in the darkness.

"Yes," Shakey spoke once at the foot of the bed.

"Is it time for my shot?" The elderly sounding female voice questioned.

"Just checking your IV," Shakey managed through clenched teeth, the pain from his wounds and the constantly growing fatigue he felt causing him to perspire.

"I've never had you as a nurse before." The woman was fully awake, and highly suspicious.

"I work for the agency." Shakey was finally at the door that adjoined this room to the next.

"Why don't you turn on the light?"

"I'm finished." Shakey opened the door. "Get some rest. I'll be back with that shot soon." He closed the door behind him.

Shakey made his way through the next darkened room. This one empty; the short trek across the room becoming much more of a challenge than expected.

With the key he turned the lock of another door stopping just inside the room as dizziness threatened to overtake him.

The light snore of the room's occupant reminded Shakey of the moment's extreme urgency. With the will of a punch drunk prize fighter, he trudged to the room's front door, stopping to brace himself before turning the doorknob and pushing the door open.

"Try it, white boy!" David's challenge filled the hallway as he quickly shed the sports coat. He dropped the piece of clothing on the ground between himself and the police officer before finally striking a fighting pose. "I got something for yo' steroid-taking ass!"

"Oh yeah, asshole?" The officer unfastened the canister of mace that was attached to his gun belt then stepped in David's direction.

"What you need mace for, ya big ole bitch?" David could see Shakey as the injured man slowly made his way down the hall toward the stairway. He quickly diverted his eyes from his friend, lest the officer turn in that direction. David knew that the dangerous charade must last a few more minutes if Shakey was to have a chance at escape. "Chunk 'em up like a man.

"Your ass is going to jail." The officer continued in David's direction.

"That don't mean we have to fight." David changed roles. "All I asked was to see Walter Lewis." He was now the innocent passerby, unable to understand his own victimization. "And you wanna spray me with mace. Black folks got rights now ya know."

"You sure this guy didn't come from the eight floor?" The officer questioned David's sanity. The eighth floor was the mental ward.

"Let's be friends." David suddenly dropped to his knees, watching as Shakey closed the door to the stairway before looking directly in the officer's eyes, hands clasped under this chin. "We can forget about all this shit, man!"

"Your ass is going to jail." The officer felt no sympathy for David.

"Oh yeah?" David held his pose.

"Yeah." The officer re-holstered the canister of mace then grabbed his handcuffs. "Stand up, turn around, and put your hands behind your back."

"Fuck that shit, you big ole bitch!" David stood quickly, playing the part of the madman again. "I ain't goin' no mothafuckin' where."

"Like hell you ain't!" The officer reached for David's shoulder, but before he could grab him, David fell flat on his back.

"Owww!" David yelled as loudly as possible as onlookers from every wing on the floor closed in. "Somebody call an ambulance!"

"Nice try, buddy. Get up!" The officer, bending at the waist, tapped David on the shoulder. "Owww!" David yelled with such volume that the officer made an immediate recoil. "My back's broken!"

"Sir." A young and hairy-faced intern made his way through the crowd. Standing over David, he asked, "Are you injured?"

"Hell yeah. I'm injured," David loudly agreed. "I was assaulted by this officer without provocation. My back is broken!"

"Sir, I'm sure your back is not broken." The intern laughed in spite of himself. "Would you like me to take a look at you?"

"Call Johnnie Cochran!"

"OK, but first let me look at you." The intern was still smiling.

"Promise?"

"Promise." The doctor repeated after David. "Where does it hurt?"

"Right here." David lifted his left arm high enough to show the scrape on his elbow. The entire crowd, including the officer and the head nurse, erupted with unrestrained laughter.

Shakey continued his painfully slow descension down the stairs. He clung to the banister, desperately trying not to tumble forward. Drenched in sweat, the stairway spinning before his eyes, Shakey moved on instinct.

Finally reaching the bottom of the stairs, he tumbled forward into the door. The frigid December air almost sent him into shock.

Resting against the doorframe, Shakey scanned the row of parked cars in front of him, searching through blurred vision for the sweet chariot of liberation.

A horn blow was heard from his left, and the engine of a large car quickly came to life. "Shake and bake." Shakey heard Smitty's call. "Let's go, man."

Shakey staggered toward Smitty's voice, the world spinning out of control now, the nausea worsening. With fast failing strength, the Handsome Intimidator fell to one knee. The spinning was gone now, replaced by the all too familiar darkness of coming unconsciousness. With all the resolve he could muster, Shakey hoisted himself back onto his feet. His wobbling knees threatening to buckle with every step.

Shakey staggered forward, unsure whether Smitty would be found there.

"I got ya." A firm grip clasped around Shakey's waist. Shakey also welcomed the brace of his friend under his arm. "Easy, man. One step at a time," Smitty encouraged as the two of them traveled the final few feet separating them from the car.

Smitty thought to himself how ridiculous a decision it was for Shakey to pull a stunt such as this one, less than forty-eight hours after such life-threatening injuries.

Smitty used his free hand to open the rear passenger side door for Shakey, carefully extracting himself from the injured man's wing then gently placing him inside the car. Shakey fell over onto the seat, motionles, leaving Smitty to lift his feet from the pavement and push them onto the floor of the car.

Smitty slammed the door and hurriedly took his place behind the wheel of the car. Moments later, the Monte Carlo was speeding from the UTMB medical complex.

"Man!" Ralphy squeezed Josephine's hair tightly with both hands, watching excitedly as her head bobbed up and down between his legs. The constantly ringing telephone was starting to be an annoyance.

"Grrrr." Josephine was on all fours. Nude except for the black bikini underwear, she growled playfully, confident that Ralphy would soon be firmly under her thumb.

"Man," was all Ralphy could say. His eyes closed now, the grip on Josephine's hair tightened. The stubbornly ringing phone was now unheard by him.

"Answer that damn phone!" Josephine's routine suddenly stopped. Pretended anger masking her devilish face, she glowered at Ralph, using the unexpected prop of the late-night caller to teach Ralphy his first valuable lesson in traversing the black widow's web: All job and favors performed by Josephine Gilbert are precipitated by the immediate following of her each and every command. With the whole of Ralphy's thinking faculties still gripped firmly in her hand, she added, "Now!"

"Hello." Ralphy fumbled with the receiver with both hands. Finally, the mouthpiece touched the bottom corner of his lip. Moments later, the caller had a much firmer grip on him than Josephine ever could. "He what?" Ralphy pushed her hand away as he stood to gather his clothes. "How the fuck did that happen?"

Josephine's nude body laid back on the floor, not the least bit shaken by the sudden turn of events. Shakey had escaped. She was sure of it. Once learning that he was still alive, she knew that Shakey would find a way to leave the hospital. She had to admit, however, that the quickness with which he had achieved his goal, was a surprise even to her.

"I'll fuckin' be right there!" Ralphy slammed the receiver onto its cradle. He ran his hand through his hair before gathering the rest of his clothes.

"What's wrong, baby?" Josephine's range of emotion now entailed curiosity. Widely she opened her legs, wanting to be sure that Ralphy would be thinking of her while on his fruitless quest for Shakey.

"Shakey got away," he responded simply.

"I guess you gotta go then." Josephine's was the face of sadness.

"I gotta find him." Ralph's voice begged her to understand.

Josephine struggled to hide the smile that threatened to blow her cover. She would allow him to stumble blindly for a day or two before instructing him of exactly how to track Jonathan Reed. She would do so in order to instruct him thoroughly on lesson number two: Nothing can be achieved without Josephine!

"I guess you gotta do what you gotta do." Josephine stood, dejectedly reaching for her robe. Her performance complete, an Oscar was beneath her.

"I'll be back as soon as I find him."

"How long will that be?"

"We'll have him by daybreak," Ralphy promised.

"How far can he go in his condition?"

You don't know Shakey, she thought to herself. "OK." She tied the robe in front of her then stepped slowly in Ralphy's direction, kissing him before saying, "You'd better hurry."

"I will." Ralphy returned her kiss then turned for the door. He was sure not to look back again, as he wanted no more reminder of his loss.

Josephine laughed aloud once Ralphy had closed the door behind him. She was certain that he would be the easiest prey she had known since high school.

"I got it," Christopher instinctively announced, though both Jessica and Cindy had retired hours ago. Pressing the pause button on the control pad, the youngster reached for the telephone. "Hello?" He un-paused the game after positioning the telephone between his chin and shoulder.

"Christopher." Shakey did his best to speak in a strong voice.

"Shakey?" Christopher dropped the control pad onto the floor.

"What's up?" Shakey couldn't help but smile at the joy in the young boy's voice for a split second oblivious to the immensity of his own pain.

"When you gettin' out the hospital?" Christopher asked innocently.

"Christopher, listen." Shakey took a deep breath before placing two more Tylenol 4 tablets in his mouth. Chewing them without water, he steadied himself for the business at hand. "Y'all gotta make a move."

"You want me to get Jessica?"

"No." Shakey drank from the cup filled with gin. "You the man, Chris. I need you to handle yo' business."

"What you want me to do?" Christopher took the responsibility bestowed upon him like the truest of soldiers.

"Wake Jessica and Cindy." Shakey started, his breath coming in gasps now. "Pack enough clothes for a couple of days. You listenin'?"

"Yeah." Christopher could tell that Shakey had been hurt much more than he had been told.

"Call Yellow Cab, ask for Isaac . . ."

"Shakey?" Christopher was alarmed by the extended silence on the other end of the line.

"When he gets there." Shakey's voice was the weakened whisper of a dying man. "Tell him I said to take you to the hideaway." Shakey closed his eyes tightly against the pain that rocketed against his insides. The tears that escaped were the involuntary protests of a body driven much too far. "You listenin', Christopher?"

"I'm listenin." Christopher had never been as afraid as he was now.

"When you get there . . ." Shakey struggled to finish. "Don't open the door for anyone . . ." Gathering himself he re-emphasized with all the strength he could muster. "Anyone! Understand?"

"Yeah." Christopher shed tears of his own.

"You gotta be a man for them, Christopher."

Christopher was now unable to speak, yet unconsciously nodded his head.

"I gotta go, Chris," Shakey said suddenly. "You the man, homie. Take care of your business." The click of the closed phone line was heard shortly after Shakey's last words.

Christopher used his palm to wipe the tears from both sides of his face. Starting to begin his task, he didn't bother to turn off the power to the Sony Playstation 3. He knew that either way things went, the games were surely over.

The coolness of the night was of no concern to the fast moving bodies that transited the corner of Thirty-fifth Street and Avenue H. Like a moundful of red worker ants, the best of the Island's hustlers, dealers, and users flexed their skills.

"Come back and holler at me, baby girl." Smitty smooth-talked a new customer, loving the excitement of Friday night on the block. "Smitty'll take care of you every time."

"I'll be back," the pretty teenage girl spoke up, never taking her eyes from the boulder in her hand. "If I make my money right."

"Shit," Smitty laughed. "You gon' make yours, then you can come back and get some of mine if you act right."

"Huh?" The girl placed a hand on each of her wide, curvy hips, observing Smitty for a long while before sounding, "We'll see." The girl turned to walk away, her large behind shifting in the tight-fitting jeans.

"What in the world is they feedin' these youngsters?" Smitty shook his head, speaking to no one in particular.

"Hey Smitty." The voice was nearly as rushed as the short and thin light-skinned man speeding in Smitty's direction.

"What's up, Herk?" Smitty greeted an old hustlin' partner turned drug addict.

"I got a sell, man." He whistled through two missing front teeth, pointing in the direction of the unfamiliar dark Chevy Cavalier parked across the street.

Smitty squinted his eyes through the shielding darkness. "That's a white girl." He frowned at Herk.

"It's cool, man." Herk was sweating profusely despite frigid night air. "She want a hundred."

"You know that bitch?" Smitty was highly skeptical of the strange woman.

"Yeah," Herk lied, knowing that with Smitty, the promise of fast money would overrule all. "The bitch got paper. She gon' spend all night. She just startin'."

Smitty hesitated for a moment. Something didn't feel right.

"The bitch just got a settlement." Herk refused to lose his fish. "Hurt her back on the job."

Smitty thought for a moment longer. Turning his gaze back and forth between Herk and the white woman before finally resting on Herk. "You gon' serve her?"

"Hell yeah." Herk's eyes widened. "I'ma serve that bitch everything I got!" He tugged at his crotch. "I'm trying to win, fool!"

"You's a nut, homie." Smitty laughed loudly then took a step away from Herk. He made his way for the two large aluminum trash cans positioned along the edge of the curb in front of Brown's Liquor Store.

"Shit, nigga, I'm for real." Herk took the dirt stained Kansas City Chiefs hat from his head, watching closely until Smitty reached between the cans. Herk then used the cap to fan himself.

Ralphy's grip tightened on his radio as the informant's signal was finally given.

"Let's do this!" He shouted his only instructions into the radio before flinging it into the car's backseat, his right hand opting instead for the 9 mm Luger.

"One-time!" The first man on the block to see the task force van coming from the alley opposite the storefront yelled loudly.

Smitty stopped in his tracks, his hand still in the paper bag filled with crack cocaine. A mid-sized sedan shot gravel behind it while screeching to a halt at the alley corner beside Smitty. The passenger side door of the car opened quickly and Ralphy's partner ran full-speed, gun in hand, toward Smitty.

"Move and I'll kill you, nigger!" The infrared beam affixed to the officer's gun was aimed at Smitty's solar plexus.

Smitty looked directly into the officer's eyes. There was no doubt the peace officer's threat was real. However, Smitty was in no way willing to be apprehended with his hand in a bag filled with dope. "I'm unarmed!"

Smitty screamed as loud as he could while snatching his hand from the bag. He backpedaled as quickly as he deemed to be safe, all the while praying to a God he had abandoned long ago.

"Face down, mothafucka!" The officer quickly continued toward Smitty, not stopping until the barrel of the gun was just beyond his reach.

"I ain't got nuthin', man!" Smitty yelled just as loudly while still moving slowly backward. He hoped to put just a few more feet between himself and the bag of dope. Finally, sensing he had pushed his luck as far as it would go, Smitty went slowly to the ground.

The entire block was infested with cops as vehicles of all types approached from every possible route. A swarm of officers, both plain clothed and uniformed, formed a dragnet that completely surrounded the block. They rousted all within their trap; dope and weapons were found, warrants were filled, and a score of Thirty-fifth Street regulars would not be seen for years.

CHAPTER 27

Acceptance is the final stage of grief. And what Shakey accepted was that his time was up. The Handsome Intimidator was finished and he knew it. His thoughts now as he walked into David's shop were only of what could be salvaged for those he cared for.

"What's up, homeboy?" David poked his head from the office in response to the bell that alerted him of another's presence.

"Nothing much." Shakey took a few steps toward the back of the building. The garage seemed much bigger now that only two cars were present. "Empty," was the resounding thought as Shakey pulled his coat closed in response to the chill that filled the hollow building. "What's goin' on?"

"Makin' it." Even David's voice lacked enthusiasm in Shakey's ear.

David frowned his concern. He appeared to be contemplating a quite serious matter but spoke no words.

Shakey, aware of the thoughts swirling in the mind of his friend, got straight to the point. "I need you to take care of a couple of things for me, David."

"Anything, homeboy."

"I bought this house in Lawton, Oklahoma for Jessica and the kids." Shakey reached into his coat pocket, producing a handful of assorted sized papers. "I didn't have time to have it furnished." Shakey handed him the first sheet of paper.

David looked at the paper. He said nothing.

"Use this." Shakey handed over a credit card. "Here's a list of some other properties." Shakey gave him another piece of paper. "Bank accounts." He placed more papers in David's hand.

David looked directly in Shakey's face. The mechanic's large red eyes posed a multitude of questions.

"The rest is self-explanatory." Shakey handed him the rest of the papers. "Just hold things down for me. I'll get in touch soon." Shakey spoke evenly though in his mind he knew that the real possibility existed that he would never get in touch again.

"Gotcha." The sadness was clear in David's face now.

Shakey offered his hand. He had run out of words.

Ralphy wheeled left on Jefferson Avenue. He passed the house marked 1321 slowly then parked a few feet up the block.

Galveston's newly crowned drug czar donned a pair of dark sunglasses before exiting the car. He scanned the block in both directions before taking the first step toward Shakey's home.

The block was quiet and the only sign of life was the elderly man working in the yard next to Shakey's. "Hello, sir." Ralphy flashed the All-American smile.

A well-aimed scowl was the old man's response.

Ralphy was unconcerned with the old man's belligerence. The narcotics officer's heart raced with the excitement of knowing that the distance between himself and his prized catch was quickly closing.

Ralphy paused to catch his breath once standing before the door. He reached in his pocket for the key that Josephine told him would surely unlock the headquarters of Shakey's empire. The officer's hand trembled with excitement while considering how ridiculous it was for Shakey to not know that Josephine had a key to his home.

Ralphy took another deep breath then reached for his gun. Service revolver in hand, he took a quick look behind him before fitting the key into the lock.

Ralphy's heart threatened to discontinue service when he heard the clicking sound made by the turning lock. He turned softly on the doorknob then pushed the portal open. His gun at the lead, Ralphy moved forward into the house, not bothering to close the door behind him.

Ralphy quickly scanned the living room for the fish tank that Josephine instructed him would give the clearest indicator as to whether or not Shakey still frequented the residence. Ralphy located the tank and his feet shuffled quickly in that direction. Both his eyes and gun were trained upon the top of the winding staircase.

Ralphy's heart sank once he looked into the oversized tank. The Chinese Beta was gone. Josephine assured him that this would mean Shakey had permanently vacated the premises.

Ralphy refused to admit failure. He moved quickly for the stairs. Gun still at the ready, he headed for the house's upper level. His mind recalled perfectly the diagrams Josephine had drawn for him. He started his search with the master bedroom and bath.

Twenty minutes later, his search was complete and Ralphy once again stood next to the fish tank. It was then that he noticed the bottle of Jack Daniels on the bar next to the tank. A shot glass had been placed bottom up next to the bottle. "Mothafucka!" Ralphy reached for the shot glass after sitting on a bar stool. Three shots and ten minutes later, the chase continued.

"This the spot?" the cab driver asked once directly in front of the old building. "Yeah." Shakey read the meter for himself then handed the man a twenty. "Keep the change." "Thanks." The man tipped the dirt stained baseball cap in Shakey's direction.

Shakey gave a quick nod in return then stepped from the cab. He placed the brown paper bag he carried into his pocket then pulled his coat closed before moving slowly forward. Exhausted, he still had much to do.

The sign on the door of the tin building said closed, but Shakey walked around the side of the building anyway. He stopped once at the gate. Shakey smiled to himself. The gate, like most of the fence, leaned inward, the base of the proposed barrier proving itself no longer able to bear its own weight. The gate was chained and locked despite the fact that a school aged kid could easily push the structure over.

Shakey shook the gate, causing the chain to rattle loudly. "Bro," he called.

A dog's bark from the other side of the fence was the response.

"Bro." Shakey shook harder.

The barking grew louder as the the dog stepped closer to the fence. Shakey could see through two planks of the fence that Bro walked slowly beside the dog.

"It's me. Shakey." Shakey spoke once man and dog were directly on the other side of the gate.

"I know who it is," the surly voice answered. A moment later the gate swung open.

"What's up, Bro?" Shakey opened his arms in jest, knowing that Bro would never submit to a hug.

"The prodigal son returns." The old man stood still in place, closely observing Shakey.

Shakey met the gaze of his long-time mentor. The years were fast catching up with Bro. There was no black remaining in the old man's hair and very little in his beard and mustache. There were long, deep lines crisscrossing the bronze-tinted skin of his face. If Shakey didn't know any better, he would have also thought Bro had actually shrunk an inch or two. Bro finally turned to walk away, and Shakey could see that the limp he had walked with when Shakey last visited was much more pronounced now.

Shakey followed Bro into the back yard. There, the Handsome Intimidator found that Bro had invested in a new picnic table. That was the only change for the oversized yard though, as the other sights were quite familiar to Shakey. There were no less than a dozen cars present, each of them in various stages of being gutted. The grass grew wild in some places and was bare in others. There were also entire patches of earth stained with oil and other fluids.

"Have a seat." Bro motioned with his hand. If the old man's words were meant to suggest cordiality, then surely his tone of voice and body language ruined the gesture.

Shakey followed instructions. He placed the bag in front of him on the table. He waited for the go-ahead to speak.

A nod from Bro was the signal.

"I got big trouble, Bro," Shakey started.

Bro nodded again.

"I need something fixed," Shakey said then pushed the bag in front of him forward until it was within Bro's arm reach.

Bro pulled the bag a little closer to him. He took a peek at the bag's contents then looked back to Shakey. "Lotta fixin'." The old man's eyes didn't move.

"Moe," Shakey spoke the name. When Bro didn't respond, Shakey continued with, "The coward from Twenty-ninth Street."

"I know who it is," Bro spat back at him.

The two of them sat in silence. Both men listened to the protest of the howling wind.

"I still remember that time you was up in Sandra Hawkins' house havin' sex with her granddaughter." Bro was looking straight through Shakey now.

Shakey remembered too. He was fourteen-years old. Patricia Hawkins was three years older. During lovemaking, Patricia Hawkins had obviously begun the messy portion of her menstrual cycle. After the act was complete, Shakey stood to find his genitals and torso covered in blood. The sight sent him into shock.

"We was all across the street at the gamblin' shack. Tunk was the game. Me, Deek, Bug, and of couple of seamen." Bro laughed to himself. "And here you come. Butt naked and full of blood." The old man's laughter was loud and hoarse now.

Shakey smiled then chuckled despite himself. Despite the fact that twenty years had passed since the incident, he was still quite embarrassed by it all.

"We ain't know what you had done. Killed, raped, or what. And you couldn't even talk. Just stood there. Tremblin' like you was having a seizure or somethin'. No sense even to cover yourself." Bro was not laughing now. Instead, his face showed how pitiful the entire sight was.

Shakey winced in pain as a gust of wind found its way between the openness of his coat and kissed his wounds. He reached for the pill bottle in his pocket, pulled the cap, and poured directly into his mouth without counting.

"Shakey Jake!" Bro shook his head while speaking the name one of the men had given the teenage boy after Patricia Hawkins found her way inside the gambling shack and explained to them all the ail that afflicted her Romeo. The name would soon evolve to Shakey. "You ain't changed a bit, boy!" Bro voiced his stern chastisement.

Shakey looked to his lap for a moment, gathering himself before returning Bro's gaze.

Bro didn't move or speak for a long while. When he did, he took the bag from the table and placed it on the bench beside him. "Fixed," was the only word that needed speaking.

Ralphy bobbed his head while the smile grew wider on his face. Josephine was dressed in pink lingerie and six-inch stilettos. She danced just inches in front of the cop.

Ralphy took a sip from the bottle of Jack Daniels while watching Josephine dance closer to him. He placed the bottle on the floor beside the bed and beckoned for his private dancer to move closer still. She obliged him, and his thoughts were of the player he had become. He reached forward with both hands, first clutching at her hips then cupping her rear in hands.

Josephine reached out with her own hands and clasped her fingers at the back of Ralphy's head. She pulled forward until his lips touched her belly button. She unclasped her fingers and moved her hands atop his head. She pushed down firmly.

Ralphy inhaled deeply then kissed at her moistness through the panties she wore.

Josephine pulled back suddenly. She placed a hand on each of his shoulders and pushed with great force, causing Ralphy to lie back on the bed. Once sure the surprise had registered clearly in his eyes, Josephine quickly shed the few clothes that she wore.

She stepped forward then placed a knee on the bed. Next the palms of both hands were placed flat on the bed and she crawled forward a little ways until her face hovered at about waist level to the narcotics officer. For her next feat, Josephine used her teeth to unfasten his belt.

Josephine knelt upright in the bed. She reached beside the bed and took a quick drink from the bottle, allowing enough time for Ralphy to finish undressing himself.

Josephine placed the bottle back onto the floor and quickly mounted her prey. Once he was positioned inside of her, she bounced rapidly up and down.

Minutes later, sure that Ralphy had spent all his excess energy, Josephine lay beside him on the bed. The jelly-like consistency of his body let her know that his ear was totally hers now. "Don't worry, you'll find him, baby." Josephine kissed him on the cheek.

"Is it that obvious?" Ralphy's thoughts turned immediately to his fruitless search for Shakey. He was totally unaware of the Jedi mind trick just played on him.

"It's all over your face," Josephine added. "When we made love it was like you wasn't even paying attention to me."

"I'm sorry, baby." Ralphy rolled onto his side in order to face her. His apology was filled with sincerity. "Really I am."

Josephine smiled at him. It was all she could do not to laugh in his face. Once regaining her composure she continued with. "Baby, I have been wanting to suggest something to you, but I didn't want to step out of place."

"What is it, baby?"

"It's about finding Shakey."

"If you got some thoughts on finding that ass-hole, I definitely want to hear it."

"I do, baby." Josephine said and did. Perhaps no living soul knew Jonathan Reed as completely as did Josephine. The first thing she knew was that whatever calamity that had befallen Trevino had not been precipitated by Shakey. He was likely part of the cover-up, but not the act. The chief reason she had chosen Trevino over Shakey was the fact that while Trevino was hell bent on personally causing the Handsome Intimidator's complete destruction, Shakey could never bring himself to hurt Trevino. She considered Shakey's position to be one of extreme weakness. "I think you oughtta try the opposite approach."

"Opposite approach?"

"Yeah," Josephine said. "You have been chasing him from behind, going places that you know he has been. Maybe you oughtta try to get to where he is going next."

"You got any ideas where he might be going next?" Ralphy grew excited.

Josephine knew exactly what Shakey's next move would be. He would no doubt be getting the white girl he had grown so fond of and the runaway living with them as far away from Galveston as possible. His most likely choice of transportation for them would be a bus. Josephine was sure that Shakey would not allow them to board a bus in Galveston for fear that someone might remember something. He would drive them to Houston. "I was thinking," Josephine started, pretending to be deeply perplexed.

"Yeah?" Ralphy was growing slightly impatient with her hesitance.

"He's going to try and get the girl and the boy out of town." Josephine sensed his impatience and got right to the point.

"Think so?"

"I know so." Josephine spoke with supreme confidence. "He'll use a bus. He'll take them to Houston."

Ralphy rolled onto his back. He considered Josephine's words. "Shit, you're right," he finally deduced. In a blur he was standing next to the bed fully dressed.

Josephine relaxed further into the bed. She could only smile while watching the door close behind him.

CHAPTER 28

The wheels of the Cadillac slowed to a crawl then stopped altogether once in the parking area beside the bus station. The car's occupants were still and quiet, the four of them staring ahead into the nothingness that awaited them.

Shakey was first to break the spell. He pulled the handle on the door then stopped when he heard the click. He took a deep breath before speaking. "Help me get the bags, Chris." Shakey was still looking forward.

Shakey pushed the door open then stepped from the car. He knew that another waiting moment would mean he could never do so. He closed the door softly behind him and stood still in place next to the Cadillac.

There was a nothing to this early December morning that nearly stopped Shakey's aching heart. There were no other human beings in sight and no cars passed along the street before him. The air was completely still and there was absolutely no sound to be heard. Shakey turned his eyes to the heavens. The grayish-blue sky greeted with its most menacing scowl.

Shakey looked to the heavens once more, this time voicing the silent curse that freed itself from his heart. He was sure that no one listened.

The trunk opened now. Shakey could only stare at the three bags inside. He was unable to move until he saw the small hand wrap around the handle of the topmost bag.

Shakey looked into Christopher's face. The youngster matched his gaze then nodded as if to say to Shakey that all would be well in the world. That despite the distance that would soon be between them, Shakey would always be loved. That Shakey was not to blame for the pain they all felt.

Christopher placed the first bag on the ground in front of him then reached for the next one. The courage shown by his young friend gave Shakey the strength to reach for the final bag. The trunk was now as empty as the hollowness in Shakey's heart.

Christopher used both hands to close the trunk. Both men stood still for a moment before Christopher gave a gentle nudge to Shakey's side. Once gaining his friend's attention, Christopher beckoned with his head for Shakey to follow. The younger man lifted two of the bags from the ground and stepped from the rear of the car.

Both passenger side doors opened at once and the red-faced women stepped from the car in unison. Shakey reached for the bag in front of him then followed Christopher. He was not yet able to look in Jessica or Cindy's face.

Christopher still led the way as the family rounded the corner. The sobs of the women were heavier now, and he could hear there pain. He would console them later; his thoughts now were only of getting them on the bus. The young man soldiered forward, gaining strength with each step he took.

Christopher pulled on the handle of the glass door then held the door open for the others. He gave Shakey a pat on the back as his wounded friend passed before him. Jessica passed next, but before she did, Christopher pulled at her with his free hand, near enough to kiss her on the cheek. Next came Cindy. Christopher reached for her also, but the pursed-lip scowl that formed on her face caused his hand to stop short. The two of them shared a quick laugh.

The inside of the bus station showed no similarity to the outside. Though barely 7:00 A.M., the bus station was alive and bustling with activity.

Shakey and Jessica walked side by side as did Christopher and Cindy behind them. Jessica reached for Shakey's hand, and the foursome continued forward. Shakey eyed the sign that said GATE TEN. Beneath it was the portal that would consume the last in his life worth living for. He could see that there were other passengers already boarding the bus. He had timed their drive to arrive at departure time. He hated long good-byes.

Shakey stopped a few feet in front of Gate Ten. He placed the bag on the floor. He turned to face Jessica.

Jessica pulled away from him. Both hands covered her mouth in a fruitless attempt to smother her own sobs. She took a series of half-steps backward.

"It's OK." Christopher was quickly at her side. He placed an arm around her shoulder.

Jessica's head shook furiously, and a cry sprang forward. She would have continued backwards if not for the firmness of Christopher's grasp.

"Jessica," Shakey mouthed while reaching forward with both hands.

Jessica's head shook again. She was unable to deal with all that was happening.

Shakey's heart stopped beating and was no more.

Cindy stepped forward and wrapped both her arms around Shakey. "I love you, Shakey." She squeezed tighter before adding, "We'll be all right."

"I love you too, baby." Shakey's eyes filled with tears. "I love you too."

Cindy pulled away then took a full step backward, not taking her eyes from Shakey until she was standing next to Jessica. It was now her turn to hold Jessica, and Christopher stepped forward.

Christopher stood before Shakey. He offered his hand.

Shakey smiled at the gesture then pulled Christopher deep into his chest. The Handsome Intimidator's sobs were clearly audible now.

The two men let go.

"You know," Shakey started but was unable to finish. "You know . . ." he tried again.

"I know." Christopher nodded slowly. "I'm the man."

Shakey offered the hand now. Christopher's shake was a firm one.

Shakey stepped toward Jessica.

Jessica's head shook again. She wanted to back away, to turn and run, anything to avoid the goodbye that awaited her inside Shakey's embrace. In the end, she found herself unable to move from her fate.

Shakey's arms opened and Jessica was now able to move. She took a step forward then collapsed against Shakey's body. If not for the muffling effects of Shakey's chest her sobbing would surely have been audible to all in the bus station.

Shakey closed his arms around her. His chin rested atop her head. In the blur of faces seated in the chairs before him he was sure there was a familiar face. The thought was a fleeting one, however, as his eyes were tightly shut.

Shakey inhaled deeply, enjoying Jessica's smell one last time. He pulled back just far enough to peer into the large green emeralds that had once shown him eternity. He placed both hands on her face, feeling the smoothness of her skin once more. He placed an open-mouthed kiss on her cheek, directly atop a fast-running teardrop. The salt he tasted from the teardrop was not nearly as strong as the sweet taste of the skin it soiled. "Jessica." He spoke her name once more then returned her to his embrace.

The two of them were instantly transported to another plane of existence. A place where nothing existed but the two of them. Their own special place in the universe. Their stay there would be short, as the unsympathetic voice that boomed through the bus station's sound system instructed that Gate Ten's final boarding call was now.

Shakey didn't notice when Christopher's hand went inside the pocket that held the three tickets he had purchased for them a day ago.

Christopher placed the tickets in his own pocket then lifted the bags from the floor once again. He walked for the gate.

Shakey finally pulled away from Jessica. Her sobs grew loud again.

"I got her, Shakey. We gotta go," Cindy said without looking at him. She instead picked the third bag from the floor. Her other hand was once again around Jessica's shoulder. Cindy led the broken woman away.

Shakey stood still in the middle of the floor. He watched silently as his world came to an end.

Christopher, who had already taken care of the trio's boarding requirements, stood by the door while Cindy and Jessica stepped through it. He then looked to Shakey, who was yet to move. The young man made a fist with his right hand then twice tapped the left side of his chest.

Shakey slowly balled his own fist then returned the gesture. His fist was still on his chest when he watched Christopher disappear through the door. The door closed behind the young man, and for Shakey, all was lost.

Ralphy placed the newspaper back in his lap. He couldn't believe how easily he found Shakey after following Josephine's advice. He also couldn't believe how broken up his prized catch seemed to be over the trashy-ass white broad and two crack babies that weren't even his. The fool had still not moved, even though they had left over five minutes ago. Could this man really be the dangerous calculating criminal he had heard so much about? Ralphy smiled to himself. One thing was for sure *I got his black ass now!*

Shakey turned to leave the bus station. A frantic movement caught by the corner of his eye caused him to look to his left. The familiar face showed again, and now Shakey was sure of the identity. Officer Ralph Stephens, next up as Galveston's Chief Narcotics Officer. Shakey's mind instantly thought of Trevino's promise of a partner.

The Handsome Intimidator stepped forward. He pretended not to see the officer. Nearly smiling, Shakey found that the edge was taken off his pain, if only temporarily, by having something to focus his anger on. "Wanna game, bitch?" Shakey mouthed the words aloud to himself. "I'll give you a game."

Shakey's Cadillac turned left off Broadway on Thirty-first Street. He took a peek in the rearview mirror. Not surprisingly, the late model Impala traveled not far behind him. What did surprise him, though, was that by all indications the young officer had yet to call for back-up. It seemed the officer was intent on apprehending Shakey alone.

Shakey brought the car to an abrupt stop about halfway between Winnie and Market Avenues. He put the car in PARK and relit the half-smoked Swisher that lay in the ashtray. He took a puff on the cigar while waiting for the cop's next move.

The Impala stopped once directly behind Shakey's Cadillac. The young cop made no effort to hide his intentions.

Shakey kept the Cadillac still a moment longer. He took another long smoke from the Swisher while looking into the rearview mirror. The two men locked eyes, and Shakey couldn't help the smile that parted his lips. "OK, hero." Shakey spoke to the face in the mirror then shifted the Cadillac's transmission out of park. He eased his foot from the brake and allowed the car to ease forward. "Let the games begin."

Shakey drove slowly until reaching the stop sign on the corner then pressed hard on the gas. He ran the stop sign and sped toward The Backtrack.

"Mothafucka!" Ralphy hurled the Impala into oncoming traffic. He swerved to avoid an oncoming car then continued his chase. Shakey would not get away from him.

Shakey laughed aloud at the shock he saw in Ralphy's face. The monster within him rejoiced with thoughts of what awaited the young officer at the other end of their game of cat and mouse.

Shields Park was but a blur to his right as the Cadillac sped forward. A few blocks later Shakey made a sudden turn right. A block later he veered left, and the Cadillac was on the dirt beside the road.

"What the fuck?" The Impala's tires screeched loudly while being stripped of rubber. Ralphy shifted the car in reverse, placed a heavy foot on the gas then shifted the vehicle back into drive. He could see the Cadillac as it veered off-road.

Shakey's Cadillac stopped once alongside a procession of train cars. He reached into the glove compartment for the weapon that would end the officer's life. He waited for the Impala to pull a little closer to the Cadillac before leaping from the car. He ran full-speed for the open train car closest to him.

"Shit." Ralphy pulled the Impala next to the Cadillac. He jumped from the car, not even bothering to close the door behind him.

Shakey ran from one train car to the next. He from past experience that many of the cars were still loaded full with undelivered cargo. As he ran, he turned over stacks of boxes behind him to hinder the progress of the fast pursuing officer. If Shakey had wanted, he could have lost the rookie altogether. But that was not the plan.

"Hey stop! I just—" Ralphy's words were cut short when he had to dodge a falling stack of boxes. "Crazy son-of-a-bitch," he fussed.

About eight train cars into the journey, Shakey found exactly what he was looking for. This car was filled with boxes. The stacks stood from floor to ceiling and there was very little room for maneuvering inside the car. Shakey would leave Stephens here.

The Handsome Intimidator slid the first stack of boxes a few inches to the left—just far enough so that he could step for the next row of boxes. He returned the first stack of boxes to their original position then did the same at the second row of boxes. He continued this pattern, cutting a diagonal path through the row of boxes that took him to the east wall of the train car.

Ralphy entered the train car. He frowned at the wall of boxes that both blocked his path and obscured his vision. He was sure he heard something slide along the floor somewhere within the train car. Instinctively, the officer reached for his service revolver.

Shakey crouched alongside the wall. His weapon also in hand, he slowly cocked his weapon.

Ralphy jumped in an attempt to gain a view over the boxes. He could see nothing. He moved a stack of boxes a bit to his left. "I know you're back there," Ralphy called before stepping forward into the maze of boxes. "Why don't you just come on out so we can talk about this?"

At this Shakey nearly laughed. This one was really stupid.

"I know he had it coming." Ralphy moved another stack. "We can work this out."

Shakey's body tensed as the rookie moved closer. His pulse quickened and a hint of perspiration formed on his brow. He was prepared to kill.

"Come on, Shakey." Ralphy moved the next stack of boxes. "You know I'm your only way out."

Shakey frowned. The kid was so stupid, Shakey nearly felt bad for him.

Ralphy traveled farther into the train car. He cocked his gun now. His nerves were frayed, and he was finding it increasingly more difficult to breathe with each pound of his heart. "I know he was playing you, Shakey. I know everything." Ralphy didn't go any farther. Instead he leaned against the next stack of boxes. He took a moment to catch his breath. He was sure he would faint if he didn't.

Shakey felt the thud against the box. The rookie was on the other side. The youngster's life would end when he moved the stack of boxes.

"Come on, Shakey!" Ralphy yelled in frustration. "What's it gonna be?" the young officer panted.

The only sound that could be heard inside the car was the officer's breathing.

"Working with me will be cool," Ralphy promised. "Just come on out so we can talk about it."

Work with you? Shakey couldn't believe his ears. The rookie wanted in the game.

"I never liked that mothafucka anyway, Shakey!" Ralphy declared. "He fucked me over too!" Ralphy took a deep breath then uncocked his gun. It was obvious to him that Shakey had the drop on him the entire time. The gun was useless. "Look, I am putting my gun away. I just want to talk. We don't come to an agreement, you walk. My word." Ralphy reholstered his weapon.

Shakey considered his options. He stood slowly, and in one swift motion, the barrier between them was removed. Shakey's gun was aimed at the rookie.

"Hey man." Ralphy's eyes widened and both hands were in the air. "I just want to talk is all."

"I'm listening." Shakey motioned with the barrel of the gun for the officer to proceed.

"Look, asshole is out the picture and it's us now." Ralphy figured his best bet was to get straight to the point. "Fair and square, fifty-fifty." When Shakey didn't respond, Ralphy continued. "As far as Trevino, I don't wanna know what happened."

"But others do," Shakey said evenly.

"Look, Shakey, I'm not going to lie to you. You got big problems."

"Tell me something I don't know."

"OK." Ralphy noticed the discernible mellowing of his prized catch. "I can fix it all," the young officer boldly promised.

Shakey tried to maintain his mask of intensity, but the interest in Ralphy's words showed clearly in his eyes.

"Don't ask me how yet, Shakey," Ralphy continued. "But I will make it all go away."

"And in return?" Shakey knew the answer, but wanted to hear the rookie say it.

"In return." Ralphy hesitated. "You do for me what you did for Trevino." He stopped then started again. "Except without all the bullshit."

Shakey hadn't a leg to stand on. He was right back where he started.

"Partners." Ralphy extended a hand. When Shakey didn't accept, he said, "Can you at least uncock the fucking gun?"

Shakey nearly smiled while putting the gun away. In another moment in time, Shakey would have thought meeting Ralphy to be a Godsend. In the present, the start of their relationship only meant for Shakey another stint in purgatory. Hell, it seemed, would make him wait still longer.

"Look, lay low for a few days until I figure some of this shit out." Ralphy instructed. He reached in the pocket of his pants for the cell phone he purchased earlier. "I'll call you here when I got something for you." He handed the phone to Shakey.

Shakey placed the phone in his pocket but said nothing.

"So we good?" Ralphy was growing excited now.

"Yeah." Shakey nodded. "We good."

"Yes." Ralphy was a pimply faced high schooler with a date to the prom.

This time Shakey did smile.

"Aw right, just do like I said." Ralphy turned to walk away. "I'll call soon."

Shakey nodded then watched as the rookie navigated the boxes.

Ralphy's smiled stretched across the width of his face. He hurried from the train car. He couldn't wait to tell Josephine of the day's happenings. Before stepping through the passageway that led to the next car, Ralphy turned back to Shakey. "I'm sure glad you came out when you did. I nearly shit my pants."

Shakey shook his head behind the rookie. He was unsure whether to laugh or cry at his predicament. It really didn't matter he concluded. Like always he would play the hand dealt to him. He would play it to the fullest.

"I knew you'd be here." Christopher ran from the bus and despite the gangsta he would like to be, he leapt into Shakey's arms. "You did, huh?" The sound didn't seem to come from Shakey, but it was distinctly his voice.

"I know you wasn't going to leave us stuck out like that." Christopher backed away long enough to look his hero in the eye.

Shakey said nothing—at least no audible sound came from him. But in Shakey's face Christopher saw all that needed to be seen or heard. The young boy saw that he would always be loved and cared for. He knew that there was someone that he could always depend on and who would never abandon him.

Christopher stepped close to his hero again. He hugged him once more. The nine-year-old squeezed hard. The embrace tightened constantly with each passing moment until two solid thuds to Christopher's own chest startled him.

"I was gonna let you make it, but you goin' too far now," a voice fussed.

Christopher looked to Shakey again, and Shakey was not there. Cindy was, though, and she was not too happy with the young boy's hug and incoherent murmuring into her ear.

Christopher released her from his grasp then sat straight in his seat. He took a deep breath to compose himself. He must deal with the pain of Shakey leaving again.

A moment or two passed before Cindy, perhaps sensing his pain, offered a smile.

Despite his broken heart, Christopher returned the gesture with equal warmth.

The two of them laughed before Christopher asked, "We almost there?"

"Yeah." Cindy turned her attention back to the book of word puzzles in her lap. "The bus driver said five minutes, about five minutes ago."

Christopher smiled then looked around the bus. The majority of the scattered occupants were sleeping. He looked past Cindy at Jessica who was also sleeping and had somehow managed to form a ball so tight with her body that she fit perfectly as she lay across the two bus seats. With her arms she appeared to hug herself tightly. The smile of perfect contentment framed her face. Christopher knew why and wished she could sleep forever.

Christopher lay back in his seat then leaned to his right until the side of his head rested against the window. He peered through the dirt-stained glass. The sun had not yet completed its rise, but succeeded in obscuring Christopher's view.

Christopher struggled against the glare and could finally see the small bus station a short distance in front of them. There was a small car parked in front of the building and though Christopher was not quite able to discern the color of the vehicle through the sun's glare he could tell it was a Cadillac.

Christopher shut his eyes tight and opened them again. The Cadillac and the man was still there. He looked at Cindy then turned back to the glass. The Cadillac was green now.

"Cindy," he called softly without turning his head away from Shakey and the Cadillac.

"Yeah." Cindy circled another word on her puzzle.

"Hit me again." Christopher said, still not looking at her.

"What?"

"Just hit me."

Cindy gave a solid pound to Christopher's shoulder with the side of her fist.

Shakey was still there.

"Again, Cindy," Christopher said loud enough that the occupants nearest them began to stir. "Harder."

Cindy frowned at him.

"Please, Cindy."

Cindy hit her crazed friend and nemesis twice more.

Shakey was still there.

"Harder!" Christopher yelled loud enough that all in the bus heard him. Even the bus driver looked through his rearview mirror in response to the commotion.

"What the fuck is wrong with you!" Cindy turned in her seat far enough to pepper his arm and shoulder with a succession of blows. "Crazy-ass boy." Her voice trailed off as her own eyes followed the path of Christopher's gaze.

Christopher leapt from his seat and quickly climbed the back of the seat in front of him; Kicking a woman in the head in the process. He made a mad dash for the front of the bus.

The panicked bus driver pressed instinctively on the brakes once the maddened boy was close to him and Christopher went crashing into the dashboard.

Unfazed by the collision, Christopher pushed away from the dashboard and leapt from the door. The bus driver was able to reach for the lever that opened the door just in time to keep Christopher from crashing through it.

Christopher's first steps on Oklahoma soil were an all-out sprint. Once a foot or so from Shakey he leapt into his arms with such force that Shakey would have fallen if not for the Cadillac behind him.

Christopher squeezed Shakey's neck so tight that Shakey thought for a moment he would pass out.

A moment later both Cindy and Jessica were reaching for Shakey too.

The four of them fused together in a constantly tightening embrace. Laughter as well as sobbing could be heard from them all. Each of them tried to speak, yet none of them were able to do so.

Shakey's arms closed completely around the three of them. His mind worked hard to record it all. The feel of their bodies pressed against his own, the warmth of their muffled sobs against his chest, and the mix of sweet smells that came from them. This moment was perfect and would forever be his refuge. Perhaps he had never before known complete and total happiness. Perhaps he would know nothing of the sort again. But he had this moment, and this moment would be enough. Enough to steady him against the assorted miseries that would surely dominate the rest of his time on earth. Enough even to carry him through his predetermined fate in the after-world. For not even the pit of Hades possessed strength or fury to take this moment from him.

ORDER FORM
URBAN BOOKS, LLC
78 E. Industry Ct
Deer Park, NY 11729

Name: (please print):_____

Address:_____

City/State:_____

Zip:_____

QTY	TITLES	PRICE

Shipping and handling-add \$3.50 for 1st book, then \$1.75 for each additional book.

Please send a check payable to:

Urban Books, LLC

Please allow 4-6 weeks for delivery